R.C. PRENTICE

False Premise

A Zoe Dill Mystery #2

False Premise
Zoe Dill Mystery Series
Published by HugelMar
Denver, CO

ISBN: 978-1-7353011-1-2
FICTION / Mystery & Detective / Private Investigators

Cover design by Natasha Brown Designs. Copyright by RC Prentice. Interior design by Victoria Wolf, wolfdesignandmarketing.com

HugelMar

PROLOGUE

MAVIS SAMUELSON had a peculiar new friend. It was actually Mavis' grandnephew, Randy, who had the friend. Randy was Mavis' grandnephew, just as Aimee was her grandniece, and not Randy's sister, but rather, his cousin, and now in his mid-thirties, a good dozen years older than Aimee. Mavis did not notice that she gushed and hovered over Duncan Pennfield, who preferred being called "Penn", rather than "Duncan", introducing him to Aimee as "that wonderful curator from the college". Randy had brought Penn home after Penn had invited Randy to "come back up and visit your wonderful donation" following his and Mavis' return from the unveiling of Mavis' gift to the small college in eastern Washington state. The gift was an early painting by the neo-cubist artist Fernand Léger, a companion to the lithographs hanging in Mavis' home. Randy and Penn spent a week together, a week of torrid lust, hedonistic indulgence in food, drink, chemical assists, and surprisingly frank conversation about politics, philosophies of life, and social presence, Penn and Randy had declared that they were, indeed, made for each other. Now, two weeks later, Penn was visiting Randy in Trestle Glen.

Aimee, skeptical of anything having to do with her cousin Randall, remained her usual tight-lipped, disapproving self, an attitude she adopted when she was forced to have anything to do with Randy except tolerate his existence in the house. But now Mavis was pleased to see her gradually soften, bantering with Penn at the dinner table.

Then, Penn dropped his bombshell. At dinner, where the presence of Aimme's Beau, Kenny was an increasingly common occurrence, with Mavis beaming benevolently on what she called "these nice friendly family get-to-gethers, even if you're not all really family" Kenny had gone on and on about a stupid incident at one of his stores, having to do with mice nibbling at electrical wire and causing an alarm to malfunction. Following this tedious recitation, the four adjourned to the living room where Randy broke out the Glenlivet for the three of them; Aimee would have some of the mint tea that she was preparing for Mavis, with a couple shots of brandy. They settled in chairs. Aimee entered from the kitchen with an oversized blue cup.

"Speaking of alarm systems," said Kenny, addressing Aimee. "I'm surprised Mavis doesn't have one. She doesn't, does she?" Aimee shook her head. "With all these valuable items, the art hanging on the wall, you'd have thought she would," added Kenny.

Penn rose. "Do you mind if I look?" he said, walking over first to one of the Léger prints, taking it off the wall and looking at the back, then doing the same with the other two and with the Braque oil.

Randy nodded but was becoming increasingly uncomfortable. Where was this going? "They all have certificates of authenticity," he said softly, and somewhat weakly.

"Indeed they do," agreed Penn. He was carefully reading the one on the back of the Braque. "'Placement of forms, use of colors known to have been used by cubists such as Gris, Braque, Picasso, Léger … consistent with paintings known to have been painted by Braque between 1909 and 1920 and with Braque's style and habits … execution of brushstrokes indicating use of a brush or brushes and pigments available at the time.' This falls just short of out-and-out identifying it as one of Monsieur Braque's original paintings." Rehanging the painting, he took his seat again.

"You mean it might not be?" queried Aimee, glaring at Randy.

Penn shook his head. "No, no. I'm not saying that at all. We have the same situation with the Léger painting you–or your aunt–donated to us. A lot of authenticity certificates read like this. Cautious. Many authenticators are reluctant to give definite opinions without incontrovertible chains of transmission between artist and present owner. And those are rare."

"But what you are saying is, it might not be worth all the bother of an alarm system and the couple hundred a month to maintain it. But what about everything else? All this statuary and sculpture?" objected Kenny. "And the dining room set? Mavis, isn't it eighteenth century?"

"Uhhh, well … that's what Randy told me. Eighteenth century, isn't it, Randy?"

Randy was silent.

Penn looked at Randy, then at Mavis. "Eighteenth century replica, I'm afraid," responded Penn diffidently.

"But what about the Légers? Those certificates do state positively that they are Légers".

"Yes. Léger *lithographs*. Unsigned. Probably done from the masters that Léger made, but sometime after Léger's death. Same with the Remington, Erté, Miro, and Chiparus bronzes. Cast from the molds those artists made, but probably long after the artist had met his maker. Quite common. The family needs money, makes new casts. Why not? They're the same pieces of art, just not poured by the artist's own hands."

Before they all went up to bed, Penn heading for Randy's bedroom, Randy stopped midway in the hall. He took out his phone and sent a text message.

Next day, Aimee went to work. Randy announced he and Penn would stroll around Lake Merritt, then spend the day in San Francisco before he saw Penn off at the Amtrak station, so he would be gone all day.

They parked at the lake, then entered an arbor formed by a pergola with a walkway that stretched in front of them, flowering vines entwining the pergola's trellis, the trellis supported by Doric columns. Each side of the walkway was planted in lush vegetation. They strolled along the path, which gave way out into the open and continued on until they came to a boathouse and concession stand. They each got a hot dog. Part of the lake was closed off, where rowboats bobbed and paddleboats circumvented the small lake-within-the-lake. They sat on a stone bench and watched the Canada geese, gulls and several varieties of ducks cluster around the concession stand. Two black swans were among them but unlike the other species that appeared to be waiting for handouts, they glided around like royalty oblivious to the riffraff.

Then Randy peeked at his watch. "Oh God! We've got to get back to the car. It's already two o'clock. Where did the time go? We've got to get you across the Bay and me back over here before rush hour starts. Sorry, but I'm going to have to just abandon you at the Amtrak station." The on-ramp to the MacArthur was stop-and-go. Randy sped up in the right-hand merge lane, entering the freeway just in front of a semi. The driver hooted at him. Randy slipped into the next lane to the left.

He dropped Penn at the Amtrak station, then inched back along city streets to the Bay Bridge. Surprisingly, the return trip was faster. He parked in front of the house and ambled into the dining room just in time for heated-up leftovers. Mavis and Aimee were sipping mint tea at the yes, replica, eighteenth century dining room table. As Randy's brought his heated-up leftovers to the table, Mavis became suddenly unusually tight-lipped. Mavis' expression was stern, her responses monosyllabic to Randy's attempt to chatter affably about the books he knew she was reading about the birth of electricity at Niagara Falls and the tussle between Tesla and Edison. Aimee, on the other hand, took up the conversational slack; she was also reading the two books, after Mavis went to sleep. Then she sat back, smirked and smiled. She let the silence build and broaden.

Then, Mavis spoke, her words delivered staccato, her voice raspy. "Why did I pay you ninety-five thousand dollars for reproduction furniture and what is probably forged or at least unoriginal artwork? And don't deny it! It was your friend Penn who spotted it and spilled the beans!"

Randy hemmed and hawed, stuttered and stammered, finally giving a gigantic shrug. "Oh bother! How was I to know?"

A week later, the following Saturday, Mavis had her usual postprandial infusion: mint tea with a couple of splashes of brandy. But she had not shared it as usual with her grandniece, Aimee; rather, it had been her grandnephew, Randy, who had prepared her tea, following a dinner of Chinese take-away: sweet and sour pork, cashew chicken, shrimp with garlic sauce, pan-fried rice, moo goo gai pan, and bean cakes. It was far more than she could eat, although Randy made away with quite a lot of it. The leftovers would do for her and Aimee, or at least for Aimee, tomorrow; she would make do with the cream of asparagus soup Aimee had kindly prepared for tonight's supper. It was hearty and nutritious; she made it with egg, which gave it protein and thickening. But the take-out food was a treat.

Aimee had gone out on a date with Kenny, her young man. They were going to an early showing of *Black Panther* at the Grand Lake Theater, Oakland's historic refurbished movie palace, then to one of their "take-back-the-Congress" movement meetings, then for a late dinner (Aimee did not yet know where–they'd decide that at the time, she'd told Mavis). Mavis was sure they would go back to Kenny's apartment; he was becoming something of a steady for her. *That's all right*, she thought. *I'll manage fine; Aimee deserves, needs a night out, a day off at least once a week.* Mavis had been surprised when Randy turned up shortly after Aimee left the house. When Randy suggested ordering the take-away, she readily agreed; the soup would keep.

This was unusual for Randy, thought Mavis. *He usually treats my home like a boarding house.* They ate a little bit on the early side, at 5:30, but that was fine; Aimee preferred eating at 6:00 or 6:30, but for Mavis, the earlier the better. "

So," said Mavis, "your fortunes are about to change! This will be good! Starting in the Anthropology program at Sonoma State College. Good for you!" He had decided to drive up there this evening after their supper, he told her. "Less traffic. There's a marvelous little B&B just out of town. They're expecting me." If the interview tomorrow went well, and Sonoma State accepted him, he would start the graduate program in the fall. Mavis observed Randy had indeed been solicitous; he had fixed her tea with which she ended every supper, and also prepared her cuppa for her bedside table. Once he had seen her upstairs, he had bid her farewell, declaring he could not stay. "On to Sonoma!"

Now, upstairs sitting up in bed, sipping her tea, Mavis reflected. *Aimee will be glad to get him out of the house*; maybe she was right. Mavis had been so pleased with Randy's effort, following his return from Florida, when his own mother had wanted nothing to do with him, complaining shrilly that he was just as bad as ever, just doing a different kind of scamming, buying what she insisted were fenced goods, stolen from unlocked garages or jimmied storage lockers, to resell at his flea market stall. Mavis placed the cup on its saucer on the night table and scooted down between the sheets. As she drifted off to sleep she rehearsed, not for the first time, a conversation that she'd never had with Nancy nor ever would: *Why, Nancy, have you not seen fit to give your own son credit for his self-rehabilitation? Why do you dismiss me as, as you put it, "a gullible seventy-year-old" because I announced that I was writing him back into my will? Yes, he buys things at estate sales to resell at the flea market or to a contact he met at an estate sale he went to. There's nothing wrong with that.*

But now Mavis heaved a heavy sigh. *There* was *something wrong with that!* Aimee had pointed out that she had undoubtedly paid far too much for the accessorizing of her dining and living rooms because so many of the pieces were not what he had led her to think they were. They were replicas. And the inflated sum she'd paid, she'd paid to Randy. "That's clear from what his latest heartthrob, Penn, as much as *told* us, Auntie," Aimee had said. *Paid too much. Yes*, she thought, *I agreed to buy the majority of the contents of that house from Randy based on one of the photographs he'd shown. Was that so bad? Afghani kilims, modernist sculptures, the Braque, the four Légers (three lithographs and that one very rare early painting that she had donated to the college art gallery).* She went over, again, the conversation she had had with Nancy, deflecting her pessimistic skepticism. *"Ninety-five thousand dollars is* not *so much to pay! It's a fraction of the insurance settlement paid out from the fire that consumed my dear-departed Arthur's and my villa and what I paid to buy this house."*

But last week, after the visit from Randy's art curator expert friend, Penn, Aimee had convinced her of what Nancy had insisted was fundamental to Randy's character: he could not help scamming, cheating, getting away with something. Mavis was so disappointed. *Mr. Cronin is coming up from San Diego sometime later in the week,* she thought. She had told him on the phone that she had wanted to change her will. *This will also be good for Randy, like his new career. No more handouts; no more easy rolling along at someone else's expense. He'll have to really work, develop some backbone.* She wasn't sure what anthropology was all about but what little he had shared with her and Aimee sounded interesting. The only question now was what to do about the will: *Should what was written in the will as Randy's share of the annuity now go to Aimee? Or should it go to some charity? Maybe to that nice little college where I donated the Léger? Mavis drifted off to sleep.*

Mavis woke up. Not as suddenly as usual, but wake she did. She turned her head to see the clock: pretty much right on time. The tea always made her go right about five hours after finishing dinner. *Yes, right on time: 12:30 in the morning.* Lying there, she thought again about how it was too bad that Nancy and Randy were on the outs with each other. *I'm liberal,* she thought. *I'm tolerant. Why can't Nancy be the same? Otherwise Nancy is a delightful person – delightful to be around. Chatty and solicitous and cheerful, the other day when she was over for tea. Dr. Jekyll and Mr. Hyde. Just shameful, the way Nancy had reacted to the suggestion that Nancy come over some weekend, maybe even stay over. Could have been a nice five-some, with Aimee's Kenneth. But* "Oh, no, not with Randy here," Nancy had said. Mavis recalled the sudden hardness that Nancy had assumed: her face in rictus, her body rigid.

Mavis started to drift off back into sleep, when her bladder jolted her with another message. *Oooh–must get up. Gotta go. Can't delay...* Mavis swung her stiff and aching legs over the side of the bed, pushing herself to a sitting position against the pillows. "Ooof!" she said with a whoosh of breath. *Dizzy. Too much brandy in the tea? Well, whatever. Gotta go.* She rotated so she could plant her feet on the floor in front of the rollator. Grabbing its handles, she pulled herself up to standing. *Oh-oh-oh! Really not good. Really dizzy. Well, once I get moving with the rollator it'll probably stop.* She navigated slowly to the bedroom door. She could move without the rollator–after all, she "chugged", as she put it, slowly down and back up the stairs every day, without it, holding fast to the baluster but for navigating around the house and for her two "constitutionals" she took with Aimee around the neighborhood, the two rollators – one upstairs, one downstairs – were extremely handy, even necessary.

Now she moved cautiously forward. *Really unsteady on my pins, aren't I?* And disoriented. Now in the hall, she was having trouble remembering just which direction the bathroom was. *Vision all screwed up: the walls, the floor, the stairwell, the railings, all dancing up and down. But gotta go.* She started off slowly, but then she knew she had to hurry. She would not, absolutely not piddle on the floor. *Oh!* But now she realized, too late, she was not heading for the bathroom; she was heading for the stairs. She pivoted with the rollator at the top of the stairs but then it happened: her right knee gave way, she lurched, toppled against the rollator. Fear gripped her. She gave a little scream: "Aieeee!" The rollator gave way. It tumbled over the top step of the stairway, bouncing, spinning, crashing, smashing all the way down while

Mavis Samuelson, vision blurred, hands reaching out to grab the banister, the spindles, the rollator, or anything at all, tumbled down after it, her last living thought, *No! This can't be happening!* as her head banged innumerable times on the treads.

1

THE PREVIOUS NOVEMBER

SACAJAWEA AND JEAN BAPTISTE
CHARBONNEAU COLLEGE

DAMIA ZOELLER DILL, preferring to present herself as, and to be referred to as Zoe, found the campus charming and comfortable, the location dramatic, and even the weather refreshing, brisk, stimulating. She would not be escaping the ubiquitous gray Washington cloudscape, and it would be colder here; the steppe-like geography and altitude made snow more likely than the constant drizzle-drip of Seattle.

In geographical location, it was indeed a backwater. But it was close to an intellectual hub, Washington State University, and the Tri-Cities--Walla Walla, Pullman, and Spokane—together offered all the amenities that could be found in Seattle. Additionally, proximity to the two rivers ensured that the campus' two swards of vast lawn–Kendall Green and Bodmer Common–were well watered. Zoe found the campus lush, verdant, and cozy in its compactness. She had a feeling of being at home here, a feeling she had never had at the sprawling University of Washington campus. And pleasantto

Zoe had been given the grand tour by one of her might-be colleagues, Carlin–Carly--Pinto, and was scheduled for dinner at the house Carly shared with another potential colleague, Mona Spradley. Carly, on the tall side with very long brown hair, worn loose, was what Zoe thought men would probably call "leggy". She had a no-nonsense, confident manner. Mona, of slight build but round and soft in body and voice, expressed a more subdued but no less confident demeanor. Another potential colleague, Gudrun Hance, embodied a knowledgeable persona that hinted at just a tad of well-meaning busy-body-ness. Veteran of twenty years' teaching, with three pre- and teen-age daughters, married to a man who owned a bicycle shop, she projected a helpful, if overconfident, solicitousness. These folks, along with the Director of the School of Art, Peter Blenheim, her possible future colleagues, seemed lively, intelligent, companionable, and just quirky enough to offer a bit of enigma and sophistication without pretension in this academic hermitage. Carly's MA was from City University of New York; Mona's from Chicago's Art Institute. With only a BA, Peter Blenheim was a holdover from the days when the college had been a women's finishing school; he seemed gentle, gracious, and perhaps a smidge overprotective. In her interview with him, he assured her that he would retire within the next year or two.

Her mentors at University of Washington, sometimes tagged with the far-from-euphonious acronym, "U-Dub", had prepared her for what they called the "job interview gauntlet": one-on-one interviews with the dean and with individual faculty members; scrutiny by a self-selected swarm of students offered a free lunch if they modified their daily agendas to constitute a reception committee; and then, finally, the "job talk" before an audience of whatever collection of faculty and students proved sufficiently interested to attend. Occupying a library carrel between interviews with the college's Dean of Faculty, Dean Fister, the Director, Mr. Blenheim, her potential colleagues Spradley, Pinto, and Hance; and the gaggle of undergraduate students over lunch, she was expected there once again to prepare her job talk, scheduled for four o'clock, in forty-five minutes. But outside was preferable to the carrel.

She threaded her way along a pea-graveled path that meandered along a water feature, a kind of infinity pool. From the pool a thin sheet of water cascaded into a stream that narrowed and deepened, then broadened into another pool. She sat down on one of the benches on the edge of the pool. The sound of the water murmuring into the shallow reflecting pool eased her mind.

The perch gave her a vista overlooking a gentle slope, with terraced swaths covered in wet brown straw. A sign informed her it was a garden maintained by students: "Cultivation by Our Generation: Organic, Local, Sustainable". It was an inspiring place to mentally prepare her talk: "A False Premise: The Role of the Swiss Art Market During World War II in the Production and Marketing of Rembrandt Forgeries". A mouthful for a title, but she hoped it would draw students and faculty interested in art, art history, history, and maybe art marketing, thus drawing from the Business School. It had to do with the erroneous assumption that several works by Grovert Flinck, one of Rembrandt's many understudies, were actually Rembrandts because they had been sold by their owners hastily at low prices to a dealer in Geneva as *not* Rembrandts, trying to keep treasured artwork out of the Nazis' hands during World War II, and also possibly so the sellers could buy them back equally cheaply after the war which, alas, of course they could not do because Hitler had murdered them. It had taken Zoe several weeks of intense research in the records of the "Monuments Men" in the National Archives and several more intense weeks of analysis of the paintings themselves–those that were housed in the Rijksmuseum and in the Rembrandthuis in Amsterdam. Several more weeks were required to write the paper, which had eventually become a chapter in her nearly completed dissertation, also titled *False Premise* which would net her a PhD from University of Washington.

Following the talk, which Zoe thought had gone well, she, Carly, and Mona were joined by a tall, thin bespectacled man, in polo shirt and jeans, youngish but with just-beginning baldness surrounded by tight pepper-and-salt curls, sporting a tightly trimmed mustache-and-goatee. Carly introduced him as James something, "a botanist" from the Sciences and Engineering Department and Carly's "companion of the moment", a designation James took in stride with a frown and a grin. The ensemble trooped over to the house that Carly and Mona shared, a few blocks from the College. In contrast to the Tudor-style brick buildings of the college, many of them emulating family homes, especially those that were dormitories, the houses in the neighborhood surrounding the college were uniformly modest, small, one-story clapboard affairs. "There are some grand houses," commented Mona in a longing tone, "up on the hill. Some faculty do live there. They date from the 1880s and '90s when prosperous farmers were piling up silver, lived in town, and had peons–mostly Chinese and Indians–to do the farm work."

They entered the small house "We're having lamb stew. I put it in the crockpot this morning. It's set on warm; I just have to crank it up. Should be ready in about half an hour," said Mona.

"Wow. Yum," affirmed James enthusiastically.

Mona walked through the hall, then through the living room. Zoe, Carly, James and Zoe followed, Zoe feeling at once eager and shy, out of place but on the cusp of being accepted. At the old-fashioned swinging door to the kitchen Mona turned around: "We don't need appetizers now with all the crackers and cheese and hummus and whatnot at your talk, do we?" Then she took in the look of discomfort on Zoe's face. "Ohhhhh. Don't tell me. You're vegan, aren't you?"

Zoe laughed. "Vegetarian. Relaxed vegetarian. I do dairy, cheese, eggs. And I'm perfectly happy with whatever else, veggies and so forth, that you're planning to serve besides the lamb."

"Oh, well, whole small potatoes, whole baby carrots, whole baby onions, sliced turnips, golden beets and celery, and home-canned tomatoes, all from the college's organic garden–but they've been cooked in the gravy with the lamb stew."

"Oh," said Zoe, waving her hand in the air, "that's fine! Like I said, I'm a relaxed vegetarian."

"Okay. Well, I'm also going to dump in some polenta and small mushrooms. The polenta gets spooned out–whatever I can get from the mélange–then mixed with a couple eggs, oregano, thyme, rosemary, red wine and some corn starch, and gets pan fried, so it's a great big, thick tortilla-like thing, then gets parmesan grated over it. That okay?"

"Hey–veggies over fried polenta? Of course! Sounds great!" enthused Zoe.

Zoe thought the meal exquisitely delicious, complemented also, as it was, by bottles of Willamette Valley wines, white and red. Polenta, Zoe knew, was tricky: cooked too long and it became mush. Undercooked, eating it was like chewing through pea-gravel. This was perfect, and she relished the crispness provided by the pan fry. Carrots, potatoes, celery, and daikon radish carried the delicate rosemary flavor seasoning the lamb. Zoe sipped her white wine between spoonfuls. She noted James taking hearty swigs of his red, refilling his glass, as he stabbed at chunks of the lamb on his plate.

Mona and Carly, like James, drinking red, filled Zoe in on how the college was structured: "decentralized" characterized it, except for the sciences and the business college, which were ruled by intransigent assistant deans. "We have our own intransigent rulers, too, here in the Arts and Human Sciences," remarked Mona, "but they have nothing to do with us."

"Ah, yes!" agreed Carly. "The Social Sciences Department. Ruled by the tyrannical triumvirate: Joe and Madison Canter and their probably-but-who-knows-lover-but-at-least-best-buddy Dora Harris. The administration has tried to break up that department ever since the de-centralization push."

"When was that?" asked Zoe.

"Long before our time," said Mona "I think, maybe the '90s?"

"Whoa! So they've been here a long time!"

"Since the late '80s, I think. Hired straight out of grad school at Columbia. What I heard was one of them wouldn't come without the other two," said Carly, wagging her head. "They're historians, but their fiefdom includes the sociologists, the political scientists, the speech pathologist–everybody like that except the psychologists. They managed to get away!"

"What about the Art School? How is it structured?"

"Oh–it's also decentralized. But that's sort of historical. There used to be a 'Performing Arts' school over in Lewiston, Idaho. They had art classes, music classes, theater, ballet. But it went bust sometime in the '70s. Weird place for an arts and performances school anyway," commented Carly. "Apparently the brainchild of a grocery store chain owner. Local boy who made good. When he died, the family sold the business, and the cash flow stopped. Charbonneau with its generous endowment was able to take it over and move it here."

"So," said Zoe, ticking off on her fingers. "There was the Arts and Performances School. What happened to the performances part?"

James, returning from the kitchen with his plate again filled with polenta, veggies and a slab of lamb, sat down and provided clarification: "It was hived off and it's now the School of Performance and Theatre, directly under the dean."

"And when the School of Art and Art History rose like a phoenix from the ashes of the girls' school, with Peter Blenheim as its director, the arts part of Arts and Performances was plugged into the classes in ceramics and drawing. We now have proper artists teaching fine arts," declared Carly, in a high, dramatic falsetto, imitating, perhaps, Zoe thought, some unidentified trustee making a pitch to a potential donor.

"And the gallery came along with it," added Mona. "But it's really like we're three separate entities, with Peter functioning as chair of Art and chair of Art History, separately, at the same time. And the gallery, under Duncan Pennfield, operates as its own little fiefdom, with its own set of donors and devotees."

"But something I'm curious about here," said Zoe. "I would be the 'old masters' instructor but you do all the Dutch ones, Mona? Isn't that unusual, for a medievalist to be doing old masters or, like, I mean, some of them?"

"Ha!" crowed Carly. "That has to do with your predecessor, Zoe!"

"That was Brandon. Brandon Laird," explained Mona. "He was—still is—very close with the gallery, with Duncan Pennfield. Penn—that's what he likes to be called."

"There's much din and clatter about a 'big donation'"—Carly held her hands high above her head and made quote marks in the air—"that he's arranged for the gallery, to kick off next Spring Quarter with a big blast of trumpet fanfare." Then she added, in hushed tones, sarcastically, "We can hardly wait."

Mona, who seemed annoyed at what Zoe thought might be Carly's over-eagerness at divulging what might be too much rumor of fuss and ado, continued her recitation: "Anyway, yes, Brandon Laird came her with considerable sway and he captured Rembrandt, the Bruegels, Rubens, Hals, and of course Vermeer and mostly all the Germans for himself, but couldn't be bothered with the minor, earlier Dutch and Germans. So we agreed to divide it by century: I got the 15th and 16th, and earlier, and he got all the rest." Mona shrugged. "So I got Cranach, Bosch, Memling and van Eyck, and van der Weyden, but that it meant I also got Durer, Fra Angelico, Raphael, Giotto, Bellini, Lippi, Velasquez, and best of all, Botticelli, Piero della Francesca, Da Vinci, Titian, Tintoretto, and Michelangelo! I really am a medievalist but I only spend the first three weeks of the course *Medieval Europe and Early Renaissance* on that period. Then it's on to everybody else."

"And Gudrun does Islamic, Buddhist, and Hindu?"

"Right."

"And I see why it makes sense for me to also be doing Native America."

"Right. You covered those cases of the illicit—or at least unethical--marketing of Native American patrimony–the pots, the masks, and so forth–in your dissertation," said Carly.

"Well, I hope students–I mean, if I get the position–I hope they'll be content with a course that's half Native America and half Europeans-trying-to-fit-classic-themes-into-Native-American-landscape. Okay. So one last question," said Zoe. "Back to my predecessor. He retired?"

"Oooooo," cautioned Carly, "Brandon Laird. Dat dere's a non-no," she insisted, imitating a Brooklyn twang. "We peons don't got much t' say 'bout that. Or him."

"Yeah, youse wanna know 'bout dat? Go scratch yer ass," affirmed Mona, imitating Carly's imitation and sticking her tongue out.

"Ladies, please do not descend into Pygmalion argot!" James affected a vaguely Boston-Brahminesque hauteur. "We must maintain our commitment to only the most educated, erudite enunciation and elocution!" Then, dropping back to the usual flat tones of the West, he declared, "He's suing, isn't he?"

Zoe pressed: "He was fired?"

"We've been cautioned not to say anything but, yeah," admitted Mona, "basically. He was– what was it–suspended? Placed on leave without pay. He's not officially, technically out, but he might as well be. That's why you're a 'Visiting' Assistant Professor. That's why we did the 'nationwide search' for a *visiting* position, 'renewable for up to three years, with possible conversion to tenure track.' But we can't really tell you the story until you're–I mean, unless ..." hesitated Mona.

"You're hired," finished Carly, making some kind of significant but enigmatic eye contact with Mona.

"There'll probably be an out-of-court settlement," said James confidently. "Chancellor Chennell will want to cut off the negative publicity as soon as she can."

"Okay. So I guess I'll never know."

Again, the eye contact between the two young women, along with faint smiles. "Look," said Carly. "You might as well know: this job is yours if you want it. So you *will* know."

"But surely you've done—or will do--interviews with other candidates."

Carly nodded. "Yeah, but the one guy is already tenured where he is, and probably wants more money than they're willing to shell out and he probably wants to be hired with tenure. They're not gonna do that. And the other candidate–well! Codpieces?"

Zoe laughed. "Ah! So that's what the students were going on about in our pizza lunch! Those girls were really outrageous, looking at the guys' laps and asking about whether they had their codpieces in!" *I have hooks I intend to use to haul the students into classes, too*, thought Zoe. *But they're better than that! I just hope students don't heat up coals to rake* me *over.*

"Yeah. It was really a dumb job talk," declared Mona. "I mean, 'Codpieces in European Art'–that's, like, maybe an introductory lecture in the Art Appreciation course, to get students' attention, hook them into the class, but it's a throwaway lecture. Not something you do for your job talk. It's like saying, 'Well, I have this one thing that I know about and that's all I'm going to tell you about because that's all I know', and 'tee-hee, isn't it naughty and exciting, even if I really do know a lot more.' Wrong message."

"So what we're saying is, we think you're in," said Carly. "But I suppose you've got interviews lined up for the Art History Annual Conference next month."

"Well, yah," replied Zoe. "I mean, this is really early for on-campus interviews. I wasn't expecting any until, like, maybe January."

Carly nodded. "I think they really want to get this behind them, turn over a new leaf, get a new fresh start, whatever. With your *Fakes and Forgeries* class, *Old Masters*, *Native America and Beyond*, not to mention your class in the General Curriculum– the 'Gen Cur'--a section of *Art Appreciation*, you'll make everybody feel better and they'll get over it."

"And *your* predecessors?" asked Zoe. "Did they leave under equally odious circumstances?"

"Oh, no," replied Mona. "Mine retired. Emmy Sibelius."

"And mine died," responded Carly. "At least, we presume he did."

"Drowned in the Mediterranean, after his little boat capsized," added Mona. "Body was never found, but he's presumed dead. He's had two books published posthumously: one on American surrealists in Paris in the 1920s."

"Derivative, turgid, not much new in there," interjected Carly.

"But his other book, *The Titian Forgeries* is kind of entertaining, speculative, but maybe part of it is true." Mona frowned. "Have you come across it, Zoe?"

"No, but it sounds from the title like I should have, maybe even scope it out for my class. Well, too bad he drowned on the one hand," said Zoe, "but on the other, you wouldn't be here if he hadn't, would you, Carly?"

"Too true, too true. What is it about an ill wind blowing?"

Zoe reflected: *This is the perfect job for me. But here be closets here with skeletons, minefields to be avoided, and hidden pitfalls. A department right around the corner ruled by tyrants. A gallery supposedly part of the Art School but going its own way. A wheeler and dealer with heavy influence with donors but who did something to get himself suspended from teaching. New girl on the block that you are Zoe, beware.*

2

TWO WEEKS LATER, NOVEMBER 2016
SEATTLE: ZOE, PHIL

IT WAS TWO DAYS BEFORE THANKSGIVING when the phone call came. Zoe and her much-more-than-companion-of-the-moment, Philip Backstrom, Assistant Professor of Anthropology at Multnomah University, were contemplating what kind of supper they would like; because Phil had more days off from Multnomah than Zoe did from U Wash, he had come to stay with her. They were in Zoe's cramped little apartment. "Yay! I've got it!" hooted Zoe.

"Hey! Congrats!" Phil hugged her. "We've gotta celebrate!"

"You know it! And we've gotta do it with food! Cooking it, I mean. More fun *cooking* and eating than just eating—like in some fancy restaurant."

"Sure you don't just want to watch Netflix's and eat bags of microwave popcorn? That's a vegetarian meal right?"

Zoe made a rude noise.

They celebrated by going to Pike Place Market where they took in the smells of the sea and its bounty, picking up scallops, squid, chilies, fresh ginger and a lime for Phil; a large eggplant, a zucchini, a red pepper, some spinach, shallots, a leek, potatoes, parsley, and cilantro for Zoe. They brought it all back to the apartment they shared. Phil measured a tablespoon of olive oil and into a cast-iron frying pan, then lowered the scallops and squid into the pan and stir-fried them with the chilies and fresh ginger along with some blanched almonds, sesame seeds, and soy sauce. Zoe left her task of slicing some of the flesh out of the eggplant and chopping the zucchini and half an onion to join Phil at the stove to give her eyes a rest as she blinked back tears. "Red onion!" she exclaimed. "Stings!" She sniffled, then draped her arm around his middle and gave him a squeeze. "Mmmmm," she said, squeezing her eyes shut and taking in the smells bursting from the sizzling pan. Phil turned off the burner. Zoe opened a drawer to the right of the stove and slid out a Teflon-coated frying pan, measuring a tablespoon of peanut oil into it and dumping garlic along with the rest of the chilies, the shallots, the zucchini, the eggplant and also almonds, sesame seeds and soy sauce into it. She opened a tin of water chestnuts and dumped them in, the brought the mixture to a simmer. After a few minutes Phil turned on the gas under his shellfish. Zoe fresh blended the spinach, potato, leek, parsley, and cilantro with heavy cream and butter for a soup, spiced with dried chervil, tarragon. She dumped it into a saucepan and turned the burner on low under it. In a perverse reversal of the usual order of dishes, the soup would come last, in lieu of desert.

Phil served up his fish fry and Zoe's veggies. "Sit!" Phil commanded. Zoe sat. Phil stood at the kitchen table, grabbed up the bottle opener, twisted the handle and popped out the cork. He poured the citron-colored wine, a Chateau St. Michelle sauvignon blanc, into two glasses, stopping when each was half full. He picked up one glass. "Here's to Professor Zoe Dill, art historian extraordinaire!"

Zoe laughed, picked up her glass, and returned his salute. Phil sat down. They both drank, then commenced eating. Zoe savored the crunch of the almonds and the water chestnuts, their persevering texture against what was almost a creaminess of the eggplant, the soft chunkiness of the zucchini. Her mind played over the previous three years: she had enjoyed many meals such as this one, setting aside Fridays and Saturdays for these indulgences, when Phil drove up from Portland, before having to drive back on the Sunday. And now it was all coming to an end, with this new beginning for her. Had she taken Phil for granted these past three years? She had certainly slipped him into her comfort zone, after encountering him, literally, on the road, discovering that he was also at University of Washington as a graduate student, sharing an adventure with him, and then relishing his playfulness, matching her own, as a bed partner. But surely they could keep up the long-distance relationship: it would be just a little longer long-distance, and maybe with fewer encounters. Well, nothing new there. Zoe knew one of her new colleagues, Mona, had a long-standing long-distance relationship with a guy, Joel something, who taught at Northern Washington.

After the meal, Phil opened a Gewurztraminer. "Well", he said, "I've got some news, too. When you arrive at Charbonneau next September, or whenever, I'll be hard on your heels."

"*What?*" Zoe was so astonished she partially rose out of her chair. "You're going to be teaching at Charbonneau?" She felt a confusion of emotions grip her chest. She was suddenly excited and taken aback at the same time There was the thrill of anticipating continuing their life together, mixed with apprehension about having her lover along with her new colleagues also scrutinizing her performance in her new role.

"No, no," Phil assured her, wagging his head. "Nothing like that. But you know about accreditation?"

"Vaguely." Now puzzlement replaced apprehension and enthrall.

"Well, all institutions of higher learning have to periodically go through the reaccreditation process. It's usually every ten years and it's pretty perfunctory. All kinds of statistics get assembled, the reviewers, usually two of them, interview students, faculty; reports get written and sent off to the accreditation people; and that's that. It often happens piecemeal, like over a three- or five-year period, because colleges and universities don't like too much time to be taken up with bullshit. So it's Charbonneau's turn and they're doing two units this year: Math and Computer Science and ..." Phil paused dramatically.

"Art History?" Zoe said querulously.

Phil wagged his head. "No, no, no. Maybe next year. This year it's Social Sciences."

"Oh."

"And apparently it's not perfunctory. The administration is really hoping that the accreditation report will turn up some solid reasons to make big changes, whether the accreditation commission recommends them or not."

"Well, that's great! I guess. Congratulations! How did you get this appointment?"

"You know Porter Harder?"

"Not personally but I know who he is and I know he's at Multnomah." Porter Harder was, in fact extremely well known. With expertise on the history of race relations, he periodically gave interviews to NPR, CNN, and the *New York Times*. He had retired from Cornell, only to be snapped up and given a distinguished professorship at Multnomah, for which he was obligated to give only ten lectures per academic year in the university's required gen ed history course. He was incredibly well published, genuinely friendly, and universally liked and respected. "Well," continued Phil, "he was persuaded to take on the accreditation review for Charbonneau. Like I said, they usually want two reviewers, so I'm the second one!"

"But that's great! Did he personally come to you and say, 'Hey, Phil, can you help me do this?'"

"Basically. But not quite like that. He went to the provost and asked who should be the second reviewer. The provost suggested me."

"But you're not a historian."

"No. But this is a social sciences department. History is only part of it. And some of the history program's courses are pretty unusual. Most history programs focus on the U.S. and Europe. But there, the European history course targets the history of how Europe invaded other places–the Americas and Africa. So it's the history of colonization as well as the history of Europe. It's a two-semester course. Students learn European history, but not just for the sake of learning European history."

"Cool!" She took up her glass and toasted him. "Now. Help me clean up this mess."

Zoe ran warm water in the sink and with clatters and bangs, shoved the pot and pans into it. She took the blue scrubby, pumped dish soap onto it, quickly scrubbed and rinsed, and handed first the pot, then one pan, then another to Phil, who, towel in hand, dried, opened the drawer between the sink and the stove, and slid them in.

"Yeah, it *is* cool," he continued, as they tidied up. "They also have a course on African history, like the major civilizations: Zimbabwe, Ashanti, Benin, Islam. There's a lot of anthropology in it, of necessity. But that's where it stops. I'm given to understand that their sections of the World History course are likely to be basically bits and pieces of the other three. They do have a European History course so if history majors take the required Gen Ed World History from that instructor, it's, like, the course they'd be taking a year or two later under a different title and number. And that instructor's a sociologist! So there are student complaints when they get into those higher-level courses that they've heard it all before. I mean, apparently, nothing on Asia! And the American History course–-this is what Porter Harder got from the provost, who got it from the Charbonneau chancellor, who really pressed for Porter to take this on–-is basically a high-school level recitation of dates, presidents, wars, etc.

Phil was drying the last of the dishes, and putting them away in the cupboard above his head. Zoe had taken up her glass of wine and now leaned against the sink. "No analysis," he continued. He waved his hand in the air. "No social history. It's like, way out of date in terms of how things are done at other places. Then they have a Native American historian but he doesn't teach the Native American History course. In fact, he doesn't teach at all. That course is also taught by the sociologist! Plus, there's been almost constant turnover in the fields outside history: they hire, then there's pre-tenure review, and they fire. They hire again, put the person through pre-tenure review, fire again. So it seems like, what was a good idea twenty years ago has gotten soured, stuck in the mud, fossilized."

"Wow! That really sucks!" She mimed a shudder, but only halfway. She was actually appalled. "I hope they're the exception to the rule. I mean, I'd like to think we in Art History are on the cutting edge, breaking new ground, launching brilliant insights."

"I'm sure you are! But Social Sciences seems like it's a sinecure for the has-beens and never-weres. The place is run with an iron hand by three tenured profs and has been for years."

"Ah yes! The triumvirate! I heard about them when I interviewed."

"Yeah, that's a good name for them." Phil paused for a moment. "Who were the original ones? Octavian, Marc Antony, and who else? It wasn't Cleopatra, was it?

"I don't think so. She was married to Marc Antony. That's how Rome got ahold of Egypt.

Let's adjourn to the couch." Phil grabbed the bottle of Gewurz by the neck and they took the few steps into the apartment's miniscule living room. Phil set the bottle and his glass down on the coffee table and sat on the couch. Zoe joined him, scooting next to him.

"Anyway, one of our mandates is to get student comments and also get syllabi and so forth so we can evaluate the quality of the courses. Our second mandate is to look at the structure of the department with an eye toward whether or not there's a pedagogical basis for detaching the historians from the other disciplines, like, all these constant hirings and firings; department morale and so forth."

"So nobody else in that department has tenure?"

"There's one woman who managed to make it past pre-tenure review and since she's in her fifth year, she'll come up for tenure next year. She'll probably get it."

"So getting back to you. Why is it *you* are doing this?"

"Well, one member of the accreditation team needs to be untenured--I guess to sort of be in the same position as the untenured faculty there, empathy and so forth. And Porter is actually going to do the four tenured faculty. I'll do the other four–the sociologist, the two political scientists, and the speech pathologist, all of whom are untenured. Another reason for me is that I'm a social scientist, but not any of those fields. I mean, if the second member of the team was a political scientist, then the sociologist and the speech pathologist might feel slighted, blah blah blah. But also, the way Porter Harder put it to me, there's enough sort of 'anthropological segues' to warrant me, somebody with an ethnological background, being the second team member.

"One of the–as you call them, the triumvirate–the guy who's chair ..."

"And doesn't teach."

"Yeah, who doesn't teach, did his dissertation on a kind of anthropological topic: trade among the tribes in the Basin-Plateau area. It was published as a monograph; I haven't read it yet but obviously I will. It looks pretty good. So there's gotta be a reason why *he* doesn't teach the Native America course. Oh–here's another thing: the second member of the triumvirate is his wife, and the third is the wife's best girlfriend!"

"Whoa! nepotism, cronyism, conspiracy to commit ..."

"Yeah, that's the third question: why doesn't Joseph Canter teach and is it the nepotism and cronyism that's driving the revolving door personnel decisions and, if so, why?"

"Did you tell Porter Harder that I'm being hired there? Is that going to throw a spanner in the whole thing, you, having a conflict of interest?"

Phil shook his head. "No. I asked. You don't know any of them, do you?"

Zoe wagged her head back and forth. "They may have come to my job talk, but no, I didn't formally meet any of them."

"Yeah. And we're not married. If we were, it might be different. Also, Porter said if you were in their department, then yes, that would be a definite no-no or if you'd been there a while and sat on committees with them or had some vested interest in their situation, then yes, that would let me out. But none of that's the case. So I'm good to go."

"Well, it should be interesting. I'd love to sound out Mona and Carly on this scene but obviously I can't."

"No, you certainly can't."

"But I wonder if they even know about the accreditation. Can I tell them you'll be visiting?"

"Yes, you can tell them that, but not anything else."

"Got it." Zoe took a long sip of her wine, finishing it, noting the bottle was nearly gone. She set her glass down on the table, drew her feet up onto the couch, shedding her slippers as she did so, and snuggled against Phil. "My grand entry into serious academia is going to be interesting."

3

SPRING BREAK, APRIL 2017
NEW HAVEN, CONNECTICUT

JOEL CURWIN, a third year as assistant professor of Anthropology at Northern Washington University, was researching the impact of the imprisonment of a Paiute chief, Natchez, on the history of the Paiute people. Natchez and his entire band had been arrested, imprisoned first in Alcatraz penitentiary, then placed under a kind of "house arrest" on the Yakima Reservation in Washington State. Eventually much of the band ended up on one reservation in southern Idaho and on another two in Central and Southern Oregon. The story of Natchez and his band had been made famous through the efforts of his sister, Sarah Winnemucca, who had toured the country giving lectures in the late nineteenth century, and had written a book about the injustices done to her family and her people. But how had the draconian measures affected Paiute culture? This was Joel Curwin's interest.

Joel was interested in the disruption to the intricate relationships of trade, economy, military alliances, and marriages that had linked Natchez's band, living in Nevada's Paradise Valley, to the neighboring Bannocks, Shoshones,

Cayuse, and Nez Perce peoples. Joel's dissertation, *Trade, Subsistence, Friends and Foes Along the Oregon Trail, 1846-1860: The Ecology of Interaction Among Indians, Overlanders, and Native Food Resources*, had languished at a university press for nearly two years while the press sent it out to reviewers, then changed editors, sent it out to more reviewers, and then finally let him know they were not going to publish it. Yes, he had quickly sliced three chapters from it and sent them out to journals to be published as articles, but the journals were all local, appealing to regional and specialty interests. He was up for mid-tenure review in the fall and he would either be recommended to apply for tenure the following year or to forget it and move on. He needed a publication in a major journal in the anthropology field that would be of broad interest to the profession.

And now he had one. He had been astonished to learn that one member of the band, a man going only by the name of "Taibo" (ironically, the Paiute word for "white man"), had participated in performances of Buffalo Bill Cody's Wild West Show first in London in 1887 and then in Paris in 1888, ahead of the grand Exposition of 1889 celebrating the 100th anniversary of the French Revolution and just prior to construction of the Eiffel Tower, on the Champs de Mar. While in London, Taibo had enlisted the sympathies and support of the Anti-Slavery Society for reparations compensating the Native participants in the so-called "Camas War" of 1878 for unlawful seizure of their resources and livelihood. The Society had sent an envoy to Idaho in 1890 to investigate. Nothing ever came of it, but the envoy had filed a report which the Society had in its files in London. Joel would have to get himself over there to get a hold of that report, but he had that covered. The University would partially compensate him to present a paper at the annual meetings of the European Society for American Ethnography, in Prato, Italy, in June. He would present a paper there, "Taibo in Paris". Due to the richly detailed reminiscences of the former prisoners of war at Yakima who had ended up in Idaho that some Columbia graduate students had researched and recorded in interviews in an ethnographic field school of 1937, he thought he now had enough to complete a paper that would be of interest to ethnographers, to historians of Indian-white interaction, to scholars of the impacts of Europeans on American domestic policies, to the growing field of human rights studies, and even to military historians, and get it accepted in a major journal.

But now he also had a mystery on his hands. As luck would have it, the previous spring, a fellow professor at Northern Washington had shared with him an issue of the *Ethnohistory Society of North America Newsletter*. His colleague had noted something of interest: an obituary for Jane Bennett, who had been at the field school in 1937 sponsored by Columbia University on the Paiute Reservation straddling the Nevada-Idaho border where the half-dozen students had collected oral histories from venerable Piute elders. He had checked: Jane Bennett had not earned any degree from Columbia. He had searched in vain for publications reflecting that summer of research; aside from one tiny article coauthored by Jane Bennett with one Stephen Stencil, he had found nothing. In fact, with one exception, as far as he could tell, all the participants in the field school had gone on to other academic venues for their PhDs: one into linguistics, another into archaeology, yet another to Florida for post-slavery narratives, and three to Africa! Only one, Stephen Stencil, had maintained his research interest in Native Americans. Three of the students had completely disappeared from the profession, including Jane Bennett.

He reckoned correctly that the journals and field notes from the field school would be in the Columbia University archives, filed with the papers of the supervising professor. His small but adequate travel grant had enabled him to use the weeks off for winter break to travel east to the Columbia archives despite the inclement weather. And, yes! There they were! They were a gold mine of reminiscences about what the elders remembered or what they remembered their elders telling them about the brief period in which horses provided transportation for people and goods and enabled economic, marriage, and defense alliances to be formed. He had found field notes, journals and rough drafts of papers. He thought it peculiar that almost none of the fieldwork was ever turned into dissertations; *maybe it was simply not exciting enough. Maybe the field school was a kind of practice course for the real fieldwork lasting months, not weeks, that each participant would undertake later.*

Joel had wondered at the time why the field notes from Jane Bennett, had not been in the files, despite her name being on the roster of students who had participated. *Had she not participated in in the research after all? Had she dropped out early on?* Now, from the obituary in the *Newsletter*, Joel learned she had not disappeared at all; rather, she had obtained her BA from Yale and a masters from London School of Economics in 1939 and had married one Stephen Stencil a year later, in 1940. *Had she*, he wondered, *studied under the great and good Malinowski?* A search for his obituary turned him up also at London School of Economics, also in 1939, as a tutor. *Had he gone there because Jane was there or the other way around? And how easy had it been for him to get the position of tutor?* They had both returned to the United States on the eve of World War II, taking up residence in Seattle, where Stencil was hired as anthropology faculty for a year. Stencil had eventually become well known; he ended up teaching at Northern Oregon University and had gone on to a distinguished career, publishing a number of books. Jane Bennett had died, incredibly at the age of ninety-nine, in an assisted living facility in Berkeley in 2016. From the obituary he also learned that she had taught sociology and anthropology for forty-four years at University of the Olympic Peninsula with her masters degree from London School of Economics. Obviously, she had foregone her career to marry Stencil and carried on a "commuter marriage" with him. They had no children.

Joel had gone out to University of Olympic Peninsula, and the Special Collections librarian there informed him that yes, Jane Bennett had taught there and yes, there was a file for her. It consisted of class rosters and grades and lecture notes; but no field notes from the Columbia University field school in 1937. So what was she doing in the Columbia University field school in Idaho in 1937? Obviously pursuing Stephen Stencil! *But*, he wondered, *did she take no field notes? If she did take field notes, where were they?*

Then, a thought occurred to him: *with her BA from Yale, might she have donated her personal papers to her alma mater?* Yes! A phone call to the Beinecke Library at Yale confirmed they were indeed there. The Special Collections librarian told him there was quite a thick file for her–term papers, lecture notes for the classes she took, and, yes, it looked like several spiral-bound steno notebooks that might indeed be journals of some sort. Although there was not much left from his little grant to travel out east to research the Columbia archives, there was enough for round trip plane fare and an Airbnb where he could stay and keep food he could prepare himself so as to stretch his grant dollars.

Now, he was ecstatic to see that his hunch had paid off: he was taking copious notes and would see if the Beinecke would copy selected pages from Jane Bennett's journals and, most importantly, the rough draft of a paper, obviously typed in fits and starts over the field season, with some marginal handwritten notes referencing "see notebook #2 (or 3, or 4), pages such-and-such." But as Joel read, a realization slowly crept up on him: *I've read something like this before.* It was not what was in her co-authored piece with Stencil, which analyzed child-rearing practices. This paper-in-pieces was a detailed account of trade and economy along parts of the Oregon Trail. *I read and referenced this material for my dissertation*, he thought, *but it wasn't in anything authored by Jane Bennett!*

He felt a little foolish doing so, but he accessed the electronic version of his dissertation, which, of course, Yale had. The Beinecke staff supplied him with the password necessary to access the library's collections. He did word searches. Yes, he knew he had referenced and quoted the work, in some cases quoting whole paragraphs. The work was certainly important for his dissertation. It represented a crucial and groundbreaking piece of research. But here was the mystery: the author of the work that he had read, cited, quoted was not Jane Bennett. *How had Jane Bennett's field notes gotten, word-for-word, into a monograph authored by someone who was not Jane Bennett?* If the answer to that question was what he thought it was, this was potentially explosive.

Two weeks later Joel was back teaching at Northern Washington, taking his at-least-every-other-weekend break, to visit his girlfriend, Mona Spradley, at Sacajawea and Charbonneau College a couple hundred miles away, but an easy drive. He told her what he had discovered. "There's just one more piece of the puzzle I need," he said. "Wanna go to London this summer?"

4

ZOE WOULD MEET THE REQUIREMENT of having her dissertation in hand and ready to defend with the date set, as the condition for her being hired at Sacajawea and Jean-Baptiste Charbonneau College. Doing so had meant non-stop work for the first seven months of 2017. But she had finished by deadline, to be awarded her PhD in August. When she got the offer from the college, and knew she would have to defend her dissertation by the end of June at the latest and make whatever revisions her committee required by the end of July.

She told Phil, "We need to celebrate with something more than just a good meal." Phil suggested a road trip, more or less replicating one they had taken three years previous to the Southwest. This time, suggested Phil, they would do it leisurely, taking two or three weeks. But Zoe vetoed the idea: she had to be at Charbonneau, as it was colloquially known, for Home Week, as it was colloquially known. It was really a kind of pre-registration boot camp for incoming first-year students, the last week in August, and prior to that, she had to prepare two courses to teach in the fall. One would be based on her dissertation and on a course that she had taken as a student: *Fakers,*

Frauds, Forgers, and Filchers: Scammed, Looted, and Unprovenanced Art. But the other course, *Old Masters* was something she knew a lot about but did not have organized material on. No time for a road trip.

Instead, she proposed nine days in London, starting the day after she uploaded her completed dissertation into the ProQuest website, which would mean her dissertation was official and would result in her being awarded the PhD. She could then have nearly two weeks to prep before the beginning of Home Week.

She had invitations from Carly and Mona as well as from Gudrun Hance to take up temporary residence with them until she could find her own place; she would take them up on their kind offers, hoping to do her preps in the library in the mornings and house or apartment hunt in the afternoons. Eventually she would have her own office at the college, but with profuse apologies, Peter Blenheim had told her that until the issue with her predecessor, Brandon Laird was resolved, he stubbornly refused to vacate his office. The space would not become her office until he did so.

~◦~

So London it was. Nonstop from Seattle, the flight offered movies, music, or old TV reruns, which with which Phil filled his ears and headspace. But Zoe was content with an old John Grisham paperback, *The Litigators*. She hoped it would put her to sleep; she knew she must sleep. But she didn't. Every now and then she would put down the paperback, hoping to nod off, but unable to do so. Instead, she accessed the screen in front of her and watch the cartoon airplane making its way over a cartoon North America, and then the Atlantic and then returned to her paperback.

When they landed at Heathrow, it was morning. They made their way by Tube to their hotel in the Gloucester Road where they stowed their luggage with the concierge who told them they could move into their room after three o'clock. They then went the few steps to the hotel next door that served a full English breakfast: coffee with half-and-half, eggs, bacon, fried tomato, toast, butter, jam.

What to do for the next six hours? Zoe knew she must be jet-lagged, but she also knew from the Rick Steves travel shows that, as he put it, jet-lag hates exercise and fresh air. With the Victoria and Albert and the Science Museum just a few blocks away, it was a no-brainer. That's where they would go.

Zoe was enchanted by the variety offered by the Victoria and Albert: paintings, a display of gowns worn by royalty from Queen Victoria to Princess Di, and a house front that was, so said the exhibit text, one of the few wooden structures to escape the great London fire of 1666. The Science Museum offered any number of hands-on interactives in the environment and epidemiology displays as well as what Zoe found to be an instructive exhibit on communication. And for lunch they could go right back next door to the V & A where a buffet offered hot dishes and salads.

Grateful for the chance to wind down in their room, they actually did take short naps, waking at seven, and walking outside into a light drizzle. For a lark, they decided to walk the few paces to a bus stop and get on the next bus that came, just to see something of London in the slowly descending evening. The bus took them to what they learned was one of London's pride and joys: White City, a collection of multi-storied interior malls and super-stores that dwarfed the King of Prussia shopping center in Pennsylvania, that had so wowed Zoe on a trip with her aunt when she was a child. When the bus dropped them around the corner from their hotel, they decided to walk up the Gloucester Road to see what they might find for supper. An upstairs restaurant proved just perfect: Zoe got an olive plate, hummus, and falafel with pita bread. Phil chowed down on gyro and a green salad with feta.

In Kew Gardens they had brunch at the Orangerie. Real old-lady garden party food: sandwiches of cress and mayonnaise, cream cheese and salmon, and scones with clotted cream! The grounds are like a plant museum, all labeled. At the greenhouse Zoe learned the gardens were established in the mid-1700s not as a beauty spot but for scientific purposes: experimentation with cross-breeding plants, new varieties and as an incubator for the bread-fruit tree native to the South Pacific and transplanted to the British holdings in the West Indies. Rubber trees, as well, were grown from seeds planted in the Kew greenhouse, then transplanted to the British colonies in Malaysia to break the monopoly on the rubber trade then controlled then by Peru and Brazil.

The following day brought them to the Courtauld Collection, Somerset House, the Wallace Collection, and the Soane Museum. Zoe was amazed at Soane, who collected stuff willy-nilly, mixing up time periods and styles, picking up bits and pieces wherever he went and having them shipped back to his house. A Constable painting hung on the wall next to a marble foot taken up from some smashed Roman peristyle!

Day four saw them at the Tower of London and Westminster Cathedral. Another day of sight-seeing took them via the Underground again to Westminster, where they crossed the bridge and strolled in pleasant mid-morning warmth along the Albert Embankment, traipsing back over the Thames at Lambeth Bridge, ending up at the Tate Britain. They returned to what they liked to think of as their neighborhood for a late lunch at the V & A, then, exhausted, they took naps.

They decided to make a late afternoon foray to Harrod's and its famous "Egyptian" escalators, not to mention its food hall with myriads of gourmet delicacies. It was with some astonishment, that, as she and Phil strolled down the Brompton Road, on this, their fifth day in London, she heard her name called. They stopped. Again they heard "Zoe!" *Must be a different Zoe, surely,* she thought. But she looked around. And there, across the street, in a restaurant with French doors opening onto a terrace, sat Mona Spradley! "Zoe!" Mona shouted a third time, waving both arms. "Mona!" Zoe shouted back. She and Phil crossed the street and mounted the steps up to the restaurant. "Join us!" invited Mona. Their food had just arrived and they were tucking in. Zoe and Phil pulled two chairs over and sat at the tiny round table. A wait person hustled over. Mona introduced Joel Curwin, her more-or-less beau.

"We already ate–really great salads at the Victoria and Albert. But how about a couple of glasses of white? Pinot gris? This is so amazing! What are the chances!" gushed Zoe. "What are you doing here? I didn't know you were going to be in London this summer!"

"I didn't either, until a few weeks ago," said Mona. "Oh, I hope you don't mind. We're incorrigible meat eaters." Her lunch was grilled salmon; his was a lamb shank. She and Joel were in London for two weeks, Mona explained, with several days in Paris, then back to London for an overnight coach trip to Bath and the Cotswolds, before returning to Washington state for Home Week at Charbonneau. "We're here in pursuit of a mystery–actually probably a case of fraud."

"Now, now, now, let's not puncture the balloon! Breathless anticipation is part of the strategy," tutted Joel.

"But how can you let out titbits before you unveil the whole scenario?" objected Mona.

"By choosing a publication for the first article that gets things out quickly and one for the second one that everybody knows is pokey slow. The first one is published right here in Bloomsbury. It's out of University College. *History and Anthropology*. *The American Anthropologist* will publish the second one; they're notoriously slow."

Mona explained to Phil and Zoe: "He's writing two articles on this anthropologist who recently died: Jane Bennett." She turned to Joel. "So people reading your first article will learn that Jane Bennett compared Kula Ring stones with–what did you call them?"

"Chert templates from Northern Nevada," responded Joel.

"As part of a paper that Jane Bennett wrote for Malinowski," added Mona.

"For her master's thesis! Which obviously a so-called scholar who plagiarized her field notes from the Yale Library archives didn't know about," completed Joel.

Phil's and Zoe's heads swiveled back and forth as they followed this enigmatic conversation, with questions bursting forth: Who plagiarized what?

Who is this Jane Bennett? Whose master's thesis? Who was the plagiarist?

"Can't answer that last question at this point." Joel wagged his head. "But rest assured, you will be astonished when the whole story comes out in publication number two. Jane Bennett was an anthropologist who had a career tucked behind her more famous husband, Steven Stencil. And it was part of her master's thesis that was plagiarized; actually some field notes and the draft of a paper she wrote while she was still in the States. I had almost all the pieces of the puzzle put together; all I needed was her master's thesis."

"If this has something to do with anthropology," offered Zoe, "Phil has a special interest. He's an anthropologist."

"So is Joel," noted Mona.

"But you can't tell us who the plagiarist was at this point?" Phil prodded.

"No."

Zoe turned to Mona. "Do you know?"

"Yes, and you'll be settled into Charbonneau when it all comes out. You'll be surprised when you find out."

"Yeah. Somebody, or several somebodies, will be shitting their pants when that first article comes out, or at least when they learn about it." Joel chuckled. "Anyway, turns out I didn't have to bother the London School of Economics people--long story--because I found what I needed at Imperial College."

"So you know who the principals are," Zoe asked Mona, following up on Phil's probe.

Mona nodded. "I know. Let's just say it's a lot closer to home than we are here. And, can I say that part two, Joel, your second publication on it, is going to be kind of autobiographical?"

Joel nodded. "Yeah you can say that. It's going to be what we call historiographical. A step-by-step revealing of how I did something using archived documents and what the process of that revealing revealed. Believe me, it's going to read like a whodunit!"

"A revealing of a revelation that rips off the masque of fraud and deception!" Zoe tried to sound like Daniel Ellsberg in one of his many interviews about the *Pentagon Papers*.

"Yeah, yeah! I like that!" enthused Joel. "Got it right here!" he slapped his hand on a saddlebag draped over the back of his chair.

"And while he's been at Imperial College, I've been at London Museum Docksides. They have a huge medieval collection." Mona turned to Joel. "But next you have to present your paper on 'Taibo in Paris'. After all, that's why we–you--are here." She turned to Zoe and Phil. "European Society for American History, annual meetings--in Prato, Italy! That's just up the street from Firenze–Florence! All those Titians and Tintorettos and Bellinis and Boticellis! So for me, it's a tax write-off," she said with a big smile.

"Ah! Through the Chunnel on the Eurostar!" exclaimed Zoe. "How exciting!"

Three more days of museums brought them to the London Docksides, the National Galleries on Trafalgar Square, and of course, the British Museum, spiced with lunches and dinners in Drury Lane, Knightsbridge, Covent Garden, and Exhibition Road. At the British Museum, Phil had them go at a snail's pace, making them stop and read almost every text, every label. At the Rosetta Stone he reflected: "Written in three languages, this pompous decree in three languages really opened up the study of hieroglyphic Egyptian, because the version in Greek made it clear that hieroglyphic Egyptian and demotic Egyptian were the same language, just written differently." At the National Portrait Gallery Phil got quickly bored. "Who cares about all these stuffed shirts and their wives from ages past?" They departed for the National Gallery, right next door.

And here, Zoe set the pace and made Phil stop at the works she really wanted to contemplate: Da Vinci's Virgin of the Rocks, Caravaggio's Boy

Bitten by a Lizard, Titian's various scenes from Roman myths, Rubens' biblical tableaux, Vermeer's Ladies, Cezanne's Bathers, Constables' Salisbury Cathedral, and Rousseau's Tiger in a Tropical Storm. *How is it,* she wondered, *that ordinary slice-of-life situations such as the bitten boy, la-di-da ladies entertaining themselves, figures in nature, and fantastical or wished-for events from various ages' treasured stories all inspired such different yet compelling artistic imaginations and the challenge of capturing the human condition, the machinations of deities, the magic of natural settings that we can now only look at, that we cannot experience, cannot enter because of the march of time, the tyranny of distance, the separation of ourselves from the immortals? When they, the artists, were drawing and splashing the colors, planting figures into rooms and landscapes and mythic, mystical majesties, were they able to do so? Were they able to enter their creations, to actually be what and where and even who their depictions presented?*

Their return flight was on Air Norway with a change of planes in Denver, then on to Seattle. Unlike the flight over to London, these air journeys lulled Zoe to sleep, with questions about the life toward which she was now racing erasing the awe and wonder of their week in the suspension of other-worldliness hovering in her consciousness on the occasions she emerged from slumber. *What did Joel have up his sleeve that would, as he put it, make him the Sherlock Holmes of academia, or at least of a little corner of it? Why were Carly and Mona so tight-lipped about the departure of their fellow scholar-teacher, Brandon Laird, who had occupied the position she was about to fill, until last year? What major scandal must have compelled the college to let go a tenured faculty member? Sexual harassment? Must have been. But why so secretive about it? In so many other venues the aggrieved parties were more than willing to expose their exploiters and harassers, and the accused were even more vocal in their righteous denials. And it seemed that there might be one of those situations. But what was it about the crash site that produced a wreck, but one that then couldn't be hauled away?*

5

CONSIDERING HERSELF thoroughly integrated into faculty life, and thrilled to be so, Zoe had indeed embarked on a marathon routine of preparing lectures, class exercises, and paper assignments for her two fall semester courses in her library carrel in the mornings. Like most college and university libraries, this one had converted itself into a gathering place. Computer stations abounded. The entire top floor was faculty study carrels on the periphery and small-group study rooms. There were no books. Well, that wasn't quite true. Half the ground floor was movable book shelving. But seventy per cent of the library's collection, she had been told, was housed off-campus in a storage facility; you submitted a request for a book in the morning and had it delivered to the circulation desk by five o'clock. Or, if submitted in the afternoon, you had it by next morning.

Her carrel, as did all the carrels sported a narrow floor-to-ceiling view; this one looked out on Kendall Green. As she pounded away on her laptop, she stopped every now and then to contemplate the view. She liked to divide the two-hour class sessions into lecture in the first hour, and class discussion or problem-solving for the second hour. The *Frauds and Filchers* class leant itself particularly to this format: project a slide and have the students, in pairs or groups, hunt for hints: genuine or guile? Ruse or real? Looted or legitimate? And why?

She planned to dress up for her first day of class by wearing her black handkerchief hemline DJT skirt with a white chiffon T-shirt blouse. The outfit would present nicely her well-filled-out-but-well-sculpted body, at 118 pounds and a height of five feet-five inches. She was young and looked it, and with her blue eyes, frizzy-styled hair, and dusky, roundish Kim Kardashian-like cameo face and a nose that might evoke Matisse's Zorah, she knew that look was to her disadvantage for being taken seriously. On the other hand, her blond-highlighted frizzy hair that looked okay even when mussed and her latte colored skin would attract eye-riveting attention. The effect was a sufficiently exotic one to get students to stare at her long enough to try to pigeonhole her on the "ethnicity and race" chart that had become so much a part of Americans' head space and once she had that attention, she would launch forth.

She would begin her *Frauds and Filchers* class with two particularly famous hoaxes. First would be a textbook example of stolen artifacts that found their way into legitimate, even highly respected venues that ricocheted with resounding rebounds through the museum world. In 1986 a gang of thieves had broken into the 16th century summer home of a wealthy member of the defunct Italian nobility who spent most of the year in her home in Rome. The summer house was piled full with collectible furniture, paintings, sculpture, and accessories. The place abounded with Louis XVI chairs, antique church pews, Bruegel engravings, works by the Master of Flemalle and Petrus Christus, statuary by Matteo Civitali, Mino da Fiesole, Jacopo della Quercia, and sepulchral objects from Roman ruins. The burglars had easily snapped the padlock off the door and carted off just about everything. The even stripped the carpets from the floors and ripped out a fireplace, columns, and parts of walls. They left nothing of even dubious value. Then, little more than a year later, vigilant Italian art police noted three items in a catalogue of a May auction in Sotheby's London: a Roman marble capita, a Roman marble child's sarcophagus, and the fragmentary front of another Roman sarcophagus. All three matched descriptions of items taken from the wealthy aristocrat's lodgings. Interpol moved to block the sale; two hours before the auction was scheduled to open, Sotheby's pulled the items from its offerings. They had been consigned by a Geneva-based company. After much investigation and negotiations between European Union representative and Swiss authorities, ten years later the company was revealed as a repository for hundreds of items dug up from Italian ruins. The revelation rumbled through the art world, leading famously to a lawsuit against a curator at a well-known art museum who was an innocent victim of the filchings, and the eventual repatriation of some of the museum's most prized antiquities back to Italy.

She would get to the case by leading the students through a little exercise questioning museums as safe havens for items of world heritage. The lesson would be clear: even seasoned museum curators could be fooled with fake authentications for family heirlooms reluctantly relinquished by this or that count or marquess in service to cash flow dilemmas. As frequent mediators in booty's transition from looted patrimony to respectable museum treasure, auction houses were particularly susceptible to the certificate-sanctioned peddling of purloined property.

Then she would begin the second hour with a standard straight lecture on El Greco, ending with a slide of a painting proudly displayed in a museum sporting the signature "El Greco". She would ask the students, "What's wrong with this picture?" It was the fact that this well-known *"nom-de-plume"* was an attribute of conversation, a nickname, an artefact of the world of art patronage, not that of art creation. El Greco always signed his pieces with his name: Doménikos Theotokópoulos, in Greek!

That first lecture had gone well, as had the exercise; she then had the class right where she wanted them. Her *Art Appreciation* class was not nearly as much fun. She was following an outline that was pretty much the same for all class sections, no matter who taught it, but she did introduce some unusual perspectives on brushstrokes as she showed the slides, drawing on her well-tutored store of knowledge courtesy of her former boyfriend, Nick Taylor, now a not forgotten but thankfully absent part of her personal history. Life felt like it was sliding into a routine. After munching a quiche or a sandwich from the Bistro Café on the library's ground floor, she devoted afternoons to apartment hunting before she returned, either to Carly's and Mona's, or to Gudrun Hance's, usually after supper time. She abjured offers to set something aside for her. They were all meat-and-fish eaters and it was too complicated. Falafel and hummus from a Lebanese take-away, or a cheese pizza or bell pepper-and-tomato pasta from Tony's, both near campus, did just fine for her.

Now, it was the beginning of the second week of classes. She had finally found a place, one large room with free-standing wardrobe and her own shower and toilet, in a big old house on the hill that had once been one of the farmer barons' mansions. She had kitchen privileges, of course, but there was also a mini-fridge and she had bought an electric crock pot, microwave, coffee maker, and teapot with infuser. The situation was almost identical, if somewhat more spacious, to the little flat she had had with Nick as an undergraduate in Connecticut. She thought she had grown up or out of sharing spaces but things were limited in the tiny town, and the trip to London had seriously shackled her credit card limits and which had accrued painful interest charges. She could occupy it as of October first.

Today, at the beginning of this second week, after classes, Mona had insisted: "You have to come to fat Tuesdays and sinful Saturdays. Come over as soon as you can this afternoon. You don't have to bring anything but we'll be sure to have at least one veggie or cheesy dish or you can come over early and fix something for yourself or to share, if you don't mind looking at us tearing into chicken or gobbling salmon skin. And we always have a green salad! Arugula is all over the backyard garden and we get grape tomatoes from the student farmers' market at the college every Thursday afternoon. We try to grill on Saturdays when the weather cooperates; Joel usually comes down and Carly's James brings stuff from a really great deli market in Walla Walla. All you have to bring, really, is a special bottle of wine."

"He lives there?"

"No, he just likes to drive down and pick up goodies. Hey, would Phil want to drive up? Could he stay with you for the weekend? That would be really fun! Joel drives down Thursdays for the weekend if the weather's okay for the weekend. You remember Joel, from London? If Phil came too, you wouldn't be odd gal out."

So now, for her first fat Tuesday she had brought a liter bottle of Austrian Riesling, very different from most American and German Rieslings because it was dry, not fruity, and her crock pot full of split pea, shallot and zucchini soup, flavored with turmeric, lemon juice and garlic cloves, thickened with egg. Carly had fixed roasted yellow, green and red peppers with sun-dried tomatoes, balsamic vinegar, garlic cloves, and canned artichoke hearts and Mongolian peanut-and-beef stir fry. "Can I ask two questions?" queried Zoe. "First, why 'fat' Tuesdays?"

"Fat," said Carly quickly.

"My husband was always going on about fat—his, mine, everybody's," replied Mona.

"Fat, fat, fat," chanted Carly.

"Fat, fat," responded Mona.

It's almost like a mantra, thought Zoe. Then she asked for clarification: "Husband?"

"Ex-husband. And I did used to be a little plumper," replied Mona.

"You mean you used to be slender instead of skinny," remarked Carly.

"I ain't no skinny. And I've got cellulite," added Mona.

"Everybody's got cellulite," objected Zoe. "It has nothing to do with fat."

"Anyway, fat Tuesdays are just kind of a joke, like, Mardi Gras? We don't teach on Wednesdays. Well, neither do you, so it's like our first Friday. And, fat is conspicuous by its absence."

"No fat," affirmed Mona.

Carly nodded vigorously. "No deserts. None on sinful Saturdays, either. So they're not sinful."

"Then Saturday is like our second TGIF, like Friday. So we make whoopee," added Mona.

"Why not on actual Friday?" Puzzled Zoe.

"James has classes all day on Fridays. Field trips, labs. Sometimes he gets back late, really exhausted."

"Okay. Now to the second question: Why was my predecessor abruptly dismissed? Was it for one indiscretion? Or a string of many?"

"A string of them. But not his. Hers," replied Carly.

"Hers?"

Mona clarified: "His wife's. Every fall she'd audit a class, something she could do as a faculty wife. She'd select a male student from the class and shag him, usually for just that term, but sometimes for the entire year."

"And one of them complained?"

"No. It went on for years. But then a new instructor, female, in the English Department *did* complain. She filed a grievance, claiming Mickie's liaison with the student was disruptive to the class."

"But that probably wasn't the real reason," amended Carly. "We think the instructor was probably put up to file the complaint by administration, to give them an excuse. I mean, yes, her husband, Brandon, was kind of complicit because without his status as faculty, she couldn't have taken the class as a faculty wife," Carly pointed out.

"But that wasn't the *real* reason, either," noted Mona in her gentle way, "it was the Vermeer that did it, and the Grassers."

"*Vermeer?*"

"The Vermeer that's not a Vermeer," said Carly matter-of-factly.

"Oh!" Exclaimed Zoe excitedly. "A genuine Han van Meegeren?"

"You've got it!

"Well, that's not so bad. It's a good teaching moment."

"Yes, well, eat your heart out. It's been taken off view. You can't use it for a teaching moment."

Agitated and annoyed, Zoe wiggled to the edge of her chair held her hands out, palms up, and shook her head. "I don't get it."

"Okay." Carly shoved her plate, with the remains of the veggie and beef stir-fries, toward the middle of the table, put her elbows on it, and brought her hands up in a kind of prayerful mode. "The Grassers are major donors. Mainly money, but over the years they've given a few paintings, mainly all those dark domestic scenes and portraits of unknowns by unknowns."

"Now that's not quite true", Mona scolded. "van Honthorst, Bloemaert, van Hoostrater, ter Borch, du Mol, van Mieris, Bramer--they were all well known in their day."

Zoe could tell that this was a subject that was not to be exhausted any time soon. She chimed in, imitating a connoisseur of haute culture: "Indeed, what makes a painting a work of gray tart?" She made quotation marks above her head.

"Yes, yes, yes," responded Carly dismissively. "Great art is in the eye of the beholder. But you know most of what's in that gallery is faculty artwork and a few pieces from former students. I think it's their policy to acquire one every year. They have a little contest for seniors' best. It's a community outreach kind of thing. A panel is assembled from the good citizens of Dayton to do the judging. But we digress. Anyway, so over the last twenty years, Florence and Melvin Grasser have given huge bucks and every now and then donated a painting or two found for them at an auction, an estate sale, somebody's attic, a junk store by guess who?"

"Uhhh ..."

"That's right! Your predecessor! Professor Brandon Laird!"

"He was their buyer?"

"Right. Their finder, buyer, art broker, procurer, whatever. Brandon Laird went charging around the world on their nickel, picking up art bargains, some of which they kept, some of which they donated."

"Aha!" interjected Zoe. "While wifey-poo amuses herself at home by shagging a series of student studs."

"Exactly."

"Isn't that, like, conflict of interest?"

"That's what we thought when we heard about what he'd been doing," affirmed Mona. "But we asked Pete about it."

"Blenheim."

"Right." Mona leaned back in her chair, apparently a signal for Carly to take up the narrative.

"The university attorney said as long as he was not being paid to *authenticate* the art works, that is, he wasn't using his position to sell his professional services"—now Carly made quotation marks in the air—"it wasn't conflict of interest. All he was doing was *accepting gifts*, travel and lodging, and *picking up gifts* for friends, who compensated him for his expenses in obtaining those gifts. Yeah, it was definitely awash in shades of grey, ethically, but it wasn't technically illegal. So it all worked. Grassers got some art, the college got some art, Laird got teaching aids and fun trips, the students got first-hand viewings of decent artwork.

"Well," continued Carly, "one of those bargain paintings he found was the Vermeer. Apparently it hung in the living room of the Grassers' ski chalet in Aspen for years; then Florence broke her collarbone in a skiing accident. It shook her up. She decided there was no point in having a pied-a-terre in Aspen -- better to trade it in for a golf shack in the Caymans. They downsized, de-accessioned. The Vermeer came to Charbonneau. Press conference, unveiling, hoi-polloi flying in from global hot spots, catered appetizers, woo-hoo!"

"You were invited."

"No. But I was," chimed in Mona. I mean, it would have been weird not to invite the resident expert on Dutch old masters."

Zoe turned to Mona. "And you spotted it as a forgery?"

"No, no, no! I wouldn't have dreamed, wouldn't have dared. But you've got to appreciate that it attracted curious connoisseurs, experts, real authenticators. And one of them spotted it. The Grassers had insisted on tests and sure enough, the paints and canvas were consistent with it being mid-seventeenth-century, *but …*"

"Had it never been authenticated?"

"Oh, yeah, back in the 1950s, by somebody long dead."

"Oooo! Major event in the forgeries world! So what tipped off the expert that something wasn't right? And how did I miss all this?" mused Zoe.

"You missed it because it was instantly hushed up. The Grassers were hugely embarrassed, angry, mortified. It was just coincidence that all this came down when the English teacher filed her complaint," explained Carly. "Anyway, this visiting expert pointed out the flaw, and Brandon Laird had to go. I mean, what else had he gotten for them that was dubious or forged or faked?"

"How was it determined that it was a van Meegeren, not a Vermeer?"

"Dendrochronology," replied Mona. "Van Meegeren had almost got it right; he'd painted it on a wood panel, just like Vermeer would have done, but the panel turned out to be from the mid-1700s; probably part of an old table he picked up in an antiques store. The tree rings on the panel matched tree rings of European larches cut down in, like, 1760."

"So what happened to Brandon Laird?"

"Nothing, really." Carly replied. "He's still around. I mean, he's not teaching, and he's on unpaid leave of absence, but he's still here, in and out. That's why you don't have an office. Because he still has one. That should be your office. But until the complaint gets adjudicated by the Faculty Senate Personnel Committee, he's only on suspension and so he gets to keep his office, library privileges, yada, yada, yada, until they give a final ruling on the English teacher's complaint."

"So when the English teacher, Minette Grisham filed her complaint about Mickie Laird taking advantage of her devastatingly handsome, highly intelligent, but—according to her--severely dyslexic student at the same time," added Mona, "that became the ostensible reason for Brandon Laird's suspension."

"You knew the student?"

Mona nodded. "Had him in class. Art appreciation."

"So this was our introduction to the quiet but innovative, on-the-cusp but highly reputable Sacajawea and Charbonneau College!" crowed Carly, pouring herself another glass of Riesling.

"These Gassers …"

"Grassers," corrected Carly.

Zoe resumed: "Okay. So these Grassers. I don't mean to sound snotty or anything but what interest do these high-flyers have in, in …"

"In podunk college in butt-fuck nowhere, right?" said Mona.

"Well, not quite that, but …"

"It's Florence," replied Carly. "She's an alumna of Rosamund Academy."

"Which is …?"

"That's us. Used to be," answered Mona. "This was a girl's finishing school until, what, the '70s?" Carly nodded. Mona continued: "They sent the girls off to Radcliffe, Barnard, Smith. Then they went gangbusters. Really expanded. First came the Arts and Performances School, relocated from Lewiston, Idaho. And along with the Arts and Performances School came Florence."

"That was in Idaho. So Florence is from Idaho?" Zoe tried not to sound incredulous.

"Her family made a fortune in potato farming."

"Ah! So daddy sells tubers to grocery store man, who endows Arts and Performances, where of course tuber man's daughter goes to school."

"Yep. And when they absorbed the Arts and Performances School, they also added a two-year college course and with all the baby boomers flocking in they decided they might as well go co-ed so they added boys and then they added another two years of college courses and here we are," added Mona.

"Apparently Melvin Grasser and Florence-whatever-her-name-was were, like, next door neighbors in Boise. He's what they call a self-made man. Made a fortune with an early word processor programs. Ever heard of WordPearl?"

"No."

"Well it was *the* program you used to write anything, before Word came along. Headquartered in Boise, Idaho! Rumor has it that Bill Gates bought him out to eliminate the competition for Word. Anyway, he's, like, been a gentleman of leisure for most of his life. They have houses in half a dozen places: San Francisco, the Caymans, Santa Fe. Flat in London. Yada yada yada."

"So it's his money that funds the gallery?"

"No, it's hers. He has other pet projects. Do-gooder things: malaria clinics in Africa, earthquake reconstruction in Haiti. They're actually good people. But they do things their way, and when things *don't* go their way, watch out!"

"And what about that *Léger* that's hanging in the gallery? Was that also a donation from the Grassers? Surely not a purchase!"

"No, that was also a donation, too," clarified Mona, "but not from the Grassers. That got its own opening and unveiling as well, but not nearly as showy. We–all the faculty–were invited to that one. What was her name?"

"Mavis something," responded Carly. "I remember because who carries around a name like 'Mavis'? She was nice. She and her nephew–forget his name–were here a year ago last March for the gifting and presentation."

"She a Charbonneau alum?"

"No," said Carly in a puzzled tone. "That was kind of strange. It was the nephew who seemed to take credit for getting his aunt to donate the Léger. I think he had some connection, but I don't know what. Maybe with Laird. He seemed very pleased with himself. Could be Laird sort of hoped it the Léger would make up for the Vermeer, but it didn't."

"That is strange," agreed Zoe. "No connection with Charbonneau what-soever? Maybe wanting to have some connection, you know, like getting onto the Board of Trustees?"

"Don't know." Carly frowned. "Don't think so. Anyway, she didn't get the chance to enjoy her potential influence. She died just about a year later. Fell down the stairs in her house. That was–what–a year after the Vermeer scam and her donation of the Léger. Just this last spring. Poor lady. Broke her neck."

"Ow! What a horrid way to go! But the Léger is real, I mean, really painted by Léger."

"I guess. You tell me. You're the fakes expert."

"Does it have an authentication certificate?"

"Probably. We can go over there sometime next week and look at it."

"Oh–and talking of donations! You don't know about our orphans-on-the-doorstep, do you?" Carly's question came off a little smugly, but Zoe sensed yet another good story. She wagged her head back and forth.

"Hey, isn't Phil an archaeologist?" queried Mona. "He should take a look at our orphaned stash."

"No. Cultural anthropologist, just like Joel."

"Well, anyway, some of this stuff seems really archaeological."

"There's a skull," affirmed Carly.

"But Phil's a *cultural* anthropologist, not a physical one."

"Still. Joel may be interested too. So let's save all that for Saturday. Phil is coming, right?"

"Right. And–I guess I should tell you–he'll actually be around here quite a bit. He'll be here for more than a week in October."

"Great!" enthused Mona. "He can be away for that long?"

"Yes, but it's work related." Zoe told them the bare bones of the accreditation visit to the Social Sciences Department.

"Wow! I'll bet heads will roll!" crowed Carly.

"Can they? I mean, those history relics have tenure," objected Mona. "But this is getting really interesting, with what Joel's told me."

Carly nodded knowingly. "I'll bet they'll pitch it like taking long-needed measures to ensure quality education, blah, blah, blah. Maybe making a few heads roll will get Charbonneau back in the Grassers' good graces."

Zoe wondered what kudos or consequences might tumble over Phil if, in fact, heads did roll and a major shake-up came about as a result of his and Porter Harder's report. *Would Porter Harder insist on a hard-hitting expose? Or would he whitewash?*

⟋⟍

Saturday came quickly; Zoe was glad to have had Phil to herself on the tail end of Friday. Now at Carly's and Mona's, a splendidly sunny, warm afternoon welcomed them into the backyard where albacore and salmon sizzled. Phil was formally introduced to James. "This is Dr. James Gambel," Carly stated stentoriously, "Associate Professor of Botany and graduate of the Gambel School of Cuisine who will demonstrate his grilling expertise by *utilizing two different kinds* of fin-equipped denizens of the marine deep." James, in a straw cowboy hat, blue apron and shorts, tongs in hand, took his attention from tending the grill long enough to give a wave of his hand and a "Hi!" Ears of maize roasted in their tinfoil wrappings. More heavy-duty tinfoil, folded into a squarish cooking pot, was also on the grill, in which hunks of summer squash, onion, blanched almonds and curry paste simmered along with fresh peas and Romano beans. Phil and Joel were sprawled in canvas lawn chairs; Zoe, Mona and Carly sat in collapsible camp chairs. They were all sipping Vivanco Rioja Blanco. "And this," she continued, taking Joel by the arm, "is your fellow anthropologist, Joel Curwin."

Phil and Joel shook hands. "Yeah," said Phil. "I remember meeting you in London. Great to see you again!"

"So these boxes," began Carly. "Two weeks before Home Week these boxes, five of them, appear literally on the college's doorstep."

"To be more accurate, on the gallery's doorstep," corrected James, turning around from his post at the grill.

"Right. Four of those big bananas boxes are shipped in and another huge box from Mayflower. Penn–that's Duncan Pennfield, the gallery manager–gets all jumpy, won't touch them, calls in the police, sniffing dogs and all that. Turns out they're clean. No drugs, no explosives. But the gallery and the Arts and Performance School don't want them."

"So you get them?"

"We've got them. But we get to choose what we accession and what we chuck or sell or give away."

"You can accession things, even though you're not a gallery or a museum?" Zoe was perplexed.

"The college, in general, can accession," explained James. "We do it all the time. It's not only the gallery that gets donations. The engineers regularly accession the exit projects of their students, the ones that get A grades, temporarily. They're put on display for a year, proudly shown off to parents of prospective students: see what wonderful constructions your child may also assemble under our brilliant tutelage. They're displayed in cases, then turned back to the students who created them. There are always some who say, 'oh just keep it,' so then it gets permanently accessioned. We've got a ton of those in "the pit", which is what se call our storeroom. Hey! everything's almost done."

They adjourned to a picnic table where six places were set; two bottles of wine sat on ice in makeshift chillers: empty paint cans. James arrived at the table with two plates heaped with the fish and the vegetables, which he set in the table's center. He plopped fish and corn onto everyone's plate along with mounds of vegetables swimming in curry gravy, except for Zoe's; she got double corn and extra stew. "So then what exactly is in these banana boxes?" she asked.

"That's where all of you come in. Your mission, if you choose to accept it," Carly frowned seriously and deepened her voice, "is to unpack, inventory, and do an informed analysis of the contents of four banana and one movers' box."

"You mean you want Zoe to do this?" queried Phil.

"Hey, we'll all do it! You too! It'll be fun!" responded Carly. "And if we all do it, like, over a couple weekends, it'll go all that much quicker. And who knows? It might be interesting. There might be some worthwhile things in there, maybe a few mystery objects."

"Like the skull," Mona nodded.

"Yeah. The arts people opened one box and there was a skull inside! They wouldn't touch it."

Phil dropped his spoon. It clattered onto his plate. "*A skull?* "A human skull? Is it real?"

"Well, that's for you and Joel to tell us!" stated Carly matter-of-factly.

"But I'm not a physical anthropologist. And I really don't enjoy handling dead people"

"Neither am I," chimed in Joel.

"But you'd know if it was real, wouldn't you?"

"Yeah, and I could probably take a stab at saying whether it was male or female, maybe even approximate age. If you'd let me, I could take it back to Multnomah and get a colleague to confirm."

A Week Later

Zoe's second sinful Saturday began in midmorning at the pseudo-Tudor building that housed the Art History Department. She, Mona, Carly, James, Joel and Phil carried four banana boxes and an oversized moving box that comprised the doorstop cache, as Carly called it, out to Phil's vintage Austin mini station wagon; he kept it in the mint condition in which it had come to him as an inheritance from his great uncle, housed in a garage, but for every-day use he drove what Zoe referred to as his "fat little Fiat." Now, however, with the Pacific Northwest enjoying a second week of splendidly sunny, dry weather, he had decided to show it off to his new friends. They drove the few blocks to Carly's and Mona's house, unloaded the boxes, and carried them around into the backyard, setting them on the picnic table in the backyard. Joel would serve as registrar, noting down items as they came out of the boxes, now labeled in black marker #1, #2, #3, #4, and #5. Zoe, Carly, Mona, Phil, and James each had their own box.

Joel would enter the item's description into the table on Carly's laptop. The task was both more interesting and more tedious than they had anticipated. Each item would be inventoried as "accession" (A); "trash" (T); "yard sale" (YS); or "don't know yet" (?). This latter entry could also generate a check in the "investigate?" (I) square. They would also inventory the containers that housed the items, when appropriate, as well as wrappings if there were any. They began with Carly's box: the Mayflower movers carton. "Okay," said Carly, "Here we have one South Berkeley Creamery milk bottle filled with little pieces of glass, minor gems ..."

When they finished three hours later, the inventory showed it to be, indeed, a combination of somebody's highly prized junk collection along with stuff that might merit the label "heirloom" or "cabinet of curiosities". The items requiring more investigation were what looked to Zoe like a ceramic "Colima" dog; nine painted wooden icons that looked like they might be pre-revolutionary Russian; dozens of tiny stone crosses that did not look as if they had been carved; a heavy tome, *Old Panama* by one C.L.G. Anderson, copyright 1911, along with a photograph of Anderson himself, handsomely illustrated "with numerous full-page plates in Duogravure," in its own box, the book inscribed on the frontispiece, *To Hector Cortez, In Appreciation of His Pride in His Ancestors' Courage in the New World, July 20, 1970, Emily V. Quattlebaum* ("What a funny name," *Mona had quipped.* "A name with character," *Carly had parried.* "I've run across funnier: Huntingforest? ffrench with two lowercase 'f's?"); a Roi Tan cigar box filled with coins, some European, but others American, including some silver dollars from the 1880s and large pennies dating from the 1850s; and, yes, a skull, plastered with turquoise tiles. All these got "accession" and "investigate" checks in the inventory list. In the dubious category were a stone Venus of Willendorf, probably fake; a small vest made of what looked like chain mail but, in gold that might have some value; a probably hand-painted set of mah-jongg tiles; the gem (or glass)-filled milk bottle; a matchbook collection; a bottle cap collection; a medallion, dated 1887 with the word "Jubilee", that appeared to commemorate the 50th anniversary of Queen Victoria's reign and seven British coins from the same year of different sizes and values; a stack of bus or commuter train transfer tickets bundled with a fraying rubber band; another milk bottle filled with marbles; a wooden box filled with toys, some plastic but some metal Tonka toys; a tattered, heavy, falling apart children's book called *Chatterbox*; various stones and fossils; a set of pocket-sized guides to butterflies, birds, and plants; and three ceramic beer steins with metal tops, the kind that are sold to tourists all over Germany, all got entries in the "yard sale" column.

The only clues to where the collection had originated were some yellowed newsprint, used as wrapping, from the Oakland Tribune, dating from the 1930s; more newspaper wrappings from the Santa Cruz News-Post, 1999; and, in a box labelled "Podesta Baldocchi, San Francisco", a funeral notice, in an envelope, for someone named Virginia Grimm along with a 1956 catalogue from University of California, Berkeley, with the name "Cortez" written in ink on the cover. The box also contained a half-dozen unframed, small canvases, some signed, that Zoe thought looked vaguely Hudson school-ish.

And then there was the skull. Covered with a mosaic of small turquoise tiles glued onto its surface, in a hat box labeled "Goorin Brothers North Beach" it was, of course, by far of the most interest. Phil looked at it and frowned. "This is a serious matter," he declared. Phil affirmed that it was indeed human; probably from a youngish female; and probably not Native American. Joel agreed.

"But didn't some Indians, like, maybe the Aztecs decorate skulls like this?" asked Carly.

"Yes, you're right. They did indeed do so," Phil answered. "But those are hundreds of years old. This is much more recent. Maybe inspired by the Aztec ones, but not one of them. You know what? Let's pack it back in that hat box with the newspapers. I'll take it back to Multnomah with me and see what my colleague Aarons had to say about it."

"Somebody decorated it with these tiles. How did they do it?" asked Carly.

Phil examined the skull closely. "Probably with superglue."

"Do you suppose it's Cortez' skull?" wondered Zoe. "Whoever Cortez was."

"Nah. Doubtful. Probably it's either not a real skull or maybe something somebody dug up in their backyard," offered Joel.

"If it's real, then it must have been dug up from a graveyard. And if it's Native American, it should be turned over to somebody appropriate for reburial," remarked Zoe.

"Hey, we'll know more once I get Ollie's opinion," declared Phil.

6

SACAJAWEA AND JEAN-BAPTISTE CHARBONNEAU COLLEGE

LATE SEPTEMBER, A FRIDAY

RANDY STROLLED ALONG THE PATH that circled the reflecting pool. He liked it; liked it much better now than the previous March when he, his aunt Mavis, and Associate Professor of Art History Brandon Laird had unveiled and presented the Fernand Léger painting to the College, and he had met Duncan Pennfield. At that time, an icy rain that turned to sleet had swept through the college grounds, whipping the bare trees and evergreens and pelting the windows in the gallery's atrium. The only good thing that had come out of that trip had been Penn. Penn had artlessly suggested, at the gala following the unveiling, after Mavis had been chauffeured back to the hotel in town, that Randy could stay with him since he lived only a few blocks from campus. With the absentminded social drinking, Randy didn't feel like driving all the way downtown, and Penn assured him he had plenty of room.

The "plenty of room" had turned out to refer to his spacious waterbed, which Randy ultimately ended up sharing with him. Penn had, in turn, visited him in Trestle Glen; Mavis was tolerant, understanding, if not exactly out-front approving. She simply referred to Penn as "your nice friend from the college in Washington." Aimee, of course, had no trouble communicating her disapproval. He would be glad to be shed of her if his application for grad school at Sonoma State panned out. Too bad Charbonneau didn't have an anthropology program; but Penn seemed to have a flexible schedule and could visit, just as he did now, every couple of weeks.

Randy reflected: *Too bad about Laird, on suspension for the duration. But the Vermeer had nothing to do with me. That was Laird's bad luck. And too bad also that the Léger had not, in the end, redeemed him, although he had seemed truly grateful to me for finding it. Now all that's done and dusted, good and gone.* It had worked nicely for a while. Randy "found" items at the sales and auctions, or from his weekend flea market stall; Laird then presented them to his clients, mainly this couple who endowed the college and its gallery but lived nowhere nearby--he couldn't blame them–but also others, as "found" by Laird himself. *Well, that was all right. Now*, he thought, *it's probably good that all that was ending just as a new life–Sonoma and Penn–is beginning.* Their back-and-forth trips between Oakland and Charbonneau, much more frequent this past summer, had made the Trestle Glen house, with its fusty circumscriptions and embosomed closeness, its miasma of cautioned patronizing and Aimee's huffy, haughty, short-shrifting tolerance, almost bearable. Charbonneau had loomed increasingly as a haven, a neutral enclave of dilettantish indulgence where consequences cascaded onto someone else. In fact, Penn actually seemed relieved, happier, when it had been announced that "Mr. Laird has voluntarily agreed to take a leave of absence while the complaint against him, involving his wife, Mickie Laird, whose access to the circumstances alleged in the complaint, had been facilitated by Mr. Laird's position at the college, is under review."

Randy had initially resented Penn for planting doubts and suspicions in his Aunt Mavis' mind those few months ago, and especially in cousin Aimee's mean little mentations. *But it's all worked out*, he reflected, *hasn't it?*

Mr. Cronin had indeed come up from San Diego, but, in the end, did not, could not change Aunt Mavis' will, as Aimee had so wanted him to do on Mavis' anticipated instructions and which Mavis had been prepared to do. Rather, he affirmed the will's original provisions. Randy and Aimee would share equally in the annuity that, Mr. Cronin assured them, would "bring you each a minimum of one percent of the principal on a quarterly basis, so never less than $2,400, and in years when the stock market cooperates or the trust's managers are particularly savvy–over which, by intention, you have no say-so–as much as $18,000, more or less, per quarter which, of course you can, and should reinvest to assure you a modest income for the remainder of your lifetimes, blah, blah, blah." *Well, not bad. I can live on that,* he thought, *and leave the profit from selling Mavis the replica dining room set, the bronzes, the lithographs, the Braque, the kilims tucked away as a fail-safe. And,* he thought, *at least the other stuff can now be reasonably assured to be secured from the peril of unwanted scrutiny, whether deliberate or accidental, from Brandon's nosy colleagues. Aimee's so dumb, so clueless. And she'll probably get Kenny to move in with her, into Mavis' house. Perfect.*

Randy had all but moved out of the house. It and everything in it belonged to Aimee now; she could have evicted him anyway. He had boxed up everything of his, not that it was much, and moved it in stages to a storage locker in Santa Rosa, to be moved again to his quarters when he got settled at Sonoma State. Penn had taken his vacation and joined Randy for the glorious last two weeks of May and they had spent numerous afternoons wine tasting in the Sonoma and Napa vineyards. In June and July he had completely disregarded Mr. Cronin's advice and spent much of his thankfully substantial quarterly income, taking advantage of reduced rates during the week in the ranch B&B outside of Sonoma. Every long weekend, Thursday through Sunday, he spent with Penn at Charbonneau.

In August he moved into his dormitory room at Sonoma State and gotten his meager possessions out of storage. Now he was snatching another precious week with Penn at Charbonneau while his major instructors–the

Drs. Pinkowski–were away at an archaeology conference in Reno. "Deucedly early this year," Ned Pinkowski had complained, "but these contract archeos run the conference now and this makes a nice hiatus for them between the trials and tribulations of the hot and dusty summer field season and the last couple of months of pleasant weather before they have to shut down their digs. But hard on us academics, who have to interrupt classes to get wherever the conference is."

So here he was, reflecting on all this, appropriately, on a bench at the reflecting pool, waiting for Penn to gather him up for lunch in the faculty dining room. Randy and Penn had arranged to meet here; then they would make their way to the mock-Tudor building that housed the student cafeteria and the faculty dining room.

~⌒

ZOE, PHIL, CARLY, MONA, JOEL; RANDY, PENN

Zoe, Mona, and Carly made their way from the Art History building to the cafeteria, Joel and Phil in tow. James could not join them because he was doing his Friday marathon of labs and small-group tutorials. Usually, Joel arrived late Friday afternoons or evenings, but some weeks, this being one of them, he was able to get away earlier, arriving Thursday evening, as had Phil. They entered the cafeteria through the line marked "faculty". There was always a *prix fixe* lunch: $6 for faculty, $3 for students, or sandwich and desert chits for $1.50 each. Drinks were free, but if you wanted Pepsi or Mountain Dew, or a bag of mini-chips, you had to plunk money into one of the machines, just inside the building, lining the outside wall of the cafeteria. Access to the faculty dining room was at the cafeteria's far end. As they stood in line, Mona explained that the chit system, as well as the placing of the vending machines outside the cafeteria was to discourage binge eating of junk foods and thereby obesity and concomitant health problems. Inside, signs at every station proclaimed, "No seconds". The rule seemed to be enforced by two monitors in which chefs' aprons roaming the space.

"Okay," announced Carly. She swept her arm out to her right, explaining to Phil, "so behind the glass doors you've got your sandwiches: ham, cheese, ham *and* cheese, roast beef, egg salad, chicken salad and your yogurts: plain, vanilla, fruits. You've got your soft drinks, your juices, kefirs, waters. Deserts: ice cream, ice milk, ice soy, sherbet, strawberry and chocolate mousse." She gestured ahead of herself. "Straight ahead in the middle, the salad buffet: lettuce, tomatoes, olives, croutons, marinated artichoke hearts, garbanzo beans, kidney beans, three different kinds of salad dressing. To your left", her left arm shot out, "your hot buffet. Looks like today, potato and cauliflower curry; roast carrots and new potatoes; pulled pork; chicken in gravy; hamburger patties; hot dogs and bratwurst. Bread, hamburger and hot dog buns. Coffee high-test, coffee decaf, hot water and teas. The faculty dining room will have prime rib roast and either pork loin or ham; they always do." They made their way into the center of the room.

Zoe looked at Phil, then peeled off to the refrigerator section. Drinks? Carly? Mona? Joel? Phil?" "Orange juice for me," called Mona after her. "My usual AriZona tea," said Carly. Zoe grabbed them and handed Phil a lemon water for him and another for herself.

"I've got my tea and my tea ball," responded Joel.

"I'll go ahead and snag a table," said Carly. Joel was hovering at the coffee-and-teas table, filling a large cup with hot water; he had a plate of pulled pork and roast veggies. As Zoe sailed past him with the drinks she said, "They have roast veggies in the dining room too, and usually a bit more, like maybe golden beets or kale."

She returned to the student cafeteria as Joel was navigating his tray of food and hot water into the dining room; he'd set a little canister and a tea ball on the tray. "I'll have some of the pork loin and roast beef, too," declared Joel.

Zoe came in the faculty dining room with a plate heaped with salad, bleu cheese dressing and the curry; she sat beside Joel as Mona, Carly, and Phil were cutting thin slices of roast beef and pork loin onto their plates alongside little piles of carrots and potatoes.

Duncan Pennfield raised a hand in casual greeting and nodded at the adjacent table as those seated at it tucked into their food. Randall Allen stared. One of the two men at the table turned. Randy caught the unmistakable shadow of puzzled recognition that flitted across the man's face as his eyes locked with Randy's. He might not have been able to exactly place who Randy was, but Randy knew exactly who *he* was: those mutton chops were unforgettable. What was *he* doing *here*? "Who are they?" Randy asked Penn.

"The three young ladies are Carly, Mona, and the new hire–forgotten her name--three-fifths of the Art History faculty. I don't know who the two dudes are. Oh, yes, I know. He's attached to one of the young ladies. I met him last year at a do when the new hire came to interview. They had a little wine-and-cheese thing after her job talk. She's teaching an interesting class– what is it now?" He paused. "'Freaks, Frauds and Phonies?' Something like that. Anyway, it's about forgeries and their makers–like the Vermeer that unfortunately was not and put paid to our mutual former friend."

"He, the boyfriend, also teaches Art History here?'"

"No, no. He's … what is he? I think, oh, yeah. He's in your newly found field of endeavor: archaeology." Penn had noticed Randy staring. "Does he look familiar? Do you know him? Maybe you encountered him at a conference. You want to go over and say hi?"

"No, no. I don't think so. I don't think I know him. What's his name?"

"Ah … what is his name? Can't remember." Penn shook his head. "I think Joe something. Can't remember if I ever heard his last name."

"But he teaches here," affirmed Randy.

"No, teaches at, I think U Wash, or maybe Northern Washington. I've seen him here now and then in the faculty dining room, and also at our Friday art lectures, when we have them."

Randy heard the man who was probably Joe and might be an archaeologist, teaching at either Northern Washington or U Wash, apparently declaiming in answer to a question, "Nope. No coffee after nine a.m. but mint tea just about every hour on the hour until supper time."

"Then it's beer or wine, right?" He heard the tallest of the three women declare. "And so you bring your little can of tea and your tea ball everywhere you go, don't you?" she added teasingly.

"That's right!" he declared stridently, but jovially, picking up the canister by the side of his plate and banging it on the table.

Yes, thought Randy, *he was the one from the estate sale, last year. And now here he is! And I'm pretty sure he recognized me. So if he recognized me, he'd be able to recognize, identify, the others who were with me at that sale. And is it his girlfriend who teaches a course on frauds and forgeries? Or somebody at that table at least. And Penn with the Léger in his gallery … And Penn doesn't know it, but it was Brandon who had "found" the Léger and planted it in the estate sale and who had declared to Penn and to the Chancellor that it had been* Randy *who had cleverly "found" the Léger in the estate sale. Attested to by Brandon, based on the authentication certificate, it was Brandon who persuaded my old biddy aunt,* reflected Randy–*sorry, the venerable willing donor, to gift it. Isn't it just a matter of time before two and two and two get put together? Well, I'll share this information with the others, and let them decide what to do about it.* He thought, *measures might have to be taken.*

He became aware of Penn making motions with his hand. In fact, he was snapping his fingers in Randy's face. "Hey, *hey*! Earth to Randy! Earth to Randy! Come in, come in!"

Randy shook his head. "Sorry. Just a food coma. This roast beef is filling."

THE FOLLOWING DAY: SATURDAY

As the academic quarter progressed, Zoe's classes were going increasingly well; the students were enthusiastic, responsive, and high-performing. After receiving a positive reply from her letter of inquiry, she had sent her dissertation off to a publisher, Felix Harrow, in London, for consideration for publication. Her colleagues continued to be hospitable, full of useful and entertaining anecdotes, gossip, and rumors from Charbonneau's past and present, and she was really pleased with her new friends. She found something enigmatic about James, but could not put her finger on what it was. Phil, quiet as he was, seemed to be fitting right in. He and Joel, especially, seemed to be forming a special bond, or at least it seemed to Zoe that Joel was making a special effort to do so.

On this, Zoe's fourth "sinful Saturday", in the nothing-short-of-miraculous third week of fine weather and also the third week of fall term, while James was unpacking the cooler from what he called his "Walla Walla run", Zoe saw Joel take Phil aside. "Let's go for a walk," he said, and they did so.

Mona had told Carly and Zoe that she thought Joel seemed nervous about something ever since they'd had the meal in the cafeteria. *Maybe that food didn't settle well with him*, Zoe thought. He'd been unusually quiet. Zoe tinkered with the salad she contributed to the late-afternoon meal, which would be taken outside in the backyard, with James doing the honors at the grill: a huge heap of cold pasta with celery, scallions, large cherry tomatoes, halved, one cup of crushed corn chips, a small jar of vegan bacon bits, and a dressing consisting of two-thirds of a cup of vegan mayonnaise, paprika, salt, and two thirds cup of olive oil, added at the last minute. "So the pasta doesn't get soggy," Zoe had explained. "The recipe called for hard-boiled eggs as well, so you can add those to yours if you want." Mona had boiled up a dozen of them and piled them into a bowl that now sat on the table.

Zoe had also noticed, without saying anything to Mona, as they sipped their preprandial wines, that Joel seemed jumpy, not saying much, his eyes darting around the assembled gathering periodically, as if he was trying to get hold of a thought, or an idea that was eluding him. Now she saw Mona watching, she thought somewhat anxiously, as Joel and Phil strolled off together. She walked up beside her. "Something up?" she asked.

Mona shook her head. "It seems like something's eating Joel. He was really fidgety yesterday and he's even more so today. I'll bet it's the Jane Bennett thing."

"Huh?" Zoe looked at her.

"He was really happy to find all this material on this historian called Jane Bennett. Remember when we were all in London together?"

"Yeah, that's right. He was like, on a high. Jazzed. Seemed like he had all kinds of good things going."

"That's what I thought. I wonder if that's it. Too many good things going. Maybe having trouble writing all those articles he's got planned."

James had everything prepared; a few minutes on the gas grill would do for the chicken kabobs, the shrimp and scallops on skewers, and the marinated slivered beef from the deli. A few minutes would also do for what Zoe had brought for her hot dish: large portabellas stuffed with thawed frozen spinach, Vidalia onion, red bell pepper-feta cheese and a panko-and-egg mixture, already cooked. Although Mona had made a Mumbai Chaat satay sauce for the kabobs and the beef, Zoe thought she might try it over a portabella just to see how it was.

Now, as James brought the grilled food and set it in the middle of the picnic table, Joel and Phil returned, both looking serious, but James twirled two kabobs with a flourish and declared, "Let the gluttony begin—the *mangiata*, the *abbuffata*, the *scorpacciata*, the *panzata*! Gourmands, gourmets, and libertines, crowd around, help yourself to pinot gris, and grab your tongs!" Each eater with his or her own tongs eliminated the clumsy two-stage serving routine that usually delayed the grill-to-mouth progress among less experienced cookout enthusiasts.

With the shortening days, the Saturday meals were now in mid-afternoon, allowing full advantage to be taken of the soon-to-be-waning sunlight and warmth; Mona had come to call the meals "dayjinners", a melding of the French word for "main meal", *dejeuner* and the English "dinner". Joel and Phil were both quiet during it, leaving the other four to produce banter about topics such as Brexit, the latest presidential tweets, a house in the neighborhood that had been scraped more than a year earlier to be replaced by a low brick wall but nothing else, the anticipated demise of plastic straws. "Let's adjourn to the terrace," suggested Mona. The "terrace" was not a terrace at all, but rather a small patch of lawn that could barely hold the three contemporary versions of deck loungers and the three camp chairs. Joel and Phil took two of the chairs; Zoe the third.

Joel, looking serious, made an announcement: "So Phil and I have discussed this and we think you guys should know. The more people that know, the better, up to a point."

"This is going to be a story?" asked Carly. "Oh, goody." She sprang up, ran into the house and returned shortly, bringing two bottles of Chablis, opened, which she poured into their plastic wine glasses.

Joel began, hesitatingly, and without his usual blustery confidence: "First of all, let me say, I'm telling you all of this out of paranoia. My dad was an FBI agent and when I was a kid–I hadn't even started school yet–we suddenly moved from Berkeley, California to Santa Barbara. We changed our names. Took my mother's name. I ceased being Joel Curwin and became Joel Magoffen. Then, five years later, we moved back to Berkeley, to our same old house, changed our names back to Curwin. I think my sister–she's seven years older than me–knew what was going on but I didn't learn the whole story until years later–I was in graduate school." Joel leaned back, took a large sip of his wine, and seemed to reflect.

"You were in witness protection," proclaimed James.

"Something like that. We'd been threatened by a Russian Mafioso. At least, that was the story. At some point the gang was dissolved, captured, deported, whatever and we went back to being ourselves. But ever since I put it all together, after my dad had died and I'd pried the story out of my mother and sister, I've been what you might call cautious. So now along comes Phil investigating the very situation that I'm about to drop a bombshell on."

"You all know I'm going to be here for more than a week, just a week from now, doing that accreditation thing," affirmed Phil. Everybody nodded.

"Well, last month," continued Joel, "when Mona and I were in London, I visited Imperial College. I'd hooked up with an old friend and colleague of someone I teach with at Northern Wash. I was looking for anything about or by a woman named Jane Bennett. I'll explain why in a minute. Anyway, this guy, Chad Beatty, had a carbon copy of Jane Bennett's thesis in his files. She had done her thesis for Malinowski and what I found was a clean, streamlined version of a rough draft, some of it typed and some of it in notebooks, that I'd found in Jane Bennett's personal papers in the archives in the Beinecke Library at Yale. Jane Bennett did her undergrad at Yale and that's where her personal papers are. It, the thesis had some additional material, but embedded in it was essentially the material I'd found in the Yale archives. Well, guess who also got her undergrad degree from Yale? Her last name, her 'maiden' (Joel made quotation marks in the air) name was Madison Freeburg. Then she went on to Columbia for her PhD where she met…"

"Joseph Canter?" suggested Carly.

"Yup. And guess what Joseph Canter's dissertation was on, later published as a monograph?"

Shrugs and head-wagging all around, except from Mona, who, with a frown on her face, was staring into folded hands in her lap. "*Trade and marriage among the Shoshone-Bannock in the late 19th Century*". And guess what Jane Bennett's master's thesis was on?"

"Oh, no! You're kidding!" exclaimed Carly.

Joel was nodding vigorously. "*Trade and Marriage among the Bannock*. And not only that, but she had a lot of rich anecdotal material from her interviews that she did when she was part of a field school out of Columbia in the 1930s. That's what I found at Yale. The Beinecke copied her notebooks for me and sent them after I'd already gotten back. That was over spring break. Cost me a mint, but it was worth it." He shook his head. "I've got page after page, word-for-word correspondence between Jane Bennett's field notes and the rough draft of what became her MA thesis under Malinowski at London School of Economics and what was published as a monograph under Joseph

Canter's name. And what's not word-for-word in his monograph is so closely paraphrased it's obvious where it came from. Needless to say, he doesn't cite her work. And to think I used his monograph for *my* dissertation! What made his study so useful was all the rich material he had directly from interviews; and it was all Jane Bennett's! She'd added some more general material on trade, economics, the function of social institutions that I guess she got from Malinowski's course, but that material from those interviews that she did in the Columbia field school in 1937 is pretty much all in that thesis."

"So Canter plagiarized!" exclaimed James.

"That. Is. Just. Amazing!" Zoe shook her head.

"And Joseph Canter is teaching right here! Chairing the Social Sciences Department! This is a lot more than just a couple old fogey faculty screwing around with hiring and firing to keep the status quo!" crowed Carly. "This is, like, actionable offense! Major scandal! Grounds for firing! Prison sentence for fraud! And it's all about to be exposed in the re-accreditation, Phil?"

"How did he get away with it?" asked a perplexed, reflecting Mona.

"Well, the way he got away with it was, first of all, who would be particularly interested in looking up Jane's thesis at London School of Economics?" responded Joel. 'And secondly, even if they did, they might not have tumbled to the word-for-word concordance between that and a monograph published fifty years later. Thirdly, if you happened to know about the Columbia field school in 1937 and accessed the students' field notes and what not, you wouldn't come across anything from Jane Bennett because it wasn't there. And why would you think to look at Yale? Plus, she didn't even send her papers to them until she'd retired from University of the Olympic Peninsula in 1984. And even though she taught, she basically retired from the profession when she married Stephen Stencil. Finally, Canter's monograph was–is–available, but it was published in a really obscure monograph series by a private publisher that's now defunct: Castilla Press, out of California. So how or why would she even come across it? I think she had no idea she'd been ripped off."

"But what did Canter do for references? I mean, surely he didn't reference Jane Bennett's field notes! But he had to reference *something*," insisted James.

"He made them up. Supposedly the material was from a combination of letters from Indian agents to the Commissioner of Indian Affairs and a lengthy military report published in *War of the Rebellion*. That's a well-known source. A lot of people use it. Why nobody checked, especially his dissertation advisor, I don't know. I guess it made sense that some of the info could have come from that. But mainly he was citing letters from Indian agents that didn't exist. I spent a week with my eyeballs falling out of my head going through microfilm and letterpress copies of Indian Affairs correspondence at the National Records Center in San Bruno in July!

"So what I've got is a historiographic essay on how not to do history that's going to blow the pants off the professions of Anthropology *and* History but also off of Joseph Canter. I've told Phil because it seems to me this kind of blatant dishonesty trumps dereliction of duty like not teaching. And for me to sit on it while reaccreditation is going on would be dishonest. But here's the reason I'm paranoid. Last week I was going through some files–we hardly have any paper files any more, but midterms are hand-written and a lot of times I print out their term papers because they're easier to grade that way. So I was looking for this one paper by this great student from a couple years ago, Ben Driscoll. Really good research on Dalits'–they used to be called 'Untouchables' in India–uses of forest resources. Really bright guy. He's in the grad program at UBC now. So I asked him if I could cite him and use his work for my *Comparative Ecology* class. He said sure. So I was going to dig out his paper just to refresh the kind of telegraphic notes I took on it.

"So I've got my desk. It's got two big deep drawers." He leaned over, placed his hands a couple of feet apart and moved them up and down on his left side. "On this side I've got my tea things: canister, pot, infuser." Then he moved his hand over to his right side. "And over here, I've got files: midterm exams, final exams, some term paper printouts. Well, I've got Ben's paper as an email attachment from long ago but it's easier to access the printout. So I open the right-hand desk drawer and start ploughing through the files to get the printout of his paper. They're arranged chronologically. So Ben's should be at the back. Well, guess what? It *wasn't* at the back. It was in the middle. And some of the other files were jumbled up, too. I mean, like, files from 2016 in front of ones from 2017. And that shouldn't be. Somebody got into those files and put them back willy-nilly. And my guess is they were looking for something: copies of Jane Bennett's thesis and the material from the Yale archives."

"But when? How? Are you sure you didn't accidently, like, misfile them?" queried James.

Joel wagged his head back and forth. "I'm sure, I'm sure. I haven't even been into that drawer since last June. I mean, why would I be? And it's really easy to get into our offices, no matter what anybody says. I'll bet you could stick some kind of lock pick in there between the door and the frame and spring the button and you're in. I mean, you can throw the bolt with the key, but who ever does that? It's easier to keep it locked with the buttons."

"Whew!" exclaimed James. "So what you're saying is, somebody got into your files who knew you had the Bennett material to keep you from using it, quoting it, referencing it for a published article! What are you going to do about this? Did you report the break-in to anybody?"

"I mentioned it to the chair of the department, but he came around, had a look, and couldn't see any sign of a break-in. So he was dubious about having it reported."

"But you are going to bring this to the College Administration here, right?"

"That's what Phil and I were just talking about. I guess first he'll need to bring Porter Harder into it when he flies in next week. I guess I'll have to be involved on some level. But this break-in thing has all gotten me a little paranoid. I mean, did Canter find out? Did he send somebody to rifle through my office? What kinds of mischief could he get up to? I don't have tenure. I mean, could he say I made it all up? Try to take some kind of reprisals? Send goons to trash my apartment, smash my computer, dump my files in the river?

That's why I've told all of you: if too many people know, too many people can blow the whistle on him if he tries anything."

"I hardly think he's up to that," said James. "He shuffles along like he's got some kind of major problem. And my students talk about him like he's a laughingstock. Instead of teaching, he comes over to the sciences twice a week, sits in a little cubbyhole of an office, and advises students who are doing the premed program and thinking of going to med school."

"Huh?" Exclaimed Phil. "What does a historian know about premed?!"

"Precisely," responded James. "It's a sinecure for a has-been that never was, so they can justify keeping him on the payroll."

"Sounds like a sad case," remarked Mona. "I mean, on some level, you feel sorry for him. But do you think he and Madison—I mean, it would have to be Madison—she runs him—would really do something? Like, hire somebody to tie you up and throw you in the river in a duffel bag with a chunk of concrete or something?"

Joel heaved a huge sigh and shook his head. "I don't know. I just don't know. Yeah, it's probably unlikely. But I feel better now that I've told you guys the whole thing. It's like … it's …"

Carly nodded, "Witness protection?"

"Yeah" Joel agreed. "Kinda, something like that. Phil convinced me to confront the paranoia thing by telling you all. It's like, the more people that know about somebody going through my files, the less likely something *really* bad is to happen. I mean, before the article gets published. Like good juju. Or before I have to appear before the accreditation people, that is, Phil here and Porter Harder."

THE FOLLOWING TUESDAY

It was Zoe's fifth "fat Tuesday" and she had fixed what she called her "wicked mushroom pasta," bursting with cremini and swimming in stewed tomatoes that Carly and Mona had put up from the college's organic garden, spiced with plenty of thyme and rosemary, also from the garden, and a pinch of ground dried Slim Jim pepper, on Carly's and Mona's stove, grated parmesan optional. Carly and Mona had prevailed upon Zoe to investigate the six small paintings from the Podesta Baldocchi and she had done so. They proved to be by early twentieth century California artists: Elmer Wachtel; Marion Wachtel; Walter E. Brehm (actually Swiss, but painted in California); Andrew Melrose, and two by Percy Gray. "Not Van Goghs, but worth a couple thousand each," noted Zoe. Each now resided in its own archive-quality sleeve, housed in an archive box used to store paper documents. "So we should draw up the accession papers and get them to the college lawyer, but should we donate them to the gallery?"

"First, the college has to agree that the department can accession them, but I say no to the gallery," said Carly. She was fiddling with her ponytail. Zoe noticed she did this when she was contemplating something slightly serious. "Pennfield could chuck them in the vault room and nobody would ever see them again."

"Yeah, I say we keep them," agreed Mona. "Get Peter to find a few hundred dollars to have them framed and hang them in the hall. They're great as teaching aides."

"Speaking of teaching aides, do you suppose there's any way I could get the gallery to put the van Meegeren Vermeer back on display, just for a few days, so I can take my class over to see it?"

Mona shook her head. "No way. It's sequestered. I don't think they even have it any more."

"Yeah–I'm sure it's in a bank vault somewhere in town," agreed Carly.

"It didn't go back to the Grassers?"

"It might have. But I doubt it. Maybe it will eventually, when they get over it. But speaking of viewing, I'm taking my class over to see the Léger on Thursday. That *is* on display. You're free at noon, aren't you? Wanna come?"

"Sure," said Zoe.

~⌒~

Two Days Later: Thursday

Carly's guided tour of the Léger was part of a unit she did on Modigliani, Matisse, and Picasso that segued into Léger, following hard on the heels of a unit on Renoir, Valadon, and Valadon-Utrillo. While she lectured the class of twelve as they ambled across Bodmer Common, moving back and forth among these seven, whom some art historians thought of as the definers of modernism, Zoe mused, not for the first time, on the fates of pieces of art that might be produced with studious care, attention to detail, dedication, and skill, but which an expert had besmirched with a testimonial of "inauthentic," "forgery," "fake." *On the other hand,* she thought, *was it not a cavalier theft, a pretentious usurpation of an artist's legacy to imitate the style, technique, subject matter of a person who poured his or her ingenuity, creativity, energy, talent, sometimes at great personal sacrifice, into making a thing of beauty that now might even be doubted as the masterpiece that it had been hailed as being, because the imitator was as good or better at the craft than the ostensible master?*

Now in the gallery, Carly continued to hold forth. Zoe meandered back through the gallery to the entryway and knocked on the door marked "Duncan Pennfield, Gallery Manager". "Yes?" Duncan opened the door and stuck his head out.

Zoe introduced herself, then asked: "I'm curious about the Léger you have. It was a donation from a Mavis ..."

"Yes, Mavis Samuelson. She donated it last year, obviously before her unfortunate accident."

Zoe then mentioned that she taught a course on fakes, frauds, expertizing and authentication, although she thought he might already know that. "I wonder if she'd had it authenticated?"

"Oh, yes, she did." Duncan Pennfield nodded.

"Do you have the authentication certificate?"

"Of course!"

"Do you suppose I could see it? Even copy it? To show my students what one looks like for a piece of art that they know, or can get to know?"

"Ah–I'm sorry, but it's attached to the back. And of course the painting itself is alarmed. I'd have to turn off the whole system to take it off the wall and show you the back."

"Ah," noted Zoe resignedly. "I see." Zoe knew the answer to her next question, but asked it anyway continuing to probe. "Was she a Charbonneau alum? Did she live around here?"

"No, and no. She lived in the Bay Area and her connection to Charbonneau was—well, circuitous and fortuitous." Pennfield smiled.

Zoe nodded. "Okay. Well, thanks for your time." Duncan Pennfield retreated back into his office and closed the door. Zoe waited to hear if he locked it. He hadn't but he seemed determined to get away from her.

Maybe, she thought, *there's another way to unpack the authentication bugaboo in a way that would bring it home and make it more than something that just "happened" in the world of art expertizing that the students did not touch and that did not touch them. Might there be some way she could apply pressure to have the alarm system shut off, just for a few moments?*

After the end of her second class, at four o'clock, she returned to her flat and Googled Mavis Samuelson in the phone book for the San Francisco Bay Area. She found an address and a phone number. She tried it. A voice mail message told her, without identifying the recipient, "Leave us a message, and one of us will get back to you." She did so, introducing herself as "Zoe Dill, assistant professor of art history at Sacajawea and Charbonneau College, where Ms. Samuelson's graciously donated Léger resides." She expressed interest in knowing more about the Léger, which no one at the college seemed to know much about, and how Ms. Samuelson came to have it. As she started to hang up she realized she hadn't left her phone number and shyly did so.

Zoe was well aware that being vegan required attention to protein, but she also had a strong value for taste, a foodie obsession she was glad she shared with her fellow twice-a-week epicureans. She had just finished up a microwaved meal of spicy three-bean mix that she had dumped into a bowl with tomato-pepper soup and mashed tofu marinated in coconut milk, tamari sauce, vinegar, ground nutmeg, and cumin, when Aretha Franklin's *Respect* ringtone sounded. Zoe heard the woman on the other end of the phone introduce herself as Mavis Samuelson's niece, or rather grandniece, "Amy Garrison. I'm also executor of the estate." Amy Garrison grilled Zoe before saying much about herself or Mavis Samuelson.

But Zoe's recital of her interests, the courses she taught, her doctoral dissertation, seemed to establish credibility and rapport. Zoe was sorry to hear about Mrs. Samuelson's passing. When she expressed interest in whether the estate's executor might know anything about the Léger that she had donated to Sacajawea and Charbonneau College, Amy Garrison opened up, telling her the Léger had come from an estate sale along with a lot of other things, that Amy had reason to believe might not be genuine. And she knew about the college: she had not been part of the donation ceremony but she had been there with Mavis and her cousin, the one who had found the Légers in the estate sale, when Mavis had donated the Léger painting to the college. Mavis' whole house was like a museum. Two Légers, lithographs, still hung on the walls.

Zoe was gratified that Amy seemed glad to talk; she was wondering what she should do with the house and its contents, which she had inherited. She had left it pretty much as Mavis had accessorized it, but now Amy's boyfriend might be moving in with her and she wanted to redo it as a joint project. And she didn't trust auctioneers and estate sale brokers because of some personal history that Mavis had had with them, indirectly through her nephew who was not Amy's brother. He's my cousin", she hastened to explain. In fact, would Zoe like to come down to Oakland and see the house's contents in person? Could she tell if something was or was not a fake? There were the two Légers, a Braque, and a lot of sculptures. Maybe Zoe could help her decide what to do about all the art and antiques she'd inherited? "Amy" assured her the house had tons of room and welcomed her to stay there.

Yes, Zoe replied, she'd definitely be interested in looking at the art, but she would probably not be able to say definitively whether any particular item was or was not "genuine". Zoe thought she could probably convince Carly to come with her and combine the visit to Amy Samuelson with a trip to UC Berkeley to find out anything she could about "Cortez" and maybe the decorated skull. But the trip would have to wait until December, or late November, following Thanksgiving. Charbonneau's peculiar schedule gave faculty and students up to six weeks off between Thanksgiving and New Year, perfect for research, writing, or traveling. But until the day before the holiday, it was full court press, non-stop. Would the week after Thanksgiving work? And could she bring along a friend?

"Sure," replied Amy. "Bring him along!"

"Actually. It's a her." Zoe thought now Amy probably had an erroneous impression about the direction of Zoe's amorous affiliations. *But what does that matter?* she thought.

7

FIRST WEEK IN OCTOBER

PHIL; PORTER HARDER; ZOE;
CARLY, JAMES; MONA, JOEL

THURSDAY

NOT EVEN HALFWAY through the term, and the week of the accreditation is looming! thought Phil, as he prepared for the short flight to Walla Walla, which he would take the following morning and thence in a rental car to Sacajawea and Jean-Baptiste Charbonneau College. He would spend a week interviewing students and faculty, pouring over teaching evaluations, plus attending classes. And at some point, Joel's discovery about Joseph Canter's plagiarism would be revealed and perhaps challenged, but probably in a very private session with Canter and the Dean of Faculty, toward the end of the week-long process. Phil was flying in on Friday morning in order to spend a say with Zoe; Porter Harder would arrive on Saturday afternoon.

In these first few days of October, the weather had now finally turned, with three days of grey skies and showers of a rain-snow mix. Temperatures were not getting out of the 40s, and were dipping to below freezing at night.

They were going to have a real fall. Carly, Mona and Zoe had remarked that the reflecting pool had yet to be turned off, but it looked like, in contrast to the previous year, it would not still be burbling in November. Saturday "dayjinners" were relegated to nostalgia, along with Zoe's and Phil's, Mona's and Joel's trips to London and beyond: artefacts of summer that recalled a distinct quality of life. They would still have sinful Saturdays, but indoors.

Porter Harder had received a phone call from Madison Canter inviting him and Phil "and their significant others" to a gathering with the department faculty. "Would it be more convenient," she had inquired, "for it to take place as a kind of pleasant preamble to what we all know is going to be a necessary but intense week of work for all of us?" or "as a repast celebrating closure?" Harder had judiciously chosen the former; he suspected nobody would have anything to celebrate by the time the proceedings had run their course, although as yet he had only hints of Joel's explosive revelation from Phil by email. So the gathering was scheduled for Sunday. This evening, at Phil's urging, Harder had accepted the invitation to "sinful Saturday", although Phil had not called it such, but had abjured the invitation to the following "fat Tuesday"; in declining the latter, Porter had noted, "I think I, at least, and probably both of us, have to anticipate working lunches and dinners and at some point some overtime with the Dean next week." However, he had notified Phil of the invitation to the Canters on Sunday and Phil planned on attending with Zoe.

Zoe called Phil. They would all assemble at Carly's and Mona's for dinner the day of Phil's and Porter Harder's arrival. In acknowledgment of the wet wintry weather, Zoe proposed two soups: hot potato-leek with heavy cream to start, and cold spinach with barley as a salad, or, with lemon-honey garnish optional, as a kind of desert.

"Sounds fine," agreed Phil.

"Does Dr. Harder have any dietary restrictions?"

No, he was an omnivore. So in addition, Mona would prepare gingered flank steak stir-fry with chili paste on the side, and Carly would do a butternut squash and bell peppers stuffed with rice, blanched almonds, and raisins, held together with egg.

Now, at Saturday's dinner, Porter Harder gave the impression of holding a reserved but powerful authority and a distinguished pedigree of arbitration and accountability. Well over six feet tall, with a close-cropped pepper-and-salt afro, still with a trim physique at well over sixty, Harder was dressed in a pale gray suit with a mini-ascot at his throat. He sat at the table ramrod-straight, but exuding a jovial warmth with a dimpled smile and a habit of lowering his head and cocking it to the side when initiating discourse or responding to questions.

As they brought out the soups, Carly enthused, "Let's use the special spoons for the soups!" Mona went to the sideboard, opened it, and took out six spoons, nested in a chamois. As she distributed five of them, she told her guests: "These were a gift from Joel, Valentine's Day."

"Lovely. Joel Curwin, who could not be with us here today," clarified Porter Harder. Phil had given him a "heads-up" on who would be at the Saturday dinner, and who was aligned with whom.

"That's right," affirmed Mona. "He's fighting some kind of flu and he just didn't think it was a good idea to drive down. But he's got a flight booked for tomorrow."

"And his information does bear directly on the accreditation process," added Phil, "even though, obviously, he's not part of the accreditation process." Porter Harder nodded.

Between soups and the main dish, Harder remarked: "You know I really congratulate you on your Saturday and Tuesday get-togethers. In these days of Instagram and Twitter and Facebook and apps and earbuds, not to say television and YouTube, we are becoming–those of us on the upper rungs of the socioeconomic ladder who can afford such devices and have the time to indulge our cyber-fiction fantasies with people we mostly imagine–an increasingly self-isolating segment of humanity. We don't hold hands and do round dances with one another. We don't spend hours strolling in the countryside together or lounging on riverbanks on blankets with picnic baskets. Instead, we stuff our faces with microwaved food packaged by anonymous people whom we underpay to shove plastic-wrapped calories through our vehicle windows or to overstock our airline-hangar-sized food warehouses with what we're persuaded is legitimate sustenance, grown who-knows-where with massive chemical assistance, processed in lands distant and unfamiliar, transported in defiance of global climate warnings, and made identical, ready and appropriately sanitized for consumption by the thousands, or in some cases, made identical, ready and toxically septic with E. coli for those same thousands!

"So I really applaud you for getting together for locally-grown, home-cooked, carefully prepared gems of feast and festival, for conviviality and camaraderie. For actually communicating face-to-face, not blasting outraged confrontation or shrieking aggravation or blatant prevarication. For weaving the tapestries of experience from whatever yarns your daily lives spin for you. You know, in our humble conversations, for millennia, we humans followed the trail of orators, epic-tellers, and just plain crafters of discourse and song. That trail took us on the long journey, a long way away from the beast that we began as and toward the human that we became, in the early days of our existence as a species."

Phil thought maybe he recognized a well-rehearsed soliloquy. From anyone else, this speech would have been overblown hyperbole, but it flowed with such easy eloquence, such unpracticed, genuine confidence, that it seemed to warm the entire group as much or more than the delicate soups that had begun the meal. "Well, thank you!" said Mona, as she, Phil and Carly rose from the table. "I'm afraid our yak-yak is more like gossip and babble than Homeric poetry!"

Phil cleared the soup bowls; Carly and Mona brought in first the salads, then the other two large dishes, served family style. Whiffs of ginger and coriander wafted from the steak stir-fry; the stuffed squash emanated exotic scent of a night in Tunisia. As they ate, Zoe filled Porter Harder in on her personal history from U Wash to Charbonneau, in response to Harder's diffident question. As Phil returned with dinner plates, he heard Harder disclaim, "I regret that my wife couldn't accompany me, but she has recently decided she can let me do my trips all on my own." He chuckled. "She knows my wily ways now and she's unconvinced that a parachute-drop here, then there, lecturing to this or that audience, which I've tried to disguise as broadening one's horizons and experiencing untried parts of the world, is worth the bother and jet lag." Then, switching tone from jovial to serious, he continued: "I know I don't have to caution you, but obviously everything you know about this situation, everything that you may have discussed among yourselves, is absolutely confidential and off limits to anyone else. I did expect to encounter Dr. Curwin here tonight, and I understand why he couldn't make it, but we will speak at some point and I know it's only natural that he will share some of that conversation with you all."

"Yes," responded Mona. "He copied me on the email he sent you. But he's really looking forward to meeting with you on Monday." Mona actually thought Joel probably had very mixed feelings; once he met with Porter Harder and Dean Fister, there would be no withdrawing of the whistle-blower trumpet.

"Yes, yes." Harder nodded. "I don't exactly know how the Dean will want to handle this but I expect that he'll want to have a preliminary meeting with Dr. Curwin, Phil and myself, and that meeting will probably include drawing up a statement about how Dr. Curwin discovered what he discovered, along with the documentation. I'm not sure, but I think protocol will then require us to inform Dr. Canter of what amounts to an accusation by Dr. Curwin, which will be joined by accusations from myself, Phil, and the Dean. At some point, a meeting of all of us with Dr. Canter and Dr. Curwin will take place so that Dr. Canter can have the opportunity to legally, so to speak, confront his accusers. He may decline the opportunity, but that will have to be witnessed, and he may have an attorney or someone acting in that capacity, possibly someone from the college present. All of you may be contacted at some point by the administration because even though your take on the situation amounts to hearsay, Dr. Canter could propose that your prior knowledge of the situation compromised his capacity to take appropriate action, although I don't see how that could hold up.

"So on Sunday, Phil, when you and I and Ms. Dill are introducing ourselves, and being introduced to, the faculty of the Social Sciences Department in the home of Dr. Dora Harris, we must be circumspect about what we say about the upcoming procedures. Those procedures have already been communicated to them, or will be communicated to them, by the college Administration; we do not need to, nor should we respond to questions about those procedures. We only need to affirm the appointments that have been scheduled with the various faculty members.

"Oh, and before I forget: I did give notice to Dr. Canter, Dr. Madison Canter, when she called on behalf of the chair, Dr. Joseph Canter, to invite me to this coming Sunday's gathering, that my wife would have to send her regrets that she would not be able to avail herself of the invitation. When I did so, Dr. Canter conveyed to me her–their–accommodation of someone else who might accompany me. She said I did not have to tell her one way or another at that time. I assume she supposed, or was alluding to the supposition, that I might turn up with a young lady on my arm, presuming me to be what we used to call a 'swinger', inviting someone into my bed to play while the wife is left at home, and I'm away. Well, nothing doing. I don't go in for that sort of unchristian duplicity. But I do want to extend that–ah–accommodation possibility to both of you, Dr. Pinto, and to you, Dr. Spradley, if you don't mind the unfortunate probable wrongful conclusions to which the other guests might jump."

Mona shook her head. "Thank you, but no. I appreciate your position. I have no interest in having anything to do with those people."

Carly piped up, "And I'd take you up on your offer out of curiosity to see how the other half lives, but no thanks. I've actually been there."

"To Dora Harris' place?" asked Zoe.

"Yep."

"That's right. I'd forgotten that. She was all in a tizzy about a piece of artwork she has?"

"Yea. She has a Juan Gris. Well, I guess it's a Juan Gris. It's probably a Juan Gris. Right after the Vermeer thing she called Peter and asked if there was anybody over here who could give her an opinion on it. He told her we don't do that. I mean, we can't say whether something is really a this or that, authentic or phony. But she said, well could somebody come over and just tell her whether or not it was something worth having. That's the way she put it: something worth having. I think she hoped that once I saw it I'd go all gushy about it and say of course it was the real thing and how wonderful and how lucky she was to have it, yada, yada, yada. So Peter said why don't I go over as a courtesy and at least ooh and ahh at her collection, which he said was impressive, although bordering on a cabinet of curiosity."

"And…?" queried Zoe.

"Well, she does have a lot of neat stuff. You'll see it. Mostly African masks, some Native American art. The Juan Gris looked fine, and I told her so, without saying, 'yeah, this a real genuine Juan Gris.'"

"Did it have a certificate?" asked Zoe.

"Mmmhmm," responded Carly, her mouth full of barley spinach salad. She chewed, swallowed. "Yeah. It was sort of noncommittal. Something about it being in the style and with pigments known to have been used by cubists such as Gris, Braque, Picasso. There was something about brushes and brushstrokes which I thought was a little unusual."

"*Brushstrokes*?" Zoe exclaimed.

"Yeah. I haven't seen that many authentication certificates but they usually stop at pigments and style and comparison with other similar works known to be by the artist."

Brushstrokes. Zoe sat back. *That authentication certificate could only be by one person. Someone I used to know very well.* Someone who had introduced her to the violent restlessness, the wild desire, the passion fraught with shocks, tremors, the kind of carnage that spewed destruction over all the mundane, functional, ho-hum robotics of everyday American life, the inspiration that made characters from a daring world, the world of art, come alive for her. If it were not for him, she would not be here. But eventually, she had realized that his excitement, his boisterousness when he talked, taught, waxed eloquent about art was a masque: it concealed his all too mundane and functional burgeoning career as an art authenticator. And his signature evaluation? One that was ambivalent, praising without commitment and–his claim to expertise–always referenced brushstrokes. *How ironic, how coincidental, how capricious, how fortuitous was it to encounter this contingent confluence of her life with his métier!* She thought.

She was just returning to the here and now when she realized Carly was replying to a question: "... from Peter that she really doesn't have to work; she's an heiress, or maybe *the* heiress to the Harris Organ Company of Harrisburg, Pennsylvania. Founded by one Jacob Mosgorovsky, who changed his name to Harris for business purposes sometime after World War II. He's gone, although I gather not long gone, since Peter learned all this from an obit sometime in the last ten years. Anyway, Dora Harris is old Jacob Harris' granddaughter."

"Well, all that is interesting," temporized Porter Harder. "But it has no bearing on what we will be doing next week and it should have no bearing on our interactions with Dr. Harris on Sunday." Harder stood, excused himself, and noting that he had texted for a Lyft car and it had arrived to return him to the Hotel Fitzgerald in town, departed.

They cleared the table. "You know, the spoons, they're not real," stated Mona quietly.

"They seemed pretty real to me," objected Phil. "I really slurped two different kinds of real soup with a real spoon and those soups in that spoon were real and good."

Mona chuckled. "I mean, they're meant to be antique, but they're not really. They're replicas."

"They're supposedly from an archaeological dig–what is it?" said Carly.

"The Somerset hoard," replied Mona. "But they're not. They're replicas. The real spoons from the real Somerset hoard are in a museum in England."

"But they are silver, aren't they?" queried Phil.

Mona nodded. "They're real silver, and good quality, well made, probably hand-cast."

Zoe shrugged. "So what's the difference? Unless Joel, like, paid a fortune for them."

Mona shook her head. "I'm sure he didn't pay a fortune for them. He couldn't have. He doesn't have a fortune."

"Where did he get them? Antiques store?" asked James.

Mona gave her head a little shake. "Estate sale, Bay Area. He was down there to celebrate a friend, actually a guy he went to grad school with, finally getting his degree, at the eleventh minute of the eleventh hour, before his time ran out! Joel likes to browse estate sales, rare print and paper shows, that kind of thing, for postcards. He collects vintage postcards. I guess this sale didn't have any, or didn't have the ones he wanted. But he spotted the spoons. Unfortunately, they were part of a whole dining room set: flatware, table, chairs. He didn't want all that, so he asked if he could bid on them separately but the auctioneer said no. So afterward, Joel approached the guy who'd gotten the set. I guess the guy bought half the contents of the house and asked if he could buy the spoons. The guy said sure. I imagine he paid maybe a few hundred dollars for them."

SUNDAY
ZOE AND PHIL; DORA HARRIS; THE DRS. CANTER

Zoe and Phil entered the house, shedding their coats that were taken and hung in a closet by a valet. Dora Harris' house, as well as the one next door belonging to the Canters, was one of those large mansions on the hill that, unlike the one Zoe inhabited, had not been chopped up into rooming houses. Phil was dressed in upscale casual: gabardines and a dark grey sports jacket over a green close-checked shirt. He had grown his beard back, *perhaps inspired by Joel Curwin's formidable mutton chops*, thought Zoe, *and he looks almost distinguished!* For the midafternoon, pre-dinner gathering, Zoe had chosen a Serengeti pleated flounce-hem blue skirt with a charcoal TBdress one-button blazer over a Calvin Klein pleated sleeveless V-neck shell.

As she and Phil entered the living room, Zoe froze. There, directly opposite her, hanging on the wall, was a mask. And it was not African. It looked to be leather, painted in bluish green, with a band of yellow running horizontally along the eye line, outlined in black, with a row of yellow dots underneath and a solid line of brownish red on top. The eyes were triangular slits cut into the leather. The protruding ears were brown, also apparently leather, attached probably by rawhide thread; yellow triangular leather earrings dangled from them. The mouth was a small red square. A profusion of sixteen stiff brownish-red, black, and yellow feathers formed the mask's headdress; a thick fringe of green yarn at the neck completed the mask. Zoe turned and looked at Phil. He nodded.

Several years earlier she and Phil had become involved in exposing a scheme to extract large sums of money from collectors who had been convinced to put up earnest money in anticipation of being selected to spend more money purchasing sacred masks, originally offered in an auction in Paris, that had been obtained, undoubtedly at some point basically stolen, from their Pueblo homes. The masks had been presented as Native American "art"; except that it was not "art" at all. The Native American "art" consisted, in fact, of pieces that were religious ceremonial items: masks used in sacred ceremonies. The mere possession of them could have constituted grounds for the FBI to consider confiscating them until provenance and provenience could be clarified. Although some items had been in the possession of this or that person or museum, they were officially "unprovenanced" for purposes of the auction; therefore, they might well have been stolen from the Tribes while their caretakers thought they were safely tucked away, awaiting their participation in the next appropriate ceremonies. The auction sellers had been anonymous.

Phil had made arrangements to return the masks to the Native American communities from which they had come; but in the end, the perpetrator of the scam had disappeared. Thirteen of the fourteen masks that she supposedly had, disappeared with her, although it was not clear that she had ever had them. So the only one that could be returned was the one that had been on display, so to speak, as an exemplar. Now the perpetrator of the scheme had obviously resurfaced along with the masks! And had sold this mask to Dora Harris! No, Zoe would have to walk that back: it was possible that Dora had bought it from someone else who had successfully bid on it and other masks at the auction. Or bid on it herself. But could this mask be returned? Zoe was buzzing with the urge to quiz Dora Harris, unpack the mask's recent provenance, and give her a short treatise on why the mask should be returned to the Tribe from which it originated. But she knew it was not her place to do so. She could not be so conspicuously assertive.

Zoe refocused her attention on the three people standing in front of them, who were introducing themselves as Madison Canter, Joseph Canter, and Dora Harris. Now Madison was leading them to little clusters of two and three people; one of them included Porter Harder. Zoe didn't catch all the names– Gerry something, Pat somebody, Jeff something, Roger so-and-so, Spencer who? Dr. Fister, who she knew was Dean of Faculty, and a jovial, stout little man named Herman. Only two of the other Social Sciences faculty seemed attached: Herman was there with Patty, his wife, and Gerry and Pat were a couple, apparently with small children, since Pat declared, shortly after Zoe and Phil had arrived, that he "had to get back and relieve the baby sitter."

"And please help yourselves to wine, beer, sparkling cider over here," urged Madison Canter. "And do grab a plate–cheese and vegetables and dip over there; the caterers are circulating with *amuse-bouche*." Phil joined the group with Porter Harder; they both would have to circulate amongst the faculty and the Dean, all of whom they would have to interview in formal circumstances beginning the following day. But as a tagalong guest, Zoe considered herself free to wander. The Juan Gris hung on a wall perpendicular to the one where *the* mask hung, surrounded by other masks that were undoubtedly African. She wandered over to the Gris, itching to turn it against the wall and read the authentication certificate that Carly had said was attached to the back. But of course she could not do so.

Clearly, the Canters and Dora Harris were trying to strike a chord between elaborate, well-planned presentation and folksy, friendly camaraderie. The catered food was impressive: plentiful and well prepared. Caterers circulated with two sorts of deviled eggs: one mild, made with mayonnaise, vinegar, sugar, Greek yogurt, and Dijon mustard, declared their bearer; the other spicy with Sriracha, black pepper, and chives. Zoe heard Madison declaring that they would have held the gathering at their home, but their dining room table was strewn with documents from Joe's latest project–something about a claim for recognition from an Indian tribe that didn't have it. Zoe knew from Phil that there were dozens–maybe even up to a hundred of such claims from groups of Native Americans that had at some point been terminated, declared "extinct," "assimilated," or "detribalized" by government fiat sometime in the past and now had to go through complicated procedures to acquire "re-recognition" through the Bureau of Indian Affairs. So the message here was twofold: Joe Canter was an active scholar and, as such, he was an advocate on behalf of the Natives. *Or is he,* thought Zoe, *perhaps preparing material for the government attorneys who were going to argue that the tribe--whichever it was, she had not caught the name–did not exist?*

Another caterer offered chicken liver, tomato-garlic, or pistachio-nut-and-pomegranate-in-cream-cheese crostini, and yet another hosted mid-sized tomatoes, finger-sized eggplants, small summer squashes and small peppers that looked like serrano peppers, but which she was assured were actually sweet, stuffed with a choice of either rice or mint and raisins; or the same rice but with chopped blanched almonds, parsley and egg. Porter

Harder loaded his plate with the tomatoes, the eggplants, several of the crostini, and both kinds of stuffed peppers and several stuffed squashes. Zoe noted Joe Canter declaiming loudly to him about Charbonneau's registrar being pokey with posting grades. "The students have a right to know their grade!" he declared. "I tell everyone in my department they should send each student's grade to them by email as soon as they've got it figured out."

Caterer number four carried chicken kabobs, with or without satay sauce; large prawns on toothpicks and prosciutto-wrapped cantaloupe; and candied watermelon chunks. Zoe turned her attention to a round-bellied man with thinning hair, in trousers that looked to be cinched so high Zoe thought they must cramp his arm movements who was talking with a younger woman with shoulder-length dark hair wearing a black skirt and a thin knit that hung to her knees. The man grabbed three kabobs, dipped them in the satay sauce and, after shoving one of the kabobs into his mouth, and washing it down with a swig from his bottle of beer, admonished the woman that she "should go. If you've never been to a Pow-Wow the one at Yakima is one of the best. And they fix up a terrific green chili stew." It looked to Zoe as if this was a recitation the woman had heard before. Was it Zoe's imagination, or did the woman actually grit her teeth?

After affable "goodbyes" and "see-you-tomorrows", Porter Harder was ushered into a Lyft car and Phil and Zoe retreated the few blocks to her flat. Zoe activated her phone; she had a text from Mona: *joel arrived still not well but come for tuesday.*

8

EARLY OCTOBER: TUESDAY

PHIL SAT IN THE FACULTY CARREL the library provided to him for the week; the dean had found an unused office in the administration building for Porter Harder. Now Phil began his review of the contents of three file folders. In one was a two-page printout from the college's Human Resources office. It summarized the personnel changes in the Social Sciences Department. The records only went back only to 2003. But there was a clear pattern. A total of fourteen faculty had been hired since 2000; those hired in 2000, 2001, 2002, and 2003 had all not had their contracts renewed following their third-year, mid-tenure reviews. Instead, they had been replaced by four more young faculty, all in the positions for political science (2), sociology, and speech pathology. Again, those four were all gone by 2007; again, four replacements had been hired. And *they* were all gone by 2011. All except two had been men; Dean Fister told Porter Harder he thought only one of them, one of the women, had filed a complaint; the case had gone all the way to an unsuccessful lawsuit. In response to his question, the dean said that when he had first been appointed, he had reviewed this extraordinarily high turnover and asked for the evaluations for those former assistant professors.

He was informed that they, of course, had been deleted by the faculty who had done them; the printouts had been shredded along with all other items in the former faculty members' paper files.

However, a replacement hired in 2011 was still here: sociologist Geraldine "Gerry" Lenahan. Another, hired in 2012, was also still here: speech pathologist Jason Bamberry. The two political scientists, Jeff Harley and Roger Keller were still here, but had not been recommended for contract renewal following their mid-tenure reviews. Academic year 2017-2018 would be their last years at Sacajawea and Charbonneau College. Obviously the Social Sciences Department had at least two, presently, and in the past, four positions that were "revolving doors". Nobody in those positions had ever been granted tenure. Now in her sixth year, Gerry Lenahan was likely to be recommended for tenure, and although Jason Bamberry's future might still be a question mark, Harley and Keller were definitely what, using a vulgar colloquialism, Phil thought of as "toast."

The second folder was thicker: printouts of four years of peer reviews of classroom performance, student evaluations, and mid-tenure reviews for Lenahan, Bamberry, Harley, and Keller. Peer review were evaluations by fellow teachers. Student evaluations for all four instructors were more or less on a par with one another; those for Bamberry and Lenahan slightly lower than those for the Harley and Keller, and several for particular courses, all taught by Roger Keller, were notably higher.

The classroom evaluations for Jason Bamberry had been done by Madison Canter, Joseph Canter, Dora Harris, and Gerry Lenahan. They were all positive, approving of organization, content, manner of presentation, use of whiteboard, elicitation of classroom participation, and praiseworthy of the knowledge and understanding thus achieved by the students. Those for Gerry Lenahan, done by the two Canters, Dora Harris, and Herman Shaftley were equally positive.

The evaluations for Harley had been done by the two Canters and Dora Harris. Those for Keller had been done by Madison Canter, Herman Shaftley, and Gerry Lenahan. All these evaluations, for both instructors, noted Phil, were in marked contrast to those for Lenahan and Bamberry. These also followed a pattern: the early evaluations ended with expressions of cautious optimism that so-and-so had the makings of a good instructor, but wasn't quite there yet; later ones directly asserted that instructor so-and-so had unfortunately not taken to heart the constructive criticism and positive suggestions given in earlier classroom evaluations.

Each evaluation was a page or more. Phil decided to compile the various assertions into a Word table. He typed a summary onto his laptop:

Lectures are not well organized; imbalance between theory and data; absence of theoretical contextualization; introduction of ideas made with no follow-up or no lead-in; lectures are o.k. but not connected to anything else;

Phil made a note at this entry: ***How would the peer reviewer know what had come before and what was to come after, unless sitting through the entire course?*** He continued typing:

Tendency to skip over theoretical points; lecture was laced with errors of fact; central theme of the class period not clear either to the instructor or to the class;

Phil made a note next to this last one: ***How would the peer reviewer know the central theme was not clear to the instructor?!*** He continued typing:

Lack of both clarity and closure characterized the handling of many of the topics; Interaction between instructor and students tended to be desultory; Class lacked elaboration on the salient theoretical points which furnished its focus;

Lecturer spoke well, students were responsive, attentive and interested (but) the theoretical relationships of spending so much time comparing the U.S.S.R and the U.S.A. of the 1970s to the topic of political science was not apparent; agap in synapse, e.g, gap between what he is thinking and what he is communicating.

Again Phil made a note: ***How would the observer know what the lecturer is thinking?!***

Anecdotes rather than the points they were meant to exemplify will be remembered; An interesting talk delivered with a firm voice, a dramatic style, and an openness to student questions and reaction (but) suspect that a number of students did not follow the line of argument.

How would the peer reviewer know the students weren't following the argument?!

Stressed details at the expense of other material essential for providing students with adequate background for continued work in the social sciences.

Another note: ***This from Herman Shaftley!***

Material from the field of archaeology in a lecture on urban enters of the New World in a political science course should not have so much emphasis; indicative of a lack of breadth and training; student response sometimes enthusiastic, at other times undetectable, thus uneven. Lacks teaching effectiveness. Reading assignments too thin.

Phil reflected on Herman Shaftley. Porter Harder had discovered in conversation with Dean Fister, that Herman Shaftley, who was among the peer reviewers, did not have a PhD; had no publications to his name; and did not have tenure. His three-year contract had been renewed every time it came up since 1995 with something called a "certificate of continuing employment"!

Over an inch thick, the third file folder was everything pertaining to complaints filed by Roger Keller. Complaint number one contested each classroom evaluation and also contested the essentially negative mid-tenure review. The complaint noted the contradiction between the peer reviews and the students' evaluations and alleged an unfamiliarity on the part of the peer evaluators with the content, premises, and pedagogy of political science. A second complaint alleged the incompetence of Joseph Canter as an evaluator, teacher, and department chair. *Well*, thought Phil, *if you want to ensure that your overlords would not have a change of heart at the last minute, and recommend you for tenure after all, attack them with formal complaints, such as Roger Keller has done!*

The complaints themselves, never mind the ancillary supporting documents, were lengthy. Keller went on and on in a long rant. He seemed especially peeved about the fact that while he was being dismissed, Mr. Shaftley was being retained–forever! He had written: "Mr. Herman Shaftley has no post-baccalaureate degrees. Yet he is teaching the arguably most important courses offered by the department: *History of Sociological Theory, Qualitative and Quantitative Methods, Writing and Reasoning in the Social Sciences, Historiographic Method*. I do not see how it can be legitimately argued that because Mr. Shaftley has traditionally taught these courses, he therefore has the qualifications, credentials, training, or expertise to do so."

In the complaint against Canter, Keller had written, "The balance of power in the department is held by Prof.'s Canter, Canter and Harris. They are the 'old guard.'" Referring to a non-committal response from the chancellor, in answer to a memorandum he had sent her, he complained, "It is evident that the chancellor considered *only* the recommendation of the chair of the Department, *not* my file or any other factors." At still another point, he complained that he was denied access to his personnel file, alleging that the denial was motivated by an effort to prevent him from seeing various memoranda or notes from whomever, that were detrimental to him. Finally, "evaluations of personnel are sometimes made on the basis of criteria that are not always reflected in a faculty member's total performance. Evaluations of teaching effectiveness are not used to determine teaching effectiveness . Teaching observation report forms themselves are DISTORTED AND DELIBERATELY FALSIFIED. Teaching observation report forms are deliberately used by those who control the department to falsify and fabricate data that they wish to use against particular non-tenured faculty. Those who control the department, by their policies against certain faculty, by their creation of an atmosphere of fear and intimidation, and by their refusal to develop a well-rounded curriculum, are irrevocably damaging the educational quality of the college."

Phil went back and forth between the voluminous complaint file, the peer review evaluations for Keller and for Harley, and the student evaluations.

Phil thought about what the basis would probably be for negative evaluations following their mid-tenure reviews: Students find them entertaining
but they just do not have the theoretical background for communicating as
effective teachers. And some of this from a piece of deadwood who hadn't
taught in, how many years? More than a decade? And from someone else
who had no degree higher than the students he was teaching? All of these
evaluations–even those by Lenahan, the most positive--relied on insinuation
and innuendo, unsupported assertions, judgments based on idiosyncratically
inspired criteria, or at worst, on a fabricated chimera. These classroom evaluations could easily derive from pique at being left behind on the sidelines of
academia, or from a follow-the-leader strategy intended to stay in the good
graces of those who held the power of tenure-or-no-tenure, of career-or-no-
career, of scholarly success or ignominious retreat into self-effacing failure
at having been unable to measure up to standards.

Student evaluations for Harley and Keller could not have been in greater
contrast: "class is extremely well-taught and organized ... Presents subject
matter in a dynamic manner. Class discussions are interesting and always
relevant to the context of the course. Supercharged with energy ... Gives help
whenever I need it . One of the few professors who has students' academic
respect ... Would not have taken this course if not for his reputation as a good
teacher. Only complaint I have is he assigns too many readings." The numerical
evaluations for the final two of ten question—"This was a very effective course"
and "This is a very effective teacher"—on a five-point scale were in the high
fours for all thirty courses that Keller and Harley had taught over the three years
they had been at Charbonneau. Phil slammed his palm on the desk. *If ever there
was a case of unfounded, gratuitous, small-minded evaluations, this has gotta
be it!* he thought. *True, students obviously don't have global knowledge about
what they are or should be learning, but they are obviously getting some benefit
from the classroom experience! These so-called peer reviews are disingenuous.*

Phil reflected on the interviews. He called up his notes. Monday and
much of Tuesday had been given over to interviewing the four junior faculty

100

members. Phil found that what Roger Keller had had to say was pretty much what he had written in his complaint; Don Harley had had a similar story, but communicated it less stridently. Jason Bamberry was a chatterbox; he was enthusiastic about everything: the sleepy pace of life in Clayton in contrast to his native Seattle; the College's architecture and landscaping; the responsiveness of the students; the opportunity to introduce students to linguistic methodology that, if they did happen to be living with what used to be called a "speech impediment," rationalized and minimized this or that speaking manner within the context of the range of sounds that could be made by pushing air through throat, mouth and nose in a comparative framework, etc. When Phil introduced the subject of classroom evaluations, he effused enthusiastic endearment for the senior faculty who went to such trouble to give pointers and suggestions for how to improve classroom performance. A question about why Joseph Canter did not seem to be on the teaching schedule either for this year or the previous year was dismissed on what Dr. Bamberry made seem perfectly logical grounds: how could he possibly do the important and time-consuming work of running the department and keep up with continuing developments in the medical field so that he could give well-grounded advice to those students contemplating a premed program and also teach? (Phil had restrained himself from asking follow-up questions such as: Just what does he do to keep up on the medical field? Or how did he get to be qualified to give advice in the study of medicine in the first place?)

The interview with Gerry Lenahan had been more measured; she tended to give short answers to his questions and seemed a little on the defensive side: she let him know how difficult it was to teach full time, to write and publish, and to care for and raise her two eighteen month-old twins, a boy and a girl, as a single mother.

Hmm, thought Phil, *so Pat whatever-his-name-was is not her husband; maybe not even the father of her twins? Clearly she was intent on making a statement: a single mother could also pursue an academic career on a par with her male, non-parenting peers. Well, that was good. More power to her.* Questions about classroom evaluations drew more measured responses: they were a bit of a distraction but necessary. Her field was the sociology of skilled labor; she turned out to have an unusual and interesting background. Her dissertation had been based on a three-month-long study of factory workers in Finland. *Why Finland?* Phil wondered, and asked. She had grown up in a cooperative of third-generation Finns in Brooklyn. It had originally been an actual commune and although the building was now a standard co-owned co-op, most of its inhabitants were descendants of the original founders. They regularly got together for communal activities such as meals, work on the building such as minor repairs and painting, and establishing a sliding scale of semiannual fees based on size of unit and income. He also asked about teaching a course–Native American History–that was so far out of her field? Did she mind? "Oh, no." She had the notes from the last time Joe taught the course. *And when was that?* There were no dates on the notes although she thought it might have been the year before she came, so seven years ago. Again, he had refrained from asking two obvious questions: *Why is it to your advantage to teach a course for which you have no prima facie expertise or qualifications for doing so? Why is it in the students' best interests to have information that is now seven years old and may be even older than that, if from Joseph Canter's early days of teaching?*

Now at Mona's and Carly's for fat Tuesday, Phil was chagrined to see how badly off Joel seemed. Dark bags puffed from under his eyes. He slumped in his chair. He sipped his mint tea silently. For supper, he was having only a bowl of soup Zoe had made specially: spinach and lemon, without the onions, turmeric or garlic she usually put in. "This soup and the tea are the only things I can keep down," he said.

"How long have you had this?" Phil asked.

"Little over a week. I can't seem to shake it. Every time I think I'm getting over it, usually in the mornings, by noon I'm reeling again."

"He's having dizzy spells and headaches and he's weak," said Mona, laying a soothing hand on Joel's arm. Phil thought she was trembling slightly. "I'm so glad you didn't try to drive." She looked searchingly into his face.

"Yeah, but even getting to the plane was a chore. Now though, I'll see it to the finish, 'cause ah eats mah spinach, Ah'm Popeye the sailor man, toot toot!" He smiled wanly.

They all laughed. Carly nodded vigorously. "A good laugh will get you through anything! You meet with the dean tomorrow?" she asked.

"Yeah. I'll bring over my laptop and they'll print out my statement, then we go to the registrar's office and get it notarized. But the dean wants me to give verbal testimony in front of a court recorder who'll take notes as if it were an actual deposition. He thinks that might be important for avoiding an actual trial if the college decides to take action and Canter fights it. I hope I can slog through it."

"And then you're going have to actually confront Canter?" said Mona. "Is that a good idea, with you battling the flu? Do you really have to spill it all out into the open right now? That's really going to shake things up around here."

"Maybe that's what's needed," declared Carly.

"Well, it's more like he has to have the opportunity to confront me, ask me questions, and so forth. Confront his accuser, deny the charges. Or admit them, I suppose. The court reporter's going to be there too, I guess. And you and Porter?" he addressed Phil.

"Yes, we'll be there. And the dean."

Joel nodded. "Well, if you'll excuse me, I think I need to be supine. You all enjoy your dinner." He rose, but lurched as he turned around and banged into the wall. Mona gave a little cry, jumped up, grabbed his arm, and steadied him. "I'll just get you settled," she said. Now, Phil noticed, she really was trembling. They walked slowly, he gingerly, while she held onto his arm and more or less guiding him, out of the room.

"That seems like a little more than the flu," observed Zoe with concern. "Has he been to a doctor?"

"No," said Carly disapprovingly. "He refuses. Mona says he was raised Christian Science and even though he professes not to believe in it any more, he avoids doctors."

"That sounds like the worst of all possible worlds," suggested Phil. "He doesn't have the support of the Christian Science community yet he doesn't do standard medical."

Carly shrugged. "I'll bet a lot of it is actually psychosomatic. I mean, he finds this case of plagiarism exciting, but now suddenly he's in the thick of this really ugly academic imbroglio and he turns out to be the star performer. That's gotta be major stress."

WEDNESDAY MORNING
PHILIP BACKSTROM, PORTER HARDER, JOEL
CURWIN, DEAN FISTER, A COURT REPORTER

The deposition took place in the dean's conference room. Joel, Phil, and Porter Harder sat around a large table in the center of the room. A court reporter sat at a desk off to the side, typing on her laptop. Joel began. " In the summer of 2016 I was researching the impact of the imprisonment of a Paiute chief, Natchez, on the history of the Paiute people. Then, I guess it was in February or March, one of my colleagues, at Northern Washington showed me an issue of the *Ethnographic Society of North America Newsletter*. There was an obituary for someone named Jane Bennett, who had been at a field school in the 1930s on a Reservation in the Basin-Plateau region sponsored by Columbia University. About a half-dozen students had collected oral histories from Paiute elders. I checked. She hadn't earned any degree from Columbia.

"I'd reckoned correctly that the journals and field notes from the field school would be in the Columbia University archives, filed with the papers of the supervising professor. I went out east and researched the Columbia archives. Sure enough, there were all the journals and notes the students had taken in the field school. They were a gold mine of reminiscences about what the elders remembered or what they remembered their elders telling them. I found field notes, journals, rough drafts of papers. This field school was apparently a kind of practice course for 'real fieldwork' later on because almost none of that work ever got into anybody's dissertation or publications.

"But I wondered at the time why the field notes from Jane Bennett had not been in the files, despite her name being on the roster of students who had participated. From the obituary in the *Newsletter*, I'd learned that she'd had gotten her BA from Yale in 1936 and a masters from London School of Economics in 1939. So I thought, maybe with her BA from Yale, might she have donated her personal papers to her alma mater? The people at the Beinecke Library at Yale said yes, there was quite a thick file for her–term papers, lecture notes for the classes she took, and some spiral-bound steno notebooks that turned out to be her journals from the field school. I went out there last April during spring break." At this point, Joel felt his voice threatening to give out. He had to stop for a moment and wipe his brow with his handkerchief; his hand trembled a bit. He took a sip of mint tea. "You'll have to excuse me; I'm still fighting a flu bug. I don't think I'm contagious but it's taking me a while to get over it."

He resumed with a shaky voice: "I asked the Beinecke people to copy the journals for me and also what looked like the rough draft of a paper that was never published. I was especially curious about that rough draft because while I was there, reading the journals and the rough draft, I realized I'd read it somewhere before. It turned out to be, page after page, word for word, identical to a monograph by Joseph Canter, published in the 1980s; it was his PhD dissertation, from Columbia. And what was not word-for-word copied from Jane Bennett's notes and journal and the rough draft of what eventually became her MA thesis from London School of Economics was so closely paraphrased that it was obvious where it came from.

"Well, I didn't mention any of this to anybody but I did tell everybody who was interested that I'd found this treasure trove of field notes in the Columbia archives and asked if anyone ever heard of somebody named Jane Bennett, who got her masters at London School of Economics, and maybe have studied under Bronislaw Malinowski. He's really well known as one of the fathers of anthropology. You can't get out of an intro anthropology class without encountering Bronislaw Malinowski. So I was really interested to learn if she'd studied under him.

"One of my colleagues at Northern Washington, Ned Roberts, an old guy who's actually retired but still has an office–he's still active in the field–said that somebody he'd known for years had done anthropology at LSE, long after Malinowski, but *his* dissertation advisor had done *his* dissertation under Malinowski. He put me in touch with this guy, also retired, or about to retire, from Imperial College, Chad Beatty. Well, I had a conference in Prato, Italy, in June, so I went over a week early, paid a visit to Imperial College, found Chad Beatty. It turned out his old professor, Loren McChesney, had given him a carbon copy of Jane Bennett's thesis because of his–Beatty's--interest in the crafting and use of stone as prestige trade items.

"So yes, she had indeed done her thesis for Malinowski and what I found was a clean, sort of streamlined version of the material in the rough draft and in the notebooks I'd found in Jane Bennett's personal papers in the archives in the Beinecke Library at Yale. Dr. Beatty made a copy of Bennett's master thesis for me. So in a sense, Joseph Canter had done an injustice to Jane Bennett twice over: he stole her work, passing it off not only as his dissertation, but also as the definitive monograph on the subject, *Trade and Marriage Among the Bannock in the Nineteenth Century* and garnered the scholarly recognition that should have gone to her. He also cheated her out of possibly publishing her master's thesis, although there's no indication that she ever tried to bring it to publication. In fact, there's nothing to indicate she knew about the rip-off that was perpetrated against her.

"Anyway, not only did Canter plagiarize, he also made up the references that he had supposedly found in letters from Indian agents to the

Commissioner of Indian Affairs and a lengthy military report published in *War of the Rebellion.* That's a well-known source. Well, I checked. The events he was referencing, that Jane Bennett recounted in her notes, were a decade or more *after* the Civil War, and I spent a week going through microfilm and letterpress copies of Indian Affairs correspondence at the National Records Center in San Bruno in July. There was nothing, nothing like what he had cited in there. So that's it."

"And let us affirm, and let you affirm, that we, myself, Porter Harder and Philip Backstrom in our capacity as accreditation reviewers, did not solicit the information that you have just provided to us," noted Porter Harder.

"That's right. I came forward when I learned that Dr. Backstrom, who is a personal friend of a personal friend of mine, or maybe more accurately, the personal friend of a personal friend of a personal friend …"

"And to be clear, those personal friends are Drs. Mona Spradley and Zoe Dill, both of whom teach at this institution," interjected Harder.

"That's correct," affirmed Joel. "I shared this with Dr. Backstrom here shortly after learning that he was one member of this accreditation team. He recommended I share it as well with his friends, Drs. Spradley and Dill and also with Dr. James Gambel, only because Dr. Backstrom pointed out that these discoveries I made were a legitimate part of my personal history and my academic profile. And there was an event to which I was party and might have a bearing on the significance of these discoveries had occurred, and had upset me greatly. The whole thing was eating me up. So it was like sharing something personal, not necessarily confiding something confidential. And the only reason I'm coming forward with this here is that I thought it appropriate for you, the reviewers, and the college administration, to have this information ahead of my publication of my findings, which is a year or more off. What I am seeking in doing this is justice for Jane Bennett, who unfortunately passed away more than a year ago, before she could see justice done." Joel shook his head.

"And," asked Porter Harder, "Is it correct that you have never personally met, do not know Joseph Canter?"

"I do not know Joseph Canter, and if I might have encountered him on visits here, I did not know it."

"Thank you, Dr. Curwin."

THURSDAY
PHILIP BACKSTROM, PORTER HARDER, JOEL CURWIN, JOSEPH CANTER, MADISON CANTER, DEAN FISTER, THE COURT REPORTER

Phil and Porter spent the remainder of Wednesday, over a working lunch and then the entire afternoon, hammering out an outline for their report. The contrast between the student evaluations for Keller and Harley and the classroom peer evaluations from faculty would be noted. The negative evaluations submitted by the two by two other junior faculty members, whose classroom peer evaluations from senior faculty were praiseworthy and positive, had to be questioned. The high turnover in faculty over the last decade-and-a-half was surely a red flag in view of the retention of one faculty member with only a BA. What was behind the indifference of the senior faculty to retaining qualified faculty with PhDs? And the unusual arrangement in teaching assignments, with apparent expertise not matching with courses taught. And how did the chair get assigned to purely administrative duties! Finally, they would have to note that this same faculty member might have secured and maintained a career at Sacajawea and Jean-Baptiste Charbonneau College under a completely false premise, that he had *not* fulfilled one of the requirements for the PhD because he had submitted a dissertation plagiarized from Jane Bennett. Prima facie evidence for that suggestion would be an appendix consisting of a notarized statement from Dr. Joel Curwin; the transcript of an oral deposition by Dr. Curwin; and the transcript of Joseph Canter's answer to the charges made by Dr. Curwin.

And that was where they now were: at the point where Joseph Canter would answer the charges made by Dr. Curwin. They had met briefly beforehand in the office provided to Porter Harder. Porter Harder shared some off-the-record comments with Phil:

"You know," he said, "it's a shame that all this could not have been handled in a way that did not compromise the careers of over a dozen teacher-scholars embarking on their careers, all to protect the egos and--I will say it--hide the truth about the personal shortcomings of a couple people. It's a shame because Madison Canter and Dora Harris? Those two wrote two pretty interesting, well-grounded books. One of them is a valuable scholarly contribution: *The Real Africa Unveiled: How Travelers' Accounts Fabricated a History that was Myth*. That was, substantially, as far as I can tell, Madison Canter's doctoral dissertation. The other, *Stories, Epics, and Folktales of the Ashanti: History as Interpretation*, seems to be substantially Dora Harris' dissertation. Those two books got each of them tenure; the monograph that Joseph Canter published under his own name but which is incontrovertibly Jane Bennett's work, got *him* tenure. But you know something? A little note in the "Acknowledgments" section of Dora Harris' dissertation thanks Madison Freeburg, Madison Canter's pre-marriage name, for providing her with the raw data! It was a library dissertation! Dora Harris has, as far as I can determine, never set foot in Africa!

"Now there's nothing wrong with that. Or there would be nothing wrong with that, except that it set me to thinking. I asked Dean Fister what he knew about the personal histories of Canter, Canter and Harris. Well, he didn't know much, but he steered me to a now-defunct in-house publication, oddly titled *Muse*, that was published weekly, years ago, featuring news, notices of events, and little anecdotes about various aspects of the college including vignettes of recently hired faculty members. Well sure enough, the Special Collections librarians helped me find issues from the late 1980s: there they were, the Canters and Dora Harris. Madison Canter basically grew up in Africa, specifically, in Accra, Ghana, where her father was administrator of loans for the World Bank. The family was there for ten years until they returned just in time for Madison to be enrolled as an undergraduate at Yale. And where did Joel Curwin find those notes and rough drafts from Ms. Jane Bennett? At Yale!

"So here's what I think is the situation. And this is strictly off the record. I think Dora Harris and Joel Canter don't have a brain in their heads. When I interviewed Madison she volunteered an explanation for why Joe doesn't teach: he's got some sort of neurological condition, which the doctors, according to her, can't figure out that causes him to have what she called 'gaps in synapse.'"

That's interesting! Phil thought. *That's exactly the phraseology she used to characterize one of Roger Keller's lectures for which she had done a classroom observation.*

Porter Harder had continued: "He may or may not have a neurological condition but what I suspect is that years of fear at being exposed as a phony plus just not being bright enough to write a PhD dissertation has, in effect, paralyzed him. He can't do anything in public. I think Madison Canter wrote his dissertation for him. It's possible he never saw Jane Bennett's notebooks. Perhaps Madison offers to go to DC and look in the National Archives to see if there's anything he can use–I mean, he may have thought of a topic something like what Jane Bennett had written on and Madison thought, wow, there's this pile of data–maybe she encountered it while she was doing a paper for an undergraduate class at Yale–just stumbled across it–that I'll help him turn into a dissertation. Who would ever know? He may actually believe he had data from the National Archives. And so what if Madison decided to help him write the thing? And falsifies the references?

"Madison Canter may also be the author of Dora Harris' dissertation. She is one bright woman. And she's got total control over two people: her man and her best friend. She's the one who supplied all those stories and epics to Dora, right? Well, maybe Dora did some of the gofering in terms of finding some of the historical events that those stories refer to, but I can see this charade, this pretension, carrying over from the dissertation level to her getting them all planted out here where there's likely to be no questioning of what might have gone on two thousand miles away. Three PhDs from Columbia! What a *coup* for a little college trying to make that transition from girls' finishing academy to well-accredited institution of higher learning.

"And I say it's such a shame because there is value in validating indigenous oral histories through reference to the received history produced through the dominant paradigm, and there is certainly value in questioning the premises of the ethnocentric and racist accounts that passed for history for decades, even centuries. It's a sorry state of affairs that those studies, not to mention Joseph Canter's sham, have come to the attention of the scholarly world under false premises. But this department has been stood on its head: the people who should be teaching the key courses are either no longer here or will not be here for long; instead, those courses are taught by the people least qualified to do so, with the possible exception of Madison Canter and Jason Bamberry; I doubt even the--what is it called around here? The triumvirate?--could manage *Speech Pathology* and *Linguistics!*"

Throughout Porter Harder's discourse Phil's responses ranged from disbelief to dawning realization, from discomfort at being privy to these suggestions to admiration for this elder statesman of academia's insight. He shook his head, winced, nodded, shook his head again, puffed his cheeks and blew air out, shook his head again. At one point it was all he could do to keep from bursting out laughing. "Amazing!" he declared. "I wonder how much of this they would ever admit to."

Now they were in the dean's conference room and it was almost six o'clock; Dean Fister had originally scheduled the meeting for ten o'clock in the morning but then had to move it to later because of back-to-back meetings during most of the day occasioned by the other accreditation review that was going on in the Math and Computer Science Department. Dean Fister opened the proceedings by introducing himself, then Dr. Joel Curwin, from Northern Washington University, and Professor Joseph Canter, and affirming that Madison Canter was present as Joseph Canter's advisor, equivalent to legal counsel. He then referred to the notarized statement supplied by Dr. Curwin. Had Professor Canter read it? Yes. Did Professor Canter want it read to him at this time, either by Dr. Curwin or by the court reporter? No. "Then," said the dean, "please proceed to comment on the charges of plagiarism and falsifying references." He introduced the court stenographer, "Miss Gee-ann …"

"Giansiracusa. Meghan Giansiracusa. Just Meghan."

"Fine, Thank you Meghan. Let's begin."

Canter sighed and shuddered. As he began, his voice seemed to break, but then gathered strength, although Phil noted that his head and limbs betrayed a slight tremor. Jane Bennett was unknown to him. He had never worked in the Special Collections of the Beinecke Library. If there was some similarity between what he had written in his monograph and dissertation and what Jane Bennett had written in her master's thesis and her field notes, it was purely coincidental. Such things happened. Two people got the same idea and searched the same sources and inevitably came up with very similar narratives.

Although somewhat atremble, Canter did not seem to be having any gap in synapse. Phil thought he was gripped by a combination of anger and fear. Despite his slight tremor, his jaw clenched, his eyes shot daggers, his face flushed red.

Dean Fister prompted him on the references: how could he explain the nonexistence of the references? Canter glared at Joel and pointed a trembling finger at him. "Just because he couldn't find them, doesn't mean they don't exist. He's a lousy researcher. He looked in the wrong place. Some satellite records center in California. My sources are from the National Archives in DC."

Joel shook his head. "The original records were decentralized in the 1970s. Records from BIA area offices in California and Arizona were relocated to the San Bruno Federal Center."

Canter seemed to want to say something, but only licked his lips and swallowed hard, Phil thought probably to allay a dry mouth. Canter seemed to be getting quickly exhausted. Phil risked a wry smile. He'd heard that people reflexively started breathing more heavily when they lied as lying causes changes to heart rate and blood flow. Sometimes liars would have trouble speaking as the mucous membranes in the mouth dried out as part of the body's response to lying.

Now Madison Canter chimed in, addressing Dean Fister: "How do you know he," nodding briefly at Joel, "hasn't made up the story that they don't exist?"

"If I may add some clarification?" asked Porter Harder. Everyone nodded. "It's not that the references don't exist. Jane Bennett had plenty of them. According to Dr. Curwin here, they were specific persons that she interviewed at specific times in a specific place, in the year 1937. Summaries of those interviews and some direct quotes are in her field notes in her personal papers archived in the Beinecke Library at Yale. Is that correct, Dr. Curwin?" Joel nodded. "They were *not* from letters from reservation officials of the Bureau of Indian Affairs to the Commissioner of Indian Affairs!"

Madison turned to Joel, and also turned *on* him: "How do you know the Indian agents didn't interview those same people, or their antecedents, at the time, in the 1870s and '80s? How do you know this, this Jane Bennett didn't read those letters and make up the interviews?"

Now Joel, who had been studiously not making eye contact with anyone in the room, sipping his tea (the dean had offered coffee or tea and donuts to everyone, but only the dean himself had taken a coffee and only Phil had taken a donut), raised his head and spoke up, somewhat wearily: "Other participants in the field school interviewed some of those same informants, on different topics. What interest, let alone the time, would Indian agents have had to sit around getting prisoners of war to talk about how great their lives had been when they were free, before they were rounded up by the cavalry?"

"I think I'm going to have to call a halt to the proceedings," said Fister. "I would like to affirm your denial, Professor Canter, of the charge of plagiarism, and also your denial of the charge of falsifying references. Part of your defense, or explanation, is that you and Jane Bennett wrote identical or extremely similar sentences, phrases, paragraphs, pages because you were both writing on the same topic, and that Dr. Curwin could not, in a search of the documents, transferred to the National Archives and Records Center in San Bruno, California, and available there since the 1970s, find the references you used in your monograph because he was looking in the wrong place. Also part of your defense, or explanation, is that you have never heard of Jane Bennett, you have never been to the campus of Yale University, and you have never conducted research in the Beinecke Library's Special Collections."

Canter closed his eyes, sighed, and almost whispered, "Correct."

Madison Canter now addressed Joel Curwin: "I don't know what you hope to gain by all this. Are you so mean, so petty, so devoid of creativity yourself that all you can do is attack an old man and fabricate a case against him that you know won't stand up in the scholarly world? You make up this supposed journal that you claim to have found in somebody's personal papers and trump it up into some sort of primary source document! *You're* the one that's fabricating something! How were you brought up? How did you get to be so sneaky, so overbearing, so self-important, so pompous? Why do you think you're so self-righteous? You want to make your own reputation by throwing dirt on someone's life-long career, his dedication to educating students at this college, his mentoring of young teachers and scholars. You have a lot to answer for!"

"I only want justice for Jane Bennett," said Joel quietly.

"I think we need to bring this encounter to a close," declared Dean Fister with finality. "You, Professors Canter and Canter, will be provided with a copy of the transcript of this meeting. At this point, there are no formal proceedings being brought against you, Professor Joseph Canter, but I cannot guarantee that they will not be brought at some time in the future. The transcript of this meeting, as well as the transcript and affidavit from Dr. Curwin and the supporting documents with which he has supplied us, copies of the notes and journals from Jane Bennett's personal papers in the Beinecke Library and her thesis from London School of Economics, will be added to it. We have sequestered the copy of your monograph from our library and that will also be added. Do you have any questions?"

A visibly shaken and pale Joseph Canter shook his head; Madison Canter whispered, "No." They left the room. Joel Curwin stayed seated, but said, "I would like to sit here for a few more minutes, to avoid an unpleasant encounter as I leave."

"Are we going to talk?" Fister asked Porter Harder. "I think we need a short wrap-up. Can we adjourn to my office?" He addressed Phil and Porter. "It's right across the hall."

Turning to Joel, Phil asked, "Do you want a ride? You could wait for us here or in the library."

"No, no. I'll walk. It's only a few blocks; fresh air'll do me good."

"It's drizzling. You don't even have a hat."

"'S'okay. I've got my overcoat, my father's overcoat! Makes me look like Sam Slade, or Perry Mason!"

"No hat?" was Phil's final objection. Phil usually wore a Mexican straw cowboy hat but for the last few days his headgear had been a floppy leather Australian Squashy.

"Nah, it's not that bad. I don't even own a hat." Joel stood, steadied himself, pulled on his overcoat, picked up his briefcase, and exited the room.

In Fister's office, they settled into three chairs. "Well, I can assure you we will secure an authorized copy of Jane Bennett's thesis from London School of Economics, but I don't see us reinventing the wheel, so to speak, to do just what Dr. Curwin has done in terms of trying to track down the bogus references. Even without the bogus references, there does not seem to be any doubt that we have a case of plagiarism here."

"So he doesn't really have a PhD?" asked Phil.

"That remains to be seen. We will, of course, notify Columbia and if they ask for documentation, we will send all the appropriate materials to them. There are options. Revoking his PhD is one, but I doubt they will do so. Reopening his graduate file noting he did not fulfill the requirement to submit and defend an acceptable and original dissertation based on bona fide research is another. He would then have the opprtunity, in theory, of doing a dissertation on a different topic, forming a committee, and scheduling a defense. But I doubt they'll want to do that either, or that *he* will. The final option would be to retroactively expel him on the basis of plagiarism, meaning the plagiarized work that he submitted would not count for his PhD. So then, yes, he would obviously not have a PhD."

Porter and Phil both nodded. "Well," said Porter rising. "This has been enervating, I must say, but also instructive. Never in my career have I encountered anything like this. But I wonder how many other cases like this there are out there."

They shook hands with Fister, then departed. "Would you like a ride?" asked Phil.

"No, thank you. I have a standing account here with Lyft and texted them just at the end of the proceedings. They're probably waiting for me downstairs." Porter picked up his briefcase and clattered down the stairs.

Phil took out his phone and saw he had a phone message from Zoe. He called her. "Hi ... You're at Mona's and Carly's? ..."

"No", he said, in response to her question. "He was going to walk. He left, oh, 30, 40 minutes ago ..."

What Zoe told him was alarming: She insisted it was at best a ten or fifteen minute walk from the college to Mona and Carly's house and Joel had not yet arrived. "We've got to do something," declared Zoe. "You know he was feeling ill."

"Okay," responded Phil, "I'll be right there."

Phil parked the car, slid out of the seat, slammed the door shut, and hurried to the house. Mona opened the door before he had a chance to knock. She was frantic. "I've called Joel's cell about a dozen times. It goes straight to voice mail! Something's happened to him. I know it. Something's happened!"

"He's been really wobbly the whole time he's been here–for days!" said Carly.

"Maybe he collapsed. What if he's lying in the dirt somewhere? He could have hit his head. Maybe even gotten a concussion!" Mona was almost screaming and was fighting back tears.

Zoe appeared behind both of them. "Look. Why don't we try retracing his route. Walk the streets to the college, then through the college to–where was the hearing?"

"Admin building," responded Phil. "So he would have walked from there, up the hill, along the path past the reflection pond, down through the two greens."

"So why don't Phil and I drive to the parking lot outside the admin building and go from there? You two start off from here. If he's between here and there, we'll find him," assured Zoe.

Phil and Zoe hurried to Phil's car and sped off. They parked and walked to the door of the Admin Building, turned around, and began walking up the path toward the reflection pool. And there they found him. "Oh, man!" shouted Phil, racing up the path, Zoe right behind him. Joel Curwin was half in, half out of the pond. His arms were spread out on the gravel path. His head lay on his left forearm. He was motionless.

Zoe lifted his head. His face was bloodied. His overcoat was soaked, whether with water or blood or both was unclear. But he was alive. He groaned. His eyes opened. "Oh, man!" shouted Phil again. "We've gotta get him out o' the water!" To get him out, they had to get in. On either side of Joel, each lifting him under an arm, they heaved and hefted and managed to push, then pull him out of the pool and onto the gravel path. They rolled him over and Zoe maneuvered herself under him, his head on her lap, which she supported under her arm. He had a long, bloody gash on his forehead. "Mona and Carly are on the way. As soon as they get here we'll get you back down to the car and get you home. What happened?" asked Phil.

"I … I was … I started up the path … was kinda wobbly … dunno what happened … on the ground, fell into the water …"

"You were damn lucky!" exclaimed Phil. "You're concussed, but you could have gotten knocked out, drowned."

Joel was trying to get into a sitting position. "Nah, nah. Can't drown in six inches o' water."

"It's more like two feet here. Clearly you fell in. Maybe the shock of the water actually woke you up a little bit. You know you were half in, half out of the water when we came along."

"Yeah, yeah. Just couldn't heft myself out o' the water."

"Joel!" Mona came running up the path from the other direction, Carly close behind her. "Oh, my God! Oh, my God!" She knelt down by Zoe, cradled Joel's head. "Call nine-one-one! He needs to go to the hospital" She raised her head, looking beseechingly at the other three.

"No, no," said Joel. "No! Just get me home. I'll be all right."

"By the time we get EMTs over here, and he gets to the emergency room and all that he's probably better off getting out of those wet clothes and into a warm tub and getting some warm fluids and getting some antiseptic into that wound asap," said Phil.

"So let's get him up and out and down to the car!" said Zoe. With two on either side, they were able to shuffle Joel, more or less on his feet, down to the car.

"My … my… briefcase …"

"Let's worry about that later," insisted Phil. They got him into the car, Mona hugging Joel in the back, Zoe in the front. "I'll go back and get his briefcase," said Carly. "I saw it in the pool. You go on ahead; I'll walk back."

"Be careful!" cautioned Zoe.

THURSDAY, 10:05 PM

Mona and Zoe had shrugged Joel out of his overcoat on the front porch, got him straight into the bathroom, where they sat him on the toilet seat, and got his clothes off, while Phil ran a bath, warm but not hot. "Oh, this is nice!" said Joel, "fondled by two nubile maidens" as they helped him into the tub. Carly had retrieved his overcoat from the front porch, draped it over a chair in the backyard, and spread out the briefcase and its contents on the backyard table: a few wads of paper, his laptop, his phone, the shattered shards of his teapot and his "Kermit the Frog" cup, the infuser, and the tea canister.

Mona had stayed with Joel in the bathroom, where she wrapped a bacitracin-soaked gauze bandage around his forehead. The rest were gathered around the dining room table. "When Joel slipped and fell," explained Carly, "he must have flung the briefcase far and wide. I found it in the pool, but on the opposite side from where he fell. His phone and laptop were in there and I hauled them out. They're sitting out on the veranda but I'm sure their innards are, like, bread dough." Zoe could tell Carly was furious. "Some papers were in there too; anyway, when the briefcase landed in the pool, the impact shattered the tea pot and cup and must have jarred the lid of the tea canister loose. Some of it spilled out into the briefcase. Papers, tea, and the rest were wadded into a greenish lump. I dumped it in the compost. I hope the bugs'll eat computer print-out. Somebody did this to him."

"Speaking of eating," said Zoe, "have you done so, Phil?"

"Hmmm, well, a donut. Now that you mention it, I'm starved." Carly disappeared into the kitchen to heat up flank steak strips and pea-with-tofu curry. Mona appeared in the doorway: "I wanna get Joel out of the bath and into bed. Can one of you help?" Zoe jumped up. She might be small, but Kung Fu, which she had started again after she'd found a class meeting at the high school every Friday evening, made her strong and agile. Confronted with Joel's nakedness, Zoe felt diffident but she realized Joel could hardly care. She and Mona got Joel into Mona's bed.

As Phil tucked into his food, Mona and Zoe reappeared. "He'd like a cup of his mint tea but I told him it was all ruined; we don't have any here."

"Would chamomile do?" asked Carly. "It's kind of old, but I'll put in two tea bags."

Mona sat down at the table. She was trembling. Zoe joined her in a chair opposite, next to Phil.

"So … so did you get any idea of what happened?" asked Phil gently.

"Somebody did this to him," Carly declared again.

Mona gave her head a little shake. "He can't remember. He says he was walking along and then suddenly he wasn't walking along. His feet went out from under him and the next thing he remembers is floundering around in the water, coughing and gasping for breath. He says he tried to shed his overcoat and heave himself out of the water but he thinks he blacked out for a while and when he came to, he was half in, half out of the pool, and feeling weak."

"I wonder," said Phil. "I'd like to know if there's any possibility that he was tripped, or pushed."

"Yeah." For the third time, Carly spoke up. "Somebody did this to him."

"*What!*" Exclaimed Mona. "*You think so?*" Everyone turned to Mona and their troubled expressions hinted they weren't sure how long Mona was going to be able to keep it together. "But *who?*" she cried.

Phil, silent a moment, took another couple of bites of pea curry. He shook his head. "I don't know," he said quietly. "The hearing was contentious as you might well imagine. But at one point Madison Canter got really steamed at Joel and made that evident. She not only denied everything Joel had put into his statement, she also kind of maligned his upbringing, like he was doing this because of some inherent character flaw."

"She resents him for not having a Jewish mother?" asked Carly.

Slumped, fatigued, but seeming relieved, Mona quipped, "Maybe she thinks he *should* have had a Jewish mother; he had a Jewish father," and nearly smiled.

Zoe caught a sense of anxiety emanating from Phil. She reflected. *Surely the Canters' machinations belied the high-minded ideals of academia, here dehumanized by the sorcery of politics.*

But Phil's countenance soon reassumed its reassuring composure. He calmly broke back into the conversation. "I can't really share any details with you but my guess is her career and her man's career are over. She's feisty and she's been calling the shots around here, at least in terms of her little corner of the world, for nearly three decades. And she's gotten away with it up until now. I could see her seeking vengeance."

"So you think, what, she hid in the bushes? Then pushed him into the pool?" queried Carly.

"But how would she know that he was going to walk and what route he was going to take?" objected Zoe.

"It was dark. It was drizzling."

"But there are lights there, at the admin building and that imitation gas lamp at the pool," suggested Carly.

"Joel doesn't wear a hat," stated Phil matter-of-factly. "He had his head down to keep the drizzle off and maybe also to help with his balance. She–or somebody--could have hidden in the bushes around the admin building and then followed him. Or lay in wait for him, knowing his route back here would take him past the pool. Joel wouldn't have noticed. He seemed pretty out of it. So she–or somebody–sticks out a foot, trips him, over he goes, bangs his head, and into the pool."

"Whoa!" said Mona. "Are you going to suggest this to Joel? I'm not so sure that's a good idea. He was already paranoid to begin with."

"Well, he may come up with something like that scenario all by himself," suggested Phil. "You can't say he didn't predict something like this happening."

9

SATURDAY

BY THE TIME SINFUL SATURDAY rolled around, Phil and Porter had hammered out much of their report, working on Friday until three, when Porter had to leave for the airport in Walla Walla. Joel had improved dramatically, now wandering around the house, chafing at being forbidden to go outdoors by Mona. "You'll catch pneumonia!" insisted Mona. But his "wobblies" as he referred to the combination of dizziness and headaches that had plagued him for nearly two weeks were gone. "Yeah," he joked. "Just get knocked on the head, fall in the drink, and lie there for a while and you'll rise up healthy and wise, if not wealthy." His laptop and phone were, of course, ruined, but Phil thought Joel could probably find a hacker wizard back at Northern Washington U who could retrieve the files of his laptop and maybe even some of what was stored on his phone. In the meantime, Joel was using Mona's computer to continue writing his paper on Jane Bennett; he'd write a chunk of rough draft, then send it to himself as an email attachment for retrieval later.

Zoe had had a full two days to contemplate the accident that had befallen Joel. Now, she had a hunch, an intuition, a guess about what might have been at work with Joel. So when she and Phil arrived at Monas' and Carly's, Zoe marched straight through the house to the back door, leading out from the kitchen, setting a Tupperware container on the counter as she passed. She had prepared deep-fried panko-coated zucchini spears in her crock pot.

Carly, who was shoving a pan of tortilla empanadas into the oven and turned to Zoe. "Spinach, raisins, anchovies, and pine nuts held together with an egg batter–sounds strange but we had them a couple of weeks ago and you'll be surprised. The ones without anchovies for you have a little glob of pine-nuts-and egg on--hey, where are you going?"

Zoe turned, her hand on the back doorknob. "You said you dumped the contents of Joel's soaked tea into the compost bin, right?"

"Right, along with the papers that were in the briefcase. They were all lumped together."

Zoe realized she would probably need a utensil. About to retreat out the back door, she retraced her steps, strode over to the stove, and removed a large, long-handled ladle that was at home with a collection of wooden spoons in a sturdy ceramic container at the back, between the burners. "Can you throw my zucchini spears into the oven with your empanadas? How long for the empanadas?"

"Fifteen minutes." Carly was now dumping a couple of dozen fat scallops into a pan.

"That should do it for the spears, too."

Outside, Zoe headed straight for the compost bin at the back of the yard. She took off the lid, leaned in, and spotted the greenish lump; scraping away as much paper away as possible, she then maneuvered the ladle underneath the remaining lump and carefully lifted it out with one hand, re-securing the bin's lid with the other. Carrying the lump back into the kitchen, she laid a double layer of paper towel onto the counter, then dumped the goopy lump onto it.

"What's that?" demanded Carly, now putting the finishing touches on the sautéed scallops, adding paprika, parsley, and lemon juice.

"That's Joel's tea." Zoe departed, standing in the doorway of the living room, where everyone else was assembled.

Joel was regaling James with a highly inventive rendition of what he now was calling his "encounter with a reflecting pool". "So there I was, making my way up the scree, or maybe it was a gravel path, the wind blowing stinging pellets of water in my face, my head down, my shoulders bunched …"

"Hey, 'scuse me for interrupting," said Zoe, "but can I borrow a sheet of paper and maybe a sharpie?"

"Sure," responded Mona. "In my bedroom, middle desk drawer." Zoe returned to the kitchen with the paper and sharpie. Carly was sliding the sheet of empanadas, decked with Zoe's zucchini spears, out of the oven. Zoe wrote: *Please do not touch! Do not remove!* She propped the sheet of paper against the food processor on the counter, where the greenish lump sat on the paper toweling. "I'd like this to dry out where it's warm and dry."

"Why?!" exclaimed Carly, spooning the scallops into a thick, purple-colored ceramic serving bowl.

"I had one of those three-o'clock-in-the-morning, a-ha moments. It's just hunch but it's worth pursuing. I'll explain when we sit down to supper," promised Zoe.

There was a scraping of chairs along the floor as everyone took their seat, waiting to hear what Zoe had to say. Carly stood over the pan of empanadas and zucchini spears with a pair of tongs, plopping generous portions of both onto everybody's plates; the scallops were making their way around the table to everyone except, of course, Zoe.

Carly sat down, forking a zucchini spear into her mouth. "So give," she said to Zoe as she munched.

Zoe bit into an empanada. "Oof! Good but hot!" She set the rest of the empanada onto her plate.

"This have something to do with me?" queried Joel.

"You bet it does!" affirmed Zoe. "How many cups of mint tea do you drink in a day?"

"Oh, uh, well, I have coffee at breakfast, but then when I get to the office, first thing, I make myself a cup of tea. Probably have two before class, then a pee, then at the break I fix myself another one, then after class, I do another quick pee, fix another cuppa to have with my lunch. Then it's the afternoon and another couple o' cuppa to get me through the afternoon class. Then back home for another before my usually lonely lonesome excuse for a dinner. I mean, it's not quite every hour on the hour but damn near. Why?"

"Another with dinner?" asked Zoe.

"No. beer or maybe red wine if it's a cold day."

"So we're looking at, like, a minimum of six or seven cups from your office stash."

"Yeah," agreed Joel cautiously.

"And you've had these flu symptoms for, what, a week? Two weeks?"

"Oh, probably more like two weeks."

"And while you've been here, you've followed more or less the same routine, in terms of having your tea."

"Well, yah, not exactly, but more or less. A little less, except for Thursday. I went over there, to the admin building, for what I thought was going to be a nine-o'clock meeting that was postponed 'til four. So I went to the library and worked on my pubs I'm hoping to get out, you know, Taibo in Paris, and a couple articles, I hope, on Jane Bennett."

"And you guzzled tea all day, in the library."

"Well, yeah …"

"Okay. So here's what I'm doing. I've got the remains of the contents of your tea canister drying out in the kitchen. Ever heard of henbane?"

"Don't think so," said Joel.

"Henbane, henbane." Mona ruminated. "An herb. A medicine. Native to Asia but came into Europe in the late Middle Ages."

"An herb, maybe, but in large doses, a poison." Zoe popped her third empanada into her mouth. Gasps and exclamations all around while she chewed. "Symptoms? Well, something of a high, some say–ah–enhanced romantic capabilities, pain relief, but along with all that comes restlessness and dilated pupils. Prolonged consistent ingestion brings trouble coordinating muscular movements, trouble locomoting, confusion, sometimes something like delirium, hypertension manifesting as headaches, nausea. Sound familiar?"

"He was poisoned!" Mona fairly shouted.

"But is it common? I mean, is it all that easy to get, henbane?" asked James.

Zoe nodded. "Hell yes! You can grow it as a houseplant, in a pot. According to Wikipedia, it was even recommended as a salad ingredient in a magazine article in *Healthy and Organic Living* about ten years ago." Zoe pursed her lips, looked around at her companions, raised her eyebrows, and fought a trembling lower lip. "We almost lost you, Joel, and it's because somebody's been spiking your tea."

"But who? How?" asked a bewildered Mona.

"Who, I don't know. But how? You remember that break-in into your office, Joel?"

Joel nodded. His expression was extremely serious; his face, what was visible amidst the mutton chops, was pale.

"Well, that rifling through your files may have been a ruse. Nobody was trying to take something *from* you; the intruder was getting in to plant something *for* you. No pun intended."

"Wow! *Wow!*" exclaimed Carly.

Zoe held up both her hands, traffic cop style. "But so far this is only a theory. That's why that mess is on the kitchen counter."

"Huh?" said Joel.

"Carly dumped the soggy mass from your tea canister into the compost bin. I fished it out just now. It's drying on the counter. If my idea is right, when the soggy mess dries, it should reveal two shades of green. In photos, henbane looks to me to be a little paler green than mint, whether it's peppermint or spearmint. My idea is that someone spiked your office canister of mint tea with henbane." She shook her head. "I can tell you, I'm calm as a cucumber now, telling you all this, but when it hit me, last night—I mean, I woke up, maybe I was dreaming, or in one of those half-asleep states where you're thinking and dozing at the same time? When it hit me, I started sweating. I guess you didn't notice, Phil. You were snoring away."

Phil shrugged, shook his head, held his hands out, palms out and started to stammer something.

"That's scary!" Mona's were wide. "Just. *Amazingly.* Scary!"

"I knew it! I knew it!" crowed Carly. "Somebody did this to you! Somebody made that accident happen!"

James emitted a slow whistle. "Yeah, it's scary, all right. And I'm not doubting you, Zoe, but I think we need to be dead sure—oh, no pun intended. Maybe I can help with that. My chemistry colleagues over in sciences might be able to do chemical tests. The stuff would test positive for the offending alkaloids."

"Great!" enthused Zoe.

Joel shook his head. Mona picked up on his skepticism and countered it. "So Joel, you might have been being poisoned for a couple weeks. It wasn't the flu and it wasn't nerves about confronting Canter. She looked around at everybody. "And the idea would be that they were trying to–actually *kill* him?"

"Maybe not kill him. Maybe just, so to speak, neutralize him." Zoe made quotation marks above her head. "I mean, like, if he was feeling too bad to come down here, he never would have talked with Phil. Phil would never have talked with Porter. Porter would have never talked with the dean. And Joel would have never been solicited to give his deposition, etcetera, etcetera."

"He could have phoned, emailed or faxed," objected Carly.

"Yes, I could have phoned," responded Joel. "But obviously the dean really wanted a notarized statement and on top of that a deposition, and then the opportunity for Canter to confront his accuser, me. At the very least, that whole process would have been delayed. And who knows? I might have tried to drive, could have driven off the road, had a traffic accident, smash-crash, end of story."

"But," objected James, "when, how would the Canters have gotten wind of what Joel had? What he was going to do? You didn't tell anybody about this, did you?"

"Well, no, not in so many words. But it wasn't a secret that I was interested in tracking down Jane Bennett," responded Joel. "I mean, I told Ned Roberts–he's the one that originally showed me her obituary–that I was following up on what he'd shared with me. He's the one who told me about Chad Beatty at Imperial College. And lots of people knew I was going to London to see him. And then when I got back, yeah, I told him about her thesis and Malinowski and all that. I mean, I never said why I was so interested, but yeah, he and a lot of people knew I was interested in Jane Bennett."

"Could he or somebody else have had contact with the Canters? Spilled the beans to them?" asked Phil.

Joel furrowed his brow. "I suppose so. It's unlikely. But it's, well, maybe not so unlikely. I mean, a couple folks from Northern regularly go to the Ethnohistory Meetings which are in mid-September; highly inconvenient for some of us but just before quarter begins in some places, and well into the fall term for others."

"And ethnohistory is …?" asked Carly.

"The use of documents and oral testimonies to reconstruct the history of a particular group of people, that is, an ethnic group, usually indigenous, that hasn't been the subject of specific historical treatment. So, yeahhh." Joel drawled out the affirmation. "It's perfectly possible either one of the Canters or maybe both of them and maybe Dora Harris too would have been going to those meetings regularly for years. And it's entirely possible that they might have overheard *my* colleagues talking with some of *their* ethnohistory colleagues about me and my interest in Jane Bennett. Maybe even in the act of doing me a favor–asking around for more leads, somebody who knew her. Maybe even asked the Canters."

"If hearing the Jane Bennett query at the Ethnohistory Meetings had rattled anyone's earpans, it would have been Madison," suggested Phil. "Porter thinks Joe Canter hadn't a clue where the Jane Bennett material came from, that he may have really thought it *did* come from the bogus references; that it was really Madison that got the Bennett material and plopped it in front of Joe for him to use. Maybe that it was her who actually wrote his dissertation. But you all don't know that. And you didn't hear it from me. But anyway, if she heard about somebody sniffing around Jane Bennett, that could have set her off."

"Right, right," confirmed Carly. "And the time period fits. They, or Madison, hear about the Joel-Jane connection. Then, maybe a few days later they, or she, makes a little trip up north to Northern Washington University and voila!"

"Yup." Zoe nodded. "And, as somebody I know–or once knew–would say, Bob's your uncle."

Joel sat back. "Wild!"

MID-OCTOBER: "FAT TUESDAY"

Joel was back teaching, at Northern Washington. He had switched to Red Zinger tea and, as he'd put it in an email to Mona, was "feeling super." Carly, Mona, and Phil had feasted on stir-fried shrimp with cauliflower and recon-stituted dried tomatoes, in a sauce of Mumbai Chaat. Zoe had spooned the sauce over honey and ginger roasted sweet potatoes accompanied by a heap of caramelized red onions with stir-fried garlic, Pequin peppers, and peanuts. A couple bottles of Clos du Bois Meristone Alexander Meritage accented the meal. They cleared the table and Mona brought out her laptop. She'd heard from Joel again. "Okay, this is kind of a long email," Mona warned. "So I'll paraphrase. This is in regard to the Ethnohistory Meetings and whether the Canters might have gotten wind of Joel's interest in Jane Bennett. No, the guy that set him up with his Imperial College source didn't go to the Ethnohistory Meetings, but another colleague, a Kelly Brennan, did. She does New Guinea.

The Trobriand Islands where Malinowski worked are part of New Guinea. Joel told her about Bennett's thesis. She was excited.

She's back from the Ethnohistory Meetings and this afternoon he buttonholed her and asked if she spread it around at the meetings that he, Joel was interested in Bennett's thesis. Yes, she did–didn't remember if she mentioned him, Joel by name, Brennan might have encountered somebody from Sacajawea and Charbonneau–couldn't be sure of a name–could have been Canter or Harris–Brennan wasn't sure."

Mona closed her laptop. "So yes, it's possible that one of the triumvirate got wind of Joel's interest and put two-and-two together. Now all we have to do," she said to Zoe and Carly, "is find out if any of them were actually there, at the Ethnohistory Society annual meetings."

"That shouldn't be too hard to do," commented Zoe.

The weather had gotten much worse by midweek, with below-freezing temperatures and on-and-off showers of a rain-snow mix, but now had unaccountably turned if not warm at least clear. Thus Joel was expected on Thursday evening and Phil on the Friday. Zoe had examined the now dry contents of Joel's canister with magnifying glass and tweezers and had sorted out enough light-green bits to validate her hypothesis: something was mixed with the mint. Now she had a little baggy prepared for James, who had found someone in the Sciences Department who would test for alkaloids.

Peter Blenheim called a department meeting. Zoe caught Carly's and Mona's eye as he revealed the latest news. Blenheim announced he had been seconded to the Social Sciences Department to serve as Acting Chair for the remainder of the term. The Social Sciences Chair, Joseph Canter, was now on leave of absence until further notice, starting at the end of the day on Friday. He, Blenheim, asked for a volunteer to serve, informally, as assistant chair (a position that did not exist) who would essentially take over as the Art History

Chair. He asked Gudrun Hance to do so, at least for the remainder of the calendar year. She responded that she would have to think about it because in three weeks' time her sister and family would be descending on them, two weeks early, for Thanksgiving, to be followed by a family trip to Florida, barring hurricanes, and if not Florida, then San Diego. And with a houseful of six teenagers, she didn't know how she was going to manage.

He then asked if anyone else might be interested. Carly piped up and said she would do it. But for spring term a formal arrangement would have to be made, insisted Blenheim, and he urged Gudrun to consider moving into the chair's position at that time, for which she would get a course release. Mona, Carly, and Zoe would have a few weeks to decide whether one of them wanted to take over Gudrun's section of *Art Appreciation* for spring term, as an overload for a little extra pay, or whether they would have to hire an adjunct. In the meantime, for what was left of autumn quarter, Carly would serve as chair's assistant, and thus as the de facto department chair.

As they discussed this new development–Joseph Canter being eased out and Peter Blenheim stepping into his position–they reasoned that Blenheim had had to be apprised of the whole sorry mess. Now they should be able to find out if any of the triumvirate had attended the Ethnohistory Meetings. Iif so, they would have had to submit a travel request and probably would have put in a request for reimbursement of expenses. So there would be a record in the college's accounting system. Peter Blenheim would be able to access that information. The question was how to approach him and ask him to do so. How much could they tell him? Should he know about the probable poisoning of Joel? Discussion of the issue proceeded over the sinful Saturday meal: a red onion, hard-boiled egg and endive salad with a Pequin pepper, orange juice and canola oil dressing with flank steak strips marinated in the dressing added to everybody's bowl except for Zoe's and Phil's; Zoe's wicked linguini with mushrooms and the last of the summer's canned tomatoes from the college's organic garden, this time also with chopped spinach, sweet Vidalia onion, and eggplant; and for everybody else, jumbo fresh shrimp quick fried in olive oil in a barely heated sherry-and-overripe mango sauce.

They decided only Phil could legitimately make the request; he would stay over and try to see Blenheim if not Monday, then Tuesday. If it happened on Tuesday, their contingency plan had Zoe driving to Multnomah on Monday, staying at Phil's place, and filling in for him with what would be an unannounced, but she hoped well-received, lecture in his Native North America class on Native art. Mona would take Zoe's Art Appreciation section ("Six straight hours of class--I'll be a basket case!" Mona had complained. "But I'll do it.") Phil would say nothing to Peter Blenheim about tea or henbane or Joel's "accident, rather, he would say simply that somehow, someone seemed to have rifled through Joel Curwin's files–perhaps while he had stepped out for a call of nature, or gone down the hall to the department office. Phil was not accusing or even suggesting that any one of the three senior faculty had done so, but perhaps someone, such as a curious, anonymous graduate student, might have done so, having overheard Joel's colleague, Dr. Brennan, in conversation with one of the Canters about a master' thesis on trade and marriage among the Bannock, on which, Dr. Brennan knew, one of the Canters had published a monograph and had rifled Joel's files looking for it.

This latter statement would, of course, be a not-quite-bold-faced lie, but very much a stretching of the possible truth. But the idea here was that if somebody had overheard the conversation and for some unknown reason, gone looking for the copy of the thesis, then maybe–just maybe--Blenheim would go for it because he would have been told enough of the Bennett-Canter-Canter story, maybe even a version of Porter Harder's speculations, transmitted through Dean Fister. Maybe Blenheim would not put some skullduggery past the principals to make a last-ditch effort to throw a spanner in the works, anticipating the revelation that would be looming, and would be sympathetic to looking into it further.

In the end, Phil, Zoe, and Mona did not have to resort to topsy-turvy logistics to cover their classes because Phil was able to get in to see Peter Blenheim first thing Monday morning. As he laid out his reason for requesting that Blenheim access accounting records, without letting Blenheim know Joel had shared this piece of information with four other persons besides Phil, he became once again aware of how thin the rationale sounded: just maybe somebody had said something about a masters thesis on trade and marriage in a North American Indian tribe? And this somebody was a New Guinea specialist? And somebody, maybe a Canter or Harris, or a zealous graduate student had been there and overheard? And then, either that person went charging up to North Washington University on the offhand chance of purloining the offending master's thesis, or had hired somebody to do so? To temporarily hamstring an investigation, the eventuality of which was inevitable? And now Phil was asking Peter Blenheim, in the first hour of the first day in his new position, to stick his nose into accounting records that were within the purview of an administrative assistant whom he had most probably not as yet even met!

But Peter Blenheim surprised him. Blenheim listened quietly, his elbows on the desk, hands folded in front of his pursed lips. When Phil had finished, Blenheim placed his folded arms horizontally on his desk, clasping his elbows. "I've been provided–no, inundated–with testimonials, legal opinions, transcripts, and of course, your and Dr. Harder's report." He took a deep breath. "There's enough in those documents to suggest a trail of actions cleverly disguised as the results of supposedly reasonable decisions that, in fact, were manipulations of academic procedures, ironically put in place to ensure fairness and equity, calculated to ensure the retaining of power by insecure, unqualified, self-important little despots. I've never seen such an entrenched, unremitting, and, I'll have to say, successful conspiracy to obfuscate, mislead, cover over weakness, dishonesty, and duplicity." He shook his head.

Wow! thought Phil. *What a succinct, eloquent statement of the case.*

"So I wouldn't be surprised at anything those scamps got up to. I wouldn't put it past them to persuade an MA students here in the Social Sciences Department to go scurrying up to Northern Washington and hang around until the opportune moment came to rifle Dr. Curwin's files. I'll have your answer by the end of the day." Phil gave him his mobile number. They stood, shook hands and Phil was able to return to Zoe's flat for a leisurely morning and a measured drive back to Multnomah. He was about halfway there when his phone chimed. He pulled over at the first opportunity. Peter had left a terse message. No, the Canters had not gone; yes, Dora Harris had done so. He called Peter back and thanked him.

～◯

MID-OCTOBER: THE NEXT "FAT TUESDAY"

By the next day, "fat Tuesday", they had the answer to their other question. James called Carly. James' chemistry colleague had been intrigued with the challenge of identifying alkaloids from the green bits. And yes, they were definitely present. Could be something like belladonna or ayahuasca, but definitely not hemp-derived, so not marijuana. "Now we have to decide what we do with this information," declared Carly, "Confront? Accuse? Go to the police?" They had just finished consuming heaps of empanadas stuffed with shredded gruyere, chopped tomatillos that were still left from the organic garden harvest, chopped mushrooms, yellow onion, jalapeno peppers and garlic, bound together with egg. Half had ground turkey added to the mixture; this time they had baked them in the oven, on two different pans, of course. Zoe had brought a crock pot brimming with her potato leek soup. The wine, a Dante red had gone well with the meal.

～◯

"I think the Canters are in enough trouble as it is. This adds another dimension–well, and another person–Dora Harris–to the mix. But she was probably in the whole mess up to her neck anyway, to begin with," noted Mona.

"What we have to make sure of," declared Zoe, "is that they don't continue to wreak vengeance on Joel. I mean, once his couple articles come out,

135

Canter's reputation, if he ever had one, will be in tatters. So will Columbia University's or at least a little corner of it, to some extent. And it also should be in the best interests of students and the junior faculty that are still being compromised by them, or whose heads are on the chopping block, that they don't have to still cower in the corner in fear of their shenanigans."

"Heads will roll!" crowed Carly.

"Yeah, I wouldn't be surprised if Joseph Canter isn't asked to simply resign, take early retirement, whatever," declared Zoe.

"Well, you don't know. Maybe those who are compromised, other than the two that are slated for contract non-renewal, don't mind so much being compromised," noted Mona. "I mean, maybe they're perfectly happy being lackeys. They might even aid and abet, do the Canters' dirty tricks for them."

"So how do we make sure they don't continue to wreak their havoc, then?" puzzled Carly "I mean, if they are behind the poisoning, they're not likely to try that again, are they? Hire somebody to run Joel off the road? You really think they'll wreak vengeance? What do we do, put a tail on them?"

"Call in the police," declared Mona.

Zoe nodded her head vigorously, "Definitely. Let's call in the police."

SINFUL SATURDAY

It was mid-morning. Detective Sargent J.P. Barnard propped up his head with his hand cupped underneath his chin as Zoe, Carly, Mona, and Joel went through the whole long story—or rather, several stories—of the henbane poisoning. They were all sitting around the kitchen table in Carly's and Mona's house. Officer Dorothy "D" Morrow sat at the table. It was a little cramped. The dried mash of henbane and mint leaves sat in the middle of the table.

JP took his hand from underneath his chin and joined it to his other hand, both resting on the table. "Ladies and gentleman," he began. "I hear and understand your concern. But where is the crime scene?" He swept his right hand around in a half-circle. "The entire campus here?" A desk drawer at another university? A house in Oakland, California?"

"All three," replied Carly.

JP shook his head. "Now I'm gonna tell ya. Here on the table we might have what we call physical evidence. The means by which the deed, at least one of them, was done. All right. But then the next question is, who had access to the means? That's one component of constructing a crime. What was the means and who had access to it? Another component is an eye witness. Who saw the deed being done? And the third big one is motive. You tell me you've got a couple people with a couple motives. But who saw who spiked the old lady's tea? Who saw who dumped this … this hen stuff, the poison, into the tea in the desk drawer?"

"What about fingerprints?" objected Joel. "Fingerprints on the tea canister in my office?"

"Get real!" replied JP. "If as you say, this was calculated, premeditated, the perp would have worn gloves. Or by now, the fingerprints would be long gone, smudged, covered over with the professors'. And you don't have any witness who can pinpoint either one of them at the scene of what might or might not be a crime. So fingerprints are useless. And as to the third component, motive, that's the hardest thing to pin down. You can't prove motive. Motive is always circumstantial. So all we have is physical evidence. We have no witnesses to anything. We may or may not have motives, but we can't prove them."

"And you know, honey, you yourself said you thought you might have had the flu," said Mona.

Officer Morrow, addressing Joel, said. "Flu has indeed been going around. And there's all kinds. Even those flu shots don't work for all the different kinds.

"If we went barging around, arresting your colleagues at the college, these professors, the Canters, we could never, never come close to getting an indictment," declared JP. "We couldn't get close to getting into court with this.

We'd be the laughing stock in six counties if we tried to treat this as a crime."

He and Officer Morrow rose. He gave two curt nods. "Ladies. Gentlemen. I'm afraid there's nothing we can do. Thank you for your cooperation." They departed.

"Well that was a bust," lamented Joel.

"Really disappointing," agreed Mona.

"Outrageous!" declared Carly.

Zoe blew air out of her mouth and clenched her jaw. "We're going to have to investigate this ourselves."

For the evening meal, Zoe made two salads: one endive and walnut and the other a kind of carrot-mayonnaise-raisin-agave compote, sneaked in as dessert. Mona made a whole roast chicken stuffed with pre-boiled rice and celery, blanched almonds, diced sweet peppers parsley and thyme with an egg binding. Extra mushroom stuffing for Phil and Zoe simmered along with the roasting chicken in a baking dish. Carly took advantage of the oven to make five kinds of crostini appetizers: chicken liver; tomato and garlic; spinach and anchovy; chili paste and peanut butter; and smoked salmon. Everything came out of the oven and out of the fridge at the same time so dishes were flying back and forth, up and down the table. A Catalunya Tempranillo-Grenache blend, an Orvieto Classico, and a Sonoma sauvignon blanc gave multiple choices as accompanying wines. All three were somewhat fruity. For the meat-eaters the Catalunya added spice and cherry to the chicken liver, peanut butter and smoked salmon. The Orvieto and the sauv blanc cut through the richness of the anchovies, the earthiness of the mushrooms and the condiments gracing the stuffing, the acidity of the tomato and the spinach, and the pepperiness of the chili paste. Both white wines brought out the subtle aromas that permeated the chicken from the stuffing. The red Catalunya, taken at the end of the meal, would intensify the compote's sweetness.

Zoe, Mona, and Carly gave Phil and James a run-down on their unproductive meeting with the police and expressed their misgivings about the triumvirate's potential future shenanigans. "Not to get you all scared," cautioned Mona, "but do you think it's worth worrying about, bothering about? I mean, the police didn't seem to think it was all that serious, or even likely, the poisoning, I mean."

"But we know it was not only likely, it happened!" objected James.

"I'll be the only reason they gave us the time of day was because they had nothing better to do on a Saturday morning and wanted some entertainment," said Carly sardonically. "So what do we do now?"

"Zoe suggested putting a tail on them, just to make sure they didn't get up to anything," replied Joel.

Zoe clarified, "I said it's not a bad idea. But I was half joking. I mean, why should we do that? And how?"

Phil piled four of the anchovy crostinis and three of smoked salmon and a ladleful of stuffing onto his plate. "Well, here's one thought. Like I was telling you last week, I can't tell you the source of this idea," he began, popping a crostini into his mouth, chewing, "but there is speculation that it wasn't even Joe Canter who wrote that plagiarized dissertation--it was his wife. It might be worth running that down."

"That's right!" exclaimed Joel. "I read over the transcript of that hearing, where he was meant to confront me, tell his version of things. I wasn't perking on all six at the time, but the transcript is word-for-word, and Joseph Canter says–and this is, like, equivalent to being in court, like giving a notarized statement–that he never heard of Jane Bennett, was never in the Beinecke Library, never knew about her thesis. Which is probably true."

"So would it be worth tracking down if that's true? If he really was never there? And if *Madison Canter was*?" speculated Carly.

"Yeah. It would be," offered Phil.

Zoe had just dug into her bowl of carrot salad. Now she tapped the spoon against her pursed lips. She entered a bubble of memory and speculation.

Ferguson. He might have retired to some Caribbean island, lounging under a cabana, getting himself cancerously tanned, sipping pina coladas and mojitos. But she remembered him as being too intrigued with picking apart schemes and scams through his career as insurance investigator to pass this up. *And,* she thought, *he profited nicely from my careful unraveling of a complicated tapestry of theft, fraud, extortion, blatant disregard for the culture and sovereignty of a couple dozen Native American communities, and even murder. And I kept quiet so he got the credit and the kudos and a nice bonus for his contracted services as insurance investigator, guaranteed a supplement to his income for the following six or seven years.*

Yes, she reckoned, *he owes me. Would he feel he owed her? He should do! And whoa! Wait 'til he hears about Dora Harris' mask! The possibility that Jane Faulks, alias Dahlia, the purveyor purloined masks, Ferguson's nemesis, might have surfaced again, now, recently! That should be a big pull.*

She reentered the here and now realizing Phil was laying out the case for pursuing the Beinecke clue. "... kind of getting away with it ... have a lot to answer for ... compromised junior faculty, tainted the educational process, derailed the careers of what? Ten, twelve scholar-teachers? Even if Joseph Canter resigns, until Joel's publications come out, they can lament that it's too bad about Joe but his health wouldn't permit him to continue on, etcetera, etcetera, yada, yada, yada."

"Yeah," agreed Zoe, "And I know just the person to follow up on this. I haven't said much about the mask."

"The mask?" queried Carly.

"Dora has a mask hanging on her wall. It probably came out of an auction four years ago." Zoe filled them in, as briefly as possible, on the auction, the sacred masks, her and Phil's efforts to get them returned to the Tribes, the extortion attempt by Dahlia-Jane. She left out everything about other principals. She mentioned Ferguson as an insurance investigator for whom she'd worked to expose an insurance fraud that was related to the extortion case, and that because she'd helped, he owed her. She explained that he had been drawn to the auction of sacred masks, advertised as "Native American art", because he had spotted someone there, in Paris. The masks had probably been stolen, over many decades, some perhaps bought up by several museums, then de-accessioned to a cadre of collectors and speculators who put them into the auction. One thing and another led him to the would-be proprietors of the shop on the Hudson where Zoe had been working at the time, who were actually imposters. Ferguson had thought the whole situation smacked of a cold case that had frustrated him a few years earlier. An insured shipment of well-provenanced prehistoric pottery excavated from several private ranches in New Mexico had disappeared between points of origin and destination. Ferguson's investigation had gotten as far as uncovering the probable of a clever woman: Jane Faulks, the woman he had spotted at the Paris auction years later, and who had turned up making a proposal to the imposters that they broker the sale of the sacred masks from the auction which she had in her possession. But he could never pin anything down, until Zoe came along and did it for him. (*Well, that wasn't quite the way it worked, but that was it in a nutshell*) She pointed out the possible connection between Dora Harris, her mask, the auction masks, and Jane Faulks. So he owed her, and the mask connection to Dora Harris might be an extra incentive for him to do some investigating, gratis.

"So you want something to hook Ferguson in," remarked Carly. "Ratchet up his interest. Pull his chain, in addition to paying you back a debt. Sounds like you've got it."

"Precisely," agreed Zoe, nodding vigorously. She turned to Joel. "Joel, when you went to the Beinecke, you had to sign in, right?"

"Right. I was surprised. It was an old-fashioned logbook that you actually signed. Name, date, time, affiliation, purpose of visit. And log out."

"So chances are good, they've got these logbooks going back, like, forever."

"Well, as far back as there were special collections. Yeah, probably. Yeah. Certainly back to the 1980s. So if Canter accessed Jane Bennett's notes, his name would be there."

"And if it was *Madison* Canter who accessed them, *her* name alone would be there, not Joseph Canter's, and twice: once when she was at Columbia and also, an earlier entry, in her unmarried name, maybe half a dozen years earlier, when she'd been a student at Yale; that would have been when she first discovered them," affirmed Zoe.

"So then how does this Ferguson person talk his way into these archived logbooks?" asked James.

"He's good at doing that. He'll figure it out."

"But are they going to buy that? He just comes along and says, 'Hi, I'm Ferguson, and I want to see your log books' and they say, 'Oh, sure, come on in?' I don't think so," objected James.

"You're right. But if he's there investigating on behalf of a client who has an interest, how could they refuse?"

"Who's the client?"

"Me," answered Zoe. "I'm the client. And at Sacajawea and Charbonneau College where there's been a major scandal, or where one is about to break, and this investigation is part of the larger one that has to stay confidential for the time being, *I* can hire him."

James was shaking his head. "Won't work. You don't have–what's the word?–standing. You don't have standing. You don't have a vested interest. You're not a stakeholder."

Zoe curled up one side of her upper lip in a sneer of chagrin at herself. She hadn't thought of that. Of course officially, she didn't know why Joseph Canter was taking leave and her chair had been moved over to the Social Sciences Department.

"But Peter does," observed Carly. "He's now chair of the offenders' department."

"I don't know." Mona shook her head. "Haven't we, I mean us, through Phil, leaned on him enough already?"

Phil spoke up. "Blenheim was pretty steamed about them. He used some pretty strong language when I told him why I thought it was worth looking into the travel request. What was the word he used? Scallywags? Scammers? Scamps! That's what he called them: scamps!"

"Sounds like little trolls, or what are those ghosts that play tricks?" commented Carly. "Poltergeists?"

"So if Peter Blenheim agrees to join all of us, you, Carly and Mona, and me, to hire him, and let's say Ferguson would agree to work for a dollar, but if he finds something that moves the case forward, then he submits a bill–negotiable–to the college? The dean would have to agree ..." Zoe was thinking out loud. "And he could pursue the mask-Dahlia thing on the side, on his own, if he wanted to."

"I don't know how he'd do that without exposing himself to Dora," objected Phil.

"Well, really!" exclaimed Carly, mockingly.

"I mean–you know what I mean! I'll bet he'll figure out a way to do it without her even knowing he's doing it. He's clever."

"Sneaky, you mean," corrected Carly.

"Yeah. You could say that."

"It actually makes sense," affirmed Phil. "It's a logical follow-up. I'll come with you. And open with Blenheim. I can say–which is true–that Porter Harder discovered that Madison, as Madison Freeburg, had gotten her BA from Yale. I mean, that's no secret." Then he slumped. "So it's another Monday-morning-try-to-get-in-to-see-Peter thing again?"

"No, no," replied Zoe. "Let's invite him over next Friday to my place. It'll be just you and me. You can tell him you've shared a lot of this with me. It's natural. I'm, like, your wife. In fact, in the eyes of the State of Washington, we probably *are* married, common-law. So we share information, can't be made to testify against one another, yada, yada, yada."

"Good. I can say something like, 'Joseph Canter may have never even heard about Jane Bennett,' and he'll know what I mean, from something Canter said at the deposition."

"I'll call him. Invite him over. See if he can stand a crockpot veg meal:

potatoes, onions, carrots, parsnips, tomatoes, garbanzo beans, peanuts, all in a split-pea soup gravy. Ask him what spices he can't stand."

In the meantime, Zoe googled Brian Ferguson. Too many in the phone cyberspace. There had to be an easier way. She called Assurance Associates. Employment information was confidential.

Oh, poo! thought Zoe. She called her old friends and employers, Cait and Robb Murray in New York. She had kept in touch through emails and occasional phone calls, but had not spoken to the Murrays at any length for some months, not since coming to Charbonneau. "Hey! Zoe! Good to hear from you!" shouted Cait into the phone. "I'm putting you on speaker!"

They spent a few minutes catching up. Then Zoe asked them if they had any idea of how to get a hold of Brian Ferguson. No, but their insurance agent, Don Barker, the original contact that had brought Ferguson to them, might.

Cait phoned back the next day. Don Barker remembered Ferguson, but he had not had any contact with him since the break-in incident, three years earlier. He had put in a call to the home office, however, and someone there had burrowed inside Assurance Associates and had indeed turned up contact information for Ferguson, although Don had said he couldn't put her in direct contact with him. "He'll have to call you," he said. Cait asked him to call back the go-between and give Zoe's contact information for forwarding to Ferguson.

The following day, she did indeed have a message on her phone from a number, with an area code, that she did not recognize. She returned the call. "Ferguson," came the answer.

"Ferguson! It's Zoe!"

"Zo ... Ah! Zoe! How be ye?" Something was amiss, like air pockets between Ferguson's words.

"You sound far away."

"That I am!"

Zoe laid out the two situations–mask and archived notes that would evidence not only plagiarism, but also actual forgery. The record of visitors to the Beinecke. Yes, Ferguson was interested. No, he was not sitting around on his duff, but he didn't have much interesting work. Yes, he imagined that anything Zoe got involved with would be intriguing, puzzling, and slightly dangerous. Yes, he would do it. "But," he cautioned, "let me look into things and get back to you with a plan. If I ha'e one, would it be worth my while to run it by you in person?"

"Certainly. In fact, if you're going to take this on, you're going to have to be here, not there, wherever there is. I picture you on St. Lucia, on a terrace with a view of the harbor and the fort, sipping frozen rum daiquiris with a nice lady stroking your thigh."

"Well, ye be na' far off," he affirmed. "Since I got those insurance fraudsters to cough up what they bilked Assurance Associates out of, I'm more or less semi-retired. Or at least taking a hiatus, ye might say. Living off that nice bonus they paid me for getting the settlement.'

"With my help," amended Zoe firmly.

"Indeed, with your help Ms Zoe."

"Well, if you can swing it, can you be here by Saturday? Friends and I have a little get-together every Saturday. Any diet restrictions? You still a carnivore?"

"Absolutely. If I can make it on Saturday, I surely will. I'll call you by the Friday."

10

LATE OCTOBER: A FRIDAY

FERGUSON DID INDEED CALL on Friday. He would avail himself of her kind invitation, if she could give him directions from Walla Walla. Peter Blenheim also seemed delighted to respond to Phil's invitation. Zoe apologized for her one-room, loft-like home, but Blenheim seemed enchanted with it. "Reminds me of when I was young and just starting out." He was something of an enigma; no one Mona and Carly knew had ever been to his place, and he never turned up to functions with any sort of partner. There was some speculation that he was gay, but there was equal speculation that he had a long-standing relationship with a woman in Pullman, a destination to which it was said he disappeared regularly on weekends and holidays. Zoe had come to the realization, or perhaps a conclusion from her imagination, that he seemed to be constantly in a state of mild deference, perhaps in recognition of being "grandfathered in" from the college's finishing school days as permanent member of the faculty, a "senior lecturer", *a status similar to that of Herman Shaftley*, she thought, *with his certificate of continuing employment. Except Blenheim has the dignity coming from having made a difficult transition, not just the smugness of being handed a sop for ass-licking in the form of a bogus academic label that he can wrap around himself.*

Minimal introductions were made and Zoe noted Ferguson presented a more relaxed figure than she had remembered him being. He was clean-shaven, tan and fit, and sported a blue serge sports jacket over a polo shirt with his Levi's. She had cautioned him on the phone to, a she put it, "dampen your natural penchant for making an exotic impression and spinning intricately detailed stories of your derring-do" and let her and Phil do the talking.

Phil began with an apology: yes, he knew the accreditation proceedings and the whole situation were confidential, but he and Zoe had been together for going on four years, and they had been through some horrendous times together, including dodging the nasty intentions of a pair of thugs that Zoe had single-handedly disabled with some Kung Fu moves. So naturally, they shared experiences, perceptions, reflections, information. Ferguson nodded in affirmation.

Peter Blenheim was suitably impressed. He sat back in his chair. "Whew!" he exclaimed. "Taking out thugs with Kung Fu! That's incredible!"

"I'm not proud of having done so," said Zoe. "Kung Fu is an art of self-discipline, of self-improvement. It's never, never, supposed to be used to harm, even in self- defense. But if I hadn't used it, things would have turned out quite differently and maybe even some of us wouldn't be around to talk about it."

So Zoe was aware, said Phil, without his having shared the details with her, that there was every reason to believe that not only was Joseph Canter's PhD dissertation a work of plagiarism, but also that he had not even written it. And it was worth gathering some more evidence that might affirm that belief. Zoe, he said, had a vested interest in following up on that possibility.

Peter Blenheim nodded "I get it I get it. So now you think, these--well, can we call them the academic equivalent of hooligans?–are even bigger phonies than we caught them being. Not only was one of their credentials based on plagiarized material, but also it's a case of forged plagiarism! Amazing!"

"Basically, that's it," affirmed Phil.

Phil now brought in the possibility–no, the necessity–of having a professional investigator to confirm that the phonies were phonier even than they appeared to be. He then turned the floor over to Zoe. She went through a reiteration of what she had told the sinful Saturdayists nearly a week earlier about Ferguson. "Phil wanted to clear it with you before we went charging on ahead. And ready to get started, if you approve. Do you need to see some IDs from him?"

At this reference to his IDs, Ferguson smiled. He was remembering a point in their history with each other where Zoe had suggested the IDs were fake. But they were not. He withdrew a bulky set of papers enclosed in glassine envelopes from this inner jacket pocket: a UK passport, two private investigator licenses from the Town of Newcastle and the State of New York, an international driving license, a UK driving license, an identification card from Europol, and a picture ID from Assurance Associates.

"In your capacity as acting chair, you could hire him for a dollar," explained Phil. "And he won't submit a bill for any further charges unless he finds something meriting further investigation, to be authorized, only, of course, by the dean or the chancellor."

Peter Blenheim had been tucking into his stew, really a thick soup, with vigor. He wiped his mouth with his napkin, nodded, lay down his spoon. "I can see that tracking down this possibility, or eliminating it, is the next logical step. I need to clear it with Dean Fister, but this sounds to me like a good idea. You obviously have a side to you that is not so obvious, Dr. Dill." He turned to Ferguson. "Just how would this work?"

"Ah!" Ferguson wiped his mouth with his napkin. "As I was tellin' Zoe on the phone before I got here, I was not surprised to discover, upon availing myself of Assurance Associates' records, that your college has a number of assurance policies. One of them, more common following the revelation concerning the private online colleges that hae been bilking their customers and the U.S. Government's student loan program, provides for compensation for legitimate complaints against it alleging provision of educational services by unqualified personnel. It is na' advertised, o' course, and it will not apply to frivolous actions. But if there is a chance a complaint will go to court, then the policy provisions will kick in. The insurance company will pick up the attorneys' fees incurred in answering the complaint as well as a settlement to the complainant, within reasonable limits. The proviso, for the college, is that it has taken all possible steps to assure that such a situation does not obtain. Doing so means not only suspending the offending unqualified personnel, as soon as the lack of qualifications have become known, but also taking proactive measures to investigate any and all other possible infractions of academic integrity.

"Your college does indeed have such a policy. The investigation I will propose will accomplish the taking of proactive measures. In this case, taking proactive measures means removing teaching personnel who did not obtain the proper qualification and documenting how and why the personnel are not qualified, so that if a student, or more likely a student's parent, complains of paying tuition for services that canna' be provided, the insurance provision can kick in. Here that means not just wrangling over the close resemblance of one piece of writing to another, but rather, not at all doing what was needed to be done—writing a dissertation—in order to obtain that qualification. Once I have my contract, all I need do is show it to the authorities at Yale."

Peter Blenheim grinned and nodded. "Sounds good! I'll let you know with a phone call or a text when everything is in place. And let me say, I respect Dr. Dill's ability to inspire such confidence and loyalty in yourself, sir, that you would volunteer to undertake this investigation for minimal payment. As soon as I get word from the dean, I'll let Zoe know and we can finalize the contract. You're staying here in town?"

"Aye. Zoe has invited me to move over to her flat when Dr. Backstrom departs for Oregon tomorrow. But not so there be any misunderstandings, Ah'll be on me own. She'll be bunking with her mates in a house nearer the college."

⟋⟍

THE FOLLOWING DAY, SATURDAY

Now, at Carly's and Mona's house, following introductions, Ferguson was sharing the Saturday repast with them and Zoe, as well as with Carly's and Mona's significant others, James Gambel and Joel Curwin: a pearl farro salad with cranberries, cubed squash, and green onions, with an olive oil, lemon juice and chicken broth dressing, with cubed turkey ham addable for those who wanted it, and a large dish of whole dismembered chicken, broccoli, pearl barley, cremini mushrooms and onion baked in a bean sauce heavily laced with garlic cloves. (Zoe had helped herself to the bean sauce, maneuvering the serving to skirt the chicken). "*Now* you can tell your stories," Zoe told him.

In his best Hebridean argot, Ferguson regaled them with his and Zoe's, and ultimately also Phil's, exploits in pursuit of the principals in the matter of what he called the "masks and Mimbres caper", including a dramatic rendering of his and four others' hours-long imprisonment in a disused coal mine on the side of a mountain in New Mexico, until Zoe's heroic rescue of them.

As they were sipping a dry Spanish Jerez, following a dinner wine of robust Willamette Valley red, Ferguson reiterated what he had told Peter Blenheim the day before about getting into the Beinecke archives.

"Great!" responded Joel.

"And now to the other matter: do you want to share with us your strategy for investigating Dora Harris' mask?" suggested Zoe. "Remember, the idea here is not to hand over a good citizen's award to her if she should decide to return the mask."

"Aye" replied Ferguson. "So here is the first step: Zoe, Carly, and Phil will offer their consensus to me on whether or not it is likely the mask on Dr. Harris' wall matches any of the masks from the April, 2013 Paris auction. I've brought the catalogue." He rose, went to the living room where he had left a slim, fake-leather carrier and fetched a brochure from it. He laid the brochure on the dining table in front of Carly and Zoe. Phil came from the other side of the table and leaned over. Zoe opened the catalogue. She turned the pages slowly, then looked up. "Any stickies around?" Mona rose and returned a minute later with a pad of Post-its. "What do you think?" She half-turned to get Phil in her vision, who, along with Carly leaned in. "Yeah," he agreed. "That could be it." Carly nodded. Zoe plastered the photograph with a Post-it. They found, altogether, three possibilities, all very similar. One was Hopi; the other two were Acoma. Zoe handed the catalogue back to Ferguson.

"All right. So we've what you might call a prima facie case," said Ferguson. "The next step is to investigate bank records for the transfer of a large sum from Dora Harris to someone sometime after that auction took place. Now there are, o' course, several problems: problem number one is hackin' into bank records–which bank, to begin with. But as you must know, such hackin' is done all the time. We would presume a local bank would be used as the originator; we canna' surmise just what name Dahlia-Jane might ha'e been using. Ah canna' do the hackin' meself, but ah'm ashamed to say, I have contacts who can do so. Second problem is identifyin' the destination account with Ms. Jane. Problem number three is establishin' the circumventin' of U.S. Customs in the importation of said mask."

"Good," said Zoe. "Now Phil has another idea that you might investigate."

"Here's my idea," Phil began. "It's an accreditation thing and also an insurance thing. It might prevent things in the Social Science Department from continuing to just go along. I mean, even if Joe Canter is pressured to retire, Dora Harris could be elected chair. The two faculty members whose heads might be on the chopping block might vote no, but the other two and Madison Canter would vote yes. Three against two.

"But here's what I'm thinking. When I was going to school in Indiana–I was in grad school, I mean–I heard about a situation at another university down the road. Back in the '80s, it really went on the skids, almost declared bankruptcy. They had to lay off a bunch of people. So they laid off everybody who didn't have tenure. Well, the whole Theater Department, which was huge, had, like, a half-dozen untenured faculty members. They all got laid off. Only one faculty member had tenure. When they did that, they had to abolish their degrees in Theater: PhD, masters, undergraduate major–all gone. Because with only one qualified faculty member, they couldn't offer enough courses for the major. It was, like, ten years later by the time they finally were able to hire enough faculty to reinstate the major. Apparently it was a matter of critical mass. You needed a certain number of permanent faculty to have an accredited major in a particular field.

"So what I'm wondering is, if Madison Canter gets caught out as being the actual plagiarist who then passed off the plagiarized work as her husband Joe's, then wouldn't that be enough to get her suspended too? And if she was out, that would leave only two historians: Harris and Shaftley. Mr. Shaftley only teaches one or two history courses. And his qualifications are dubious at best. No MA. No PhD. In order to keep their social sciences major they would have to keep the two that they were going to axe, which it seems Dean Fister might mandate, but wouldn't they have to put the history major on hold? And if they didn't do so, wouldn't that, like, be a prima facie case for somebody bringing a legitimate complaint about not getting the education they were paying for? Like those private colleges that had unqualified teachers doing the online courses and got dinged for, essentially, fraud?"

"Aye, that could do it."

"Brilliant!" exclaimed Joel.

"Creepy." Mona shuddered. "I mean, here we all are, sitting around conspiring to get a fellow faculty member in trouble, get a major abolished."

"Too true," agreed James. "But it sounds like they've sort of done it to themselves. I mean, they got away with pulling the wool over everybody's eyes for years, feathering their own nests at others' expense."

Joel agreed. "What goes around, comes around."

"Pigeons come home to roost," added James.

"As ye sow, so shall ye reap," offered Ferguson.

"What's good for the goose is good for the gander," crowed Carly.

Zoe couldn't quite see the relevance of this last quip. She thought the many worn-out aphorisms, platitudes and clichés probably set a record for getting fit into a three-minute segment of conversation. But she said, "So, Ferguson, does this sound like something you can do? Check into whether or not offering majors and degrees with too few qualified faculty was one of the things that got those private colleges in trouble? And whether or not there's anything to this critical mass criterion for offering a major, from the same insurance angle about indemnity against a complaint?"

"Aye, that can be done. But I don't think I can do it on the same contract as the Yale investigation."

"But we four–Peter Blenheim, Carly, Mona, and I could once again hire you, on a separate contract, on the basis of having standing with regard to the general issue of the college's reputation," insisted Zoe. "And if it turns out to be an insurable event, or situation, if it arises at the college anywhere, it would affect all of us, the whole college, faculty and students, right?"

"Aye. But this will take a number of hours of research." Ferguson shook his head. "Ah dunna mind trying to track down Jane Faulks. That's the bee in my bonnet, my obsession, my pet peeve, but I'm not sure I can do *this* task on the same dollar, or even another one."

"Okay. So here's an idea," suggested Zoe. "I can spend a few hours on the net looking into what tanked those private colleges, if you, Ferguson, can only find out if, in general, offering a major with not enough faculty and presumably, then, not enough courses offered often enough would qualify for this special kind of insurance indemnity."

"Aye. That I can do. On the same dollar."

"Now here's one last thing. Joel here was poisoned."

"Poisoned?" Ferguson sat up and leaned forward.

"Aye!" Zoe's eyes twinkled; she smiled. She then launched into the tale, beginning with their finding Joel, they thought half-dead, at the reflection pond. Everybody chimed in on the telling, with Joel providing a synopsis of the rationale for the poisoning: the derailing of his damaging testimony.

"Hah!" Ferguson grimaced and gave a little laugh. "I can see why this matter intrigues you, Miss Zoe! Has she told you all about the matter of the spears and the poisoning of one of the Mimbres miscreants with curare? No? Well, that's a tale for another of your Saturdays. But I dunna see any way of tracking this down. I could do some breaking and entering of the two houses looking for a potted plant. But I wouldna want to do so. And finding some way to establish that one of them, from her, went to your university, there, Joel, during the time frame, would be almost impossible. If the person used a credit card, and one could access credit card receipts on the off chance that they stopped to refuel on the way up or down, maybe. But this would be a calculated move, and the person would ha'e paid cash. I think we need to let that one go, even though it's the most criminal act of all of them."

Zoe nodded. "You're probably right. But here's one more thing, probably unrelated, but a bunch of boxes showed up on our, I mean the college's, doorstep, just a few weeks before I arrived, last summer, with a bunch of stuff in them, including a decorated skull. We'd like to know who that skull belonged to."

Ferguson raised his eyebrows at that. "Are ye asking me to look into this as well?"

"Hey, you know, I was kind of looking forward to playing Miss Marple on that one," objected Carly. "Don't give that one to Ferguson, too! It can't have anything to do with the Canters."

"Yeah. You're probably right about that. Forget it, Ferguson."

LAST WEEK OF OCTOBER: THE FOLLOWING WEDNESDAY AFTERNOON

The meeting with Peter Blenheim took place on Tuesday, after classes. The contract was signed. Ferguson left town. He would get back to them as soon as he had news. Fat Tuesday had been postponed; they would get together, but on Thursday. Zoe stretched out on her bed, in chemise and panties, with a glass of wine and her iPad. She made a list:

November/December: Find colleagues, Guide; email; anyone know? re bankruptcy, Theater dept, no faculty, abolish major critical mass. If yes, have to get notarized statement: Ferguson. Then she erased "Ferguson" and wrote: make trip.

November-December: net search: private colleges scams: role of not enough qualified faculty: send to Ferguson.

December: Leger: What's really behind Pennfield's reluctance to show the authentication certificate? Answer at Mavis estate. Firm up visit.

December: Bay Area: skull. Cortez. 1956 UC Berkeley. Joel help? Mona? Where stay?

After Xmas: Meet Phil? Wine country?

~⌒

LAST WEEK OF OCTOBER: A FEW DAYS LATER

For a postponed "fat Tuesday", Zoe brought a roasted root veggie hash. She had chopped the vegetables, boiled them in the crockpot, drained the water, mashed the veggies into four pancakes and fried them, one after another, in oil and salt in the bottom of the crockpot. It had worked. She's taken each out with a plastic spatula, put it on a plate, repeated the process with then three more patties that she'd lowered into the crockpot with more salty oil. Then she'd thrown the others back in, and off she went to Mona's and Carly's. Mona had made curried-gingered whipped sweet potatoes, reinserted into their jackets. Carly had found elk bratwursts, frying them split. Found where? "Walla Walla. James brought them up last Saturday." She'd also fixed polenta mixed with egg and spinach, fried in the bratwurst fat. Wines were a choice of Z red blend or Friuli Pinot Grigio.

Carly stuck her fork into a bratwurst. Oily fat oozed from the burst skin. She cut a slice, popped it into her mouth, and chewed. "MMMM, yum!

This fatty fat is really fit for a postponed fat Tuesday! But where did I read somewhere that eating wild things that feed on wild things like forest forage is healthier than eating lazy things that are farm raised? Now tell us about this curare thing."

Zoe shrugged. "It's either an agonizingly long story or a short one."

"How about the short one?" suggested Carly. "We've got enough long going around here to keep us tangled up in stories for the rest of the academic year!"

"Well, okay, short version: Why did a guy who may have been dealing in fake Mimbres pots and double-crossing his partners in crime suddenly keel over dead? It was one of those little titbits of information gathered from an anthropology course. Curare is common in the Amazon. It works on the nervous system. Somebody likely jabbed him in the palm of the hand with an Amazonian spear coated with curare."

"And curare is a poison?" clarified Mona, digging her spoon into her curried sweet potato.

"It's a poison," confirmed Carly. "And it gave you the idea about henbane. But how did you get from curare to henbane?"

"I backed into it. I googled alkaloids and plants in a single search and I got a bunch of hits. Mandrake, deadly nightshade, belladonna, Datura, henbane, as well as ayahuasca and curare. But henbane seemed the most likely culprit because of the color of its leaves and its relative availability as a potted houseplant." She had a double portion of her veggie pancake on her plate; she cut a double slice and moved it into her mouth, chewed. "Now, change in subject: First, Ferguson might phone any minute. He was going to be getting into the Yale archives this afternoon. Second, I'm going to propose a possible field trip for our other project: finding out whose skull we've got and what its connection is to this Cortez person."

"The name on the UC Berkeley catalogue of classes, from the banana box," affirmed Mona.

"I mean," continued Zoe, "wouldn't it be neat to have an excuse to spend a couple weeks in Berkeley, San Francisco? I'd also like to track down the authenticity of the college's Léger painting. And the answer to that question is also arguably in the Bay Area, where the Léger's deceased donor dwelled. I've got a standing invitation to visit the donor's heir and have a look at another couple Légers she had. Mona? Carly? Either of you interested?"

"Not me." Carly shook her head. "This acting chair thing is really tying me up, or down, or whatever. Boring chairs' meeting last Friday. Faculty Senate meeting on Gen Ed requirements tomorrow. Regularly scheduled meetings, workshops, right through mid-December. Guess I'll have to forego playing Miss Marple."

"Pooh!" responded Zoe. "But Mona, you might come along?"

She shrugged. "Wouldn't you want Phil to come along?"

"Don't think he can; Multnomah has classes through December 14th. But I might have to figure out how to get my butt out to Indiana if it turns out there's anything to this lack of critical mass of qualified faculty for a major thing. I mean, if I turn that up as a reason for some of those private colleges getting their accreditation pulled, and it would apply to us, here–I mean to the history major. But hopefully I can pull enough off the internet."

"Right, right." Carly shoved a forkful of bratwurst and veggie hash pancake into her mouth. "But why are you so hung up on the Léger?"

"I went over to look at it. I wanted to see its authentication certificate. The gallery manager, Duncan Pennfield, was kind of evasive. He really didn't want to trouble himself to turn off the alarm system so he could take the thing off the wall and show me the certificate on its back. There may be nothing to it. But remember Dora Harris' Juan Gris? You told me *that* authentication certificate had something about brushstrokes. Well, when I was a grad-undergrad in Connecticut I lived with a guy who did that: authentication certificates. He was really secretive about it, though. I mean, he wanted me to be his 'partner' (Zoe made quotation marks in the air) in doing them, but he wouldn't tell me that that's what he did for a living. I found out just by accident. Anyway, he was so sneaky about the whole thing. He wanted me to make a commitment to him and give up the idea of doing a PhD. That got me suspicious. You know, little Zoe, the expert (quotation marks in the air again) on frauds and fakes gives panache and credibility to Nick Taylor's authentication of this or that painting because with a girlfriend like that anything he authenticates must be God's own truth, right? And he's got some signature wording for all of them: ambiguity and brushstrokes. He'll say something like 'in the style of … using pigments and canvas typical of the times … consistent with other works identified positively as …' And the key phrase always references brushstrokes. Supposedly he was going his dissertation on the examination of brushstrokes as an identifier of authenticity. Well, you told me Carly, that you remembered that the certificate for the Juan Gris mentioned brushstrokes. I'll bet anything the certificate is a Nick Taylor. *And* didn't you tell me that my predecessor, what's-his-name Laird (Yea, Brandon Laird, Carly confirmed) went all over the place finding art for the Vermeer donors–the Grassers? Well, maybe he found the Gris for Harris and the Léger for *its* donor, Mavis Samuelson."

"And just maybe he and Nick are–were–in partnership. Laird finds the art and Nick authenticates it," continued Zoe. "So I thought it would be worth tracking down this Mavis Samuelson to see what else she has and if it's got authentication certificates."

"She's dead," Carly pointed out.

"But her estate's still intact. And I've been in touch with her niece, who inherited the house and its contents. She invited me down to have a look at the stuff. Anyway, I thought it would be worthwhile to find out what else she had and where she got it, and whether or not her estate includes art with authentication certificates."

"And then what?"

Zoe shrugged. "I don't know."

Respect sounded. Zoe grabbed her phone. "Speaking of phone … here he is … yeah … yeah…. great! … Amazing! Well I don't see how she can wriggle out of it. What would be her explanation for why she accessed the file the second time?... yeah … yeah … the date sets the scene, for catching the mischief of the sneaky queen," she paraphrased. "Yeah, thanks. Thanks *a bunch!*"

She set her phone down, took a bite of polenta, a bite of curried potato.

"Spill!" insisted Carly impatiently.

Zoe nodded, swallowed. "Yes. She accessed the Jane Bennett material twice. Madison Freeburg once, and six years later, Madison Canter, several times in the same week. The entry indicates that copies were requested. Ferguson's getting a copy of each of the two entries. He'll print out his own statement about why and how he accessed the log book. He'll bring back the hard copies, but he'll scan them all and send them directly to Peter."

"Wow."

"Double wow," remarked Mona. "Will Phil get copies? Can Joel?"

"Don't know. But just knowing that things are on the move again should give Joel a big boost. Madison Canter's strung the bow too tight," paraphrased Zoe. "The worst committed offense of one bad little mouse, admitting of no modification, has encouraged the commission of many more."

PART TWO

11

MID-NOVEMBER: THE LAST SINFUL SATURDAY OF THE AUTUMN TERM

"SO YOU KNOW I'VE GOT an invitation to go down to Oakland on the Thursday after Thanksgiving. Phil can't come and I know you can't Carly, but Mona—you could, couldn't you? And maybe we can stay with Amy long enough to make some headway on the skull-and-Cortez mystery."

~⌒~

LATE NOVEMBER: A WEEK AFTER THANKSGIVING

Zoe and Mona drove to Multnomah and stayed with Phil; Mona brought along a sleeping bag and camped on the floor. They came south on I-5 to I-80, entering Oakland on the 580, from the 680, through a thin haze that smelled of acrid smoke. Trestle Glen, the neighborhood of modest but spacious homes tucked away on canopied streets, reminded Zoe of some parts of Seattle, but without the dreary drip that made so many similar neighborhoods there gloomy and uninviting. Amy, a cheery, bosomy woman a couple years younger than Zoe, with a helmet of short brown hair, met them at the door. "Welcome to Trestle Glen! Sorry it's so smoky–all those fires–like, hundreds of them, all over the state."

It was clear to Zoe this was a person she and Mona could do serious bonding with. After introductions, Amy said, "and it's actually A-i-m-e-e, kind of an unusual spelling, not that it's important," and suggested they go in together on meals when it was convenient, in terms of planning and preparing and buying the food, "and you can stay here as long as you like. You said you're doing some work on a collection of stuff you have from somebody here in the Bay Area? My boyfriend, Kenny, will be over on the weekend, but otherwise it'll be just us."

"Your cousin doesn't live here?"

Aimee shook her head. "Used to, but–thank God–he's up in Sonoma getting a degree in anthropology. You haven't eaten, have you?" Zoe and Mona had been on the road for twelve hours and although they had bypassed the major cities, they had finally had to fight crunch hour coming through Martinez. Now it was nearly 7:30 p.m. and they had eaten only several rounds of egg salad, turkey ham, and tuna sandwiches with bar-b-que potato chips. Zoe thought she might rather topple into bed and forego sustenance, or if they could get away with being bad guests, fall into dreamland right after eating.

"Are you vegan?"

"Vegetarian," responded Zoe.

"But I'm not," Mona hastened to clarify.

"Lucky thing," said Aimee, shrugging her shoulders. "I made a mushroom and barley soup, sautéed chicken breasts with cherry tomatoes and shallots in a vinegar and basil sauce and acorn squash halves baked with pear-ginger puree. Interested?"

"Sure!" enthused Zoe.

"It won't take me a sec to heat it up. You must be zonked. You can fall into bed right after we eat. Beds are all made up. Make yourselves at home!"

Zoe reflected in a sleepy way as they waited for the meal to be heated up. Oakland was not far from where she had experienced her first love, been treated to her first trip abroad, been honored with a portion of a housing estate being named after her, and experienced her first lesson in the lengths to which some people would go to seize what they thought was rightfully theirs, yet wasn't. But all that was in the past. It could not, and should not be revisited.

LATE NOVEMBER: THE FOLLOWING DAY, THE FRIDAY AFTER THANKSGIVING, A WEEK

Zoe and Mona, tired from the long drive, rolled out of bed in late morning. "Let's have a sort of brunch," suggested Aimee, "then go over to the Grand Lake Lucky's and stock up. I don't have to go anywhere today. I'll give you a little grand tour, then we'll shop."

Brunch was frothy eggs whipped with butter and capers plopped onto an odd kind of waffle: crisply fried turkey bacon slid between slices of a hearty whole wheat bread that were slathered with butter on their tops, then pressed in a waffle iron for Aimee and Mona. "Poor Aimee's version of croque monsieur."

First thing they did was drape a visitor badge over the rearview mirror of Zoe's Civic parked on the street, next entering the detached garage, which Zoe thought looked newer than the house. Zoe was surprised to find that Aimee drove a brand new 2017 Mercedes SUV. Aimee chattered away as she took them on a tour: around Lake Merritt, downtown, which was calm now that the morning commute had been accomplished, where they parked and strolled around Jack London Square, then back to Lake Merritt. "I work at data processing company over in Emeryville. It's really boring–inventories for a contractor for eBay; but the nice thing is, I can work when I want to. Technically, I could do it from here, but the contractor is paranoid about hacking so we have to do everything on secure computers." Now she drove up a steep hill and turned onto an even steeper alley. She stopped the car in the middle of the street. "You really get a great view from up here: the whole lake, the park, the neighborhoods around it, and the other hill opposite." She turned her head toward the stately old mansion that was on its own hill. "My grandmother lived there." She pointed. "Nice room, teeny tiny kitchen, bathroom down the hall, tons of stairs. She loved it. The view was great and even on mornings when the whole city was blanketed in fog, her house was above it; the sun would be shining brightly and the tiny kitchen would be flooded with light. She loved to sit there."

"You lived here?" asked Mona.

"No. We lived in a posh residential suburb called San Anselmo in Marin County. You probably came through it, or close to it, on the interstate. But my parents liked to come to San Francisco for shows, symphony concerts, movies. They'd drive over the bridge, park me here, then Mom would pick me up the next day or a couple days later. We lived in a dump here in Oakland for a few years but then they got the San Anselmo house; they were going to remodel the garage for Gramms, but she wouldn't hear of it. She liked her eyrie, way up here. And it was hard for her because it had a tons of steps, inside and out, and she had a bad hip, walked with a crutch. I think maybe that's part of the reason I volunteered for Mavis. She reminded me of my Gramms, my Mom's mom."

At Lucky's, they loaded up on organic: vegetables, fruits, greens, bulk grains and beans, and a big humanely raised pork loin that would last Mona and Aimee, that, Aimee declared, even with inroads from Kenny, for the better part of a week. And the usual coffee, fresh orange juice, eggs, shredded wheat, milk, butter, raisin bread, the whole wheat bread they'd had for breakfast, more turkey bacon and packages of sliced turkey ham, canola mayonnaise, and Maille mustard. Zoe plopped two tubs of hard tofu and two bags of salted, roasted Virginia peanuts into the cart.

After unloading the groceries, it was lunchtime. "How do you feel about wine in the middle of the day?" asked Aimee. "When I'm not working, I figure, what the hey. Or we could have just water, or tea, mint tea. I usually have that at night, after dinner with a shot or two of brandy."

"Hey! It's a luxury, drinking wine in the middle of the day!" said Zoe. Mona nodded.

"Chablis?"

"Sure!"

"Do you mind eating here in the kitchen again? Afterwards I'll give you a tour of the house and the collection and you can tell me what you think."

Aimee led them through the old-fashioned swinging kitchen door into the dining room. "These old houses are kind of peculiar. There's a lot of wasted space. I mean, I really don't know what to do with the pantry and the kitchen is huge. There's two living rooms!"

"Living room and parlor," suggested Mona.

"Right. Okay, so here's exhibit one: eighteenth century French table and chairs. But your curator, Pennfield, said it's a replica."

Zoe and Mona both did double-takes. "Pennfield's the gallery manager, not a curator. But you say he was *here*?" Mona said incredulously.

"Yeahhhh." Aimee drawled. "Couple times. He and my cousin Randy were–maybe still are--an item. They met at your college and, well, it seems like they've been in each other's pants ever since. I'm surprised you haven't run across Randy up there. He was going up there regularly all summer, 'til he moved to Sonoma."

"We really don't have much to do with the Art and Performance School," replied Mona. "I mean, we have nothing against them, they're just in a different place and in a different circle."

Aimee opened pocket doors and led them into the parlor. "Most of the art is in here." She pointed out more than two dozen bronzes on several credenzas and buffets against a wall. It was really over the top. Zoe thought she spotted sculptures by Miro, Remington, Chiparus. On the wall opposite were two obvious Légers, but lithographs, not oils. Zoe walked over and examined them. One depicted a man in a beret, with mustache and striped sailor shirt, with brawny arms, carrying a bicycle on his shoulders against a thick black vertical stripe on his right; the man and the bicycle bled through a vertical red stripe with a protruding plug and three short yellow stripes. The other was a pastiche of a red gear cog, a yellow guitar-shaped image, a vine, three playing cards—a five of diamonds, a king of hearts, and a five of spades that seemed to be assaulted by three bowling balls colored taupe, sienna and green, crisscrossed with a gray vine, a green bare-twigged bush and a couple of insects resembling snails, all against a background of gray and blue blobby shapes, contained by a wobbly taupe frame. A white hand, index finger raised, pointed upward on the painting's extreme left.

Zoe walked a few steps over to where the Braque hung. It was a typical Braque: all squares and lines and blocky shapes. "Do you mind if I look at the back?"

Aimee shrugged. "Not at all."

Zoe turned the painting around. Yes, there it was: an authentication by N. Z. Taylor, with all the ambiguous language and the reference to brushstrokes that marked his signature verifications. "… Placement of forms, use of colors known to have been used by cubists such as Gris, Braque, Picasso, Léger … consistent with paintings known to have been painted by Georges Braque between 1909 and 1920 and with Braque's style and habits … execution of brushstrokes indicating use of a brush or brushes and pigments available at the time …" Zoe sighed. "I lived with this guy for a few years. Nick Taylor. He's made a career out of doing ambiguous verifications like these, always referencing brushstrokes. I think his analysis of the use of brushstrokes by painters is nothing short of brilliant, but he's really misused his talent. I'll bet anything the Léger hanging in the Charbonneau gallery that your aunt donated has an authentication from Nick Taylor."

"And that means it's not genuine?" asked Aimee.

"No, not necessarily. It just means that it *might* not be. Works by Braque, Léger, Corot, Rembrandt, and of course now Vermeer are among the most misidentified, to put it gently–read forgeries--in comparison to the works of theirs that are absolutely definitely provenanced to them."

"So what about all this other stuff? There's a few bronzes in the living room too, and large rugs."

"Did this all come out of the same estate sale?" asked Mona. "The kilims, the dining room table, the paintings and these Léger lithographs, and the statuary?"

"Yeah. That's right. Randy convinced Mavis to get rid of a lot of the fusty furniture and vomit-green rugs and poster art that she and Uncle Arthur filled the house with when they moved up here in 2004. Their house outside of San Diego was like a villa. It even had a little vineyard! But it all got burned to a crisp in the Cedar Fire of 2003. It hit Uncle Arthur hard. He didn't last long after they moved up here–maybe three, four years. About three years ago Nancy, the aunt that was living with me in San Anselmo, said she'd gotten a call from Aunt Mavis asking me if I'd be interested in being Mavis' full-time caregiver. This was after Arthur'd passed away. She'd had a minor upset--fallen and sprained her wrist. She didn't really need full-time caregiving, though; just cooking and some cleaning. She had, still does, I mean I do, still have a cleaning service once a week. But, you know, wiping dribbles off the toilet seat, loading the dishwasher, doing the laundry. I did all of that. It was perfect timing. I'd just gotten my part-time eBay job. Corliss and I, that's my ex, had just split up. Then–echhh–a year after I moved in, along came Randy."

"He lived here?"

"Moved right in. And do you think he lifted a finger to give any sort of help to Mavis? Not on your life! And she was so giving, so *forg*iving. I mean even his own mother didn't–doesn't trust him."

"Why not?"

"He's slimy. I mean, he's very charming. Entertaining, even. But he made his living running drugs from central America through the Caribbean. Florida finally caught up with him and he did time for it, but not the time that he should have done. Maybe I'm just prejudiced. People seem to like him. Your friend Pennfield sure does."

"He's not really our friend," clarified Mona. "I mean, he's not a not-friend, we just don't know him all that well."

"Well, anyway, Randy persuaded Aunt Mavis to buy the whole estate from this sale, lock, stock, and barrel, or a large chunk of it anyway, and that's how we got all this stuff. What do you think all this should have cost if it was real? I mean, genuine, authentic? Pennfield was the one that actually blew the whistle on Randy. I guess he didn't know he was doing it, but he's the one that fingered the dining room set as a replica and the bronzes as–what did he call them? Recasts. Apparently what happens is the heirs of the artists sell the molds, and then these replicas are churned out by the dozens."

Zoe nodded. "Hundreds, more like. Usually in India. Sometimes in Mexico. They get sold to dealers for a few bucks each. Did Pennfield have much to say about the Braque?"

"No. And it kind of surprised me. But you should have seen the look on Randy's face when he said 'recasts' and how easy they were to produce–same with those two Léger lithographs."

"Doesn't surprise me," stated Mona. "I've heard that Pennfield absolutely disdains all the modernists–fauvists, cubists, abstractionists. Loves the impressionists. Goes off on tangents and tantrums when you get him started on the downfall of art in the twentieth century. So he could care a fig if the Braque was real or forged. All the same dreck to him."

Zoe strode over and looked at the Légers. "Yea. They're okay, but they're not as crisp and sharp as they could be. I mean, they're probably the second or third hundredth printing. Still worth having, still good art."

Aimee now opened the set of pocket doors and led them into the living room. "Here's the rest of it–this large rug and a few more bronzes."

"What about the furniture?"

"Yeah, she got the stuff in the parlor through Randy too, but it didn't come from the estate sale. It came from an antiques store in Petaluma. He charged her for that, too. Well, okay, to be fair, she *insisted* on paying him a finder's fee. Fifteen percent. So there's another five or ten thou. But she had this sofa set specially made. The red and orange plaid supposedly accents the bronzes! The only holdover from the 'pre-Randy' days is Uncle Arthur's recliner in the other room. So how much do you think all this would have, should have gone for?"

"Whew!" responded Zoe. "Hard to say. I mean, if the Braque and the Léger oil that the college has were peddled as unconditionally genuine, it could have been eighty, ninety thousand just for those. But that doesn't go with the estate sale format. Estate sales are held to move stuff quickly, stuff that otherwise would be a tedious pain to unload. And my former buddy's authentications are geared to satisfying some dealer's presentation to customers or to calm the qualms of a collector who wants to be able to say with confidence at his cocktail parties, 'Yeah, it's a Braque all right.' So let's say we cut that in half, then add maybe another three, four thousand for the kilims, the lithographs, the sculptures, the dining room set—say, forty, fifty thou?"

"He charged her ninety-five. Ninety-five thousand dollars!" Aimee plopped herself down in the middle of the sofa. "The day after Pennfield's visit, Randy went off to some more of his estate sales, or to somewhere. Meanwhile, I googled Léger, Miro, Remington, Chiparus and found out about recasts and lithographs. I sat Mavis down for a long talk. I could see that she was displeased. I finally pulled it out of her that he'd demanded ninety-five thousand dollars. And he never, ever hinted at the possibility that the bronzes were recasts and that lithographs can be reproduced by the dozens. She thought she had some really valuable items and had gotten a bargain. I think it was the dining room set that really got to her. But you know, it wasn't just the money. It was Randy's cavalier nonchalance, the assumption that of course she would, and should automatically trust him. At first, she was really unhappy with his mother, my Aunt Nancy basically writing him off, insisting that he was still a no-good little sneak just like he'd been when he was doing all that druggie stuff in Florida. He'd probably been doing druggie stuff for a long time. He lived in Haight-Ashbury while he went to college, San Francisco State. Mavis told me that according to Nancy that's where he started dealing. Then he branched out, got a contact who had contacts in Europe. He even got Nancy and her new man—new then—over there with him as a kind of cover while he set up the contact. Nancy was really steamed over that. Says he was doing nothing but using them—happy little family takes a trip to Europe. Who would suspect? Mavis insisted Randy'd reformed. But that turns out not to exactly be the case. Now it turns out Nancy was right. He was still doing illegal stuff, or at least had maybe, like, switched from illegal to illicit. Scamming instead of dealing.

"Mavis didn't tell me what she was going to do, but that evening, at supper, she announced that Mr. Cronin, her lawyer, was coming up from San Diego the following week; she'd called him earlier in the day. Clearly, she wanted Randy to know that she was not happy and he should at least own up to what he'd done. But he didn't."

"And what was it that Mr. Cronin was coming up for?" asked Mona.

Aimee sighed. "She didn't say anything more, but there could be only one reason that he was coming up here: so she could change her will. And Randy must have known that the change wouldn't be favorable to him."

"But you have no idea what that change was?" asked Zoe.

"Well, yah, I can guess. I mean, she had her accident before she could change it, so it would have been something other than what it was, or is. My guess is that she was going to cut him out of the dividend. As it is, I got the house and everything in it. And we each–me and Randy–get a quarterly stipend from her investments. I mean, it's like a guaranteed income. It goes up and down because it's, like, a dividend kind of thing, but it's always there. So Randy has it made in the shade. Well, I guess I do too."

"Otherwise, if she *had* been able to change her will, would she have given it all to you?"

Aimee shrugged. "Maybe, or maybe give it to a charity? Maybe to your college! So now I've got all this stuff and two houses. What am I gonna do with two houses?"

"Two? What's the other one?" asked Mona.

Oh–the San Anselmo house. My folks were killed in a traffic accident when I was eleven, coming back from a concert in San Francisco. It was a double whammy. My Grammy Edith died a year earlier. Heart attack. It was really sudden. And I really, really missed her. So Aunt Nancy became my guardian. She'd recently divorced from her husband,"

"Randy's father?"

"No, no, second husband. Randy's father was killed in the war. Aunt Nancy moved into the San Anselmo house and took care of me. It wasn't like having parents or my Gramps but it was better than nothing, I guess."

"So you and Randy grew up together?"

"No again! He's almost twenty years older than me. His father was killed in Vietnam, actually before he was born. He was long gone by the time Nancy moved in."

"And you say he was doing drug smuggling in Florida?" said Mona.

"Yeah, presumably, although his cover was antique dealing."

"Really!" exclaimed Zoe. She sat down on the sofa next to Aimee; Mona sat on Aimee's other side. "I worked in an antiques store for three years. So Nancy rents the house from you?"

"Yes, I guess, sort of. It had to go through probate. My folks had life insurance, of course, so the mortgage got paid off. It seems there were always hearings and meetings with lawyers and all of that–none of it involved me, though. It's my parents' estate that owns the house, and the estate sends me a little check every few months. I guess it's the rent that Nancy pays. She's got a new guy now—well, he's not very new, she's had him, for, like, the last ten years--and they're living in the San Anselmo house together."

"So Nancy is almost kind of like a mother to you? And this—what you called her new guy—kind of a father substitute?" Zoe knew she was probing but she was wondering how Aimee had managed what she called her "double whammy".

"Oh, no! No, no, no, no, no! I rebelled against Nancy. I acted out. I was a real pain in the ass. A maniac. Manic. Depressive. Got into drugs–weed, E. I was a mess. And I only met her new guy, Frank, a couple times. Don't remember him very well. He's kind of a bluff." Her gaze was riveted to a point on the floor. "I was cutting school. I was cutting myself. I think Nancy was tearing her hair out. Then I started doing guys. I already had these." She pushed her hands under her breast so they jiggled fetchingly. "Smaller versions, of course, but I'd also already gotten my period. I did one guy, then another guy, then another guy, then another...."

"Not all at the same time?!" said an astonished Mona.

"Oho! Oh, Yeah. I did that too. Nancy'd gotten a job waitressing at a restaurant-bar right outside San Anselmo, so she'd be going out the door as I was coming in after school and that was fine with me. It was insane. I was, like, fifteen years old. I got a couple guys over that lived in the neighborhood. So, yeah. We'd take some E, or something else, I don't know what, then we'd get naked and I'd get them on the floor, like, their feet around each other's necks, and I'd do them both at the same time–yeah! On the floor. At first they just, you know, squirted. But then I got them so they'd hold it, or at least one of them would. Yeah, we did that over and over again, like every day, for a month. I couldn't get enough. I enjoyed it, I think. But then once, well–the last time, I barely remember it now, but I know I passed out on them and had to be hauled off to hospital. They'd given me too much of whatever it was. Then I remember something happening to me that really hurt; I think they did a D & C on me. Basically an abortion.

"That's what really did it. Nancy and the estate attorneys got me into a special residential school for wayward girls in San Rafael. I think Nancy freaked, basically read the attorneys the riot act. Like, get this asshole beast of a girl outta' here. But the school? Best thing that ever happened to me. They strong-armed me out of the drugs. Well, not exactly. I don't remember half from that period of my life. But I do remember cutting myself and they had to subdue me and restrain me and then they got me into other drugs."

"Oxycotin?" suggested Zoe.

Aimee shrugged. Maybe. Probably. I remember asking what the drugs were but they kept changing them. I only remember a couple now–the ones with funny names, like Diazepam, Stesolid--like 'stay solid?'–Ketagan, like 'get a can?'. Then they got me off of those and got me interested in computers and they made me see how you can get addicted to something good that kept me off the street, like programming. I made some friends there, too. I was one of twelve. You really get to know people when you interact with the same ones on a daily basis. I guess my parent's insurance money paid for it. I know Nancy wouldn't have.

"I think I was–or am–probably a little autistic. Not autistic, exactly, but that other thing–Asperger's? But I came out of that school with a couple good friends and a reason for not messing up my life and everybody else's. They gave me a mantra I could use to monitor my own behavior and my attitude. And you know what? At one point somebody brought me a book. Maybe it was Nancy. She'd come every now and then. It was a book about the ancient Sumerians; full of pictures. They had queens–queens who wore gold helmets and headdresses with, like, gold flowers and leaves! I would imagine myself one of those queens!" She giggled, crossed her arms over her chest, shook her head. "Can you imagine? But I really was cared for there, and cared *about*. I think achieving that realization and the responsibility that went with it was a large part of why I jumped at helping out Mavis. I wanted to give back."

"So did you ever get back into regular school? You must have done," said Mona.

"Oh, yeah. I was only in Colville for nine months. Next fall I was back in middle school. I went into my own little world, a Sumerian queen, with my mantra and my computer puzzles. I was a computer geek, a real nerd, and I kept it up through high school. Got Cs in almost everything except computer classes. I got As in them. I also got a bit of a pudge in my tummy, not to mention a big ass; I think it was a defense mechanism against attention from boys that might have gotten back into excessive humping again. But I made my peace with Nancy. We kind of went our separate ways; I played video games in the evenings for hours on end. Experimented with cooking good but light. Got my diploma. Eventually I got the data entry job." She shook her head. "Why am I telling you guys all this? I hardly know you! And why do you want to hear all this about me? You must be bursting with good auras!"

"Whew! You *have* been around the block!" remarked Mona. "But you've got something to really be proud of in terms of getting your shit together."

"For sure!" agreed Zoe.

"Well, hey!" said Aimee. "You didn't come here for an earful of my life story. Getting back to Mavis ..."

"Okay, getting back to Mavis," agreed Zoe. "Mavis fell down the stairs before she got a chance to change her will," recapitulated Zoe. "Was there any suggestion of foul play? Like, she might have been helped." Zoe made quotation marks in the air, "down the stairs?"

Aimee nodded. "That was my first thought: helped along by Randy. But afterwards Randy insisted he'd driven all the way to Sonoma that evening. That whole period is a blur. Anyway," Now a sob came into Aimee's voice. "I made an early dinner for Mavis–soup—and ... and ..." She tried to take a deep breath but she was starting to cry. "If I'd been here ...." Now she was racked by huge sobs. Zoe and Mona, both at the same time, put their arms around her, Zoe around her shoulder and Mona around her waist. Aimee buried her head in Zoe's shoulder for a minute, then rose, went to the end table next to the sofa, took several tissues, wiped her eyes, blew her nose.

She sat back down between them. "Kenny and I went to a matinee at the Grand Lake, then to a gathering, a kind of political meeting, then to a late dinner, then to his place. We were going to go to a Beyonce and Jay-Z concert over in Santa Clara the next day. I stayed the night with him. I did that a lot. So we went to the concert, then fooled around some more because it was Sunday and he dropped me off here around four." Aimee sniffled and dabbed at her eyes again. "It was ... it was awful ... I came in and there was Mavis, all tangled up in her rollator, at the bottom of the stairs. Then the next few days were just, like I said, a blur. At some point Randy came back. The police came. They questioned us. Turned out he'd had dinner with her. He'd brought Chinese take-out for her. Then–this was his story–he'd gotten in his car and driven to Sonoma. It was weeks before I had the energy to track down his story. He supposedly stayed in a B&B outside of town. I called every B&B in the Sonoma area and finally found the one he stayed at. And yes, he really had arrived the day of Mavis' death, around nine o'clock. The owners remembered him; even looked in their guest book. There he was: Randall Allen. Spent Sunday going around to the wineries. Then I guess he had his appointment at Sonoma State on Monday. Nobody seemed to be able to get a hold of him, or didn't think to try, until Monday night. Actually, I guess they got a hold of Nancy first, and then she called him. Anyway, his story checked out."

"So, like, he couldn't have hung around, or even driven back that night, after checking into the B&B? hauled Mavis out of bed, chucked her down the stairs?"

"No, no. The B&B is a kind of ranch. It's gated. Guests have to be in by ten thirty. Then the alarm is set, automatically and doesn't go off until six thirty the next morning. You can't get in or out in between those hours without setting off the alarm. The coroner determined that Mavis had died no later than four in the morning and no earlier than about midnight–rigor mortis and all that. And the owners of the B&B actually sat up with Randy and a couple of the other guests, drinking complimentary sherry and giving them a rundown of their favorite wineries. They all didn't go to bed until after eleven. So, no. Iron-clad alibi."

"That must have been awful for you, finding her like that," sympathized Mona.

"Yeah. I was a basket case for weeks. I got really run down, got the flu, had to take days and days off from work. I couldn't work. I couldn't see straight. I had trouble driving. I couldn't even *walk* straight. I finally got over to Kaiser to see a doctor, they gave me antibiotics, and it finally cleared up, but it was weeks.

177

"Hey, it's way past lunch time. Let's make us some nice sandwiches. I'll put that roast in the oven. Then, sorry to say it, but I think I'll be ready for a nap. Just revisiting all that has wrung me out."

⟋⟍

SATURDAY MORNING

Friday's meal had been roasted pork loin. Zoe ate the apples that had been roasted with the pork and they all had green bean amandine with Dijon mustard and a baked dish of wild rice, portabella mushrooms and leeks with a cream cheese and parmesan crust. A Lodi Merlot had complemented the meal. "It's nice to have somebody to cook for again," Aimee had said with a small bite of pork loin in her mouth. "I mean, sometimes I cook for Kenny, but mostly we eat out, or he brings pizza. How about some dry sherry? Or my favorite: mint tea with brandy?" They were sitting in the living room, Zoe and Mona on the sofa, and Zoe on the matching short couch.

"Mint tea!" Mona had exclaimed. with an exaggerated eye roll. "Not mint tea!!"

Zoe chuckled. Aimee looked perplexed. "What is it about mint tea?"

"It's too complicated to explain," Mona said, laughing.

They had sipped their mint tea, chatted about this and that, mainly more about Aimee's family and her young life in Marin County, then gone upstairs to bed. But as she was falling asleep, Zoe reviewed the various conversations of the day. Then it dawned. A realization. An impossibility. No, a *possibility*.

⟋⟍

SUNDAY

After a simple breakfast of shredded wheat and milk, Zoe broached the subject. They were still sitting around the round kitchen table. "Yesterday you said right after Mavis' accident you caught the flu. What were your symptoms?"

"I was dizzy, every time I stood up or took a step or two; my vision was really blurry. Things kept bouncing around. I was nauseous and I had horrendous headaches."

"And you went to Kaiser and they diagnosed flu."

"Yeah. They gave me antibiotics and blood pressure medicine. My blood pressure was through the roof. I'm off the blood pressure meds now."

"Did you vomit?"

"No. I got the runs, probably from the antibiotics, but I never threw up."

"And I'll bet you were drinking mint tea throughout. Probably even upped your intake."

"Yeah. They told me to drink fluids. Fluids, fluids, fluids. So yeah, I was drinking five, six, eight cups a day."

"And this was the same mint tea that Mavis had the night she tumbled down the stairs."

"Well, yeah ..."

Zoe bent over, head in hands. "I can't believe this! It's impossible!"

"Joel!" exclaimed Mona.

"Joel?" Aimee was perplexed.

Zoe raised her head, sat up straight. "We were wrong! We were so wrong!"

"*About what*?" Aimee was obviously becoming quite exercised.

Zoe heaved a huge sigh. "Okay. Remember when we rolled our eyes at your offer of mint tea, yesterday evening, and said the thing with mint tea was really complicated? Well, it just got even more complicated."

"Or simpler," corrected Mona. They went through the whole story about Joel's poisoning through his mint tea being laced with henbane, including whom they suspected of doing the lacing and why. "It's quite a story, isn't it?" concluded Mona.

"Yeah! Wow! What a story!" agreed Aimee.

"But now, it seems like we were all wrong. I mean we might have been going along on the basis of a false premise," said Zoe. "Let's go over the events for Mavis on the fatal day. Randy came over that afternoon, right?"

"Right. The coroner quizzed both of us, separately, but it all checked out. He said he brought Chinese for both of them. She never ate the soup I'd prepared. There were Chinese takeaway cartons in the trash."

"And he would have made her one, two, three cups of mint tea."

"Well, yeah, I guess so," reflected Aimee.

"Then, he left for Sonoma. Ironclad alibi. When did Mavis tumble down the stairs?"

"Well, probably a little after midnight. She always got up some time between midnight and one to go to the bathroom."

"And you usually helped her to the bathroom?"

Aimee shook her head. "No. When I first moved in, I did, or tried to. I'd hear her get up, throw on my robe, come rushing out, ready to help, but she was always there with her rollator and she would always say, 'I'm fine Aimee. Thank you, but I don't need your help.' So after a couple weeks, I'd still wake up and listen for her, like if she fell or something, but she had that rollator and she seemed to be doing it okay on her own, so pretty soon I wasn't even waking up any more. I slept through it."

Zoe stared into the middle distance, furrowed her brow, then nodded. "Henbane poisoning. Henbane leaves in with the mint tea"

"Henbane poisoning? You mean the same thing that was mixed in with the tea this ... this ... your friend ..."

"Joel," supplied Mona. "He had the same symptoms as you. Dizziness, blurred vision, nausea, and he ended up collapsing into a pond."

"Yes. Exactly," confirmed Zoe. "Same symptoms you had. And I'll bet, the same symptoms your Aunt Mavis had, which ended up tumbling *her* down the stairs. So even if you had been here, you couldn't have done anything. She's wobbly, she's dizzy, her vision is blurred, she's confused, she tumbles down the stairs. And if it was *you* drinking the contaminated tea as well, if *you* had gotten up and helped her that night, chances are *you* would have tumbled down the stairs, too. And afterwards, you *did* drink the tea and you *did* get the same symptoms: dizzy, wobbly, headaches, trouble locomoting." Zoe nodded. "Yep. Henbane poisoning."

"Whew!" exclaimed Aimee.

"So we've got three related events here. Mavis drinks henbane mint tea and tumbles down stairs. You drink henbane mint tea and get headaches, blurred vision, and the wobblies for weeks following, probably until that batch of tea is gone."

"Yeah!"

"Then, months later, Joel Curwin gets the same symptoms. And we know that *was* from henbane-contaminated tea because we had it tested." Zoe turned to Aimee. "Where do you get your tea from?"

"Teas on Telegraph. Over in Berkeley."

"Mona, is it possible that Joel gets his teas from there as well? I mean, he surely could have gotten them there whenever he visited his mom. And maybe they still ship him a canister, like, on order?"

"Yeah, yeah, very possible." Mona rose and headed for the stairs. "I'll call him and ask." Joel wasn't answering his phone, but she left a message.

"And the tea that Joel was drinking came from his stash at the office?"

"Well, I don't know. But it's possible–probable. Because during the summer he would have been drinking a fresh batch from his house. But the office batch- -he might have gotten it in, say, April or May, stashed it in his office, not gotten into it again until September or October. Yeah, yeah. Very possible," agreed Mona.

"So we may be looking at a batch of contaminated tea from the tea place, perpetrated by who knows who, and our nefarious academics had nothing to do with it," she said to Mona. Addressing Aimee, she asked, "Had you just gotten a new batch of tea in right before Mavis had her accident?"

Aimee shook her head. "Like I said, that whole period is a blur. I don't remember. It's possible. But who would have spiked a whole batch of Teas on Telegraph's mint tea? And wouldn't we have heard? I mean, wouldn't a whole bunch of people have gotten poisoned?"

"I don't know the who of it," replied Zoe. "Or even the why of it. But I know sick people do all kinds of sick things. Anthrax in envelopes, bombs in packages. And maybe everybody who drank the tea thought the same thing you did: 'Oh, I must have the flu.' If anybody did figure it out, they would have probably just thrown the tea out, without it ever occurring to them that it was laced with something like henbane. If they did figure it out, that it was the tea that was making them sick, they probably would have just made a complaint to the tea shop and the tea shop would have thrown out that batch, if they still had any of it left. Is this worth a trip over to Teas on …"

"Telegraph," responded Aimee. "Sure, why not. If nothing else we can stroll around the shops, Sather Gate, the campus, Strawberry Canyon."

Parking was dicey with students zooming in and out of spots, but they found a place and were tempted to stroll in and out of shops: a couple vintage clothing shops, a Japanese dollar store, and a designer sneaker shop, before ending up at Teas on Telegraph. The wiry, fortyish-trying-to-look-thirty man at the cash register seemed truly appalled at the suggestion that his teas might have been contaminated. With many gestures of hand and face, he effused copious apologies on hearing of Aimee's health troubles. "If I thought our products were in any, *any* way responsible, I assure you, we would more than make it up to you. Here, here." He opened a drawer behind the counter, rummaged, drew out a gift card, scribbled $50 in the box, then signed it, and handed it to Aimee. "But nobody, none of our customers have said anything, *anything* about any sort of illness from any of our products." He shook his head back and forth, back and forth. "I'm certain, I'm absolutely *certain*, a customer would have told us, we would have heard about it, if any of our products were making people sick."

They thanked him and exited. "Well, that tells us that nobody complained. But it doesn't tell us that it wasn't Teas on Telegraph's batch of tea that did it to you and Mavis and Joel," insisted Zoe.

"Hey–can we get something to eat?" suggested Aimee. "I'm starved! Shredded wheat doesn't go very far." They found an Ethiopian restaurant on Telegraph. Zoe had a veggie special: red lentil, split pea, potato collard greens, cabbage, string beans and carrots in a spicy sauce; Mona and Aimee, the spicy chicken, beef, and lamb combo that they scooped up with plenty of injera bread. Afterwards they strolled back in the direction of the campus, ending up in Strawberry Canyon. They found a bench near the bank of the little creek and sat. Mona consulted her phone. "Ah! Joel responded." She dialed him. This time he picked up. "Hi! ... Yeah! You should be here! ... You did? ... but not now ... Yeah, our host here had the same symptoms you did, that's why ... No? ... Okay. Hey, love ya!" She punched end.

"Nope. He *did* get his tea here when he lived here, but he's been getting his tea from a local shop right off campus at Northern Wash U since he moved up there."

"Shit! Back to square one." Zoe shook her head. "It just doesn't compute. Too much coincidence."

"Unless Mavis really *did* just happen to lose her balance for whatever reason," suggested Mona, "and Aimee really did just have the flu. Could Mavis have had a stroke?"

Aimee nodded. "Yeah, I remember the coroner asking me if she had any history of heart trouble, high blood pressure. She did take blood pressure medicine and she had mild diabetes and took some meds for that, too, every morning. But then I remember him saying even if she had had one, a stroke, it would have been the fall itself that would have killed her, knocked her up so bad there'd be no use in doing an autopsy."

Zoe gave a huge shrug and sighed. "Ah, well. So much for that idea. So it wasn't Randy who poisoned the tea and it wasn't some anonymous person who did it. It's looking like maybe the tea wasn't poisoned at all. At least *your* tea wasn't. Mavis lost her balance or had a stroke or whatever, and you really did have the flu. So on to our second mystery? Or is it our third?"

Mona responded, "The skull. And Cortez. That's really three mysteries: who's the skull? Who put the boxes on our doorstep? And why?"

"Fourth mystery, if you want multiple mysteries: Who's Cortez? And what's his, or her, connection to the skull?"

"Whaaat?" Aimee complained. "You guys have more mysteries? I feel like I'm living in an Ann Cleeves novel all of a sudden."

"Let's go home and we'll tell you all about it."

"Or, since you've been keeping it under wraps all this time, I mean these last couple days, you can save it 'til tomorrow for when Kenny comes over."

TRESTLE GLEN AND BERKELEY

Zoe, Mona and Carly were feeling the belated effects of the long drive and the tension of their now multi-faceted mystery. They turned in early. At one point during the night, Zoe was vaguely aware of doors opening and closing, of footsteps in the hall. Next morning, after they had risen late, Aimee cautioned them to have a simple breakfast because they would have an early lunch, basically dinner. They were going to have the last of the pork loin more or less at noon.

Until then, they decided to stroll around Trestle Glen and were pleased to follow Aimee's advice to "just go out the back door and you'll be on a bike-and-hiking path that takes you to a nice little park in one direction and downtown Berkeley in the other." When they returned, they found Aimee at the stove and a black man seated at the kitchen table whom Aimee introduced as "Kenny Yarborough, my beau."

Kenny explained that, as manager of a big box drug store, he officially had Saturday off, going on duty at five. "But I never get Saturday off these days anymore," he complained, "I've always gotta be on call and there's always at least one emergency on Saturday night. So I just go in early and hope I can douse the hot spots before they turn into grass fires." With a kiss on Aimee's cheek, he departed shortly after they'd finished eating.

The meal done, Zoe went out to her car, fetched the large Mayflower box, and brought it in. It contained the bundle of bus-and-train transfers, the 1956 catalogue of classes, the sheets of newsprint from the *Tribune* and *News-Post* and of course, the skull in its hat box. "Any idea?" she asked Kenny. Kenny shook his head. Aimee took up the bundle of transfers. "Hey, these are kind of cool. I remember Mavis talking about the Key and East Bay Transit System. There were trains and street cars all over the place. There was a train that ran right through Trestle Glen, through peoples' backyards, over the Bay Bridge and into San Francisco. Mavis remembered it from when she was a kid. I guess that was the 'Trestle' in 'Trestle Glen', like, a train trestle."

"Well I guess I'd suggest the obvious," said Kenny. "Go over to the campus and see what you can find out about this Cortez person."

Mona had been thumbing through the catalogue. "Ah! Here! Cortez circled these classes. I guess he meant to take them, or actually did take them: *Folklore, Form and Content*, Instructor: Mr. Dundes. *General Anthropology*, Instructor: Mr. Olson. *North American Indians*, Instructor: Miss *Oldermeyer*."

"Could have been a she," noted Kenny.

"Huh?" Mona looked up.

"Cortez could have been a she."

"Oh, right."

MONDAY

In Berkeley once again, they had to park in a parking structure, but it was close to the campus. A map on a billboard directed them to the anthropology department. They found the main office, with a barely post-teen young woman at the desk, who knew nothing about Cortez, Dundes, Olson, Oldermeyer, or 1956. They roamed the halls until they found a door ajar. The name plate told them it was the office of Dr. Laura Nader, Professor. They knocked gingerly. "Come in," said a voice from inside. They entered, tentative. A sixty or seventy year old woman, swiveled in a chair, turning from the desk at which she sat. "Yes?"

They introduced themselves and, without saying much about why, Zoe said they were trying to track down someone who had been here as a student in 1956 by the name of Cortez, who may have taken courses from Professors Dundes, Olson, and Oldermeyer. "Alan Dundes is unfortunately no longer with us and I never heard of Olson. But you're in luck with Ruth Oldermeyer. She's–I think–a hundred or maybe even a hundred-and-one-years old, but still extant. We brought her in for our colloquium series what–three, four years ago? Sharp as a tack! She lives pretty close, over on Channing Way. And she likes visitors! I don't have her phone number or her exact address but you can get it from Doreen in the main office."

They started walking down the hall back toward the main office. Then Mona stopped. "Hey, do you suppose she's any relation to *Ralph* Nader?"

"Oh, the old radical rabble-rouser from the sixties? Why don't we go back and ask!" said Aimee. They did so.

"Yes. I'm his infinitely better-known younger sister." They all laughed, then again headed for the main office, where the young woman insisted they could not give out addresses or telephone numbers of faculty. Another desk with the nameplate "Doreen" was unoccupied. But as they were about to start remonstrating with the young lady, a heavy-set woman dressed conservatively in a white blouse and brown slacks, with styled and undoubtedly dyed brown hair and plastic-rimmed glasses stepped gracefully into the office and over to the desk. "Can I help you?"

They stated their mission, invoking Laura Nader's assurance that they could get Ruth Oldermeyer's address from the main office. Doreen sat down at her desk, held up a finger, and picked up her desk phone receiver, punching a button on the set. "Yes ... yes ... certainly ... bye." She wrote something on a little pad. Then, activating her computer, she looked up at Zoe and Mona. "And you are Drs. Zoe Dill and Mona Spradley, from Sacajawea and Charbonneau College, with friend Aimee?" She clacked away for less than a minute. Then, before they could answer, she tore the sheet off the pad, wrote something else, tore off that sheet, and handed it to Zoe. She picked up her desk phone receiver again. "Here's her address," she said, handing the post-it to Zoe. "I'm sure she's home. She never goes anywhere these days. She even found a doctor that makes house calls! Go on over; I'll call ahead for you."

Channing Way was a hodgepodge of stately Queen Anne mansions turned into flats, low-rise apartment houses that dated from the 1940s, and twenty-first century fake-stone-faced monster duplexes. Amongst these sat Ruth Oldermeyer's small, one-story blue bungalow. They rang the bell. It was opened almost immediately by a thirtyish Eurasian woman in a fluffy white pullover and jeans. "Hi! Come on in! I'm Jeanine. Dr. Oldermeyer is waiting for you." They followed her into the living room. Propped up in an overstuffed chair was a tall but thin, frail, fragile-and-feeble-looking woman with thin gray hair. A large-plaid green-and-blue blanket draped her legs and a thinner blanket draped her shoulders. "Hello! Come in! I'm Ruth Oldermeyer!" Her voice was anything but feeble; it was resonant and loud, almost booming. "You're looking for a student who might have been in one of my classes?" She held out her hand. They all shook hands.

They introduced themselves again without giving the details of why or how, they asked her if they knew a student named Cortez who was at UC Berkeley in 1956. Ruth Oldermeyer invited them to sit on an old, worn sofa. "Jeanine," Ruth instructed. "Get the files for–let's see–1953 through 1959. If this Cortez took a class from me, it could have been as a freshman or a senior or anywhere in between." *Clearly*, thought Zoe, *this lady's mind is anything but feeble*. "When I started here in 1948 they told us to keep our records for a year because that was the time frame within which a student might file a grade appeal. I've kept them all a bit longer than that!" She chuckled.

Jeanine exited the room, then returned shortly. She laid eight thin files on Ruth's lap. Zoe realized this lady was not wearing glasses! But she now did so, placing them on her nose and around her ears from a chain dangling from her neck. She scanned a sheet from each file in turn. "Not 1953. Not 1954. Not 1955. Yes, here he is. 1956. Hector Cortez. North American Indians. Lotta students in that class! Lotta boys! Probably matriculated in that first cohort after the Korean War. Can't say I remember him. Got a B." She looked up. "That's all I can tell you."

"Thank you."

As they got up to leave, Ruth called them back. "Wait, wait. I *do* remember. I don't remember Hector, but I remember Paul. Paul Cortez. I remember him because he told me the reason he was taking my class was because his father had taken the same class twenty years earlier. Now I retired in 1979, so that would have been the last year he could have taken a course from me." She turned to Jeanine. "Bring me 1976, 7, 8, and 9, could you?"

Jeanine scooped up the eight files, then returned with four. Again, Ruth Oldermeyer went through each sheet by sheet. "Ah, yes!" she proclaimed. "Here he is! 1978. Did better than his father. Got an A-. By this time they were giving us print-out rosters that included everything except their fingerprints. Social security number, admission rank, gender, phone number, address. You couldn't do that now! Privacy Act. I remember him especially because a year later, the year I retired, I got an invitation to his wedding. It was quite lovely, in Tilden Park." She paused, staring off into the middle distance. "That's up in the hills, the Oakland hills, above Piedmont. Can't remember his bride's name."

"So there's an address there, in the print-out?" asked Mona.

"Yes. Here it is." She handed Mona the roster sheet. Mona typed the address into her phone, googled Paxton Avenue. It appeared as a crooked little branch off a long through street called Fruitvale Avenue. "I doubt he's still there!" boomed Ruth, laughing. "Why doesn't anybody stay in one place anymore? Well, *I'm* in the same place! Have been since 1948!"

They shook hands once again, then departed. Paxton Avenue turned out to be not an avenue at all; rather, it was a barely block-and-a-half-long cul-de-sac. The Cortez house was at the end, a one-story place set back from the street, aluminum-sided. They did not see any name on the mail slot. They rang the bell. Nobody home. Mona took out her phone, tried the phone number they had for Paul Cortez from the forty-year-old print-out.

Somebody answered, but clearly their first language was not English. A clear and distinct enunciation of "Paul Cortez" brought a spate of vowels and consonants that was not English, and Mona knew, also was not Spanish, French, or German, languages she knew. "Well, that's that," said Mona. "Another dead end."

"We can't give up on these great mysteries!" insisted Aimee.

Zoe affirmed agreement. "Let's go back to that stationery store we saw a few blocks back on Fruitvale. Let's see if they have one of those big flip chart things—you know, for meetings in the boardroom kind of thing." They did so. The store did so. They drove back to Trestle Glen. After lunch, Zoe set up the flip chart on a dining room chair in the living room. Aimee and Mona sat on the couch. Zoe played CEO with the flip chart and a sharpie.

"Actually, like you were saying, Mona, we have a bunch of mysteries here." On one side of the chart she wrote:

Grassers
Duncan Pennfield
Brandon Laird
Nicholas Taylor
Randall Allen
Mavis Samuelson
Aimee Garrison

Then she drew double arrows between Grassers and Duncan, Laird and Duncan, Grassers and Laird, Allen and Duncan, Allen and Mavis, Mavis and Aimee, Randall and Aimee. On the right-hand side she wrote:

Gallery
van Meegeren Vermeer
other gallery paintings

antiques
Leger
Braque

She drew arrows between Duncan and gallery, gallery and van Meegeren, gallery and other paintings, Laird and van Meegeren, Grassers and van Meegeren, Mavis and Léger, and Mavis and Braque.

"You should add 'art and' to the antiques for Randy."

Zoe did so. Then, in the middle between the two lists, she wrote:

Henbane tea
Estate sale
Charbonneau
Joel Curwin

She drew arrows between Duncan and Charbonneau, Laird and Charbonneau, Allen and Estate sale, Estate sale and Braque, Mavis and Léger, Henbane and Mavis, Henbane and Aimee, Henbane and Joel, Joel and Charbonneau, and Allen and Charbonneau. "So we have all these connections. Now: what if we also have connections between Nicholas Taylor and Brandon Laird and between Randall Allen and Brandon Laird?" She drew them in, but in dotted lines. "What if, in the arts and antiques dealers' world, or at estate sales, Randall Allen and Brandon Laird encounter each other? What if, at some point, Brandon Laird encounters authenticator Nicholas Taylor? Nicholas Taylor becomes Brandon Laird's go-to authenticator. When Brandon Laird spots a bargain painting at an estate sale, he brings in Nick for one of his conveniently ambiguous authentications, in this case, for the Léger and the Braque. Who knows? Brandon Laird may even have recommended to Duncan Pennfield that he bring in Nick to re-authenticate the Vermeer."

"Wow! Cool!" enthused Aimee. "A conspiracy! A real conspiracy!"

"Okay, I can see all the connections but the only connections for Joel are the henbane and Char--wait a minute! *Wait. A. Minute!! The spoons!*" exclaimed Mona.

"Okay. You're doing it again. The spoons? Give!" Aimee folded her arms across her bosom.

Mona shifted on the sofa, turned to her. "Joel gave me some spoons for Valentine's Day, a year ago. He got them *at an estate sale!* Originally some other guy got almost everything in the sale, including a dining room set. The spoons came with the dining room set. I'll bet anything, *your* dining room set. Joel said the guy who got the dining room set didn't seem to know anything about the spoons but the guy he was with said they were from an early Renaissance collection–the Somerset Hoard dug up in England some years ago. But they're not. They're replicas. I haven't had the heart to tell him. They're still nice. I happen to know the real ones from the Somerset Hoard are in a museum there. But Joel asked the guy if he could buy them off him so the guy sold them to him."

"*Oh. My. God.*" Aimee's face went deadpan. "The estate sale was *the* estate sale and the guy he bought the spoons from was Randy!"

Zoe shrugged. "It's a possibility. Or let's say it's a really strong possibility. A certainty?" She drew an arrow between estate sale and Joel and Joel and Randy, and wrote "spoons" in the middle column. "We now have all the connections we need if we draw an arrow from Randy to henbane. If we hypothesize that Randy at some point got paranoid that Joel would recognize him from the estate sale, then Joel might, just serendipitously, find out about Mavis' demise and, through Mona, get to Pennfield, not knowing that Pennfield is already, literally, in bed with Randy. Joel says, 'Hey, that Léger was in the same estate sale where I got those spoons.' Pennfield, maybe totally unaware of Laird being–probably not literally, but you know what I mean–in bed with Nick. Pennfield calls in another authenticator. Whoops! Now there's doubt about a second painting. It gets taken off display. Bad for Pennfield. And, worse than that, bad for Laird if it comes out that Laird has been peddling who-knows-how-many Nick-authenticated (she made quotation marks in the air) paintings to who-knows-how-many-collectors. Laird's reputation is in question. Collectors call in other authenticators. Nobody trusts him anymore. Nobody trusts Nick's authentications. Randy's conduit for stuff he finds at estate sales–Brandon Laird–has too much egg on his face to be trusted anymore. Randy's nice little scam-scheme, so carefully constructed over the years, collapses."

"Wow! *WOW!*" exclaimed Aimee. "So Randy gets paranoid and poisons Joel's tea? So we're back to Randy as the bad guy after all!"

"But why would he care, now that he's got this stipend?" objected Mona. "And we've established that he *didn't* poison your Aunt Mavis' tea."

"Hah! You don't know Randy!" expostulated Aimee. "Enough is never enough for him. The stipend fluctuates, goes up and down. Now he's into anthropology, probably thinking he'll expand into the black-market trade in illicitly gotten archaeological artifacts, once he gets his union card, his master's degree. I'll bet he's got grand plans. He's not really gonna become a grunt archaeologist."

"And the effects of henbane are slow but cumulative. He could have been poisoning Mavis' tea for weeks," observed Zoe.

"And he thought he needed to take out Joel the same way he took out Mavis–with henbane tea, hoping Joel would drive off a bridge or off a cliff in the throes of an attack or dizziness and blurred vision," noted Mona reflectively. Her voice hardened. "And he almost did. Not drive off a cliff, but he fell down, got concussed, almost drowned in a pond. Oh! That makes me so *MAD!*" Mona was clenching her fist. Hot tears, surely of anger, frustration, and sympathy for Joel welled out of her eyes.

"So, raunchy Randy somehow encountered Joel at Charbonneau, recognized him, drove up to his university, broke into his house, mixed the henbane with his mint tea?" Aimee shook her head. "Diabolical. *Diabolique*, after successfully using the same tactic against Aunt Mavis and me."

"Broke into his office, actually. The tea was from his office. Even easier to sneak into," corrected Mona.

"So what do we do with all this? Go to the police?" suggested Aimee. She stood up, hands on hips.

"With what?" Zoe also stood, paced in a circle, threw her hands up in frustration, then sat back down on the short sofa couch. "All we've got is potential, putative connections between some people and some places and some events. We can't *prove anything*."

"I guess you're right," replied Aimee softly. She sat back down. "Like, they, the police would just say: how can you prove, this long after the fact, that Mavis was poisoned? How can you prove that you were poisoned? How can you prove you didn't just have the flu? Shit!"

"Especially since you have a recorded doctor's diagnosis of flu."

"And even though we know Joel was definitely poisoned, and we can probably show how, how can we ever prove by whom?" agreed Mona.

"Yeah. We went through all this when we thought it was the Canters," added Zoe. "Canters are the professors at Charbonneau that Joel exposed as plagiarists. Anybody can take a trip to some place; the only thing we still could do is try to find somebody who saw someone of now Randy's description wandering around the Northern Wash campus. We didn't have time to follow up on that at the time. It seems like maybe we just need to drop the whole thing."

Aimee rose and walked a little circle. "Then why did we do all this?" she said angrily.

Zoe sighed. "I guess because I'm a fanatic, obsessed. I had to figure it all out. And there's still the chance that we could unravel at least part of it to somebody who might care, even if nobody can do much about it."

Aimee sat back down. "All right. But let's not give it up. We can leave the other mysteries 'til tomorrow. They're simpler anyway, aren't they? Let's do dinner. I'm starved. Hamburger patties for us, Mona?"

"And I'll do stir-fry tofu slabs smothered in pureed carrot mustard-garlic sauce and three fluffy twice-baked potatoes with peanuts," offered Zoe. "Would that sauce go well on your patties?"

12

ZOE WAS NOT WILLING to give up on the henbane-Randy-Joel idea, but the other enigmas seemed less fraught with personal reference points for the self-appointed investigators. After another shredded wheat breakfast, they adjourned to the living room once again. Zoe flipped over the chart to a fresh sheet. This time she started with the middle column, writing *skull, UC Anthropology, Santa Cruz News-Post, Podesta Baldocchi* and *Charbonneau?* In the left-hand column she wrote *Hector Cortez, Paul Cortez.* "Wait a minute! Wait a minute!" Exclaimed Aimee. "I'm so dumb. I'm so, so dumb. Paul Cortez. Uncle Paul. I mean, *maybe* Uncle Paul. Could his last name, Cor-tez, actually have been pronounced Cor-teez?"

"Anything is possible," admitted Zoe. "But highly unlikely. I mean Cortez is kind of a household word–you know, Montezuma, and all that. And, I think, spelled differently. I mean, wouldn't Cortese be C-O-R-T-E-S-E?"

"Yeah, but what if he wanted to distance himself from all that. From his Mexican roots and their legacy. I remember when I was at State I had a sociology prof named Dick Cortese. I asked him if he had any relatives named Paul. He didn't, not that he knew of, but I asked because of Uncle Paul."

"How did he spell his name?"

"I don't know. But we can find out." She rose and pounded upstairs.

"If he's the one that decorated that skull, it hardly seems like he wanted to distance himself. I mean, the turquoise decoration. It really quotes 'Aztec,'" observed Mona. "But what a coincidence! How likely was it going to be that Hector's son, whose wedding Ruth Oldermeyer went to, would turn out to be Aimee's relative?"

"Maybe the decorated skull could indicate that he identified more with the Indigenous than with his conquistador ancestors."

"Ah! Good point. So he'd rather be taken for Italian than Hispanic, but wanting to forge a connection with the Indigenous. Wasn't there a famous movie director or producer named Cortese? And he *was* Italian."

Aimee returned with a heavy photo album. "I found it. It's a family reunion photograph. My mother had family reunions every couple years–maybe every year. Anyway, I found a photograph of one of them. Somebody on my father's side was an amateur photographer. Or maybe he was semi-professional. Anyway, I remember always taking a group photograph. This guy Paul Cortez is in the photograph because he was married to my Aunt Nancy. He's the guy she divorced before she moved in with me. The only reason all those Cortezes are in the photograph is because he was married to her! Me and my family had hardly anything to do with them. They were there only because my mom liked big family parties, in-laws and in-laws of in-laws invited!" She had her finger inserted in the album and now laid it on the chair with the chart, opened it, and pointed. "I'm pretty sure that's Uncle Paul and I'm pretty sure if we can pry the picture out without tearing it we'll find names on the back." It took them several minutes of careful peeling, but eventually they did tease it out. "The old-fashioned albums were better–you know, with the little corners you pasted in, then slotted the photos into them. These ones from the '80s and '90s with the pages that you just plaster the sticky plastic over are really convenient and destructive!"

They sat on the sofa and looked at the back of the photo. Names were written to more or less correspond to the images on the front. Aimee read off the names: "Mavis, Claudia Cortez, Emma Rummel, May Rummel, Kate Rummel–I think those were her Grandma Claudia's sisters–never married. Maiden aunts, like. My mother's maiden aunts. Let's see--Sandoval Cortez, Brenda Cortez, Paul Cortez, Nancy Cortez–there they are! Nancy originally Allen, when she had Randy–then, Randy Allen, Arden, Elmer–my parents–Robert Cortez, John Cortez, Paula, Lucille Fenton, Bob Fenton, Todd Fenton, Edith O'Rourke–that's my Grammy, my mother's mother–Arthur Samuelson. That's Mavis' husband. And these kids, all sitting in front–there's me!" Aimee turned the photo over, then turned it back again: "Hayley, Stephen, Todd, Little Bob, John Jr, Aimee. Those are my cousins."

"Hector's not there?"

"Nah, I guess he was already dead by that time. Funny. All the adults have last names except my parents and Mavis, and this Paula person."

"Maybe she wasn't a relative?" suggested Mona.

"Nah, she probably was. We'll ask Aunt Nancy."

"And *Paul* Cortez--he was your uncle?" asked Mona.

"Not really. Remember, I said Aunt Nancy had just gotten divorced when she moved in with me and took me over? Well this is the guy she was divorced from."

"Do you remember anything about him?" queried Zoe. Aimee shook her head. "But your Aunt Nancy would."

Aimee nodded. "Yeah, probably."

"Are you in touch with her?"

"Not really."

"When was the last time you saw her?"

"At the funeral. At Mavis' funeral. Hardly anybody was there. A couple of

Arthur's relatives–really old. Nancy and Randy. They hardly spoke to one another. Or maybe didn't at all. The lawyer, Mr. Cronin. He called us all in, here, right here, to read the will. But I hardly remember. Like I said, those days are a real blur."

"Do you have a phone number for her? Can we go see her? She's still in your San Anselmo house, right?"

Aimee rose and retrieved her phone from the kitchen. She entered, scrolling. "Nope. But I'm sure Mavis would have. I'll get her little red phone book." Again, she pounded upstairs, returning after less than a minute. She sat down again, opened the little book, punched in a number. "Heh. No longer in service. She's changed her number."

"Hmm," said Zoe. "Well, maybe we should go on with our chart. In the right-hand column she wrote *Oakland, Paxton Avenue*, then rose. "I'll have to get my laptop for this last clue." She returned with her laptop open. "Holy moly! I didn't tumble to this at the time! I mean, I'd never heard of this place, so it didn't stick. But look at this! She highlighted something, hit copy, opened another Word file, blew the screen up to 200%, and stuck the laptop in Aimee's face. "This is from an inventory that we did last summer when we went through the boxes."

"That's *my* address!" Aimee exclaimed. "That's my house! 5969 El Cerrito Circle, San Anselmo! What's 'blue-bordered parcel post'?"

"Do you remember, Mona?" asked Zoe.

"Yeah, yeah, yeah. The Podesta Baldocchi box had a label pasted on it with this address. And we found a little booklet of these parcel post labels in the stash. It looked like something from the '50s."

"What's Podest–podest what?"

"I googled it," replied Zoe. "Apparently it's a flower shop in San Francisco."

"So, flowers were delivered to my house in this box in the 1950s?"

Zoe puzzled. "Not necessarily. In fact, maybe not at all. If that were the case, would the booklet of labels be in the same cache with the box? I mean, whoever *sent* them would have had the little booklet, not the recipient of the flowers."

"And that means ...?" queried Aimee.

"That means that someone was trying to send us a message. Somebody was trying to point us to your house. The answer to whose skull that is, in the box, is at your house."

"Creepy, cropo crapola!"

This conundrum is right smack in the middle of at least one of the others, thought Zoe. *This thing is layered, multiply embedded, nested, like those little wooden egg puzzles.* She walked over to the corner of the living room where they had placed the Mayflower box. She opened it and lifted out the skull. She sat on the sofa again, turning the skull upside down. "It's a little hard to see, but my friend Phil brought this to one of his anthropology buddies where he teaches and the guy pointed this out: the skull's been broken right around the nose. Phil's buddy thought it wasn't from a blow; it wasn't just a broken nose. He thought it was from penetration of a minutely thin blade, a penetration that would have gone straight into the brain and killed whoever belonged to this head. Oh, yes, and it's a *woman's* head. So not any of the Cortezes. So, we've got, like a half-dozen enigmas here. Who belonged to the head? Who killed her with a thin blade? Why? Who then plastered the head to look like a decorated revered Aztec skull? And who decided to send it to us? And why is your childhood address on a box, stuffed with unframed painted canvases that was dumped on our doorstep at the same time the skull was?"

"That's a quadruple, quintuple mystery," observed Aimee.

"Right, right."

"Can we go up there? To your house in San Anselmo?" asked Mona.

"Yeah, sure. I have every right to be there."

"Do we go now?" suggested Mona.

"Yeah. Now would be the perfect time. It's still early, but mid-morning–a lull in the commuter traffic. I guess we should bring the photo along, maybe to jog Nancy's memory? I mean, maybe she's the one who dumped the boxes on your doorstep, but it could have been one of these other Corteses–Cortezes as well." Aimee tucked the photograph into the album between two glassine cover leaves, hoping it wouldn't stick.

13

SAN ANSELMO

5969 EL CERRITO CIRCLE was a rambling, one-story, mid-century modern, 1950s structure. Aimee led them up the steps and was about to insert her key in the lock. "*What's this?*" She was looking at a code box to the right of the door.

"It's an alarm code box," observed Mona.

"How dare she! And this security door is new!" She tried her key. "And of course, my key doesn't work! She's locked me out of my own house! She has no right to do this!"

"She probably didn't specifically lock you out," suggested Mona. "She probably just installed a security system for whatever reason."

But Aimee was clearly angry. No, enraged. She pounded on the door. Pounded again. A curtain was drawn back briefly on the window to their right. The inner door opened, then the security door. An over-fiftyish woman in a pair of nondescript black pants and gray pullover, hair piled on her head, exclaimed, "Oh. Aimee. Hello."

"What. Is. The. Meaning. Of. This?" Aimee stated icily.

"I'm … I'm sorry," Nancy Cortez, or whatever name she was using now, stammered. "We … we installed this security system about a year ago because of Frank's business."

Aimee barged past her, shoving her aside so violently Nancy Cortez almost lost her balance. "*You'd better give me the code and you'd better give me the keys to these new locks!*"

"Yes, yes, of course! Are you moving back in? Who are these people?"

Mona and Zoe introduced themselves. Zoe felt kind of badly for Nancy Cortez, even though she could certainly understand Aimee's indignation. Nancy closed the doors. Nancy shook their hands. "Pleased to meet you. I'm Nancy Hennessy. Would you like something? Coffee, tea, something stronger?"

"*First of all,*" Aimee spat, "*these are my guests and we intend to stay here tonight. Second, just what is Frank's business?* And who is he? Who is this Frank? Have you married him? Is that why you're not Nancy Cortez anymore? Or Nancy Allen?"

They were now standing in the living room. Zoe was astonished. *Here's yet more art, valuable if it's genuine,* she thought. A Modigliani, and several more paintings that she couldn't immediately identify hung on the walls.

"He's a … an accountant, but he's kind of a … an inheritance accountant. He specializes in untangling estates that have multiple heirs and either no will or an ambiguous one. Probate and so forth. And no, Hennessy isn't *his* name; it's *mine*. It was mine before I was Allen or Cortez."

Aimee seemed to have calmed down. She shrugged. "I guess I forgot. Or never knew."

Zoe sensed a break in the icy fog that seemed to surround them. "Is that a Modigliani?" she asked. "And the others?"

"Right. Two are by Utrillo; the prints are Foujita, and these are a couple of Charles Russells. They actually belong to one of Frank's clients. The guy who owns them is sort of storing them with us while his brother's estate goes through probate. He's pretty sure it will be resolved in his favor, but in the meantime, we're kind of the custodians. That's why we installed the alarm system, obviously."

Aimee glared at Nancy. Zoe thought she was not even noticing the art. She seemed to have re-assembled her anger. "Get me that key. Write down the code and your new and unpublished phone number," Aimee said stonily. Nancy departed. Aimee leaned over, put her head in her hands. "I can't believe this."

"Look," said Zoe, "this will all get straightened out. Let's tell your aunt why we're here, about the boxes and the photograph, and that we thought we'd combine it with a trip up to savor the wine country, stay maybe a day or two. Ask her about the people in the photograph, especially about this Paula person. And let's really do it--visit some wineries this afternoon, some more tomorrow, then go back. Process all this, after we get Nancy to tell us about Hector Cortez and Robert Cortez. You and she are obviously related to them, if only by ex-marriage. And ask if she's the one that dumped the boxes on our doorstep."

Nancy returned with a key and a slip of paper on which she'd written the code and her new phone number. Her hand shook a little, Zoe noticed, as she handed both to Aimee, who all but ripped it out of her hand.

Zoe decided some judicious temporizing was in order. "Mrs. ... Ms Hennessy, we *would* like to stay here tonight if possible, if it's not too much trouble."

"We have a *right* to stay here!" Aimee spat.

"Yes, yes, of course. You're all welcome. We'll find room for you," Nancy Hennessy assured them.

"But I think right now we'd like to get up to the wine country and get to a couple of wineries while the light is still good and before they close," said Zoe hastily.

They were barely an hour from the beginning of the wine country on the freeways. Zoe drove. Aimee was still steaming. She called the estate attorney. "Well tell him to get his ass *out* of the meeting and get him on the phone to me! She ended the call.

A few minutes later her phone rang. She answered. After a few minutes of talk from the other end of the call, Aimee said into the phone: "But she can't shut me out! … She can? Right to privacy, right. But she can't keep me out of the house … You didn't know she'd changed it?" She took the piece of paper, which she had stuffed into her jeans, and read Nancy's new number into the phone. "Yeah, yeah … okay … thanks, Mr. Quinn." She turned in her seat. "He didn't know she'd changed her number or the locks or put in the alarm system. And she does have what he called the right to privacy. I mean, she can put code locks on her private rooms, if she wants."

"I can understand why she put in the alarm system. That Modigliani is worth millions, if it's genuine. I mean mega-millions: like, thirty, forty, fifty, maybe more."

"Really?" said Aimee. "Wow! Do you think it's real? Do you buy her story about the guy making them the custodians?"

Mona shrugged. "Don't know. I suppose it could be."

They drove to the top of the wine route, stopping first at Chateau Montelena, then Clos Pegase, and finally at Beringer, alternating the designated driver between wineries and tastings, on the theory that the one of the two of them who did taste would dissipate blood alcohol level as she sat in the car between wineries; probably not a realistic assumption, but one that they followed. Snacks with the tastings provided enough sustenance to tide them over.

It was about eight thirty when they pulled into the driveway of the house, so Nancy would surely be home, settling into her evening. They used the code and the key to enter the house and Nancy met them in the living room, arriving from somewhere else in the house. "Nancy," said Aimee. "Aunt Nancy! I'm so sorry I flew off the handle like that earlier." She took both of Nancy's hands in hers. "I really lost it. I was such an asshole. This was just such a surprise. After Mavis' accident and all that—I've been kind of what do they way? At sixes and sevens?"

Nancy half-smiled. "I understand."

"And we actually came here to share a peculiar event with you."

"Why don't you bring your things in, and then maybe we can have a drink and talk about your peculiar event." She looked alternately at Zoe, then Mona. "I'll move into Frank's room, and you two can have mine, if you don't mind sharing a bed. And Aimee, your room is still there for you, just like you left it."

"We got some wine for you." They brought their things in. Aimee extracted the album from her duffel and three bottles of red wine they had gotten at each of the three wineries. They were all sitting on a couch and chairs in the living room. They told Nancy about the banana and Mayflower boxes and the course catalogue from Hector Cortez as well as a few of the other things. The stone crosses, they had found out, were naturally occurring staurolites, much sought after by rock collectors.

"Ah yes!" said Nancy. "Hector's junk collection: his cabinet of curiosities."

"So you know it? Did you ever see it? Was it a real cabinet?" asked Aimee.

"Yes, yes. It was a real cabinet, full of all sorts of weird stuff. Tortoise shells, geodes, rocks he said were fossilized dinosaur poop, little statues. I mean, do you remember that classic old silent horror film? *The Cabinet of Doctor Caligari*? I mean, he had bones in there. Skulls. What can I tell you? Hector was an eccentric, a clown, a joker. He would pretend that he was going to open his own 'collectibles shop', then come home with some more weird crap."

"Skulls?" said Mona.

"Oh, yes."

"We could use a visualization," quipped Zoe. "Were any of them human?"

"No, you don't want to know what this cabinet really looked like. I had to live with it day in, day out. But no." Nancy laughed. "None of the skulls were human. They were animal skulls. I know there was a cow. And a couple with long snouts–probably coyote. When Hector died–that was just about the time I was breaking up with Paul–Hector's wife, Claudia packaged it all up. She couldn't bear to throw it out, but nobody really wanted it. I don't know what ever happened to it."

"So you didn't get them, the curiosities," affirmed Aimee. "You're not the one who boxed the things up and left the boxes at Charbonneau College."

"Char–what?"

"It's the college where Zoe and I teach," explained Mona. "It's in Eastern Washington, kind of in the Tri-Cities, area. Walla Walla? Pullman? Spokane?"

"Sorry, no! It wasn't me! I don't even know where those places are! Wouldn't know how to get there if I tried. No, no, it wasn't me. Claudia probably gave it to one of her kids, but it wasn't Paul. Maybe it was Sandoval or Lucille. Maybe one of her grandkids: that would be John or Robert or Paula."

"And they live where?"

"Gosh, I have no idea. Salvador was an engineer. He had something to do with transportation in Chicago. Lucille's husband Bob, that would be Bob Fenton got a job with IBM and moved to somewhere in New York State. "

Aimee brought the photograph over to Nancy.

"Yes, yes, I remember this gathering!" She looked at the back. "Yeah, this was really unusual. It must have been summer vacation, and the Fentons and Cortezes were out visiting. From Chicago and from somewhere in New York, just north of New York City. That's the only time I ever met them, except a couple years earlier for Hector's funeral. I mean, except for Paul, of course."

"And this Paula person? She's in the photo. And she is …?" Asked Aimee.

"Paula Cortez. One of Sandoval's children. There were three: John, Paula and Robert."

"And Paul had no kids," affirmed Aimee.

Nancy shrugged. "Well, not with me. But Paul could have had kids with somebody else, after me, and so could Robert and Paula."

"What ever happened to Paul?" asked Aimee.

Nancy shrugged. "Don't know. Shortly after we divorced, he disappeared."

"So you never got alimony?" affirmed Aimee.

"Not a penny. Probably why he disappeared, to avoid paying any."

"Can I see the photo for a minute?" Nancy reluctantly handed it to her. Zoe scrolled on the phone. She was looking at the backside of the photo. "Nothing in white pages for Robert Cortez, John Cortez, Paul Cortez, Paula Cortez. Not in New York City, Westchester County, Rockland County, New York. Or for Lucille Fenton, Bob Fenton, Todd Fenton, Stephen Fenton. Not in greater Chicago, either. Wherever they are, they're not where they used to be. Not anymore."

"What about Paula? What ever happened to her?" asked Aimee.

"Well, I don't know about her either," replied Nancy, "but I think she was just about to get married in that photo. Her fiancé couldn't make it. He didn't live nearby. And I have no idea what his name might have been. So she could have had kids, but I wouldn't know what her or their last name would be now."

Zoe was still scrolling. "Also nothing for Paula Cortez, Robert Cortez, John Cortez in either the San Francisco or the Oakland (Alameda County), or Marin County white pages. Nothing for Sandoval Cortez, Brenda Cortez, Deana Cortez in the Cook County white pages. This whole family has just disappeared."

"You know," said Aimee, "I think we'll get out of your hair tomorrow; do the rest, or some more of, the wine country, then head straight back to Oakland."

Nancy shrugged. "Whatever. Sleep well."

Aimee slept in her room. Mona and Zoe were shown to the guest bedroom. Now, each stood on either side of the bed. "This is a really small bed, isn't it?" said Mona, smiling, her eyes twinkling.

"Yeah," responded Zoe tentatively. "If that's a problem, I can ask Nancy to find a sheet and a blanket and bunk on the couch in the living room. Too bad I didn't snatch Phil's sleeping bag when we were there. Or maybe Aimee's bed is bigger."

"No, no." Mona suddenly seemed disturbed. "No, that won't be necessary. Aimee's had a bit of a shock. She's probably feeling territorial. Let her get her sense of place back in her own bedroom. And I think," Mona continued, "for whatever reason, Nancy wants us tucked away, back here." Mona slipped her blouse over her head and unzipped her trousers. *No bra*, noted Zoe. *But I knew that. Nice, firm, round breasts.* Mona was stepping out of her trousers.

Zoe drew her blouse over her head, unzipped her jeans, kicked them off. "Um … I didn't bring a nightie. I … uh … don't own one, actually. I usually sleep nudie. T-shirt on cold winter nights."

"That's fine!" responded Mona. "That's great! I didn't bring one either because I don't own one either! And so do I! I mean, sleep nude." She slipped off her panties, then her socks. Zoe did the same. She walked over to the wall switch, doused the lights, walked back over to the bed, and drew back the duvet and sheet. She slipped into the bed. Mona did the same from the other side.

Zoe turned toward Mona, propping herself on her elbow.

Mona did the same. "Are you sleepy?" she asked. "I don't want you to do anything you don't want to do," she said softly, "But–is something like this all new to you?"

"Well, yeah, but I'm not sure what 'something like this' is going to be."

Mona turned over on her back and placed her hands behind her head. "You know that Carly and I came to Charbonneau at the same time–actually believe it or not, on the same day! We didn't have our place yet, any place, so they put us up in a dorm. Can you believe it? And the room only had one bed! I was feeling elated; just got the PhD, just got the job, but also just got the boot from Mr. Spradley."

"Oh! So that's not actually *your* name!"

"No. I mean, I'd already established my career as Mona

Spradley–dissertation, couple publications, presentations at conferences, professional visibility. So it seemed too complicated, too fraught with effort to change back to Mona Zimmermann. Anyway, I was feeling excited, sorry for myself, needy, adventurous all at the same time."

"So you and Carly ...?"

"We talked and giggled like schoolgirls and then suddenly there I was all crying boohoo about my stupid marriage caving in and there was Carly, all arms and hugs and sympathy and then our nighties were hiking up and we were rubbing each other and I was ...." Mona gulped. "I was fingering her and then she rolled on top of me and I just about jack-knifed I came so hard. I really craved real affection. Guess I must have been kind of horny, too."

"And so you and Carly ..." Zoe knew she must be sounding like a porno-voyeuring Alice-in-Wonderland.

"We did, for a while. But there's something about big-muscle masculine and Rambo-rod-ramming that can't be matched with rubbing and fingering and nipple licking-and-pinching. So, yeah, we decided by mutual agreement we'd go looking for males. James was easy for Carly to find. It took a big longer for me to find Joel, wandering around the North Wash campus while I was at a Basin-Plateau Art Historians mini-conference. So yes, Carly and I still cuddle maybe once or twice a month, usually after one of those fat Tuesday dinners with plenty of wine."

"And you don't get kind of ...?"

"You mean, does cognitive dissonance ever set in? We don't let it. If it starts to, we joke."

Zoe was remembering an experience she had had with her friend L'Estelle, both of them pre-teen. But she asked anyway: "So, so ... How do we go about this?"

"Are you sure you want to?"

"Well, I can't promise any jackknifing orgasm, but ..."

Mona laughed. "Then we'll start like this." Mona began massaging Zoe's breast.

14

Wednesday Morning
San Anselmo

MONA AND ZOE had taken the bed apart and they had all packed up everything; their luggage now sat in the kitchen.

"I'm not big on cooking. Sorry," said Nancy, smiling. "Crispy critters, coffee or tea, orange juice, granola."

"Granola and coffee is fine for me," said Zoe. Mona and Aimee nodded.

A disheveled looking man, full head of white hair going in all directions, shuffled into the kitchen in slippers and deep blue terry cloth bathrobe.

"Good morning!" chirped Nancy. "This is Frank. Frank, this is my niece Aimee and her friends, Zoe and Mona."

"Oh, hi! Pleased to meet you!" He shook each of their hands. "Frank McGinnis."

"Coffee, Frank?"

"No, no, not yet–shower first. If you'll excuse me, I got in kinda late last night."

"Oh, from where?" asked Aimee.

Nancy gave just a little shake of her head. "Oh, uh, Portland, actually. Well, off I go–Mr. Clean."

"We'll probably get on the road in a few minutes, so nice to meet you," said Zoe.

On the road, Aimee said quietly, "Did you notice that little exchange this morning?"

"Yeah," replied Zoe. "What was that all about?"

"Well." Aimee sat back in her seat. From the back, Mona leaned forward to hear. "First of all, last night, I stayed up late. I tried all the Fentons and Cortezes on Instagram, Twitter, Tumblr, snapchat. Blech–I had to join all those. What a pain. I'll get buried in junk messages. But I found one of them on Facebook: Stephen Fenton. I left him a message, long lost cousin, blah, blah, blah, please get in touch. Nothing yet but I'll check in a minute. Okay, so I was just settling in. Gone to the jacks, lights off. But I left the door open a crack. I was still awake when I hear the front door open. I hear, 'Nancy? Nancy! Back from the Hole!' The voice comes closer. 'Wyoming's great in winter as long as the sun is shining, snow….' Then I can't hear anything except sss, sss, sss–whispering. Of course it's Frank. Then this morning, I got up, prowled around. Frank's office is alarmed with a code box. I go down into the basement. They've remodeled the basement, made the storage room into something. I mean, it still looks like it's a storage room, but it was unfinished. Now it's finished. And it has a sturdy door with guess what–a lock and code. Also alarmed."

Mona leaned up as close as she could. "So what do you make of that?"

"I make it that something's in Frank's office and something's in that storeroom that they want to protect, that they don't want me or anybody else to get access to."

"Hole," said Zoe. "Wyoming. Frank had just gotten back from Wyoming. Jackson Hole."

"And?" queried Aimee.

"Major art destination. Major money destination. Wyoming's answer to Santa Fe, Squaw Valley, Aspen," replied Mona from the back seat.

"Meaning?" asked Aimee.

"Not sure," answered Mona. "But clearly, Frank does something important and on a regular basis in Jackson Hole. And probably he's got more valuable artwork in that code-locked office."

They visited Stag's Leap, Far Niente, and Beaulieu, ending up at Sattui. By that time it was four thirty in the afternoon. They decided to buy salami, cheeses, olives and a crusty ciabatta and call it supper. They commandeered a picnic table provided by the winery. "So let's raid the deli for all sorts of goodies," enthused Aimee.

Zoe and Mona sat. "I think we'd like to just sit here for a bit," said Mona. She looked at Zoe and smiled softly. "You go ahead and so your raiding, Aimee."

"Oh. Right. Okay. I'll just go get everything." She rushed off.

"About last night ..." Began Mona.

"It was wonderful. Exquisite. Different. Thrilling." Zoe nodded without stop.

"Things ... Things haven't been going so well with Joel ..." Mona offered. "He's fidgety, on edge, rough. I mean, it's probably all this awful stuff with Jane Bennett and the Canters and the henbane poisoning." She shook her head. "He gets excited, then can't ... And he's been acting weird. Like the last time I visited him, he would like, walk down through the campus, students all around, spouting all sorts of weinsteiny mcp stuff, like 'Mona, Mona, all this flesh. What am I going to do about all this flesh?'" She heaved a huge, wet sigh. "He arranged for me to come with him to visit his mom at Christmas and she's expecting us, me, and I don't want to let her down. So I'll definitely do that. Maybe it's all going to heal. But in the meantime, it was really nice, with you. Last couple of times with Joel, well, he was so anxious, he just popped before I had a chance.... But I don't know if you want to ... to ... I don't know how well this fits with ... with you and Phil."

"Well, it would be the first time for me, but it's not like people haven't played back-to-back doubles before. So I'm cool with it for now. No, more than cool. Phil might not make it up for some weeks, with winter coming on."

She saw Aimee approaching with the food. She dumped out a bag with the salami and wrapped packages onto the table. "Here we go! I got lemon water, too. No sense taking a chance on alcohol, sun going down and all?"

"Right, right," agreed Zoe. "So let's get back to our serious, ever burgeoning investigation. I didn't put this on our flip chart," said Zoe, "because I didn't know what to make of it. I still don't know what to make of it. But now I have an idea of its significance. Just a sec." She marched over to the car, opened the boot, opened her luggage, and extracted her laptop. She returned and set it on the table, popped three olives into her mouth, and opened it. "I hope it still has enough juice." She opened the laptop to the inventory with the header, "Doorstop Boxes." Okay, here it is. She turned the laptop around so Mona and Aimee, sitting opposite her, could see. They squinted to see the full entry in the inventory table. There again was Aimee's San Anselmo address, but this time along with a name.

"Yeah," said Aimee, "there's my address again. But who's Suzanne U-trill-oh?"

"Suzanne U-*treell*-oh," corrected Zoe. "That's the name on the blue address label on the Podesta-Baldocchi box. But that's just it. Suzanne Utrillo *isn't*. Remember those paintings we saw at your aunt's–I mean, at your house, Aimee?"

"Uhhh ..."

"Well there were two Utrillos. Maurice Utrillo was a painter in Paris in the early twentieth century. His mother was Suzanne Valadon. You probably haven't heard of her, but I guarantee you've seen her. She was Renoir's model, and probably mistress, at least for a while, and for other artists too."

"Ah!" said Aimee. "She's one of the nudes on the bank of the river!"

"Exactly," replied Zoe. "Well, eventually she parted from Renoir and lived for years with a guy named Utrillo. They had a son together. I think Utrillo went back to Italy, or maybe he died; I can't remember. But Suzanne and Utrillo's father never married. She remained Suzanne Valadon, an accomplished artist in her own right. So Maurice Utrillo was actually born Maurice Valadon. Suzanne raised him on her own. He only took the name 'Utrillo' at some point when he found out who his father was. So there never was a 'Suzanne Utrillo'. Then why the parcel post label on the box with her name and the address of your San Anselmo house.? My guess is, that label was not originally on that box. Somebody pasted it on pretty recently, before the box got to us. It's really unlikely it was Nancy who dropped it on our doorstep. It was probably somebody who wanted *to lead us to* Nancy, and to the Utrillos."

"Why?" puzzled Aimee.

"Don't know. But I suspect it's because somebody knows, or suspects, that the Utrillos, the Foujitas, the Russells, the Modigliani are actually forgeries. I think this little piece of information should stay with us. This is turning out to have all sorts of twists and turns and coincidences that are really awesome."

"The plot thickens," noted Aimee.

"But the thick plottens," quipped Mona. "We're making pretty slow progress."

"The plot curdles," stated Zoe emphatically. "We *are* making progress, but every time we do, there's another twist. I guess we should get on the road, and back to our flip chart."

They stashed the remains of the meal for tomorrow's lunch in the boot. Mona drove. Aimee looked at her phone. "My cousin Stephen replied," she told them. "Says, 'great so happy to be in touch again, am school teacher in Pasadena, am in the white pages, call after 4:30 p.m.'"

Aimee did so. After much catch-up, she asked him if he knew about Hector's cabinet of curiosities and what had happened to it. "Well, I remember when Grandma Claudia was trying to get rid of it. Nobody wanted it. But I did! It was cool! It had that big bottle of marbles, that awesome little dog, those skulls …"

"Human?" asked Aimee.

"No, no of course not!"

"But you didn't get it, the cabinet of curiosities."

"No. I was really steamed! Robert got it because *he* had skulls. A whole collection–cats, rats, mice, little turtle shells–so Mom said something like, 'Let him have it. I don't want all that creepy stuff in *my* house.'"

"So Robert got it? Where's he now?"

"Robert died quite suddenly, a heart attack, not long ago, in oh–I think maybe 2015."

"And what happened to the curiosities?"

"I have no idea. Maybe trashed. Or maybe they went to Paula."

"He had no kids?"

"No idea. He could have had."

"And Paula? Where's she now? She was married, right? Is she still around? Did she have any kids?"

"No idea. I'm sorry I can't be more helpful. But it's all I can do to keep up with my own kids and my brothers and sisters and their kids. Don't know what ever happened to Paula."

"No problem. Hey, we're coming onto the bridge. It's gonna get crazy. We'll be in touch!"

EARLY DECEMBER, THE FOLLOWING DAY: THURSDAY

The Sattui late lunch did them for dinner and getting to Oakland was a crawl. Exhausted, they fell into bed. Mona in hers, Zoe in hers. Next morning, they again made do with shredded wheat; Zoe suggested the next stop be Santa Cruz and the offices of the *News-Post*. "It's evident that wherever and whenever that skull came from, it came after my cousin Robert Cortez got a hold of the curiosities." said Aimee. "And the skull was wrapped and packed in those '90s newssheets from the *Santa Cruz News-Post*. So let's go to the beach."

They found the *Santa Cruz News-Post* office. It was all but deserted. A woman in her late-twenties sat at a desk. "Can I help you?"

"We've got a kind of odd question for you. Have you worked here long?" Zoe knew she couldn't have.

"Ten years. First part-time, receptionist. Then, full time–part-time receptionist, part-time accountant, then ad-copywriter. Now. I'm everything: receptionist, accountant, advertising director, copy editor, sometime writer." She moved her head from side to side. She took off her glasses, came from behind the desk. "Jenna Blatchley."

They shook hands. "Zoe Dill, and this is Mona Spradley and Aimee Garrison. Do you own the paper?" Zoe regretted the question as soon as she'd uttered it; she'd sounded incredulous.

Jenna guffawed, "God, no. It's just that everything's online now. I mean, I hardly see a reporter. But people still come in wanting to place ads. So if they don't have a mock-up, I do that. And every once in a while the editor says, 'Hey, Jenna, got a lead on such and such. Can you look into it? If there's something there, write it up and send it to me.'"

"Sounds like a lonesome job," observed Mona.

"It is. Sometimes instead of day-care I bring my kid in here just for company."

"Well, here's our odd question: would any of your reporters have covered a kind of bizarre incident, sometime in the 90s?"

She shrugged. "I'm sure they did. But what kind of incident?"

"Well, maybe a peculiar death, possibly a murder."

"Oh?" She cocked her head.

They decided this lonesome woman deserved a spike in her day. So Zoe told her about the boxes and Aimee told her about the collection, and the *News-Post* newspapers sheets as a clue they were following up. They had decided to keep the existence of the skull to themselves but mention vaguely there was reference in the materials in the boxes to someone who had died in mysterious circumstances in Santa Cruz in the 1990s. Aimee would not mention her connection to the Cortez family, but said it would fine if the newspaper people brought it up.

Jenna Blatchley nodded her head. "Interesting, interesting. And this death was reported in the newspaper?"

"Not exactly. It's this:" Aimee showed her the funeral notice. "Virginia Grimm. Hmmn. And your college is where?"

"Eastern Washington. It's close to the Tri-Cities area, but we're really kind of in the boonies."

"So from Santa Cruz to the boonies of Washington. Yeah, that is interesting. I don't know who Virginia Grimm was, but I would probably find out. You think she may have had a questionable death? How much of this could I write about?"

The three looked at one another. "Well, I don't think it's meant to be a secret that we have the boxes, what we're calling the Cortez collection. Whoever left the boxes at the college did so pretty openly. Maybe a little article on it would bring forth some useful information," replied Zoe.

"Okay. Thanks. The editor likes little odd 'human interest' stories like this that connect Santa Cruz with other places in the world. In the meantime, you should probably talk with Carole Branson. She reported for the *News-Post* for, oh, gosh, maybe thirty years. Retired in 2014, as she put it, so she could avoid the last round of layoffs. Tell you what; I'll call her and tell her about this. I'm sure if there was a questionable death in Santa Cruz in the 1990s she'd have known about it and probably reported on it. And she'll be really interested in this, especially if it's some folks in Eastern Washington that are curious about it!" She typed on her computer. "I'll give her a call."

Yes, said Jenna, Carole Branson would most certainly see them. They found the house easily from Jenna's directions: a small, fading one-story pink clapboard house on a street that dead-ended at a cliff; through the fog that swirled, moved in, moved out, parted, closed in again, they could see a staircase with railing that led down to the beach. They gave each other a glance then headed to the door and knocked.

"Come on in." Carole Branson was of slight build, late sixties, dressed in the bottom of a track suit and a loose cardigan. "Coffee? Tea? A dram of bourby?"

"No, no thanks, nothing for me," replied Zoe. Mona and Aimee shook their heads. They went through the story once again. Zoe showed her the funeral notice that was in with the *News-Post* sheets.

"Ah! Virginia Grimm. Yes, that *is* interesting! Just a sec." Carole Branson coughed a short, rattling cough.

She retreated to the back of the house, then returned with a manila file folder. She took some folded yellowed news sheets out of the folder, handed them around. "So here's what happened back in 1995, also 1998. Big fire in 1994 in the Santa Cruz Mountains. Torrential rains in 1995. Floods. Same thing in 1998. I covered them both."

She retreated once again, returned with a packet of cigarettes and a lighter. Giving out another cough rattle, she drew a cigarette out of the pack, lit it. "Trying to quit, of course–isn't everybody? I'm down to five, sometimes six a day. One after every meal, two in the afternoon. I can get through the morning on coffee but can't get through the afternoon without a c-stick or two." After a cough and a drag on the cigarette and another cough, she continued: "The 1998 flood was the more severe one. Whole houses were washed away up there, roads out. One cabin was smashed flat and washed down the mountain with somebody in it."

Aimee was reading one of the articles. She nodded her head. "Ronald 'Smokey' Packer."

"Right. Body never recovered. Now here's the bizarre thing, where maybe you guys come in: *a* body *was* recovered. But it wasn't his. It was a woman's body. And it was a body without a head. At the same time, a young woman had disappeared. Well, guess who? Virginia Grimm! She'd gone missing a few days before the flood and all the landslides. But it was never firmly established that it was Virginia Grimm because nobody could account for what she was doing in the mountains and after weeks in the mud, there was nothing to identify her. I mean, the head would have been crucial for the dental work and so forth. Packer was a recluse--probably sold drugs, but no visible means of support. A lotta people up there lived like that then. Off the grid. No known connection with Virginia Grimm, but who knows? Her boyfriend was, of course ..."

Aimee read from an article: "Robert Cortez."

"Died a couple years ago. You knew him?" asked Carole.

"My cousin, sort of," said Aimee.

"Interesting! Well like I said, the body was–well, a body. All mashed up, no clothes, kinda came oozing out of the muck and mud, I think, like weeks later. Flesh was peeling off. Not quite a skeleton but close. No way to tell when or how she died, but, like I said, headless, so no police artist's sketch, no tattoos or scars. Did she lose her head in the crush of the landslide? Maybe got crossways with an errant shovel or axe? Coroner couldn't say." She drew on the cigarette, rattled out a cough.

"I interviewed Cortez. He said he hadn't seen her since a couple days before the floods. Purported to have no idea why she might have been in the mountains. I didn't write this–couldn't–but my idea at the time was that she'd gone up there, up to the mountains, to get some drugs, maybe for herself and the boyfriend, or maybe just for herself. Other hypothesis: she was having it off with Smokey."

"Oh, wow. And Robert got jealous and killed her?"

Carole Branson shrugged. "And cut off her head? Anything is possible, especially around here."

"Was Virginia from around here?"

"Don't think so. Where did I say she was from?" she drew on her cigarette.

Indeed, Aimee noticed, all the articles on the situation carried her byline. "San Mateo."

Carole nodded, drew on her cigarette. "Yeah. That's right. She and Robert Cortez were both in a commune together up in the mountains. At some point they left the commune, moved to–where was it? Felton? Yes, I think so. I think it was Felton. I didn't follow up on him so I don't know where or how he ended up, but at the time he was enrolled in the History of Consciousness program at UCSC. I'm not sure how together they were when she disappeared. But the coroner and the Grimm family decided they might as well assume it was Virginia. She was young; you see her picture there–not a very good one–but she was attractive." Carole shrugged. "I suppose she could have just disappeared and then when she learned she was more or less officially dead, just never bothered to resurrect. Robert Cortez did show up at her funeral."

"So that's how this funeral notice got into the box. I know Robert died in 2015 of a heart attack," said Aimee. "But my family had lost track of him. I'm not sure they knew he was living in the Santa Cruz area."

Carole Branson shrugged. "Well, good luck on your quest." She frowned "Not that I'm sure just exactly what it is. But yes, indeed, boxes with Cortez family heirlooms and this obit showing up in Eastern Washington. That is a real Ellery Queen mystery!"

As they drove back to Trestle Glen, Zoe reflected: *It's not outside the realm of possibility that Robert Cortez stabbed Virginia, perhaps in a fit of rage or a heated argument, beheaded her, then buried her body. The flood and avalanche come along conveniently soon after and wash away her body, and also any clues to the reasons and means of her demise. Well, it's probably not worth the time and effort or the psychological trauma to the family to dredge up the possibility of the twenty-year-old crime. But that still leaves the rest of the mystery. Who dumped it on Charbonneau's doorstep, and why? Simply to incriminate Robert Cortez? Perhaps acting out a decades-old vendetta? And why lead us first to Aimee's San Anselmo house with the address label and the strange addressee?*

Could Nancy Allen-Cortez-Hennessy have had something to do with Virginia Grimm's death? But is it not really the paintings that the box-dumper wanted to call attention to?

Zoe shared these thoughts as they drove back to Trestle Glen. "It's pretty creepy." Aimee shook her head. "I mean, I didn't really know Robert Cortez, but it's creepy to think he killed her, lopped off her head, took it away with him, and then buried the body? Then along comes the rain and the floods and the avalanches and he's off the hook. You really think that's who we, you, have in the hat box? So why would he do that? Chop off her head, then *decorate* it?"

Mona shrugged. "Remorse?"

"And how did he get the … the skin and hair off? I mean—ick!" expostulated Aimee.

"Dermestids," responded Mona.

"Domestics?" said Aimee incredulously.

"Der-mes-tids. Beetles. The bane of museums. Not so much art museums, but for sure natural history museums. They're beetles that feed on organic material. Museums set traps for them. But back in the day, medical schools used to keep stocks of them. When they were done with the dead bodies they used for dissection classes, they'd sic the dermestids on them. The dermestids would go to work on them. Then, the medical schools would use the skeletons for anatomy classes. I'll bet you can still buy dermestids wholesale from somewhere, or you could in Robert Cortez's day, and he probably did so. If Robert was into having his own little skull museum, he'd probably find the odd rabbit, fox, bobcat skull, still with skin and fur on, plop them into the dermestid box, and …"

"Bob's your uncle!" completed Mona. "He could have done the same thing with Virginia Grimm's head."

"Creepy, crappy, crapola. But how would we ever find out if that's what he did and that's who she is?" puzzled Aimee. "Try trotting the skull around to the dentists in town and see if any one of them has a match for the dental work? That could take weeks and still not give us any results."

"Yeah," agreed Zoe. "So let's concentrate on the other. We've got two mysteries in the boxes. One as to why somebody wants us to know about this head, and the other, why somebody wanted to lead us to your San Anselmo house. And I wonder if the two things are connected? Even though Nancy says she never had anything to do with Hector's, or Robert's collection."

"Not to change the subject, but I wonder what Frank's trip to Jackson Hole was all about?" said Aimee. "Did you catch the body language yesterday morning? You know, one thing all this sleuthing has done is make me a lot more mindful of what's going on around me. So their – Nancy's and Frank's– body language told me they didn't want us to know he was in Jackson Hole. And that fits with what I heard–or didn't hear–the night before when Frank got in. First the booming voice, then all that susurrus. At the time, I just thought it was something like Nancy didn't want Frank's booming around to wake us up. But now I think there's something more to it."

"So you think our next adventure should be Jackson, Wyoming? And what do we look for when we get there?" queried Zoe.

Mona was fussing with her phone. "We'd better do it quickly. Five-day forecast has a storm coming in Sunday night or Monday--frigid temps, freezing rain turning to snow. Nasty."

"Ooops! Even if we left this afternoon, we couldn't get there until late tomorrow, I don't think", observed Zoe.

"Yes," agreed Mona. "But we could make it to Winnemucca–no, to Wendover, Nevada-Utah border. Then the next day get into Jackson. But what do we do when we get there?"

Aimee cocked her head, smiled and raised an eyebrow. "I think I know."

15

Oakland to Jackson
The Following Day

THEY WERE ALREADY PACKED; they left the luggage in the boot. "Let's grab undies and then go." Aimee grabbed three carrier bags and handed one each to Mona and Zoe. All three ran upstairs and stuffed undies into the bags. "Maybe better take everything you might need," yelled Zoe, "just in case we get stranded or have to charge back to Charbonneau."

Aimee ran back downstairs and placed another item in the bag with her undies. They raced back to the car, Aimee locked up, and they were off. "I think we'll just beat the afternoon commute. At some point, can somebody raid the goody bag from Sattui and make sandwiches?"

⁓

They actually made it to Grantsville, Utah, finding a motel a few minutes after ten. They had changed drivers twice, and during Mona's stint, Zoe unwound a long narrative for Aimee of who Phil was and the series of events that had brought her and Phil together, including who Ferguson was and his role in them.

An early start the following morning got them through Salt Lake City before the worst of rush hour and put them in Jackson at a few minutes before two; the Sattui eats were now nothing but crumbs. Aimee suggested, "Let's park and visit galleries and shops. Then we'll find a place and have us a good meal." Aimee insisted to the other two that she had a plan for ferreting out just what Frank McGinnis was doing in Jackson and why or why not it might be important.

They came into town on route 89, Broadway, turned left on Glenwood, then right on Center, and found more than a dozen art galleries clustered within a few blocks of downtown Jackson. They parked. "Okay," said Aimee, "follow me." She grabbed her undies bag from the back seat.

"This may take a while," noted Aimee. They made what Zoe saw as a determined tour of gallery after gallery, walking around each one, peering at the art, until someone asked, "Can I help you?" or Aimee zeroed in on a proprietor, clutching her carrier bag. At each gallery, she gave the proprietor or salesperson the same spiel. "Hi. I wonder if you know Frank McGinnis?" The answer was always similar: "No, can't say that I do." "Sorry, no." "I don't think so, is he an artist?" "No, does he live here?" When pressed, Aimee would say: "He's sort of an uncle of mine, comes up here a lot; I think he has a place here." And: "My girlfriends and I are just taking one last road trip before the weather sets in; we have a few days off. I just thought I'd look him up." Nobody seemed to think it strange that she did not have an address or directions to where this "sort of uncle" lived. Occasionally the question produced a smirk from the gallery personnel--the kind of smirk that said, "He's your sugar daddy and you're his piece on the side but here at home he doesn't want his wife to know."

At the sixth gallery, with plenty of Native American art and non-Native American art depicting Native Americans, they found joy. When Aimee asked him if he knew Frank McGinnis, the proprietor drawled, "Yeah, I know Frank."

Now Aimee launched into a different spiel: "Well, he's sort of my uncle, and I've got something that he said he didn't know much about, even though, you know, he's got those Charles Russells. I wonder if you would." The gallery proprietor nodded. Aimee set down her carrier bag and, from the lump of panties in it, withdrew a small bronze: a cowboy riding his mount, swinging his lariat. "He said–you know he comes up here all the time …"

The proprietor nodded again. "He took the small bronze, turned it over, studied it. "You wondering if it's genuine?"

"Right."

He shook his head. "Can't tell you." He gave her an odd look, and the smirky half-smile that she had gotten used to. *Probably thinks this is a ruse so I can find Frank without the mythical wife having a hissy fit.* "But matter of fact, Frank was just here."

"Yeah, I know." Aimee nodded vigorously. "We were just there, at his house, down in San Anselmo when he got home. This has been in my family for about a half-dozen years and Frank said he deals in art, but this has no provenance, and he said he uses an authenticator who's sort of based here. So he suggested we try to look him up, and we needed one last road trip before we have to hunker down for the winter, so why not Jackson?"

That was really winging it, thought Zoe.

"Well, I don't think his authenticator is actually based here, but when he and Frank have some business to conduct, they do meet here sometimes." Then the proprietor shook his head. "But I think this fella does paintings, not sculpture."

"Oh." Aimee made her face fall.

She's good, thought Zoe. *This is working!*

"But tell you what I can do. If you give me your card, I can contact–well, somebody here who'd know this authenticator fella's schedule, and maybe he can contact you. Are you here for a while?"

Aimee shook her head. "Me and my girlfriends are here for just probably today. Like I said, we're just taking one last road trip while we have a few days off before the weather sets in. And I don't really have a card." She laughed. "But I'll give you my phone number." The proprietor walked over to a small table where a stack of cards advertising the gallery sat, brought one over, and handed it and a pen to Aimee. Aimee took both and wrote her name and phone number on the card. "Thank you so much. Wish we had more time to look around, but we're trying to do a crash gallery tour here!"

Aimee lowered the bronze back into her panty bag. They exited. After walking a few paces, Aimee lowered her head and tried but failed to stifle a snigger. She managed to convert it into a silent giggle, her chest heaving. "I think we've got what we came for," she said quietly.

"That was really good!" said Zoe. "Well done! Clever you to think of it and I guess it's semi-legit. Do you mind he has your name and number?"

Aimee shook her head, "Nah."

"Whoa!" said Zoe suddenly, pulling both her companions into a recessed doorway. "I don't believe it!" She peered cautiously at three figures that had just exited a bar half a block away. The figures sauntered slowly up the street, looking behind them, as if they might be wanting to cross the street. "That's Nick! And Dahlia!"

"Who?" said Mona. "And the third is–I'm quite sure–that's Brandon Laird ..."

"Quick, quick!" said Zoe excitedly. "Aimee, can you march quickly up to where they are? I mean, don't run. Just march up there like you know where you're going and determined to get there. Don't look at them. Look at the car and memorize the license plate. Just keep marching along the street, turn left, come back here."

Aimee did so. Zoe watched her striding along, her boobs thrusting, bouncing, jostling under her wooly. *Was she doing it on purpose, Zoe wondered?* She seemed to be attracting the attention of the two men; each paused–one with his hand on the driver's side door handle, the other on the passenger door handle, and seemed to cast their gaze at Aimee as she bounced by, before the one slid into the driver's and the other into the left-hand back passenger's seats of a black

Cadillac Escalade. The woman–Zoe was sure it was Dahlia-Jane, Ferguson's nemesis, who had slithered out from Ferguson's grasp three years earlier, due to his own foolish folly, maybe with thirteen sacred masks—got into the car's back seat. The car pulled out into the street and drove slowly away from them. Two minutes later Aimee came striding up, breathless, chanting, "One-one-four-five-six-N, One-one- four-five-six-N, One-one- four-five-six-N."

Zoe entered the number in her phone. "Great! Let's get back to the car and see if we can track them. They headed straight, then disappeared in traffic. It's a long shot that we could but we might as well try." The Civic was parked several blocks away. Of course, finding the Escalade proved next to impossible. Crisscrossing the town up and down the streets brought them no joy. Mona located the hotels surrounding Jackson; they drove slowly around the parking lots of nine inns without spotting the Escalade. Finally, at the Super 8, Zoe suggested, "We might as well give it up. We're not going to find them. Let's check in here; we're going to have to stay somewhere."

Dinner was at a restaurant called The Blue Lion, of French onion soup, stuffed mushrooms, a kind of Waldorf salad with nuts and ratatouille for Zoe, and grilled elk tenderloin with asparagus and a mashed potato scoop for Mona and Aimee.

"Whew!" exclaimed Mona. "This soup is really piping hot, once you break through the crust!"

"But the crust is scrumptious," affirmed Aimee. "If you take a bite of this creamy-dreamy salad and then a spoonful of soup, you've got, like, a chewy barque floating along a crunchy silk road."

"And this elk should be on the menu as 'tender-er-loin," declared Mona. "You hardly have to chew. How's your ratta? And the Waldorf?"

"The ratta's just okay," replied Zoe. "I make a better one. And you never know what you're going to get with a Waldorf salad. Same with a Caesar salad. Do you know it was invented in Tijuana? The only thing you can count on when you order one is the raw egg. Which is why I never order it. Wish I'd gotten two or three of these stuffed portabellas. "

They shared a bottle of Alexander Valley Merlot and over the dinner, reviewed their findings. Zoe had called Ferguson and left a message with the astonishing news that Dahlia was right here in Jackson, traveling in a Black Cadillac Escalade with license plate 1-1-456-N, "probably a rental," Zoe had added, with two men, but also with the news that they had not been able to track it.

"By the way, the wine's on me," affirmed Aimee. "We'll pick up another bottle from that liquor store we passed on the way in for our room tonight."

"But let's make it a white," insisted Mona.

"Good! And that'll be on me too!"

"No, no, that's too generous! Too extravagant!" objected Zoe.

"Hey, the extravagant fairy dumps pennies from heaven into my account every couple months, remember?"

Now, they had a lot to talk about. Zoe set the agenda: Zoe would fill in the gaps about Dahlia-Jane. Mona would explain to them who Brandon Laird was, and again, Zoe would fill them in on Nick Taylor, the here-to-fore "authenticator" that Aimee had made up out of thin air, but who, Zoe told them, turned out to really exist. And who apparently really *did* meet up with Frank McGinnis here in Jackson!

Dahlia-Jane was probably in possession of thirteen—no, maybe make that twelve if Dora Harris' mask was one of them—-sacred masks that should never have been placed, along with fifty-nine others, into an auction in Paris in 2013. She failed in her attempt to flog them to collectors in the Santa Fe area in 2014, but had most likely intended only to collect the "down payments" the collectors were expected to make on them, then run off. Somehow– through Brandon Laird?–one of them most likely sold to a faculty member at Sacajawea and Charbonneau College based Zoe's suspicion upon seeing it hanging on her wall, and matching it with an illustration from the auction catalogue.

Brandon Laird was, up until December 2016, faculty member at Charbonneau. Now officially on suspension, Zoe was his one-year, 2017-2018 but probably permanent, replacement. The reason for this suspension was ostensibly in response to a complaint against him by another faculty member because his wife, taking advantage of a faculty spouse tuition waiver, had taken a class from said complainant and had seduced a learning-disabled student who was also in the class. But really, he was suspended because he regularly scouted art, sometimes for Charbonneau, but more frequently for a set of wealthy donors, the Grassers, and had scouted a Vermeer for them, which they had subsequently donated to Charbonneau, that turned out to be a forgery.

Zoe took the napkin from her lap, folded it, and laid it on the table. "Let's continue this conversation back at the Wyndham Eight," said Zoe. Now in the motel room, over plastic glasses of Indian Creek Mountain Syringa dry white, they did indeed continue.

Zoe recapitulated what she knew about Nicholas Zachary Taylor during the time she lived with him: "I finally found out where he periodically disappeared to. He was going off here and there. I never really knew exactly where, or who his clients were, except for once when he went to provide authentication certificates for paintings, based, ostensibly, mostly on the nature and quality of brushstrokes." She knew definitely, based on some information from their colleague Carly Pinto, that the same faculty member that had the mask, also had a Nick-authenticated Juan Gris painting. She had seen the painting, too, although she hadn't had the nerve to turn the thing on its front and look at the authentication certificate that was most likely affixed to its back. And of course she suspected that the Léger painting in Charbonneau's gallery, Mavis' donation, as Aimee knew, also had one of Nick's authentications affixed to it, although the gallery manager had not wanted to temporarily deactivate the alarm system so she could verify her suspicion.

"Okay. My turn," began Aimee. "We know nothing about Frank McGinnis. I met him for the first time with the two of you. But I do know a lot about Nancy and her son, Randy. I mean, I guess I actually don't know much, but when I moved in with Mavis, he came on the scene a little while later. I thought it was strange that here he was living with her and couldn't be bothered to provide some minimal degree of caregiving. But then I realized, it just wasn't in his nature. Plus, he was gone a lot."

Zoe nodded. "Off to estate sales."

"Right. So it all fits together, doesn't it? I mean, Randy goes off to an estate sale, buys up a bunch of stuff, calls in–what's his name?"

"Brandon," supplied Mona.

"Right. Brandon comes along, says, 'Hey, Yeah, I can flog this stuff to so-and-so.'"

"Like the Grassers." Mona nodded.

"Or, like, maybe he goes to them with a kind of shopping list," suggested Aimee.

Zoe nodded. "Could be. And then he 'finds'—she made quote marks in the air--what the client wants, and if it's a painting, he, Laird, calls in Nick to authenticate."

"But, then, where does this Frank person come in?" Mona pointed out that his and Nancy's roles were not exactly clear.

"Well, I think I can guess," suggested Zoe. "I think maybe Brandon *pretends* to have this really savvy contact, Randy Allen, who scouts for him. But in reality, it's Frank who has the important contact: a forger, who periodically supplies him with Modiglianis, Utrillos, Russells, whatever, that he hangs on the walls of Nancy's house so the paint can dry. He brings a forgery up here, liaises with Nick Taylor, gets the authentication certificate, and passes it on to Brandon Laird!"

"Who flogs it to clientele like the Grassers! Concluded Mona. "What a racket!"

Aimee laughed uproariously. "And then I, we, come along and spoil it all! It all fits together!"

Mona was frowning. "Well, not quite. I mean, Joel's poisoning …"

"But I thought we, you, decided it was the spoons–Mona's spoons–that are fake, that would tip you guys off to the fraud angle. Randy didn't want

Joel coming around to my place and seeing the furniture and the paintings and remembering who sold him the spoons."

Mona shook her head. "It doesn't compute. I mean, why would it make any difference, and to who, that Joel picks up a few replica spoons at the same estate sale where Randy got the stuff to peddle to Mavis? And how would Randy even know that Zoe and I would eventually hook up with you?"

Zoe nodded. "I think Mona's right. There's something there that doesn't make sense. I mean, it does, or might make sense that Mavis needed to be removed because she got pissed off at being taken advantage of and was about to change her will. But why would Randy even suspect that we'd ever contact Aimee because of the spoons? I can see the Léger leading us to Aimee–which it did–but why even bother about the spoons? And even so, if the spoons led us to Mavis, Aimee, the estate sale, and Randy, so what? You could accuse him of peddling replicas all you want but with Mavis gone, you wouldn't have—what's it called—standing?—to initiate legal proceedings, even a civil lawsuit. And like you say, Aimee, proving that it was henbane that was Mavis'—no pun intended—downfall would be impossible now; and it would be even more impossible to prove that he's the one who slipped it into her tea."

Mona sat back, sipped her wine, made a face. "So we're back to the Madison Canter theory? And coincidence? Mavis having a stroke and tumbling down the stairs and Aimee really just having the flu?"

Zoe shook her head. "No, that doesn't make sense either. Especially when we plug in the orphaned boxes and the San Anselmo address. I'm sure it all does fit together. Yet at this point, I can't quite see how." But Zoe's thinking was definitely perking on a distant coil. She recognized the lineaments of getting things wrong, so wrong, all wrong because, even though the real indicators of what was what were right there in front of her, she couldn't see them because she was looking past them, or in front of them, or to the left or right of them.

She realized Aretha's signature song was going into its call-and-response chorus. She retrieved her phone. It was Ferguson. She told him about their discovery that Dahlia-Jane, Nick Taylor, and Brandon Laird and Frank

McGinnis were all connected. Ferguson wanted to know if they "have any pictures of any of these people?"

"No, but I can undoubtedly get one of Brandon Laird once I'm back at Charbonneau," said Mona.

Zoe spoke again into the phone. "We can get you one of Laird in a few days and well, yah, I deleted all the photos of Nick but I've got a photo or two printed out from our Europe trip that I kept … Frank McGinnis?" Aimee shook her head. "No … okay, bye."

She addressed the others. "Needless to say, he was astonished to hear that his old nemesis, Dahlia has popped up again and basically in our faces and in cahoots with my ex, with the guy I replaced at Charbonneau, and probably with Aimee' aunt's latest lover."

"What's his plan?" asked Mona.

"Och, ye've once again decided mah fayte for me. Ah'll ha' to go out there." Zoe tried her best to imitate Ferguson.

"Does he really talk like that?" Aimee wrinkled up her nose.

"When he wants to," replied Zoe.

"So he's coming here?"

"Right, but it'll be after we leave. He was really excited that we got him back onto Dahlia-Jane's trail. He's nothing if not thorough. He'll come here to Jackson at some point, then to San Francisco and see if he can find a couple people we encountered in that little adventure with Dahlia. One of them, Will Adrian, was Dahlia's dogsbody and Ferguson hopes maybe he kept in touch with Dahlia, and might know if Dora Harris got one of the sacred masks through Dahlia. Then he'll go to San Anselmo and poke around.

"He was really interested to hear about Brandon Laird. He thinks Laird may be the new go-between for Dahlia and potential mask customers. So your San Anselmo house, Aimee, might be the new *entrepot* for the masks that Dahlia has. Frank McGinnis may just be a fellow traveler in subterfuge, helping out your Aunt Nancy. It's not unlikely he's the kingpin linking her, Nick, Brandon and your cousin Randy together." She shrugged. "Exactly how

Dahlia got into that mix is anybody's guess."

"Hey, I hate to throw ice on the fires of creative speculation ever burning," interrupted Mona, who was scrolling on her phone. "But we've gotta make tracks pretty early tomorrow morning. You know that storm coming down from Canada? Well, there's another one coming in from the coast. Warm rain meets icy storm, just about, like, between here and Charbonneau."

"Whatever happened to global warming?" observed Aimee.

Mona scrolled on her phone some more, then looked at Aimee. "This *is* global warming. High temperature in Alaska today? Forty-two degrees. Like, hundreds of thousands of acres of wildfires there, all summer and fall. Now, warm weather up there is pushing the cold weather down to here. And I don't see how we can get you back to Trestle Glen and get us back to Charbonneau before it hits. I mean, five-day forecast is ice, snow, more snow."

Aimee laughed and shook her head. "That's okay! Like I said, I work when I want to, and that's the only reason to get back. Can I camp in your digs at Charbonneau?"

"Sure," said Mona. "No problem. We've got a little tiny pine-paneled bed-sit. I'll call Carly and persuade her to have a nice, sinful Saturday meal ready for us when we get in."

"Sinful Saturday?" queried Aimee.

"A parody on abstinence. Meals without desert."

16

CARLY AND JAMES had decided to do a post-Thanksgiving repast with two three-pound roasted turkey breasts with gravy, twice-baked sweet potatoes, two with store-bought candied jalapenos for James and Zoe, who relished spicy hot; twice-baked fluffed mild-curried russets; two kinds of cranberries, one with allspice, nutmeg and blue agave, the other–again for James and Zoe–with agave and more of the candied jalapenos; mashed-pea-pistachio-and-edamame bean flour tortilla empanadas; "French" pea-and-onion soup with a browned cheesy-bready crust; and a mango-avocado-jicama-agave-olive oil salad that could be eaten alongside, or afterwards as desert. For wines, Carly selected a Chateau Saint Michelle dry Riesling that would not overpower and of the dishes and a Gewurztraminer to end the feast. "We're always doing marathon grading," Carly explained to Aimee. "End of term–finals, papers, yada yada yada. Phil and Joel too, right? Midterms before the winter break? Too bad they couldn't make this." But Zoe,

Mona and Aimee had rolled into the driveway in the midst of a vicious ice storm, and first Joel, then Phil had phoned and said no way. They might get there okay, but they would each have to brave the elements to get back for last week of classes before break.

During and after dinner, in fits and starts, Zoe, Mona and Aimee filled James and Carly in on what they had done, experienced, discovered. "So," said James. "Summing up: you raised more questions than you answered, you uncovered more mysteries than you solved, you exonerated the doers of misdeeds, only to implicate them again, and hauled in more potential doers of misdeeds who weren't in the mix when you started all this."

"Well," said Zoe, somewhat deflated, "when you put it like that …"

"Let's do the numbers, so to speak, like they say on that NPR show," suggested James. He started ticking off with his fingers. "You've maybe solved the skull mystery but there's no way to verify your theory. It may or may not be this Virginia person. You've still not solved the 'who-left-the-boxes' mystery, except to maybe narrow it down to this Paula person?"

"Right. Paula Cortez."

"And in not solving *that* mystery, you've raised another one: what happened to Paula Cortez and where is she now? Okay, so, number four, if you will, why was Aimee's address on the flower delivery box? And, maybe five, where and how did it get there? You think recently, long after Aimee moved out. And you think that whoever used this obscure, early twentieth-century artist who didn't use that name, but had a son who did use the name and ended up doing paintings that just happen to end up hanging on the walls of Aimee's house, now inhabited by Aimee's aunt Nancy and this mysterious Frank guy, wanted to draw your attention to the house and the paintings? Because they might be forgeries?"

"Yeah. We didn't get very far with that one, did we?" admitted Zoe.

"And that generates another mystery. How did this Dahlia person, from your past, get together with Brandon Laird, your Nick, and Uncle Frank? And by extension, with Aunt Nancy?"

"He's not my uncle," corrected Aimee.

"And he's not *my Nick*," stated Zoe forcefully.

"All right, but he's there, the Frank guy, in the house with Aunt Nancy, and he's also in Jackson with this Dahlia person and with Brandon Laird, from here! And with your past paramour, Zoe! Now you're probably right about why those two, the authenticator and the finder, are partners in dubious art, and this Frank character fits, too, but it all hangs on whether or not all that art you saw on the walls is forged."

"It's *got* to be," insisted Carly. "There's *no way* some multi-million-dollar art finds its way to a tacky little house in the burbs."

"Hey! It's not tacky!" objected Aimee. "I enjoyed growing up there. I had good times there." She was beginning to tear. "Got into a lot of mischief, but it all turned out okay, didn't it? I mean, I'm okay, aren't I?"

"You're *more* than okay. I'm sorry," offered Carly. "I just mean, how likely is it that this supposed accountant, Frank, has a client who inherits an estate that goes into probate and just happens to include all that fabulous art?"

"There are some pretty fancy mansion ranches around there, right on the edge of wine country," responded Aimee. "But I know what you mean. And Zoe thinks maybe there's more forged art in an alarmed room in the basement and maybe that's where the rest of the masks from Zoe's adventures from a few years ago are too."

"So there you've got yet another mystery, or at least a question: what's in the locked room? And," ticking another finger, James continued, "You decided, first, that it was this Randy person, Aimee's cousin and Nancy's son, who poisoned poor old Joel's tea with henbane and Aimee's aunt's tea, too, but now that he probably didn't. Because you can't figure out why, if Randy just happened to spot Joel around here–and you didn't know he was around here so much 'til Aimee told you he was going hot and heavy with Duncan Pennfield, the gallery manager–why he would have gotten so freaked out that Joel would recognize him as the dude that he bought the spoons from at the same estate sale where he got all the stuff he used to bilk Mavis. Aimee, you pointed out yourself that if he did spot Joel, by the time he did, the bilking Mavis thing was a long-gone moot point. I mean, he's already inherited, right?"

"Right," Aimee replied softly.

"So now you've re-opened a closed case!" crowed Carly. "We know Joel was poisoned with henbane. So if he, this Randy, didn't do it, who did? Back to the Madison Canter theory? That might now hold more water, now that Ferguson's discovered she did indeed access Jane Bennett's notes just at the time she and hubby Joe were writing–well, she was writing hers and probably forging his–dissertation."

"Which you will never be able to prove," observed James. "So if we grant that Mavis just got a heart attack or a stroke and tumbled down the stairs and Aimee just got flu, that still leaves yet another mystery, or at least a question."

"But I think Peter really will confront her with the circumstantial evidence, so to speak, and marrying that to Joseph Canter's presumably truthful testimony that he never saw the notes and journal and never heard of Jane Bennett, which is what Phil told me, confidentially, that came out in the contretemps between the Canters and Joel, that's sort of, like, circumstantial evidence that Madison really *did* write Joseph's dissertation by copying Jane Bennett's notes and papers. I mean, like, either he told the truth or he committed perjury," affirmed Zoe.

James shook his head. "But not that she poisoned Joel because he found out, or was afraid he *would* find out. It doesn't make sense. You yourself, Zoe, said that henbane poisoning doesn't act immediately. It's cumulative. Madison Canter didn't *know* Joel had found out about Josephs Canter's—or her, Madison Canter's—use of Jane Bennett's field notes to forge Joseph Canter's dissertation when he was poisoned."

"Ah! But it has been established that Dora Harris went to the Ethnohistory Meetings where she could have overheard Kelly Brennan saying that her colleague Joel Curwin was curious about Jane Bennett!" declared James.

"That's right!" agreed Carly. "Then Madison Canter sends a graduate student up to Northern Wash, who just happens to be able to nip into Joel's office when he's not looking, and plant henbane in his mint tea! You've got to credit Madison Canter with some diabolical and careful planning!"

Zoe frowned. "If that's what actually happened. I suppose *stranger* things have happened."

"And then," continued James, "you've got a few, what you might call, ancillary questions, like, how did Nancy and this guy Frank meet? How did Brandon Laird meet them, or at least Frank? And when and where and how did your lover-boy Nick stumble onto Brandon Laird?"

"*He's. Not. My. Lover-boy. Any. More.*" Said Zoe, almost viciously, then sat back, taking a long sip–maybe a gulp–of wine. "I'm sorry, truly sorry. I guess I've got my stupid ego really involved. I mean, we have all these signs. Real ones, like objects, and these persons, who are like icons. They symbolize things–issues, questions, situations, relationships. And you want to put all the signs and objects together and make sense of all of them. I'd just really like to figure it all out. Or I'd like all of you to figure it out. All of us to figure it out. I guess all this mystery juggling is getting to me. You're right. There are so many threads in this mystery tapestry that it's unraveling!"

James was silent, looking contrite.

"You put all this together really well, Dr. Gambel!" Aimee's praise was a salve and a save.

James smiled and shrugged. "We do this kind of thing a lot over there, in engineering. Before we actually build it, we have to design it. Like Legos, or the old erector sets: finger bone connected to the hand bone, hand bone connected to the connected to the arm bone," he chanted.

Everyone laughed. "I wish we had our flip chart," lamented Zoe.

"Yeah–hey–run over all this again, James, and I'll send myself an email; when I get back to Trestle Glen, whenever that's going to be, I'll put it all on the flip chart."

"But Aimee, maybe you want to stay here for an extended time? I just checked the airports–Spokane, Pullman, Walla Walla, even Portland–they're all reporting cancellations, delays due to bad weather," cautioned Mona.

Aimee shrugged. "Like I say, I can work or not work whenever I want. That's the only reason to get back."

"*But!*" exclaimed Mona, still consulting her phone. "The trains *are* running! We can get you on an Amtrak bus early, early tomorrow morning from Pullman to Spokane, you get the train there, you get to Seattle at 4:15. Oh. Not so good. You've got to sit around all night in Seattle 'til nine the next morning; you get into Emeryville at ten at night. Not that we'd not rather have you stay here in the knotty pine room, but ..."

"Hey, you can stay with my parents in Tacoma," offered James. "I'll give them a call. My dad will pick you up, take you back next morning for the train to Oakland-Emeryville. He loves trains and train stations! And actually, that'll make it a little easier. You can get the train there from Tacoma at 10:30 next morning."

"Yes!" affirmed Mona. "Tickets are available. I'll get you one. And this is on me! It'll cost just about what you paid for those two bottles of wine in Jackson."

"Yeah, okay, okay!" affirmed Aimee. "And Mona, you and Joel are going to be down there in, what, a week or two? So I'm hoping I can see you, and I know Kenny's getting antsy to have me back. His mom will put on a huge spread for Christmas and another one for New Year's!"

Carly had risen from the table and exited. Now she reappeared and handed two fat volumes to Aimee. "If you get tired of looking at the scenery, these may keep you occupied. Thriller-mysteries."

Aimee looked at the titles. "Tana French, *Faithful Place*. Elizabeth Ironside, *Art of Deception*. Thanks!"

"I'll go make up the knotty pine bed for you," announced Carly, rising. "All three of you are probably zonked."

"No need," said Mona quickly. "She can have mine. I changed the sheets just before we left."

"But ..." objected Carly, turning.

Mona had risen, turned, and come around to where Zoe was sitting.

She stood behind Zoe now, her hands on Zoe's shoulders. "I'll stay with Zoe tonight. Maybe for a couple days."

"Oh," said Carly quietly, her eyes all but popping. James had raised his eyebrows, shifted his gaze sideways, and formed a small "o" with his mouth.

Two Weeks before Christmas

Phil was off to Indiana for Christmas; he'd invited Zoe, but she politely declined. She liked Phil's parents, but the one time she'd committed to an extended stay there had proved tense and frustrating. Phil's mother was an intense Catholic and would not allow "unmarried cohabitation". They'd had to sleep in separate rooms. James was also off to extended family gatherings in Seattle, and, as Carly stated it, "we don't exactly celebrate Christmas, but my mother expects me and my sister there for the annual visit this time of year," so she was off to New York. Mona was looking forward to a couple of weeks at Joel's mother's place in Berkeley. "I get along with her better than I do with my own mother," she stated, "and it'll be fun to do stuff with her and Joel. We'll include Aimee, if she wants to be included."

Zoe had two invitations for Christmas. One was from Ellie Bortz in Croton Corners, New York, to whom she referred as her "aunt", although she was not; Ellie had raised her, but was no relation. The other was from Ellie's long-time friend and, at one time, business partner Coco Vanderjagt in Santa Fe. Zoe had renewed their friendship with her three years previously and entertained any number of imaginings about what a "Southwestern Christmas" would be like. Her father might have been okay with her at Christmas; but New Year kicked off the busy season in Hawaii, and he would be running around fifteen hours a day, seven days a week keeping his resort and hula school on the big island primed for the tourists. As to her mother? She never knew when or from where she might hear from her as she shuttled among various play spots in the Caribbean and Florida. She usually found out on a weeks old postcard. Certainly Christmas was not on Damia Zoeller's radar.

But then just a week ago, an email from a publisher in England, to whom she had sent two chapters of her dissertation along with a precis, had arrived. They were indeed interested in pursuing publication. How soon could she get a full manuscript to them? Zoe had been warned by her professors at University of Washington that a dissertation did not a book make; extensive revisions, cutting, reorganizing, rewording would be necessary. Well, there was nothing for it. She would have to spend the following three weeks getting the dissertation completely morphed into a book. Preparation for the following semester's classes was also upon her. She had her tasks cut out for her: revise the dissertation, chapter by chapter; outline her course lectures; get her in-class activities sorted; and mock up paper assignments, tests, quizzes. And maybe at some point she could let herself once again plunge into what James had rightly noted were now more like six or seven mysteries, not just two or three. Perhaps Ferguson would phone with news.

FIVE DAYS BEFORE NEW YEAR

Aimee and Kenny had gone to a small family Christmas gathering in Livermore, California. Aimee had inserted the photograph she had carted up to San Anselmo back into the photo album and had brought it along. The family members looked at it and reminisced. One of them, Bob Fenton, remembered something that Aimee thought might turn out to be important. She got Mona and Joel over, put it onto the flip chart, but waited until she could phone Zoe to share the news.

"So we were sitting around going through this and that–Aunt Lucille said Uncle Sandoval is in bad shape–he's in a rest home in Florida and Aunt Brenda's there too, with Alzheimer's. John and his family live nearby, in Clearwater. And get this–Paula disappeared, like, fifteen years ago."

"Disappeared disappeared?" asked Zoe.

"No. She got married, moved somewhere. Out of Chicago. Uncle Bob thought maybe around here, the Bay Area. *And* they talked about someplace called Brookdale. They weren't sure if it was a house, a place, or a town, but Mona and I looked it up and it's not a town. But it's either in or near Felton, near a fish hatchery. They used to spend summers there–Sandoval, Lucille, Paul. And then later, they would come out for a few weeks each summer with their families, so with all their kids–John, Robert, and … Paula! Bob remembered it well. A big, old, rustic, rambling wooden structure. He said the fish hatchery was just down the road. It was a summer kind of place–no heat, but indoor plumbing, and they'd swim in the little creek at the back. It was meant to be a river, the San Lorenzo River, but there was never that much water in it. Well, when Hector died, Claudia wanted to sell it, but it turned out she couldn't, because Hector had specifically left it to his kids and the grandkids that had come along at the time. Bob Fenton said he thought Sandoval and Brenda and their kids continued to come out and stay during summers and that *Robert* lived there all year long until he died in 2015."

"So it's still there? I mean, the family still owns it?" asked Zoe.

"Yeah, but Bob wasn't sure what shape it was in. He thought it had been empty ever since."

"So probably vandalized."

"That's what I said, but he said probably not. In the meantime the fish hatchery's been turned into a posh resort-conference center kind of place with a few year-round cabin-condos. Last time they were there–that would have been for Hector's funeral in–what 1998, 99?–the fish hatchery, which is still called THE FISH HATCHERY, had hired a private security firm to do 24-7 patrolling. You know, I think I went out there with my folks then. I remember a big rambling place, hardly any furniture, lots of redwoods and eucalyptus all around. And there was a creek. I was warned not to go anywhere near it."

"So, so, so–you think maybe Paula's been holed up there? Like, maybe she moved in after Robert died? Or maybe even before."

"It's worth checking out."

"Yeah! Do it."

Now Mona was on the phone. "We were hoping maybe you could come down. It seems like we three should go out there together."

"Oh, oh, oh. Nice thought. But I'm not sure I could get a flight. And besides, I'm really into my course preps right now," averred Zoe.

"And if you did you'd pay thousands for it!" That was Aimee, now. "The flight, I mean. Can you get away after New Year?"

"My flight back is on New Year's Day," noted Mona. "Only one I could get. Nobody likes to fly on New Year's Day. So that won't work."

"We've got a few long weekends--MLK, Presidents' Day–we could try one of those if the weather cooperates."

17

BUT THE WEATHER DID NOT COOPERATE. Classes resumed, "fat Tuesdays" resumed, but Saturdays resembled Tuesdays because, although James was always there, neither Phil nor Joel could make it. The weather on the eastern side of the cascades brought, annoyingly and predictably, a snowstorm every weekend. Each week, by Thursday a weak sun would be shining and temperatures would peak in the 40s, sometimes even the 50s, only to plummet with icy rain or snow, weekend after weekend.

Carly, Mona, Zoe, and Peter Blenheim did indeed file a complaint, as members of the faculty, with Dean Fister, on the basis of what Ferguson had discovered about Madison Canter accessing Jane Bennett's notes in the Beinecke Library at Yale in the 1980s, and thus likely having written the dissertation and monograph attributed to her husband. The complaint was not against Madison Canter per se, but rather, was against the college's administration generally, for not sufficiently investigating the claims for higher degrees when hiring faculty. Now, the complaint pointed out, the entire college's credibility was potentially at risk. It mentioned nothing of the accreditation review, and stressed that the complaint was not a formal one requiring adjudication; it was, rather, simply a statement of these particular faculty members' annoyance at a situation that the college had seemed to allow to develop through negligence. But of course, they knew that Dean

Fister would put this complaint together with the testimony from the accreditation, which they did not officially know about, of course, of Joseph Canter that he had never heard of Jane Bennett and never been to Yale's Beinecke Library, and would use the complaint and the testimony to leverage a concession from Madison Canter: her and her husband's resignations in exchange for the college's promise to permit them full retirement benefits and not to seek retroactive sanctions. They, and Dean Fister, knew that anyone at the college or in the professions of history or anthropology who cared to do so would put the whole story together once Joel Curwin's two articles were published.

The weather pattern--icy rain or snow, weekend after weekend--kept up through February and into March. Finally, five days after the equinox, the morning dawned bright, sunny, and verging on warm. Miraculously, the weather got ever progressively clearer and warmer as spring break arrived.

Zoe called Aimee. "Hey, can Mona and I come down?"

"Sure!" enthused Aimee. "This'll be exciting! I'll get the flip chart ready! When?"

"Spring break, which is, like tomorrow, if the weather holds."

SPRING BREAK, 2018
ZOE, MONA, AIMEE; PAULA CORTEZ

Spring break was glorious; snow melted off peaks, rivers and streams swelled with runoff, the sun shined brilliantly, and lilacs budded. Zoe called Phil. They invited Carly along, but she had begged off. "With this extra class that I had to take over from Gudrun, I'm up to my ears in syllabi and grading curves."

Zoe and Mona drove down in Zoe's Civic and overnighted at Phil's on the Friday. Saturday morning was good, with Phil putting on an admirable performance just at sunup, climaxed with body-satisfying finishing strokes for Zoe, followed by a fine send-off breakfast for all of them: browned home-fries, a generous onion-pepper-tomato omelet, crisp-fried, thinly sliced tofu, fresh-squeezed orange juice.

Arrriving in Trestle Glen, exhausted, late Saturday night, even as tired as they were, they nevertheless resolved to venture down to Felton the next day and find the fish hatchery and Brookdale. Sunday late morning found them coming into Felton where an inquiry at an old-fashioned pharmacy-with-so-da-fountain got them directions to the Fish Hatchery, and found Brookdale, just visible behind a copse of redwood trees. It was a two-story log cabin. "Easy-peasy," proclaimed Aimee. Aimee maneuvered her Mercedes SUV left into a narrow, long dirt driveway, parking next to a blue BMW. Exiting the car and walking up the wide wooden steps, they were met by a petite woman standing in the open doorway. With shoulder-length styled brown hair framing a finely sculpted face, wearing jeans and a soft, light-blue T-shirt with some sort of logo on it, Zoe noted that her breasts would have been small on a larger frame but under her T-shirt, they protruded pleasantly, just short of swelling voluptuously. *She's pretty*, she thought. *Her age?* She looked anywhere between twenty-five and forty. But Zoe knew, *it must be closer to forty*, if she was, indeed, Paula.

Zoe turned and looked at Mona. Mona seemed rooted to the porch, even though the woman was holding the door wide open, an inviting smile on her face. But Mona was swallowing, gulping air. Finally she spoke: "*Mickie!*"

The woman did a mock curtsy. "At your service. Paula Mickie Cortez Laird." She stuck out her hand first to Aimee, then to Zoe. Zoe took it, confused. "Excuse me, you're who?"

Mona turned to Zoe, and said, "This is ... this is ... Mickie Laird! Brandon Laird's wife!"

"Sadly, yes, still. Come on in. I was wondering how long it would take you to find me. Congratulations! Good Sherlocking!"

Yes, thought Zoe. *She's certainly forty if she's a day. But well-packaged and well preserved. She could certainly appeal to post-teenage male fantasies. Hah!*

this is really coming full circle! Maybe now we'll get some answers to some questions, or maybe all the answers to all the questions. Hopefully not more questions.

"This isn't exactly the Ritz, but let's go into the kitchen and have a cup or a glass of something. I've got the space heater on. The old pot-belly's great for really cold weather but I have to go out and find wood for it somewhere." They followed her down a hall and through a drafty dining room with a large deal table and a smaller one framed by picnic benches. "This was meant as a no-nonsense place to accommodate gobs of people who were mainly camping out–I mean, even the bedrooms upstairs are more like your summer-camp dorms." They sat at a round table covered in oil cloth.

Mona shook her head. "So … so … you're … you've been living here …"

"Yes, indeed."

"And … and you're the one who dumped all those boxes on our doorstep," said Zoe, hoping an affirmative answer would at last set them on the trail of several of the mysteries with a jackpot at its end.

Paula-Mickie gave her head a little nod. "The very one. Guilty again, as charged."

"So … so … can you tell us? I mean, you're kind of my aunt." said Aimee. "I'm Aimee Garrison. Robert Laird was married to my aunt, Nancy Hennessy, she is now. How … how did you get involved in all this … this … whatever it is?"

Paula looked at Zoe. "Who are you, exactly?"

Mona shook her head, as if to clear it. "I'm sorry! This is my colleague, Zoe Dill, from Charbonneau, and this is Aimee Garrison, our friend from Oakland."

"I lived with Mavis Samuelson, another aunt, my great aunt, for a while."

"Ah yes! The donor of the Léger!"

"And my Aunt Nancy was married to Paul Cortez—your brother?—for some years, before I really knew her."

"My cousin." Paula frowned. She looked from Aimee to Zoe to Mona and back to Aimee again. "And how do you all know each other?"

"Well, it's bit of a story, but let's just say that Mavis and the Léger are the connecting points. So can we hear *your* connecting points? You do have some connection with the house in San Anselmo, right? And Nancy Hennessy, formerly Cortez?"

Paula nodded. "Right"

"I lived in that house until I was nineteen," interjected Aimee, "with my aunt Nancy. I guess you're sort my aunt, too, aren't you?"

Paula nodded. "Maybe aunt once removed?"

"Ex-cousin-by-marriage once removed," corrected Zoe.

"Sounds complicated. But now the connections are indeed coming clear." Paula smiled. "Well, how far back do you want me to go? I met Brandon Laird at a party in Berkeley when we were both students. I was bowled over. You may or may not have noticed–we–my family tends to want to get married right off the mark. My only deviation–well, I guess my cousin Robert's too–is, we didn't produce kids straight off. Anyway, eventually Brandon got the job at Charbonneau." She looked at Zoe and smiled. "Your job, now. And I don't have to tell you about Brandon's métier on the side."

"He peddled himself as an art finder," affirmed Mona.

"Right. And at some point he bumped into my quasi-ex: Nick Taylor, art authenticator," interjected Zoe.

"Oh, really? Nick's your ex?"

"Kinda. We lived together for three-and-half years when I was an undergraduate student. Well, I was pursuing an MA with a BA on the way, in Art History."

"Yes, yes. That made Brandon's job a lot easier. He could trot your Nick out to assuage anxieties about not so much the art itself but about questions that somebody might ask about a particular painting down the line. Then my cousin Randy came barging in. Well, I guess he's my what—step-cousin?"

"He's my cousin, too." Aimee nodded.

"Anyway, this was, what, four, five years ago? He'd just gotten out of prison and wanted to get into the kind of business Brandon was in, but more antiques and accessories than fine art. So Brandon trotted him around to estate sales, under-the-radar dealers, auctions and so forth."

"But how did he get hooked up with you?"

"Nancy. Paul's ex-wife. Randy's her son by a previous marriage. Anyway, Nancy called me. Could we give Randy a break, take him under our wing, give him a second chance, get him set up in the antiques business, blah, blah, blah. Would you like something, by the way? I can do coffee or tea, or maybe some dry sherry? It's not quite noon, but getting there."

"Sherry, sure, that would be fine," Mona replied. Aimee and Zoe nodded. "But hey, I thought Nancy and Randy didn't get along."

"Oho! Yes, everyone was indeed meant to think that, or rather, Mavis was, and by extension you, too, Aimee." Paula-Mickie took out four juice glasses and a cut-glass decanter from a battered sideboard cupboard, poured. Zoe and Mona stood and took the two glasses from her; Paula-Mickie returned to the table and gave Aimee hers.

"That was all part of Randy's plan. He wanted to go off on his own, distance himself from Nancy and Frank and Brandon, once they set him up with a little bit of know-how and some contacts. Just exactly why, I'm not sure. But I think he saw Nancy as maybe horning in on his turf, once she hooked up with Frank McGinnis and the forgery thing kicked in. I think he got nervous. I think now maybe they really *are* on the outs with each other. At least Randy seems to be trying to get into the archaeology business so he can go off on his own without the Nancy-Frank-Brandon cartel calling the shots."

"I … I just can't get my head around this. I mean, the whole time I've been at Charbonneau—I mean, most of the time, until this past fall, you've been … been Mickie Laird, there," Mona objected.

Paula-Mickie laughed. "So I was! And Paula Cortez! But I never liked the name 'Paula'. 'Mickie' was much more evocative, exotic. Oh, and by the way, you know the complaint has been withdrawn? My little dalliance was with a consenting adult. The complaint was frivolous to begin with. It was cooked up as an excuse for bowing to the wishes of the Grassers because they were steamed that Brandon was stupid enough not to get a second opinion on the Vermeer. But it would have been from your friend Nick if he had done!"

"And that would have been almost worse than no opinion!" offered Zoe. "So … so … the boxes…" She was determined to keep the story on track.

"Well, that was Hector's old collection, from what he called his cabinet of curiosities. Robert, my father, fell heir to it and then when he died it fell to me. Even though he left me and my mother and I hadn't seen him since I was a tiny tot."

"Including the skull," affirmed Zoe.

"Oh, yes, including the skull."

"And is that …? Is that really … that Virginia person?" queried Aimee.

Paula-Mickie shrugged. "Your guess is as good as mine. But yes, it is probably Virginia Grimm."

Mona shook her head slowly. "How grisly! And who decorated it that way?"

"Probably Robert. He was really fascinated with the Aztecs, wanted to try them on as his ancestors, rather than the conquistadors."

Aimee took a gulp of sherry. "And did he … did he …?"

"Kill her?" Paula-Mickie wrinkled her brow. "Again, who knows. But the scenario might be that he discovered her *in delicto flagrante*, maybe with a recluse-hermit guy, Smokey, that she used to get drugs from, she and Robert. Or maybe with somebody else."

"And Robert stabbed her in the face," declared Zoe.

"Well, maybe."

"Well, *somebody* stabbed her. We've confirmed that," stated Zoe.

"Well, okay. That's certainly a possibility."

"Then out of remorse, honored her as an Aztec ancestor!" exclaimed Aimee.

"So you were trying to get some kind of closure on Robert Cortez and Virginia Grimm?" queried Mona. "That's why you brought the boxes to us? But why *us*? Why not somebody local? And how did you know we'd investigate?"

Paula shook her head. "No. I had no interest in the skull or Virginia Grimm or who might have done what to her. But I thought that skull would get your attention. What I really wanted you to do was nail Brandon and his forgery scheme. I knew Brandon's successor—that's you, Dr. Dill—would have a keen interest in the forgery angle once you saw all those paintings hanging on Frank's wall. And I hoped that Dr. Pinto would tumble to the Suzanne Utrillo anomaly and between the two of you, you'd follow up on the address thing." She turned to Aimee. "I had no idea it would lead to him through you, Aimee. I mean, I knew you existed; I just didn't know how or why you'd have anything to do with the Charbonneau people."

"That's another story," stated Zoe. "Or another part of the story."

"But you're the one who pasted that bogus label onto the Podesta-Baldocchi box, hoping it would get us to Aimee's house in San Anselmo, headquarters for the Brandon-Frank-Nancy cartel," said Mona.

"Precisely. I thought if anybody could finger the forgery scam it would be you folks. And I thought the names Valadon and Utrillo would pique your curiosity."

"It did," affirmed Zoe. "Now, two questions. First of all, what tipped you off to the fact, or the probability, the suspicion, that there was a forgery thing going on? And second, what can you tell us about Dahlia?"

"Who?"

"There's this woman–I know her by several names, Dahlia, Jane Faulks, Cricencia Morgenhouse, but who knows what name she's using now. She's somehow in partnership with Brandon Laird and Frank McGinnis."

Paula-Mickie shook her head. "Can't help you there. I don't think I've run across her."

Zoe took a sip of sherry. "Okay. So the forgeries …"

"Well, every time we went there–not that I was there that often–there were paintings on the walls. A lot of them were Utrillos. I just happened to notice on one occasion that at least one of them was not the same one that had been hanging there a few months earlier. The story always was …"

"That Frank was storing them for their owner in his capacity as accountant." Aimee filled in.

"Right, right. I didn't say anything, but it got me thinking: If the Utrillos were constantly changing, what would that mean? Forgery could be the only answer. Somewhere there was someone cranking out Utrillos and that probable process seemed to be lasting an awfully long time!"

"Right. Not to change the subject, but what made you come here?" asked Aimee.

Paula-Mickie shrugged. "Where else? This place was going to rot. Nobody was living in it after Robert died. After Brandon and I split, I had no place else to go. And also," she added, "my–the student that ... that I became friends with, transferred to College of San Rafael. They have a very good program for... for people like him. God, I hate the term disabled! So, this isn't exactly close, but it's closer than eastern Washington."

"So, getting back to Robert. He lived here the whole time?" queried Aimee.

"He moved in shortly after he came here from Chicago, as far as I know, after he left me and my mother. From whom he never got a divorce, by the way. He lived in a commune in the hills for a year or so, then moved down here. He probably didn't have the legal right to take possession of the house, but nobody else was using it, so who was going to object?"

"So what would you have us do, what action did you hope we were going to take with regard to what was going on in San Anselmo?" asked Mona.

"Well, I thought at the very least you might get a look at those paintings, hung on the walls to season them. Do they still have the Utrillos up? Needless to say, I haven't been there for almost a year."

"Yes, the Utrillos are still--well, they're probably different ones–but yes, they're there and also a Modigliani and some Russells."

"Modigliani! Wow! They're really getting ambitious!"

"So here's one more thing." suggested Mona. "You know Mavis Samuelson supposedly had an accident. Fell down the stairs. Do you think it's possible she could have collapsed from having a poison fed to her in her tea?"

Paula-Mickie wrinkled her nose. "Whew! Where does that come from? I suppose it's possible. But who? Why?"

Zoe jumped in. "The idea is that …" Then she stopped herself *Oh. My. God! She thought. We—I—have got it all wrong!* She clamped her mouth shut.

Mona looked at Zoe strangely. "So why is Brandon still hanging around the college?"

"I think I can answer that," offered Mickie. "Brandon keeps partial files in two different places: on his home computer in his place in Pullman, and also on his office computer. It's like a kind of code. He can't keep all his contacts in his head, but he can put one part of a contact's information into one place, then the rest of it into another. Anybody accessing one file and not the other would find gibberish, but for Brandon, they're mnemonic devices."

"Has Brandon ever been here?" asked Zoe.

"Ummm … yeah, yes. We came here once, early on, when we were first married. Robert was still alive and John and Wendy were visiting with their kids from Sacramento, and Sandoval and Brenda were out here from Chicago. Kids camped out in the yard and the rest of us piled into these old drafty bedrooms with heavy sleeping bags! Then we came here again the summer right after Robert died. Brandon did quite a thorough recce–noting leaks here and there, gaps in the walls needing to be chinked. Asked what was going to happen to the place. I told him we all–the kids, grandkids--all owned it together so it would probably just sit until we all got together and decided to sell it, or not sell it, or whatever. I think now he might have been scoping it out for his operations. But he'd have had to somehow arrange for one of his fronts to buy it--Frank, maybe. But that was just about the time you moved out of San Anselmo and into the Trestle Glen house with Mavis. So what the hey, problem solved!"

Zoe's phone burped. "It's Ferguson!" She rose and retreated to the living room. "Yeah … no, I'm right close by … well, yeah, I suppose … wild! I've got lots to tell, but … really? Wow!... I know, you're nothing if not persevering … awesome … amazing … Far out! Yeah! I remember Cait and Robb going on about what a hoot she was with Jen and Thad–after they got to be friends–I mean Cait and Robb and Jen and Thad. Jen and Thad told Cait and Robb about how she practically ordered lunch and drinks for herself, like from a menu, when she made her transaction with them … Yeah, but what do we do, bust down the door with a battering ram and come storming in, shouting, 'Blackguards! Stay where you are! The gig's up!' And they say, 'Oh, gosh. Curses. Foiled again…?' You really think the folks in … where is it? Saint John's Wood? They're going to welcome us in with open arms, and say, 'Oh, we're so glad you're here to persuade us that this piece of art we're about to buy from Dahlia is a piece of forged junk?'…. You've got Dahlia on the brain … Hey, hey! Don't get all arsed … Yeah, yes. It's worth a try. I guess then they couldn't say, 'well, nobody tried to tell us …' You think so …? Yeah, I could probably recite it by heart … Okay, okay. Right now? … Address? Okay."

Zoe came back into the kitchen. "Ferguson's outside a house in San Francisco, a neighborhood called St. John's Wood Dahlia's in the house, with, probably, and a large object in a portmanteau. There's a chance to catch Dahlia out, if we move fast."

"Who?" queried Paula.

"It's a long story." Zoe replied.

"St. John's Wood. Isn't that in London?" puzzled Mona.

"It's Saint *Francis* Wood," corrected Paula-Mickie. "Very posh. Not quite Pacific Heights, but, " she shrugged, "I guess kind of like Trestle Glen. Subtle, but some big money there. What's going on in St. Francis Wood?"

"Well," continued Zoe. "I've asked a friend, a private investigator, to kind of keep tabs on your San Anselmo house, Aimee's house, for the last three months. Renting a different car each day, driving into the neighborhood, disguised as a woman! Different suit for each day of the week. Camera with telephoto lens, binocs. Today, Dahlia arrives in a taxi. Within the hour, she and Frank load two items into Frank's Toyota Camry, drive into the city to this address." She showed it to the others. "Ferguson wants me to turn up asap; says it's just the client's luck that I'm here because after the fact it would be much, much harder to do anything. They could sue, get the FBI in, yada, yada, but a big hassle for the client. But if we go in now, the client can back out before the sale goes through. So he thinks if he turns up on their doorstep with me, a forged art expert, ready to expose Nick's authentication certificate plastered to the back of whatever it is, without even looking at it, it might convince the client. Dahlia and Frank are caught red-handed. And Paula–can we commandeer you for our little caper?"

Paula-Mickie laughed. "Of course! I feel like I sort of started the whole thing–at least part of it, in some way! If there's a chance to catch Frank red-handed ..."

"So, Paula, could you drop me off at this Saint Francis Wood place?" asked Zoe. "Oh–and here's the other thing Ferguson said. About once a week sometimes more, one of them, or sometimes all of them, would go hauling off from the San Anselmo house up to Sonoma to a ranch. It seems Randy's involved too, Ferguson said. Sometimes a kind of rangy, lanky, younger guy turns up at San Anselmo, but mostly he seems to be at this ranch place, on weekends. And that might be Randy. Anyway, Ferguson thinks something's being built at this ranch–construction crews and trucks, building materials, cement truck–and he thinks what they're doing is building a secure fortress where they're going to move their operations to, out of the San Anselmo house, because they've been found out there."

"But how did Ferguson get onto them? Did you sic him on them?" puzzled Mona.

"No. That's a good point. Maybe he tracked down Dahlia and she led him to them?"

"No. *I* did," said Mickie-Paula.

Mona's jaw dropped "How and why did this Ferguson guy find *you*?"

"Hey–later," interjected Zoe. "I wanna hear this story but I've gotta boogie. Can you get me to this St. Francis Wood place, Paula? I'll get Ferguson to ferry me back to Trestle Glen, or maybe up to San Anselmo depending on what you guys find up there."

"Sure, sure."

"Good. So. Aimee and Mona, can you see what's going on up at San Anselmo?"

"Sure. Get in touch with us once you and your Ferguson have things sorted," said Aimee.

~⌒~

SAN FRANCISCO
GARETH FOSTER, MARTHA FOSTER, "GWEN AUCHENPAUGH", FRANK MCGINNIS;
BRIAN FERGUSON, ZOE DILL
4:17 PM

Gareth Foster reflected. he was pleased with the decisions he'd made in life, not the least of which was to accept a buyout as Eubanks Coffee's CEO just at the time when all the organic-fair-trade-vanilla-roast-Starbuck's-Seattle-etcetera were making inroads into the market and the board had wanted to blame it all on him. Well, fine. He'd said yes. At fifty-five he was able to get out, get up, and make more good decisions: such as to getting cautiously, judiciously into stocks and real estate just as everybody else was getting out because they were afraid the underwater mortgages and bank bankruptcies were going to topple like dominoes onto them. Another good choice was to listen to Martha's advice, and to get majorly into twentieth century continental art. "The pictures brighten up the place, don't you think?" Martha said periodically, when they were having their pre-dinner drinks. Martha, his wife–that was another good decision, made just a little too late for them to have a family, but good nonetheless. And of course the hous. It beat living out of a footlocker like he'd done for thirty years.

Now he looked around at the Kandinskys, the Delaunays, the Soutine. *Yes*, he thought. *Additions in the same vein will be good decisions*. The caterers had just brought in bacon-wrapped shrimp, pigs-in-a-blanket wantons, open-faced cracked crab and tapenade sandwiches, and avocado crostini. "Oh," said one of his two guests, "another martini to add zing to these yummy deliciocities would do just nicely."

"Mr. McGinnis?"

"Another Anchor dark, if you don't mind. I'm strictly a beer man." Martha, Mrs. Gareth Foster sat demurely on a damask-upholstered chair, sipping a hearty port. She shook her head when the caterer looked at her.

"Me too," said Foster, holding up his empty bottle. The doorbell rang. "Mrs. Poarcher? Could you get that, please?" A caterer returned from the kitchen with the martini on the rocks, McGinnis' beer, and a Fat Tire for Gareth. Gareth could hear some kind of commotion at the front door: voices rising. He rose and entered the vestibule.

Poarcher had just slammed the door shut. "There are some peculiar people out there, one with a suspicious way o' talkin' and a young lass who looks no better than she ought to be."

Gareth chuckled. Strange lingo? Poarcher should talk. "What did they want?"

"They still want. They want in. They're goin' on about how you, sir, are about to purchase a fraud and they want you to hear reasons to reconsider."

Gwen Auchenpaugh, for that was the name she was now using, had appeared at Gareth's side. "Oh, I think I know who they are. Their opinions may prove useful." She looked up at Gareth. "I think you'll do all right by letting them in."

Gareth Foster nodded. Poarcher opened the door. "We're sorry to bother you," began the man, glaring at Gwen Auchenpaugh. "I'm Brian Ferguson, private investigator, and this is …" Ferguson stuck out his hand. Gareth Foster took his perfunctorily, then let it drop.

"Zoe Dill," offered Zoe, doing the same. "Dr. Zoe Dill. I'm an art historian. I teach at Sacajawea and Jean-Baptiste Charbonneau College in Eastern Washington, the Tri-Cities area."

"Better than that, she's an expert on frauds and forgeries," added

Ferguson, dipping his head in what Zoe thought was a bit of a pompous, know-it-all nod.

"Well, Ferguson! You finally decided to show yourself!" exclaimed Gwen Auchenpaugh. "I knew you were lurking about somewhere! Are you going to be of assistance to us once again?"

"I was, as you put it, Dahlia, of assistance to you only under duress and for a specific purpose."

Gareth Foster turned to Gwen Auchenpaugh. "Dahlia? Who's Dahlia? You know these people?"

"Oh, my yes," Gwen assured him. "Ferguson likes to use that nickname for me. He says I'm just like a great big many-petaled, flamboyant flower; blooming larger than life. He and Ms Dill like to follow me around. As usual, they're a little johnny-come-lately-on-the-scene, but they may have some interesting things to say."

"Well, uh, come on in. I'm Gareth Foster." Gareth stuck out his hand first to Ferguson, then to Zoe. Each shook it. He ushered them into the living room, followed by Poarcher. "And this is my wife, Martha. Martha? These are a couple of art experts invited here by Miss Auchenpaugh to give us their expert opinion on the two items that she has on offer to us."

Martha Foster gave a wave with her hand. "Oh! 'Scuse me if I don't get up, but I'm planted in this chair and don't feel like uprooting!" She giggled.

And this is Frank McGinnis"

Zoe took a few paces toward the portmanteau that was sitting on the floor, propped against a large, overstuffed chair. From the portmanteau's interior stared the hollow eyes of a *Katsina* mask, similar to the one Zoe had seen in a different living room in a different house in a different place, three years previously, and to the mask on Dora Harris' wall, and to masks that she had seen on the bodies of dancers in a ceremonial ritual in a Pueblo village. On the chair, propped against the back was, not an Utrillo or the Modigliani that she had expected to see, or maybe even one of the Charles Russells, but rather, the Foujita print, from the San Anselmo house. Frank McGinnis was standing to the left of the chair. Gareth Foster, Gwen Aughenpaugh and Brian Ferguson clustered behind her.

Dahlia-Gwen intoned from the group's rear, "Dr. Dill can vouch for the authenticity of this piece of art. And she can probably also give us her expert opinion on the provenance of this fine Foujita print."

Gareth broke the silence. "Well?"

Zoe said quietly, "The item in the portmanteau is indeed a sacred mask, a ritual ceremonial object used in Native American ceremonies. It was undoubtedly, at one time, stolen from one of those villages, possibly spent some time in a museum or a private collection, then was put up for auction in Paris in April 2013. It should, rightfully, be returned to its origins, to the Puebloan people."

"Oh!" said Gareth, with profundity. "Did you know this, Miss Auchenpaugh?"

She shrugged. "I just thought when Mr. McGinnis mentioned you might like to branch out into something truly primitive, this might fill the bill. I'm an art dealer, not an ethnologist."

Gareth Foster was not a religious man, but he liked to watch programs on the Discovery channel that showed rituals of primitive peoples. *Amazing that they were still performed, in this day and age,* he thought once again, as he did so every time he took in his mini-art gallery. The art hanging on the walls of his house reminded him of those primitive ceremonies. "Ah! Yes! I understand. If it were to be returned, would that be a tax write-off?"

"I suppose ..." Zoe said in a small voice.

"You know, we weren't intending to make any purchase today," temporized Gareth. "Mr. McGinnis was just showing us what he might be able to get for us. Really, this was meant as just a getting-to-know-you session, getting acquainted." He gestured at McGinnis. "He brought this pretty print just as a teaser. But we might actually like to have this little prize today."

"Yes," trilled Mrs. Foster, holding up her glass. "We've gotten to know this splendid little Fouji and we rather like him." A caterer refilled it with

Amontillado. "Getting to know you, getting to know all about you," she half-sang, half chanted. Zoe figured she was half-knackered, or getting there. "Friendly get-together, with snacks!" She raised her glass again, this time in a kind of toast.

"But would you care to cast your opinion as to the genuineness of this Foujita print? You may be familiar with it," offered Gwen-Dahlia smugly.

Zoe walked slowly over to the print. She had a sinking feeling this would not have a Nick Taylor certificate on its back. She lifted it, turned it over. On the back was glued what looked like part of a paper bag, with stains on it. She read out loud the inscription, in somewhat sloppy handwriting: "'Signed and numbered by Foujita, here at Kiki's and Man Ray's studio, 31b rue Campagne-Premiere, Paris, France, witnessed by (signed) Jed Kiley, 05 May 1925, with lots of good cheer.'" Zoe could imagine Jed Kiley, whoever that was, drunk as a skunk or stoned or both, painstakingly guiding his hand to write the inscription. "This looks to be quite genuine," noted Zoe quietly. She turned it back to its front, placed it back on the chair.

Zoe could tell Ferguson was doing a small boil and might explode at any moment. "I think we should be going," she said to Gareth Foster, nodding at Martha, Gwen, and Frank. "We have another expertizing to do. Nice meeting you all."

Outside, Zoe followed Ferguson to his illegally-parked and now-ticketed car. They got in. "We've bodged it. This was a ruse. Dahlia bested me once again." He shook his head. Ferguson was obviously angry at having been mocked with a set-up, totally fooled by a carefully constructed fizzle.

"Why?"

"I think we were led onto this red herring because the really important events are happening back at the house in San Anselmo."

"Aimee–well, you don't know Aimee–but you know Mona. Mona and

Aimee were headed there when Paula and I left Brookdale. Paula's following up. I would have supposed that you didn't know Paula either, but I think you actually do. Anyway, that's where they were headed. So I guess we'll all converge on the San Anselmo house?" Zoe phoned Aimee, then Mona, but both went to voice mail. She didn't have Paula's number.

SAN ANSELMO: AIMEE, MONA; BRANDON LAIRD; ZOE, FERGUSON

On the way up to San Anselmo, Ferguson caught Zoe up on what he had been doing since they had last talked in December. He had gone to Jackson, Wyoming, made the rounds of galleries, and eventually tracked down an address for Frank McGinnis, in San Anselmo. "I could have told you *that*," said Zoe.

"Aye! But here's the important part: I continued surveillance …"

"As a woman?" interrupted Zoe.

"Aye, as a woman and as several other personages, in several different vehicles, cruising around the neighborhood, and occasionally following one of *their* vehicles to another destination. And the important thing is that I spotted Dahlia in and out of the San Anselmo house and the other destination, in and out of the various vehicles driven by Frank McGinnis and another bloke I must assume was your friend and colleague Brandon Laird."

Zoe frowned. "He's not my friend or my colleague. I don't even know him."

"All right. Your colleagues' former colleague and maybe also former friend. At any rate, the important thing is that I was able to keep tabs on Dahlia."

"Which is how you were able to follow her and Frank to …"

"Precisely. To Gareth Foster." He shook his head. "And it was a total set-up! Ah dinna know she must ha'e been havin' a tail on me as well."

Zoe speculated but didn't say anything. *Could the tail have been one Nicholas Zachary Taylor? Ferguson had never met him and wouldn't necessarily recognize him as a tail.* "So you've been able to finance yourself for four months of non-income?"

"Oh, well. I've gotten a few little jobs here and there. And you know, that annual bonus I've been getting from Assurance Associates for leveraging the payback to them from that insurance fraud has done nicely for me."

The insurance fraud in the faked disappearance of ten million dollars' worth of Mimbres pottery, stored in a fortified mine shaft and dribbled out slowly to jet-setter consumers who turned a blind eye to ethical considerations, thought Zoe. *Grave goods that never should have been dug up in the first place.*

SAN ANSELMO. 6:35 PM

When they turned onto the street leading to the cul-de-sac on which the San Anselmo house was located, Ferguson braked and pulled over to the verge. A black-and-white was parked on the other side of the street, another car a couple of lengths behind it. Zoe recognized it as Paula's. In the middle of the street was wreckage. Two cars. One of them was Aimee's SUV. Both cars looked irretrievably disabled. Aimee was standing by her car, her face streaked with the remains of tears and Mona and Paula each had an arm around Aimee's waist. Ferguson and Zoe climbed out of their vehicle. The cop in the police car looked up briefly through the windscreen, then went back to scribbling on his pad or his phone or whatever it was. Zoe ran to Aimee. "What happened?"

Aimee gulped, sobbed. "He rammed me!" Then Zoe noticed Brandon Laird standing on the sidewalk, leaning against a light pole. As he strode over, he remarked, "It was an accident. Yeah, her car is wrecked, but so is mine. The airbags worked. Nobody's hurt. The cop isn't even going to write us tickets. No traffic laws violated. It's just one of those things that happened. Something for the insurance companies. We're just waiting for the tow trucks."

A fuming Aimee yelled at him. "You're a liar! You deliberately rammed me! You could have *KILLED* me! You bastard! You're a *bastard*! *Shit on rye*! You're running a forgery scam out of *MY* house! I'm going to have you evicted!"

"You can't have me evicted. *I* don't live in your house." Brandon Laird did not yell. He projected his voice loudly, as if he were lecturing in an assembly hall. "It's my business partner, Frank McGinnis, who lives in your house."

"Which I have a feeling now may be a moot point," remarked Ferguson. He walked over to the back of Aimee's vehicle, squatted down, then rolled onto his back, slid under it, then slid back out. "Aye." He stood up, walked over to where Aimee, Mona, and Zoe were now huddled. "Dahlia learns from experience. Or maybe she was always savvy about tracking. There's a GPS transponder affixed to the underside of the carriage of your vehicle. At some point somebody installed it and she, or they have been tracking you ever since."

"How did they get it there? You've got a garage," queried Zoe.

"Yah, but I work, in Emeryville." Aimee sniffled. "I park in the parking lot. I guess they, or somebody followed me there and popped it on."

"I was pretty shocked when I came on all this wreckage." Paula had been silent until then. "I walked up to the house. It's only a few blocks. There's nobody there. What do we do now?"

"Yes, and I'll wager there's nothing in there either, except furniture and crockery and toasters. Absolutely nothing incriminating. It's all been moved to a ranch outside of Sonoma," affirmed Ferguson. "You all stay here. There's the chance, just the chance, that there may still be something we can do up there. Perhaps you can take Ms …"

"Garrison. Aimee Garrison. We haven't met." She flicked a tear from her left eye, stuck out her hand.

Ferguson took it, pumped it. "Brian Ferguson, at your service. Ah would ordinarily say it's a pleasure, but these dunna be pleasurable circumstances."

"Can we meet you back in Trestle Glen?" asked Zoe. She was puzzled by the fact how and why Paula and Ferguson seemed to already know one another. "Paula, can you take Aimee and Mona home, once the tow truck has done its thing?"

"Sure thing!"

"It's probably important to check out this ranch place," insisted Zoe. She and Ferguson did so. Binoculars and the telephoto lens revealed two vehicles parked outside a barn, but otherwise nothing seemed to be going on. One of the vehicles was a small Budget rental truck. Ferguson nodded. "Aye. I'm quite sure while we were on the wild good chase and Aimee was being gotten out of the way, the principles loaded up the remover van with portmanteaus containing masks and portfolios containing forged artwork, and transported them here to the newly-constructed storage vault."

"Yeah. Apparently there's a storeroom in the basement of the San Anselmo house that's been made off-limits with locks and alarm codes," agreed Zoe. "So this is it. They've gotten away with it. Obviously, three years ago, when we were wondering whether or not Dahlia had the other thirteen masks she purported to have, she did. She *did* have them. And she's been selling them off, one by one to Gareth Foster, Dora Harris … who knows to who else? And now if there are any masks left, they're over there in that ranch house, along with a lot of forged art. Look," said Zoe, turning to Ferguson, "instead of staying in whatever crummy motel you've been bunking in, why don't you take me back to Aimee's house in Trestle Glen. I'll bet anything she'll be glad to have you can stay there too. You can park in the driveway," continued Zoe. "She's got lots of room. We can hash this all out tomorrow."

It was 8:30 by the time they negotiated the bridge, drove through Oakland, and drew up in front of the Trestle Glen house. Paula's car was parked in the driveway, but when Aimee opened the door and looked out, she said, "Hey, I'll open the garage and Paula can store her car inside. Ha! I won't need that garage for a while. Turns out my car is totally, *totally* totaled."

"I'm really sorry, Aimee!" said Zoe, wrapping her arm around Aimee's middle and giving her a short embrace.

"Aye. Ah feel somewhat responsible. Dinna have me thinking cap on when ah was gettin' so focused on stalking Dahlia."

"Aimee, can Ferguson stay here? We can figure out all the sleeping arrangements."

"Sure! Come on in. Kenny picked up a couple of pizzas–there's a veggie one. Plenty left over. I'll heat 'em up in the microwave."

They entered the living room. Paula and Mona were seated on the sofa. Kenny Yarborough was sitting on the couch with Mona and Paula. They all adjourned to the dining room and sat around it, while Aimee set places for Ferguson and Zoe and busied herself in the kitchen.

"Before we collapse for the night," said Zoe, "I've gotta run something by you all." Talk about acting on a false premise! I think I've–we've really gotten it all wrong! We've been trying to pin two poisonings, or at least one, on the wrong, wrong person, or persons. It's not Randy. It's not Madison. It's Nancy!!" She pounded the table with her fist and began laughing almost hysterically. "*So, so wrong*! Now we know that the supposed falling out between Nancy and Randy was a ruse. They've been in cahoots the whole time. Nancy gets rid of Mavis. Then a few months later, Randy spots Joel at Charbonneau on one of his visits to Pennfield. He tells Nancy; Nancy goes into attack mode."

She turned to Aimee. "Aimee, Nancy visited Mavis?"

Aimee shrugged. "Yeah …"

"How often?"

"Oh, once every week or two."

"So she could have–most likely did–visit Mavis within a week of her death. Maybe had visited every week for the previous month."

"Oh! Are you going where I think you're going with this?" queried Kenny.

"Probably. It was *Nancy* who put the henbane in Mavis' tea. And it was *you*" Zoe thrust her fork at Aimee "that she was after as much as Mavis!"

"*Me*?! You mean she wanted to kill *me*?"

"Probably not. She wouldn't have been sure you'd drink that much tea. Mainly, she was trying to make sure that you would inherit this house sooner than later. And with Mavis out of the way, you would do so. With this house, you wouldn't need, or want, the San Anselmo house."

Aimee nodded. "Leaving Nancy and Frank to turn my house into a forgery factory."

"And Joel? How and why did she want to get rid of Joel?" queried Mona.

"That's something we have to check. Can you get him on the phone, Mona? I know it's late, but only just 9:30. He's got still be up."

She did so. "Joel. This is Mona. I know you're deep in the heart of grading. But this is important. Really important. Please pick up or call me right back." He picked up. "Yeah. Hi! Well. Well. It's going well but not so well. Long story. Aimee's brand-new vehicle got totaled, but we finally found a Cortez and who dumped the boxes ... Yeah, yeah. But later. Unbelievable story. But right now we need some info from you. Remember that estate sale where you got the spoons, my spoons? Well, you said you got them from a guy who got most of the other stuff in the estate? ... Yeah. A sort of young guy, but going bald?..." She looked at Aimee. Aimee nodded. "Well that was Randy, Aimee, her cousin ... Yeah, small world indeed. But here's the sixty-four-dollar question. Was he all alone? Or was he with somebody? Yeah ... Yeah... What did they look like? ... Wow! That sounds like...! Yeah ... Yeah ... That's the guy. And the other three guys ... Ha! ... Hey–will you be down next Saturday? We'll be back at Charbonneau ... Great! We'll show you pictures of both of them ... The second guy? Older, white hair, kind of heavy-set? Right. And the third guy? Younger, not much hair ... Okay. And the fourth guy? ... The other guy, the shorter guy, Randy's age? Tall, full head of nice, dark hair, spiffy-looking? ... Yeah. Hey, hey, Joel–gotta go. Happy grading. We'll fill you in on all this in a week." She rang off.

"There were four of them. At first, he thought the younger guy, Randy, was just the bidding dogsbody for the older guy. Well guess who the older guy was."

"Frank," affirmed Aimee.

"Yes. And the other guy, I'll bet anything, was Brandon Laird!" said Mona. "Remember, Joel often gets here on Thursday afternoon before I'm out of class. Orla lets him into my office and we meet there, then go home. In the meantime, he doodles around on his laptop or his iPad. Well, can't you just imagine it? Joel, hail-fellow-well-met encounters Brandon in the hall on one of the occasions Brandon came into his office? Or in the loo? 'Hey, hi there! Remember me? From the estate sale? The spoons? Blah, blah, blah.' He may have even said something about the Léger from the sale ending up here and isn't that a coincidence, yada, yada, yada."

"And there was a fourth guy," said Zoe. "Youngest of the three. Spiffy. Confident-looking. Joel said he had that kind of in-the-know look that people have when they know they're players but nothing is at risk."

Mona nodded. "Your Nick."

"He. Is. Not My Nick!!" said Zoe emphatically.

"Yeah," okay, sorry," said Mona. "But anyway, so there you have them. The art finder, the art broker, the supplier of forgeries and fake antiques, and the authenticator."

Zoe picked up the narrative. "And Brandon freaks. Or Randy freaks, especially if *he* encountered Joel, which he might have done. Now Joel's encountered two of the four, here at Charbonneau. And he tells Nancy, and she freaks. Or they all freak. Because now that art fraud detector Zoe is here, and art fraud is written all over Brandon's professional persona, Vermeer leads to Léger leads to Brandon leads to Nick-the-authenticator and to Randy-the-supposedly-wayward-son-who's-thick-as-thieves-with-mom-the-partner-with-the-forger-finder! They were probably afraid that eventually I, or somebody would turn up on their doorstep asking questions about just where that Léger came from. Which is, of course, just what happened! Even though it didn't happen the way they thought it would.

"I arrived at Randy for the miscreant through a pattern that seemed to underlie all the misdeeds, but didn't." Zoe shook her head slowly. "It was

Nancy, not Randy, who put the henbane into Mavis' tea, probably days, or maybe weeks before she tumbled to her death. The stuff built up in her system. It was only a fluke that Randy happened to come over with his Chinese take-out and fixed her tea that particular night. He may have known nothing about it. And acting on a tip from Randy, it's *Nancy* who goes steaming up to North Wash U, pops Joel's office door open, slides the desk drawer open, pops open the canister, dumps in the henbane, mixes it all up. Maybe on a Friday when Joel's here, or she waits for him to leave on Thursday–who would notice with all sorts of people, students, faculty around?"

"Shit!" exclaimed Kenny. "Because she, Nancy would never expect you guys to phone Mavis! Mavis was dead! And you'd never come up with 'Aimee Garrison' because … well, how could you? Just a fluke she never got rid of the landline and the answering machine."

"But once I did get a hold of you, Aimee, I pursued what I thought was a semblance of order despite the *assumed* causes of events being rooted in completely *different* causes."

Aimee put her arm on the table and cupped her chin. "So Nancy's a murderer twice over," she said glumly.

"Yes! She poisoned Mavis and tried to kill Joel just on the off chance that he might have put you onto Brandon and the estate sale and the Léger!" Mona was angrier than Zoe had ever seen her. "Why hasn't she tried to kill *you*, Zoe? Or all of us?"

"I don't think she tried to kill Joel. I think she wanted to confuse him, keep his mind on his supposed illness, off Brandon and frauds. Yeah, maybe with luck he drives off the road into a ditch, gets banged up, but probably doesn't get killed. Just gets put out of commission for a while. Which is sort of what happened. Maybe by the time he gets back on track, Brandon has completely transitioned out of here. And maybe she just couldn't figure out how to get to me without being too obvious."

"Now it *is* late," observed Kenny. "I've gotta run damage control tomorrow in the showroom. Bedtime for me."

"I was going to take off as soon as you got here," said Paula, "but Mona and Aimee have been persuading me that I'm part of the–what did she call it? The Baker Street irregulars? And so I should stay over and tomorrow morning we–you–can begin to sort all this," said Paula.

"Zoe and I can bunk together," offered Mona. "I mean, I think we'd kind of like to, and Paula can have the room I was staying in."

"There're four bedrooms upstairs, so you get one all to yourself, Ferguson, if you want to stay," offered Aimee in a nearly inaudible voice. "Meantime, I'm, Kenny and I are going to bed. I'm zonked."

They did so, then climbed the stairs. Mona and Zoe each stripped off their clothes and crawled into bed. "I'm too tired to ..." began Mona. "But I want to be held."

"That's fine," responded Zoe. "I've got my period anyway, so it would be messy." *I'm over-tired* she thought, *but the adrenalin won't quit.*

They melded together like spoons. Zoe placed her fingers strategically and cupped Mona's breast. "Do you mind if I rub, just a little?"

"Please," replied Mona. "But I'll just melt away into sleep, if you don't mind."

18

MONDAY STARTED SLOW. Kenneth was the first to stir, leaving the house quietly at 7:30 in the morning. When Zoe and Mona came down two hours later, they found Paula in the kitchen, crunching through her second slice of raisin bread with butter and draining her second cup of coffee. "Ferguson left about a half-hour ago," she told them. "He's going to run surveillance on the gang again today, but he said it's kind of useless because, like, his cover's blown."

"Tell me about it," exclaimed Zoe. "We're all blown!"

"But Ferguson has a plan. Maybe a plan," said Paula

Mona and Zoe poured coffee for themselves, put raisin bread slices into the toaster, and sat at the kitchen table with Paula. Aimee appeared at ten. She wasn't dressed. Her hair was sticking up and out in six different directions. Her face was puffy. She slumped down into the free chair.

"Coffee?" offered Paula getting up and reaching for the pot. Aimee shook her head. She opened the fridge and took out the raisin bread. "Raisin bread?"

"Not hungry." Aimee rose, walked into the parlour, opened the pocket doors to the living room, entered it, and flopped face down on the sofa.

Zoe thought she recognized the signs. Depression taking hold. She'd seen it before, in college. Girls coming to class in the same baggy sweatpants and hoodie day after day; sitting in class fiddling with their phones; not taking a single note; not really comprehending anything happening in the classroom; and then they were gone. Flunked out, or worse, Zoe had assumed. And she knew Aimee had been there, done that. She hadn't said, but Zoe wouldn't be surprised if there was a suicide attempt or two in her post-parents' death-and-boarding-school past. Given Aimee's history, it was evident she was regressing to her twelve-year-old self. They couldn't let Aimee go there. Zoe couldn't let her go there.

Zoe rose, made a quick gesture with her head, then trailed Aimee into the living room. Mona and Paula followed. The three of them squeezed onto the small couch.

"Everything's *fucked*!" Aimee turned over on her back. She drew up her knees, spread her legs. Her nightgown billowed out above them. Zoe was glad Ferguson had already departed. *This is an Aimee who is not mindful of the moment she is in*, thought Zoe.

"My car is gone, my phone is fucked, my aunt, my *good* aunt is dead, and my *other* aunt, *that bitch has gotten away with murder!*"

"You mean Nancy," affirmed Zoe. Aimee didn't reply. "What happened to your phone?"

"Got banged around in the crash."

"The tow truck guys said both cars are essentially wrecked," explained Mona. "The front ends were smashed. No steering; axle bent. It'd take thousands to repair."

"And Brandon banged into you to prevent you from getting to the house, so you wouldn't catch them loading up all the goodies into a rental truck. Ferguson speculates that all the incriminating evidence has been removed. If you went back now all you'd find would be bad taste in furniture," said Zoe.

"My car's totaled, my phone's fucked, my aunt's dead, my cousin's a self-ish, conniving bastard, his mother's a murderer," Aimee cried angrily, then sobbed, "and Kenny's lost his job!"

"*What? Why?*" exclaimed Zoe.

"He's all but lost it. Payless is going under," said Aimee, staccato.

"But it's a huge chain!" objected Zoe.

"So is Sears. Look what happened to them."

"Sears is still sort of around. But look at Monky Ward," supplied Paula. "That's a better example."

"Monkey who?" queried Aimee.

"Montgomery Ward. Long-gone department store chain. Huge." replied Paula.

"*You guys are bad luck!*" Aimee spat. "*It all started with you, all of you.*" She glared at Paula, Zoe, and Mona in turn. "Your fucking asshole husband, you two sticking your noses in, bringing 'round that phony detective …" Aimee was heaving with sobs, her body turned away from them, her face buried in the sofa's back cushions.

Yes, thought Zoe, *definitely diving into depression. Lashing out. Going destructive and self-destructive.*

Zoe rose, walked the few paces to the sofa, sat down on the floor, and started lightly massaging Aimee's back. "Do you want us to leave?" she asked softly.

Aimee wrenched her around so she was facing Zoe. Through great, heaving sobs, she choked out a strangled reply: "No, no! Don't leave! You're the only things I've got left!"

Zoe turned and grabbed Aimee's left shoulder and pulled, so that Aimee's head was cradled on Zoe's shoulder. It was an awkward pose; soon they'd both be on the floor, but it had its effect. Aimee straightened and slid down off the sofa, next to Zoe on the floor. They repositioned so they were both sitting with their backs against the sofa's dust ruffle. Zoe put her arm around Aimee and hugged her to her. Paula was standing over them, offering Aimee a box of tissues.

"You've still got Kenny. And Kenny hasn't lost his job *yet*," offered Zoe. "With his experience, surely he'll pick up another managerial job."

"Yeah." Aimee blew her nose, wiped her eyes. "Yeah. He'll be okay. I mean, he can live with me here and he'll get unemployment. It was a stressful job anyway. He's better than that. I mean, he's talented and sensitive. Being a manager sucks."

"He could go back to school. Get a degree in something else. Something he really likes," suggested Paula.

"Yeah. He could get a degree in art history!" Mona laughed softly.

"Yeahhhh!" trilled Zoe. "He could get a degree in art history and go on wild goose chases running after forgers and traffickers in illicit objects!" She and Mona broke into giggle fits.

Aimee started with a sob, but then also broke into great guffaws and giggles, almost hysterically. "Oh … oh … oh!"

Paula had reseated herself on the small couch next to Mona. "And you know, your input into this whole complicated situation is important, could be crucial. These two have to go back to jobs and put this on hold. You've got time and flexibility. I do too, up to a point. I don't pay rent.

And I'm getting some help from … friends. If you guys are the Baker Street irregulars, I can want to join!"

"Ferguson explained a lot to me this morning. He's got a plan," continued Paula. "He ran through your and his experience, Zoe, at the home of Gareth and Martha Foster and the reason for the ruse of taking away your attention from the San Anselmo house while Nancy, Brandon Laird, and probably Randy scuttled away with anything and everything incriminating, trucking it up to a building that Ferguson described as a 'barn within a barn' that's constructed at the ranch outside of Sonoma. Ferguson only decided to follow up on the Cortez-skull mystery because he was getting pretty bored sitting around waiting for something to happen in San Anselmo."

"Hey, something that's puzzled me--you guys seem to already know each other. How so?" asked Zoe.

"Ha! He took you seriously when you said offhand you wanted to find Paula Cortez. So he found Paula Cortez by examining property tax records for *Hector* Cortez. There were only two, the house on Paxton Avenue, Oakland and the Brookdale house. And he found that for the last two years, one Paula Cortez had taken over paying the taxes from Sandoval Cortez. He followed his hunch, and it brought him here."

"Why didn't we think of that?" pondered Zoe.

"No matter. Ha! He discovered Paula Cortez," Paula responded.

"So you've been following us following you and Robert and Hector Cortez through Ferguson's following us! Why didn't he tell us?"

"He decided it was more to the point for you to investigate the San Anselmo house rather than getting detoured to me. He didn't–still doesn't–know I'm the former Mickie Laird. He just knows I was one of the Cortezes. You didn't need to know I was Mickie Laird to get a handle on what was going on there. Truth to tell, I haven't particularly wanted that gang to know I'm here. I mean, I know a few things about Brandon and I remember Nancy and Randy from years ago, but I've never encountered any of these other people in the mix–Frank, this Dahlia person, and what's his name?"

"Nick," supplied Zoe. "And Just how Dahlia, now calling herself Gwen, and I think the last name is something like Ochenpaw–got into the Nancy-Randy-Frank circle is still unclear, I mean, even to Ferguson. But here's a theory: after the kerfuffle in Santa Fe, Dahlia was able to disappear. But one of the principles–well, not quite–the lover boy of one of the principles–held a sale, actually a kind of auction, of the stuff in his gallery. My sort-of-pseudo-auntie, Coco, went to it. She said Dahlia's partner, or guy Friday, or whatever he was, a guy named Adrian, was there and helping out. He and the gallery proprietor, Plumm, seemed chummy. Plumm then moved out of town. Coco's idea was that Adrian went with him. Plumm is gay. Where would you go if you were a gay guy in the rough-and-tumble frontier west? You'd head for civilization! San Francisco! And would Dahlia be far behind? Maybe not! They may not have been very public about it, but my guess is that Dahlia and Adrian have kept in touch.

"So if Dahlia still had the masks from the Paris auction–and now it's pretty certain that she did–where would she find contacts who could put her in touch with possible customers? At auctions and estate sales! And who's she gonna meet there? Randy or maybe Frank or maybe even Brandon or maybe all three. I don't know how long Frank McGinnis has been in the forgery business but one thing forgers need is seasoned canvases. If you're faking early-to-twentieth-century works you need canvases from that time period. Frank goes to auctions, like Bonham's, and bids on bulk lots of okay but not well-known artists who painted in that time period. Either Frank or the forger scrapes the canvases, and voila…."

"Bob's your uncle!" completed Mona.

Zoe noted that Aimee had at one point tuned back in and had been following the conversation with interest. *Whew!* Zoe thought. *That's so good!*

Now Aimee piped up. "Can you really do that? I mean, how easy is that to do?"

"Easier than you'd think, with solvents and a palette knife. And you'd be surprised how many artists reuse canvases: they may start a painting, don't like it, scrape it, paint something else over it."

"So what's Ferguson's plan?" queried Mona.

"He was up late last night" replied Paula. "Well, you might as well know, I was up with him! He discovered, again through property tax records, that the place where the goodies are stashed, the ranch belongs to a Francis and Frances Giacometti."

"Francis and Frances? And Giacometti? For real?" giggled Aimee.

"Yeah. Isn't that a hoot? He's Francis with an 'i' and she's Frances with an 'e,'" responded Paula.

"Hey, not so strange. I knew a couple people when I was at the Art Institute, Betty Jones and Nero Jones," offered Mona. "They seated us in the first basic class alphabetically by last name. So guess who ended up sitting next to each other? They decided they liked what they saw and got married, not even having to go through a name change or the hyphenated thing."

"And I remember reading about a nineteenth-century English guy with the hyphenated name, Hughes-Hughes. He married a cousin and so their kids were Hughes-Hughes Hughes-Hughes."

"Hughes squared," quipped Mona.

"No!" shrieked Aimee. "And if *they* had a kid and named him Hugh, he'd be something like Hugh Hughes-Hughes Hughes-Hughes!"

"Okay, okay, okay, you guys, enough," Zoe temporized. "Enough."

"And so?" asked Aimee, swallowing her giggles.

Paula chuckled. "Right! Anyway, his idea is to appeal to their better natures, and bring them in on doing the surveilling. He pointed out that none of you–us–can do it because we're all known to one or more of the gang. And now that *his* cover is blown, he is too. Even with disguises, they're know who it was driving around, lurking around. His idea is that the Giacomettis can do so."

"Yeah, and so what?" Aimee folded her arms on her chest. *She's still in negative space*, thought Zoe.

"He wants to catch the evil-doers in the act of selling a forgery," said Paula.

"Right!" affirmed Zoe. "See, until they actually collect money, they're not breaking any law. It's not illegal to paint something that looks like it was painted by somebody else. It's not illegal to have such paintings. But the minute you try to pass it off as having been painted by somebody else, and you do it for money, then you've committed an illegal act."

"And what about murdering Aunt Mavis? And trying to murder your… your …" Aimee looked at Mona.

"Poisoning Dr. Joel Curwin, associate professor of anthropology at Northern Washington University," supplied Mona.

Zoe nodded. "Right. Two probable murders that we can't prove. Well, the strategy is this: you confront the miscreants with the circumstantial evidence that they've done something bad. They protest and stamp their feet. You point out that even if such-and-such can't be proven, you can wreck their reputations, in this case, in the fine art market. It was a substantial mistake on Dahlia's–or Gwen's, as she's calling herself now–her and Frank's mistake to have led Ferguson and me to the Fosters. The Fosters undoubtedly have friends. They're connected. He probably belongs to a club. You let it be known that they were burned–or let them know that the folks they thought were going to supply them with fine art were prepared to burn them–and Frank and Brandon and Randy will never do another sale. He thinks this is also going to work with Madison Canter. Confronting her with the circumstantial evidence that she was in the Beinecke Archives at just the right point to write her husband's dissertation and her husband on record as insisting that he never heard of Jane Bennett and never went anywhere near Yale could force her hand and she'll capitulate and resign on her own."

"Canters?" queried Paula. "*The* Canters? From Charbonneau?"

"Oh, yeah–that's right; that all happened after you left. We'll have to fill you in.

"And as for Nancy, you–we–also confront her with a little bag of henbane-laced tea, which we have, from Joel's poisoning. We find somebody who saw Nancy Allen sneaking and lurking around the anthropology offices at North Washington, and get a sworn statement from them. and even though it's circumstantial evidence, you get them into a kind of plea-bargaining position."

"But nobody did see her," objected Mona. "Joel tried that on his own and nobody saw *him*, Randy. Joel never asked about a woman."

"Right," said Zoe. "So he'll ask about somebody seeing a woman and hopefully turn somebody up. And for Ferguson, the tradeoff with Dahlia is that she gives up the sacred masks to me and Phil to return to the Tribes. We lean on Brandon to cough up back alimony for Paula. For you, Aimee, Nancy and Frank give you back control of your house, and the three of them–Brandon, Frank, Nancy--pay you something for the totaling of your SUV, cough up enough for you to get a nice, new replacement, and from Randy, maybe you can get a certain percentage of whatever he inherited from Mavis. You know, we could bring Kenny in on this and maybe leverage a four-year college stipend for him."

"It could be a two-year; his management degree is from a two-year community college. Credits would probably transfer. Now that Kenny isn't shackled with a nine-to-five, he can be brought in to do surveillance, too," suggested Aimee.

"But Kenny's 'known'" objected Zoe–she made quotation marks in the air–"too; Randy's met him here on numerous occasions. And doing surveillance? He'd stand out like a sore thumb."

"You mean because he's Black," noted Aimee. "Yeah, I guess you're right. There aren't a lot of Black people in San Anselmo or Sonoma."

"But he could do things behind the scenes. If I'm right about how Frank McGinnis is getting the canvases for his forger," proposed Zoe, "then he's got to *get* those canvases *to* that forger. Kenny's only known to Randy and African-American people are all over the place, in metropolitan areas, obviously. Ferguson's fifth column people, the Giacomettis, could send the word, and at then some point, Kenny, hovering nearby, but outside San Anselmo, picks up Frank or Brandon or whoever and tails. Or maybe he and Ferguson switch. Kenny surveilles Dahlia-Gwen. Perfect for him. She'd never suspect--she'd maybe even think Ferguson had given up on her. Keeps Ferguson out of the gang's eye. Keeps Kenny from twiddling his thumbs. Does he have any idea when he's going to get laid off?"

"He thinks they'd probably be doing it, like, right now. He walks into his office and there's the pink slip, on his desk. Or the two-week notice, or whatever it is. So we could bring him on this, too?"

"Well, it's an idea. Maybe he could, with luck, trail Dahlia to wherever Adrian lives and maybe, just maybe, that place also turns out to be where our forger also lives. I'm not sure exactly how it would work, but the idea here is that the forger also gets confronted with circumstantial evidence and persuades the forgery cartel to do what we want so he or she, the forger, doesn't get exposed," explained Zoe. "Forgery is a dicey occupation. When confronted, the forger can say, 'Oh! I just paint these pretty pictures, and this man comes along every now and then and says, 'Oh, what pretty pictures. Can I buy them?' But I don't know what he does with them.' On the other hand, if this is a regular occurrence, and the forger constantly paints pictures that resemble the work of this or that artist, and the forger's works can be documented as being sold as this or that artist's work, then the circumstantial evidence is that the forger knew his forgeries were being sold as the genuine work of the such-and-such artist. Ferguson gets a statement from the forger to the effect that they regularly turn out paintings, on demand, for Frank and Brandon, that are in the styles of such-and-such artists."

"Kenny will have to be filled in, and we'll have to propose it to him. And to the Giacomettis, too. We'll need to have a filling-in-and-proposal-for-spying party!" exclaimed Aimee.

Zoe laughed heartily. She felt so good, so happy that Aimee had retreated, reversing back along the path leading to sadness and perhaps oblivion, anger and possible self-destruction, and back to the fork leading to engaged, optimistic, self-confidence. *Back on track*, she thought. Planning *with enthusiasm*.

"And hey, Paula–do you prefer Paula or your other name?"

"Mickie? I don't know. I didn't like Paula because it was such an ordinary, a family name. Like Robert, Bob. Paul, Paula. And I don't want to be Laird or, forgive me, Aimee, Cortez. So maybe Mickie."

"So where did Mickie come from?" pressed Mona.

"Mickie Faye DeMoss. She was a women's basketball coach where my mom went to college--University of Kentucky. My mom liked her a lot. I think she credited her with hauling her out of a bad depression by getting her to play basketball and getting on the team. I guess she really admired her, so, I figure the name has good karma." Paula smiled. "Even though being Mickie Laird probably doesn't."

"Hey!" exclaimed Aimee. "I'm *starved*! How 'bout I make us a huge omelet, prosciutto on the side for them that wants it!"

19

ZOE PHONED FERGUSON with the idea. He'd thought it was "Grand, terrific!" It turned out Kenny had indeed been given notice. When Aimee told him of their plan he brightened and said, "Hey, that *would* be something to do! I'm up for doing something different, something new."

Ferguson phoned the Giacomettis, introduced himself as someone who, along with Zoe Dill, had assisted Frank McGinnis and Gwen "Ochenpaw" with expertizing of a couple of items for a potential customer. When confirming the arrangements with Zoe, he characterized what he had told them as "a bit of a white lie, but mostly true," and persuaded them to accept his and Aimee Garrison's invitation to what he called an informational dinner at which they would learn a tad more about their tenant. Aimee, in whose house the couple were living who were renting a portion of their barn and had gotten their permission to construct a special, secure, alarmed room within, would share with them some suspicions about what their barn-renters were really doing with the room in their barn and several fellow diners would share with them some disturbing things they had learned about them. Their reaction was an expression of horror: "Oh, no," Frances had said. "Not drugs, I hope? Or something really icky like human trafficking. They told us it was art." Ferguson had assured them it was indeed art, "but perhaps not everything about the art is on the up-and-up, plus we have reason to believe they are sequestering some items that had been stolen from some Native American tribes. But ye'll would have to hear the whole story and decide for yourselves whether or not you can help."

The Giacomettis agreed they could make it on the coming Wednesday; Mona and Zoe would have to depart on Friday, so that would work out. Aimee opted for Tuesday evening for Ferguson to lay out the details to Kenny for what he would be doing.

Sweet and sour pork was Kenny's favorite, but he assured Aimee that chicken would be just fine, in a sauce of Sriracha, ketchup, vinegar, peanut butter, agave, red bell pepper and green onions with sesame seeds, bound together with a whipped egg and cornstarch. "Add a good handful of peanuts and more bell peppers and the sauce'll do it for me," said Zoe. She made a spinach and artichoke dip, with sour cream, cream cheese, shredded mozzarella and grated parmesan, crisped under the boiler for three minutes. Instead of commercial, she opted for homemade garnet yam and golden Yukon potato chips, sliced thin, and quick-fried in oil.

Ferguson thought bringing Kenny into the surveillance was a good idea, but "one thing I've been wondering," he said, "is just how local this scam is. If Utrillos, a Modigliani, Foujitas, Russells were all hanging on the walls, that means they are trying to appeal to two, maybe three distinct markets. And I can't believe that the small world of local gallery proprietors would not only provide a consistent market for forgeries but also supply a sufficiently diverse customer base that somebody in that small world would not behind to ask questions, especially if the forger might be a local artist known for his or her art in its own right. So I suspect some of this art goes out long-distance, especially if your phony authenticator, Zoe, is based on the East Coast. I'll bet some of this forged art goes out periodically with either Frank or Brandon as custodian and broker. The question is how, when, and how far."

Kenny listened thoughtfully, then offered a comment: "I'll bet running forged art is like running drugs. It comes in small planes where the pilots may not even file flight plans, or even if they do, air traffic control is not obligated–they're even prohibited–from revealing those flight plans to anybody except law enforcement, and even then, only for good reason. Perfect! It just so happens I've got an inside track on that particular topic, at least for the two airports they're likely to be using, if they *are* using small planes now and then."

"You've got a pilot's license? Awesome!" declared Zoe.

"No, Zoe. Not me."

Aimee pointed her finger at him and exclaimed, "Doug!"

"Right! Doug! My ex-brother-in-law. He's got a small plane and runs a courier service out of the

Oakland airport. And he regularly flies folks up to Napa for the wine train. He's been flying out of Oakland for years; if there's somebody there who regularly flies this Frank guy or the Brandon guy out of either airport, he's gonna know the guy who does it."

"Have you flown with him?" asked Mona.

"Sure thing! Back in the day, back in my previous life, me and Gladys, my ex, used to fly up for the wine train a couple times a year."

"By the way," asked Mona, "How did you two meet? You and Aimee. If you were really housebound, Aimee, taking care of Mavis." she said coyly, "if you don't mind my asking."

"We met in a Payless drugstore!" Aimee and Kenny crowed, almost in unison. "I'd turn up at least once a month to get Mavis' medicines," continued Aimee, but really oftener, because you know, Payless has other things, groceries and such, so I'd go over there probably once a week."

"And I was store manager at the time."

"And it was a few months after I moved in here with Mavis. I saw she was having trouble getting around and asked if she wanted a wheelchair and she was adamant. 'Absolutely not!' But I thought maybe something–like installing handholds in the house? Anyway, every time I went to Payless I noticed there was always this cute guy buzzing around, so I asked him if he had any ideas."

"And I suggested a rollator, or maybe two–one for downstairs, one for up. It's not quite a wheelchair but it helps you get up and around, and you can carry things with it."

"So I got the rollators, and Kenny offered to deliver them."

"And I just asked, like, off the top of my head, if she'd consider going out with me."

"And I said I didn't really do 'out' very much, but maybe he'd like to come in? I invited him to dinner and, well ..."

Zoe and Ferguson chimed, this time in perfect unison, "Bob's your uncle!" Everybody laughed.

SPRING BREAK, APRIL: WEDNESDAY

For the Giacomettis, Aimee and Paula-Mickie made Mongolian beef in a sauce of soy, agave, sherry, hoisin, sambal chili paste, ginger, garlic, lots of green onions and peanut oil, along with diced zucchini in rice. First course was a double recipe of two types of flour tortilla empanadas: potato and curried mashed chickpeas with a cucumber-onion-yogurt raita on the side. "Are just those okay for you, Zoe? asked Aimee as she sliced sirloin steak into thin strips.

"That's fine," Zoe assured her. "Save some sauce for me for the zucchini rice." The Giacomettis–Zoe thought they were probably in their late fifties, both lean, fit, and outgoing–expressed astonishment at the possibility that their new tenants were peddling forged art. "That's just so wild! But we did think it was kind of peculiar; they turned up just when we were wringing our hands, desperate for something to keep us going," said Francis.

"Francis is third generation there," said Frances seriously. "We wanted–still want–to keep the ranch going. That's why we turned it into a kind of dude ranch. But we can't grow all the feed we need for the horses, and they need constant care–shoes, medicines sometimes, new tack–that's why we thought doing the B&B might keep the wolf from the door."

"And it did do for a while," added Francis. "But there are also costs there. You're expected to provide breakfast, and we've got our own eggs from the chickens, but, you know, people want bagels, they want granola, they want fruit. And then we had to hire somebody to come in and clean the rooms. I mean, Frances was doing that for a while, too, along with the breakfasts."

"It was too much. Then, it all stops right before Christmas. And it's dead, for the next three months 'til just about this time of year," observed Frances.

"And this past season the fires hit!" Francis shook his head and rolled his eyes. "I mean, we really need that shoulder season; sometimes it's busier than summer. But *THIS PAST SEASON! OOF!* I think everybody thought we'd been burned out, and even if we weren't, who wants to take the chance of *getting* burned out!"

"And even never mind getting burned out. Who wants to drive around and see the sights and sip wine when you're choking on smoke and toxic fumes! So those fires just about did it for us."

"But the fires didn't actually threaten you?" asked Aimee.

"No," replied Francis. "We were okay. The first were peculiar. They'd get started in places you wouldn't predict. I mean, yeah, some of them were, like, forest fires from maybe campfires or in ranches from burning trash, controlled burns getting out of control, lightning. But *these* fires were in the *suburbs!*"

"But now we know a lot of it was PG&E." Frances shook her head. "Faulty electric wires coming down. All those fires in 2015, 2016, 2017—the Butte Fire, the North Bay Fires, the Camp fire--anyway, when one of our now-and-then B&B-ers…,"

"Randy?" asked Aimee, knowing full well it was.

"Right," continued Frances. "So when Randy approached us and asked if we'd consider having his parents–well, his mother, and whoever–the Frank fellow–as tenants in our barn if they could have a special room built *inside* the barn, totally at their expense, and they'd pay us rent, starting whenever the construction started, and for a year, payment in advance, well! It was the answer to our prayers! Just when the fires had chased away everybody, all our customers. So we said, yeah, sure. They presented themselves as dealing in wholesale and retail art and needed safe, secure storage, blah, blah, blah."

"Which is not exactly untrue," noted Ferguson. "It's just that they're doing so with questionable goods."

The Giacomettis agreed to keep Ferguson and Kenny equally informed about the comings and goings of Frank and Nancy and to let them know if Brandon or Randy came around, too. Either Ferguson or Kenny would then go into action.

Kenny moved out of his apartment and by Saturday boxes surrounded the replica dining room table and chairs in Aimee's house. Ferguson made the house his headquarters. Paula-Mickie returned to Brookdale. "But you have to keep me in the loop," she had insisted. "I really want Brandon to get what's coming to him for all his shenanigans."

20

First Weekend in May

BACK AT CHARBONNEAU, sinful Saturdays in the back yard were about
to resume; Joel and Phil were planning to drive in. "How do you feel about
Joel, now?" Zoe asked.

"It's going to require some getting used to. I told him I'd like to take it a
little slow. Of course, I didn't tell him about us. What about you and Phil?"

Zoe kissed Mona on the cheek and put her arm around her waist. "It's
been lovely with you, Mona. "I've really loved being with you. I really love
you. If you can continue to do the both of us, I can."

"I'm not sure I can," admitted Mona. "It's just, I just–if I kick Joel out of
my life, I want to be sure. I mean, he and Phil really get off on talking anthropology when they're both here, and Joel can be fun, funny–you know how he
is. It's just, he's so intense. But he's interesting. I mean this whole Jane Bennett
thing is just really interesting. So ... so, I don't want to just let him go."

"I get it," insisted Zoe. "I totally get it. Just, when he's back up at North
Wash, could you put up with me around?"

Mona circled Zoe's waist with her arm and kissed her on cheek and
mouth. "More than put up with you! Either it's going to be great with Joel

and I'll miss him when Sunday rolls around and I'll really need you, or it's going to be shitty with Joel and I'll need you."

"On the rebound!" Zoe giggled, letting go of Mona.

"No, no—not like that, but I'll be … lonesome."

"So will I!"

"And if it all goes sour with Joel, well, I'll *really* need you!"

~⟋

Joel had driven down on Thursday and Mona had assured Zoe it had gone wonderfully: "He was tender, gentle, relaxed, attentive to all I had to tell him, which was a lot." Phil also drove down, arriving late Friday evening.

Mona fixed what she called "Aimee's sweet and sour chicken" and with extra peanuts that could be donated to Zoe's plate and the raita and the potato and chickpea empanadas they had made for the Giacomettis. That was dinner. A white Spanish Rioja complemented the meal.

Aimee had called Zoe on Friday saying she had quite some news and would call on Mavis' landline that night, set on speaker phone, after the sinful Saturday dinner. She did so. She, Kenny, and Ferguson clustered around it on their end. Zoe, Phil, Mona, Joel, Carly and James clustered around their end as best they could.

The Giacomettis had called Kenny two weeks ago, Aimee said, and reported activity at the barn: it looked like Frank had loaded two wrapped framed paintings into his car. Kenny had developed the routine of driving to Sonoma on a daily basis, arriving around ten, getting a coffee in town, then driving around in the vicinity of the ranch and, if there was no activity, returning to town for a leisurely sandwich, then returning to Oakland in time to beat the traffic.

Day after day was spent thusly. Aimee went to work in Emeryville; Kenny went "to work" in Sonoma. But on a Monday, when Frances called to say that Frank had arrived at the barn and was loading stuff into his vehicle, Kenny charged out of the café in town, drove as quickly as he could, just in time to reach the junction where the turnoff to the ranch was located. Frank barreled past him; Kenny pulled a U-turn and, at the required distance, tailed him to Oakland airport. Kenny called Doug and alerted him. Two days later Doug called him with the news that one of his light plane buddies had indeed called him with a report that a man matching Frank's description, with minimal luggage but two well-wrapped large, flat items had commissioned a flight to Jackson, Wyoming.

The next day, Ferguson had taken commercial flights with two changes out of Oakland and had spent the following day roaming the galleries in Jackson. Eventually, he found what he suspected he'd find: two Russells hanging in a gallery. The gallery proprietor told him one was already spoken for and the gentleman had merely to come in, hand him a check, and walk out with it. Prices? $18,000 for one, $20,000 for the other. "Bargains," the proprietor told him. The proprietor was pleased to turn them over and show Ferguson the two Nick Taylor authentications. So, yes, they were certainly the two that had been hanging, "to season", on the walls of the San Anselmo house. Did Ferguson think the gallery proprietor knew, or suspected, they were forgeries? *Not at all*, Ferguson thought. Did Ferguson take any action, say anything to him? No. It was indeed frustrating. Ferguson couldn't see any way to convincingly argue that the gallery proprietor shouldn't sell them. "It would have just turned into a shouting match," averred Ferguson, "with me being thrown out of the gallery." Ferguson had taken photos.

At the end of the week, the Giacomettis reported an older lady turning up with Randy, in Randy's vehicle. Frances Giacometti then entered the barn under the pretense of tending to the horses. Well, it was not a pretense. She really did have to feed them, check up on them. As the two exited the room, situated smack in the middle of the barn was Randy with a duffel bag slung by its drawstring over his shoulder, Frances approached them and chatted them up. Was everything satisfactory? Did they need anything? Wasn't the hot, dry weather just awful? It was time enough for Kenny to get there, drive past, park, wait, and spy with Ferguson's binoculars. He was able to tail them, amazingly, all the way into the city where they double-parked in the Castro district. The older lady–clearly this was Dahlia-Gwen, added Ferguson–rang the bell of one of the "painted ladies" that had been carved into flats. Kenny reported that a youngish man answered, then accompanied Dahlia to Randy's vehicle, retrieving the duffel bag. He and the lady entered the building. Randy drove off. "That could easily be Adrian," Ferguson declared.

Kenny then drove to the end of the block and also double-parked. Fortunately, he did not have long to wait. The woman soon exited the building and walked a few blocks to the terminus of the Market streetcar line before she boarded the trolley. Kenny drove slowly down Market Street, following the streetcar, until he encountered a parking space. He threw as many quarters and dollars into the meter as it would accept, then marched quickly down the street until he encountered the pokey street car and spotted the woman in a seat on the car's far side. He got on, paid the fare, and sat down. The woman glanced up as he did so, but then resumed her contemplation of the action outside the car's window. *Who would take notice of one black man,* he thought, *in a sea of men who were black, brown, white, and everything in between?* He chuckled.

Kenny reported that she got off and stood on a street corner at a SamTrans bus stop. Kenny walked over to the stop and asked her, "Does the bus for San Mateo stopped here?" "It does indeed," she'd answered. The had both gotten on the bus. He had gotten off the bus when she did, but only after the driver had closed the door. "Sorry, this is my stop after all," Kenny shouted. The driver opened the back door again. Kenny hopped out and was able to just spot the woman turning a corner, then entering an apartment building. "Looks like she's got a bed-sit in San Mateo," said Ferguson. "So that's good. We know Frank is flogging some of his forgeries in Jackson, and we now know where she lives. And I'm ninety-nine percent sure we also know where Will Adrian apparently lives and that he's involved in this somehow. My guess is she was delivering blank canvases, and who else to except to the forger?

Or forgers? And we can also assume that Adrian is the kingpin, the contact person for that forger or forgers."

The Giacomettis also reported sometimes Frank, sometimes Nancy turning up, entering the alarmed room in the barn, then exiting with a large carrier bag, going behind the barn, and then reappearing with the carrier bag. "Ask her or Francis to go behind the barn and see if they can spot any color on the ground," Zoe advised.

"Color?" repeated Aimee.

"I suspect they're scraping canvases. There should be some evidence."

"Right," answered Kenny. "Will do."

"But in the meantime, we've got to have a better plan than simply following them around," averred Ferguson.

"Agreed," said Zoe. "I'll think on it. I think I can come up with a plan." She rang off. "Don't know how much of that you were able to hear or follow but here's the gist." She filled them in on the developments, then said: "So what do you-all think about a sting?"

"How would it work? Somebody poses as a customer looking for scarce avant-garde art like Utrillos, Modiglianis, Van Goghs, Corots, Matisses?" asked Carly. "How do you get the somebody to the San Anselmo people? And who is it going to be? Like, you hire an actor?"

"Answer to the first question yes. Answer to the second question, possibly. But I'd rather have somebody we know and can rely on and who knows them, or about them."

"But anybody who knows about them is also known *to* them," objected Mona.

"Too true."

"What about sending in James? They've never met him," Carly pointed out.

Zoe shook her head. "Won't work. Their contact person could be Brandon. Or, he could be part of the team. He'd recognize James straight off." Zoe reflected. "I know who would be perfect: my pseudo-auntie in Santa Fe, Coco Vanderjagt." Zoe shook her head. "But she won't work either. She's also known, *really* well-known to Dahlia! But I know two people who are *perfect* to do this and are *not* known to them, at least not recognizably known. We'd have to give them fake names, but … yes! The Murrays! They would be perfect!"

$$\sim\!\!\mathcal{O}$$

ZOE; CAIT; JESSICA

Zoe rang Caitlyn and Robb Murray, her friends and former employers at their shop in Croton Corners, New York. Cait picked up. "God almighty! It's great to hear from you! I'm putting you on speaker phone!" Zoe outlined her plan to them. They couldn't both do it, but Cait was enthusiastic: she would do it.

"Ferguson will send you the money for your ticket," Zoe promised. "And I'll get Ferguson to cough up his hundred-dollar-a-day per diem. That's not much, I know, but he's already got one person on the payroll at that rate; I'll argue this is going to be the turning point. I've got another thing to run down–where you're going to stay–and I can't pick you up myself. But I'll get my pal Aimee to pick you up at the San Francisco airport."

"This will be perfect! Just perfect," Cait insisted.

"Poetic justice," noted Robb.

"We'd have to change your name, which might take some doing …"

"I can go back to my unmarried name. Kernberger. Caitlyn Kernberger. I even have a passport in that name."

"But surely it's expired."

"Yeah, good point."

"And we'll have to figure out how to draft a story for you, like who you are, and why."

"That's easy. I'm Caitlyn Kernberger proud of being at least sixth generation Pennsylvania Dutch –- born and raised in the heart of antique country, Bucks County, Pennsylvania. And of course, I'll add, we're not really Dutch. We're Deutsch –- German, or at least originally German-speakers. I've got a whole little speech that I've honed to a cutting edge. I give it at least once a week to one or more tourists who wander into the shop. And I can add, 'My husband and I had to split up. It was just something we had to do. Doing antiques shows half the year, the other half the year scouting for stuff, living out of our van or in fleabag motels. After fifteen years it just got really old, I told' … hmmm let's see–what's a good name for my dumped ex? Can't be Robb. How about Irwin? Irwin. I'll have to remember to remember that. 'I told Irwin I just couldn't do it anymore. So I moved out here.' And where is 'here'?"

Zoe laughed. "That's great! We'll have to figure out just where 'here' is going to be, but when we do, we'll get cards printed up. Maybe even get you a website. They're really cheap, like ten bucks. Now all we have to do is figure out a legit address for you, what we're going to put on the cards. Having you in an actual physical place should go a long way to head off any obnoxious probing, like, for your social security number or your driving license. In fact, maybe we should make that part of the story: You never got a driving license because you were raised in this really conservative quasi-Amish household where women weren't supposed to be out-and-about careering around in vehicles. You were completely dependent on your husband. So add something like that to your pitch, your story."

"Yeah, I can do that," affirmed Cait. "Like, 'even though my grandmother was French they integrated her into our really conservative Mennonite community, blah, blah, blah. And I'm sick and tired of antiques and I want to get into fine art.'"

"But we have to think of some story to get you out here. Got any relatives in California?"

"'fraid not."

"Hmmm, we'll have to get you some, or one. I'll ring you back when I've got this sorted."

Zoe went to her computer and googled *Jessica Keegan, Photography*. Sure enough, there she was: *Jessica Keegan, Photography, Guerneville, California,* with a phone number and a studio street address. *Let's see*, thought Zoe.

What's the story here? Jessica's métier was photographs of old, decaying, abandoned, and quaint, picturesque, anachronistic rural structures She had met Jessica three years earlier at a campground while she and Phil were sojourning in the American Southwest. *Surely the quest for such would have brought her to Amish country*, thought Zoe. *Hell, maybe it even had.*

She called the number, left a message: "Hey, Jessica. This is Zoe Dill. Petrified Forest National Monument? Teepee Curios, Corrales? Remember? Can you call me back?"

Jessica did so. After a lot of catch-up with a follow-up of "guess-what-happened-to-us-after-we-left-you-and-found-Teepee Curios", interspersed with "Wows!" and "Awesome!" and "Fucking A!" and "Amazing!" from Jessica, Zoe outlined the bare bones of what they hoped to accomplish and how they hoped to do it. Amidst more exclamations, Jessica agreed to the plan. "Wow! How exciting! But how is this all going to play out?"

"Let me get this sorted a bit more, and I'll get back to you." Zoe then rang Aimee. She picked up. "Hi! Can you see if Kenny can tail Adrian for a few days–see where he goes, especially if he frequents any art galleries? I guess you'd have to clear it with Ferguson to take him off the San Anselmo folks but here's what I'm thinking …"

SECOND WEEK IN MAY

Kenny did indeed tail Adrian, undetected, and found that he did indeed frequent at least one art gallery. With a large portfolio, Adrian took the Market Street car into the financial district, Kenny getting on the car a block later after a sprint down the street. Kenny followed him closely enough to see him enter a gallery a few blocks from the Museum of Modern Art. He exited less than a half hour later without the portfolio. He seemed to be heading back to Market Street. Kenny entered the gallery. He found a mix of well-known early twentieth century modernist artists: fauvists, cubists, early abstract expressionists and unknown, at least to Kenny, late twentieth century and twenty-first century ones. There were three small abstract canvases by one particular artist. Kenny thought they were reminiscent of Miro or maybe Duchamp. The signature was largely illegible but seem to be something like "Zassy". A small sign announced one of them as sold. The proprietor sidled up quietly next to him. "Zassy?" he queried.

The proprietor nodded. "Zassy. He's hot right now. I just got two more in the back. This one will go out this afternoon. I was afraid of—what do you call it? Market saturation? But so far he seems to be only in demand."

Kenny reported all this to Ferguson, then to Zoe. In the meantime, Aimee had picked up Cait and after a night and a day in Trestle Glen, she and Cait had driven in Aimee's rental car following Zoe's directions to Jessica's photography studio in Guerneville. Large, framed black-and-white photos lined two walls and half of the back wall. There, Jessica welcomed them with a smile that seemed to take up half her face and presented Cait with a box of cards. "Sorry; they would only do a thousand." Jessica Keegan was nothing if not striking. Tall and sturdily built, with chestnut brown hair cascading to well below her shoulders, she wore skin-tight leggings of blue triangles outlined by beige borders and an almost sheer bright pink top over a white turtleneck. She led Cait to the back of the studio where a small desk would be Cait's headquarters, from which she would construct her identity as an ex-antiques-dealer-wanting-to-get-in-to-twentieth-century-modern-artists-looking-for-an-inventory. Jessica had found Cait a bed-sit nearby and promised Cait that Mitch, her boyfriend, would check in with her daily, each morning, to see if she needed or wanted to go anywhere. If anybody asked, Cait and Zoe had further embellished Cait's story by inventing an elderly relative, on the French side of the family, who had died childless and left some money, the proceeds of the sale of a house in the extreme east of the country, to distant, far-removed cousins, including Cait, that enabled Cait to break with "Irwin" and move out on her own.

They also invented a contact (Coco Vanderjagt, in Santa Fe, but name undisclosed) who had clients (names not disclosed) who were looking for "modernist" fine art. Cait had now transferred an undisclosed amount of euros to an American account, so the story went, for ready use as a bridge payment, should a prized item come available. Jessica would make some wall space for whatever Cait could acquire and hang. But of course, Cait would need to let it be known she was seeking such art, and in a way that would not threaten the business of other, well-established gallerists. She would be especially looking for Utrillos, preferably paintings, rather than lithographs, but also for similar items by different artists for people with similar tastes. Mitch, Jessica's partner who created blog logos, would be happy to chauffeur Cait around. Their first stops would be galleries in Sonoma and Marin County. Their second would be selected galleries in San Francisco, and certainly a modernist gallery located a stone's throw from the Modern Art Museum. Cait would distribute cards freely, writing, "Utrillo, Dufy, Matisse, Vlaminck, Miro, Gris" on their backs. They hoped to attract Frank McGinnis, Brandon Laird, or Randy Allen.

21

MID-MAY TO MID-JUNE

THE LAST MONTH OF THE ACADEMIC YEAR brought denoue-
ment to several simmering crises--or perhaps they were merely vexing dilemmas and difficulties, rather than true exigencies. At Sacajawea and Jean-
Baptiste Charbonneau College, Peter Blenheim requested a meeting of the
Art History faculty, cautioning them to observe the strictest confidentiality.
Without mentioning himself or Zoe, Mona, Carly, and James by name, he
noted that certain faculty had brought an informal complaint to Dean Fister
concerning some circumstantial evidence of further misconduct on the part
of faculty members in the Social Sciences Department. Combined with
certain sworn testimony provided during the recent accreditation process the
previous autumn, the information had urged yet another retirement from the
Social Sciences Department, although on a "buyout" arrangement that would
involve no teaching but by which the faculty member would retain salary and
library privileges for the coming academic year. In the coming autumn term,
procedures would be initiated to advertise for a candidate in mid-career to
replace Joseph Canter, who was retiring. The following year, candidates to
replace Madison Canter would be sought and interviewed. Of course, all of

this information was only for the benefit of Gudrun Hance: Mona, Zoe, and Carly had already anticipated all of this, or rather, had hoped for it. They were gratified to learn that hiring Ferguson to provide documentation of Madison Canter's accessing of the Jane Bennett records at Yale at the time the Canters' dissertations were being written, had produced results.

Blenheim also announced that two members of the Social Sciences faculty who had been expected to leave the college's employ as of July had, in fact, had their contracts renewed for the following academic year on the basis of complaints they had filed with the Faculty Senate Personnel Committee. Without directly recommending such, the committee had noted that the administration might want to look into the possibility of another year of teaching for both, while additional information on their teaching effectiveness was gathered. Further, Dean Fister had decided that certain allegations in their complaints would be further investigated, and perhaps their teaching, scholarship and publication records might be rereviewed by a special committee constituted outside of the Social Sciences Department. Zoe was gratified at this news. She was sure these developments could be credited to the thoroughness of Phil's and Porter Harder's accreditation report. Peter affirmed that he would continue as Acting Chair of Social Sciences.

At Northern Washington University, Joel had put out the word that he was actually looking for a *woman* who had been sneaking or lurking around the anthropology department in the previous term, probably in October 2017. Aimee had sent along a scan of a picture of Nancy, although much younger than she was now. In May, he had a visit during his office hours from a tall, lanky second-year grad student who had said, yes, he and a couple others had been coming back from what they called "the avenue" after a night at the bar. It was drizzling, so they had cut through the building to their cars, parked in the lot across from the building. "It was sometime after ten, probably around eleven." The building was locked up overnight, but the exact time varied with the finishing up of their tasks by the cleaning crew. The students had encountered a woman, of slight build, wearing dark slacks and an equally dark hoodie, apparently closely studying a bulletin board. They couldn't see her face because of the hoodie and also because they weren't paying much attention. He showed him the picture. "Could be," was the student's response. Joel emailed Aimee back that he thought it was a valid positive ID.

Paula-Mickie had also phoned with news that was not expected. She had been awarded an out-of-court monetary settlement on the basis of legal action she had threatened to bring–essentially the outlines of a lawsuit–against the college alleging defamation of her character when the English teacher's complaint had been revealed to, or rather discovered by, the local press. "Just in time," she'd told them. "Ray's parents were really generous with me, gifting me sums every now and then to tide me over for gas money, groceries and paying the attorney's fees. Well, I'm not going to insult them by trying to pay them back for the groceries and such, but now I can pay them back for the lawyers' bills." She had not told them about her lawsuit-in-waiting because she had agreed, gladly, to a gag provision barring her from talking about the case with anyone except Ray's immediate family.

Caitlyn Kernberger (Murray) had left her cards, advertising her interest in paintings by Utrillo, Dufy, etcetera, at more than a dozen galleries in downtown San Francisco, in the Castro district, and in downtown Sonoma. Initially, no responses were forthcoming. She and Jessica's significant other, Mitchell Johns brought her around regularly to check in with all the galleries over several days, each week. Other days were spent with Jessica on photography shoots. "I sort of hate to be making art out of peoples' tragedies," Jessica told Cait. "But fire-damaged structures make really good subjects." She made it a point to give out her card to anyone she met in the vicinity of these wildfire shoots, she said, telling them, "If you think my photos could be useful for insurance purposes, please let me know. I'll be glad to provide them, free of charge." She posted a similar message on her website.

SECOND WEEK OF JUNE
GUERNEVILLE; OAKLAND;
SAN FRANCISCO; SAN ANSELMO

But now, things were happening. Cait called Aimee, cautiously excited because she had gotten a call from a man who would not identify himself, asking if she was still interested in modernist art, and if she had customers lined up to buy them. She had told him yes, and he had said good, he would be contacting her. "So I told Ferguson and warned him he might have to be ready to spring for a large bank transfer pretty soon if this pans out." The man called back a couple days later, asking if he could bring something over to show her; she'd said yes. It turned out he was in Guerneville, and if it was convenient, he would be right over.

"He" turned out to be Brandon Laird and he carried a large portfolio. He opened it, took out a framed picture, wrapped in brown paper secured with tape. He carefully undid the tape, unwrapped the painting, and asked if there was a chair he could set it on. Cait quickly dragged one over. He set the painting on the chair. It turned out to be a "Raoul Dufy". "You may want to take photos to show your client," he suggested. "And do you have a standard contract form? I mean, setting out your broker's fee, and so forth?" She told him she did so, but she would have to run home, "just a few steps away," to get her camera and print out the form. Luckily, she had anticipated being asked for just such a form and also being asked to run home and get it. Clearly, Brandon Laird would use the window of her away time to snoop. She had left her expired passport in the middle drawer of the desk for just that event; she hoped he would indeed snoop, find the passport, and satisfy himself that she was indeed who she said she was and thus that everything else she represented herself as being and thus would take everything else she told him about herself at face value.

She returned ten minutes later, handed him the form, which he perused, and took the requisite pictures. Despite moving well to the side of the chair on which the painting was propped, Brandon Laird would appear, along with the painting, in at least two of the shots. Cait declined his invitation to lunch, begging off for an appointment at a gallery in the city "And since I don't drive–it's one of those activities my very conservative Pennsylvania Dutch–and of course you know we're not Dutch–we're Deutsch, German–-anyway my parents didn't approve of young girls driving so I just never did get my license–although I intend to. But for now, my partner, Jessica--she's not exactly my partner, she's my landlady, I guess! This is her studio. Anyway, her significant other, Mitch–he' s my kind of taxi service, I pay him, of course–says he doesn't mind, likes a trip to the city or to Sonoma now and then. Anyway, he's scheduled to pick me up in about twenty minutes. Sometimes Jessica comes along and we make a day of it …" Babble, babble, babble.

Laird wrapped up the painting again, and good naturedly, said he would call her and make an appointment for the transaction, but she thought he was kind of anxious to get away from what she had presented as her kind of dingbatty self. "And of course you'll be prepared to effect the bank transfer," he had cautioned her.

"Of course!" she assured him. "I've got an account right here in town. So yeah, just give me a call." He had done so. The transaction was scheduled for the Thursday of the third week of June.

〜

Second Saturday in June - Beginning of Third Week in June

Ferguson called Zoe. They needed to hold a strategy meeting at Aimee's house in Oakland, and it had to be soon. Cait had called and said a transaction for a (purported) Raoul Dufy was scheduled for the coming Thursday. Could she come down? And wasn't there a faculty member there who was an expert on early twentieth century artists, especially on the catch-all category, "modernists"? Could she come along as well? Zoe put it to Carly. Yes, Carly would be jazzed to get in on the action, rather than just hearing about it. They had suspended get-togethers during the two weeks of June for final exams and grading, but on the second Saturday in June, they had celebrated "TGIGS–Thank-Goodness-It's-Graduation-Saturday". Grades were in, summer vacation was on, and the entire sinful Saturdays contingent wanted to get in on whatever was going to happen. Joel came down and parked his car in Carly's and Mona's driveway and then he and Carly piled into James' Jaguar, caravanning with Joel and Mona traveling with Zoe in her Civic. They all overnighted in sleeping bags (except for Zoe) on Phil's floor, then continued on, with Phil, to Aimee's place. Ferguson offered to move out into a motel.

Aimee was her old, perky self. Kenny had really gotten into the cloak-and-dagger tailing business. Aimee had finally gotten a replacement vehicle. The insurance company had offered her half of what her brand-new Mercedes SUV had cost her but it was enough for a used but serviceable Subaru Forester.

Aimee declared they would celebrate "fat-Tuesday-at-Aimee's" with a feast. She insisted everyone have a role in preparing it. Phil would cut thin slices of flank steak and sear them. Carly would prepare a sauce of chili paste, fresh ginger, garlic, soy and sherry for the seared steak stir fry, and also a veggie version with bok choy, chopped by Zoe. James would prep shrimp and anchovies for a stir-fry with raisins, onions, cherry tomatoes, sliced blanched almonds, a cup of chicken broth, basil and dried pepper flakes. Ferguson was put to work mashing and then pureeing black beans and huge amounts of garlic for a sauce of chicken broth, Thai basil leaves, and dry sherry that would go over broccoli and mushrooms, also for roasting in the oven, that Kenny was busy chopping, along with peeling and then keeping an eye on boiling potatoes that Mona would cool with cold water and chop into chunks for the salad. Joel devoted himself to chopping copious amounts of baby arugula leaves and cherry tomatoes for the salad. Paula prepared the dressing: yogurt, canola mayonnaise, olive oil, basil, parsley and dill. Sunflower seeds would be sprinkled on top. Aimee assumed the role of *chef de cuisine*, directing everyone else, and also tended to tomatoes and onions roasting in the oven for a vegetable bullion-based soup. "Lucky thing this is a great big kitchen," she quipped.

As they mashed, mixed, chopped, boiled, seared, and roasted, they laid plans. Ferguson declared that the Giacometti ranch, Dahlia's bedsit in San Mateo, the Cait-Jessica studio in Guerneville, Aimee's San Anselmo house, and the Castro district house where, presumably, Adrian lived in an apartment with the forger-painter, would be targets. The Castro apartment because hopefully they would find partially or nearly completed ersatz "modernist" paintings, perhaps even catching the forger in the act. The Jessica-Cait studio in hopes of catching Brandon or Frank or Nancy or all three taking payment for a Nick-authenticated ersatz modernist painting from the Castro house studio. Dahlia "because it's her that I'm really after," Ferguson said. The ranch in hopes of witnessing one of the three actually taking one or more painting out of the barn. And the San Anselmo house just on general principle, as a fail-safe, just on the off-chance that some of the paintings might have been retransferred back to the house. Ferguson assigned the targets: he and Kenny would take Dahlia because Kenny knew where her bed-sit was located and Ferguson because, well, it was Dahlia that he was really after. "And I will get certain documents," he told them, "certain statements drawn up for a couple of the principles to sign and attest to: one for Cait, to affirm that she has been offered a painting to buy—photo attached—by a certain person; another photo attached. One for our forger to sign, attesting to his being commissioned by certain persons to produce certain paintings in the styles of particular well-known artists, again, photos attached; and a general form for gallery proprietors and collectors, such as the Fosters and with luck the place in Jackson, attesting to having been sold, or offered such-and-such a painting, purportedly painted by so-and-so, presented by one or more of the principles, Frank, Brandon, Dahlia-Gwen. Then we or I—will mention how interested the FBI is in forged art and in the importation of stolen Native American ceremonial objects without going through customs."

"But you have no intention of siccing the FBI on Brandon and Frank et al.," affirmed Zoe, as she chopped mountains of bok choy. "You have something else up your sleeve."

"Ah canna' say yay or nay t' the first, but I wou'na be Ferguson"—he rolled the "r"—if I wou' ha'e to say 'nay' t' the second."

"So, this time you really will get Dahlia-Jane to turn over the masks, and Phil and I can return them to the Tribes?" Zoe asked. "You'll offer her the opportunity to avoid the imminent FBI raid on the masks if she turns them over to you, and you'll also eliminate her from the FBI's fraud division investigation with regard to the marketing of at least four faked paintings: the Dufy that Cait is ostensibly going to purchase, the Léger that came along with the Randy-facilitated purchase by Mavis and was subsequently donated to Charbonneau College, the Braque that Aimee still has on the wall, and with luck, a forged Charles Russell that is still hanging on the wall of a gallery in Jackson, right?"

"Something like that," agreed Ferguson. Zoe knew it was as close to a promise that she would ever get out of him. "Oh," added Ferguson, "and there's a Vlaminck that the Fosters just recently purchased."

"You've been in touch with them?" asked Mona, dumping the potato chunks into a large bowl with the arugula leaves and tomatoes.

"Aye. If all goes well, Zoe and Carly and I will go over there tomorrow or the day after and get them to sign a statement. So could I suggest that it be you, Carly, who confronts the forger, whoever that happens to be? Based on Kenny's sleuthing work, I'm keen on the idea that the forger is an artist who signs his own paintings 'Zassy.' It's a gamble, but if you can get into the building—ring the outside push-bells until somebody buzzes you in—then you can hopefully find the door behind which Zassy is busy at work by knocking and crying out his name. Kenny has the address of both the home and studio in the Castro district and the gallery where he shows, should you need that. That leaves the ranch and the San Anselmo house for anybody else who wants to be involved. Oh, and we also need a kind of 'operator central'--someone with a phone who can receive calls from all of us and pass along information as needed. Someone stationed north of San Francisco, south of Guerneville. This will smooth the communication process, rather than all of us trying to call all the rest of us for whatever reason."

I'll be happy to be that person, but I'll need a vehicle, because presumably Zoe will have hers in Guerneville," offered Phil. "These are done," he added, turning off the gas under the flank steak slices.

"You can use mine," piped up Paula. "And Aimee, if you want to be the San Anselmo house point person I'd be happy to go with you. Do you want this dressing on the salad now or for people to serve themselves, Mona?"

"Why don't we put both on the table," chimed in Aimee. "Also the soup— there's a great big bowl in the cupboard to your right and a ladle in the drawer. I think everything's ready. Everybody grab a bowl and a plate. Silverware's set. Dinner rolls on the table. Wines, too: Yellowtail Shiraz, Prosecco Brut, Willamette Valley sauvignon blanc. And yes, let's you and me go up toe San Anselmo, Paula."

"Hey, what do you say, James--wanna to be the breakers and enterers at this ranch, wherever it is? I can borrow my mother's car," proposed Joel.

"Well, pooh!" pouted Mona, sliding a spatula under some flank steak slices and dumping them on her plate. "Everybody's got a purpose in life except me!"

Carly laughed. "I just assume you'd come along with me! We'll take the BART over to the city, then hop on the Market Street car. You want broccoli? Funghi?"

"Yes and yes," replied Mona.

"And I know you do," said Carly, grabbing pieces with tongs. She plopped some on Mona's plate and some on Zoe's.

When they were all seated at the dining room table, spooning slurps of soup and forkfuls of veggies or steak or shrimp into their mouths, Carly asked, "How exactly is this Dahlia person implicated?"

Ferguson chewed and swallowed. "She's calling herself Gwen-something now. And she's implicated because I think when Carly confronts Adrian, with Zoe not far behind, it will turn out that Adrian, either genuinely or conveniently, nurtured a relationship with a painter of quite some talent whom Dahlia-Gwen persuaded to turn his expertise to turning out forgeries on demand by Frank McGinnis, for clients cultivated by Brandon Laird. It was a deliberate act on her part, intended to result in paintings that could be passed off as genuine to unsuspecting, or unquestioning, gallery proprietors, dealers, collectors," Ferguson replied. "That's a crime. "The Fosters bought what is undoubtedly a fake Vlaminck from Frank McGinnis, with whom they know her to be associated. So her involvement in that will be my point of leverage to get her to admit to having, and selling, the sacred masks.

"So we've got targets identified," Ferguson had stir fry steak and bok choy and salad on his plate in front of him and a bowl of soup at his elbow. He was tackling all three in a round robin of eating. He continued. "Now as I said, we should keep monitoring the ranch, but James and Joel, if ye be the ranch watchers, ye may need to do some breaking and entering. The Giacomettis dinna answer their phone, on my numerous tries. We have to surmise that maybe they have been locked away, perhaps in the 'room within a room' in the barn without the phone and without the code to get out.

Zoe piped up, swallowing a mouthful of generously sauced broccoli and mushrooms. "Ooof! That's hot!" she exclaimed. "I'm the logical one for surprising Brandon when he shows up in Guerneville to deliver the fake Dufy, since you set that whole thing up, and I know Cait and the Jessica who has the studio where everything's going to happe."

"Have ye actually met Brandon Laird, Zoe?" queried Ferguson.

"No." She forked potato chunks into her mouth quickly, slurping the dressing as she did so. "He was already on suspension when I interviewed. I guess he's around, right, Carly, Mona?

Carly bit off a large shrimp hovering on the end of her fork. "Yeah." Mona nodded.

"But our paths haven't crossed," continued Zoe. She took a sip of white wine. "After all, he's still got what should be *my* office! I saw him from a distance in Jackson, but he didn't see me."

‿◡

KENNY AND FERGUSON
THIRD THURSDAY IN JUNE
SAN MATEO

They departed for San Mateo at seven o'clock In the morning. Ferguson figured the surprise factor would put them at the advantage. "What if she doesn't open the door?" objected Kenny.

"I'll shout her out. Threaten her with the FBI. Give her the choice: open up to me or suffer a FBI raid poised to descend upon her."

By 8:45 a.m. they were outside the apartment building. They were in luck. Just as they walked up to the door, a dark-skinned man in black pants and a hoodie exited the building. Kenny caught the door and they walked up the stairs. They stopped in front of a door. "This is it," Kenny announced. Ferguson launched forth with his harangue while Kenny pounded incessantly on the door. They stopped and listened. There was no response. They repeated the routine. A door opened down the hall. "Stop all that racket!" An old woman was poking her head out. "Who are you? Where did you come from? How did you get in?"

"Ma'am, we're really sorry, but we need to talk to the individual behind this door."

"There's nobody there. Left last night. Up and down, up and down, up and down the stairs *at two in the morning*! Waking up the whole house! And now you come along and do it all over again."

Kenny and Ferguson walked down the hall. "What do you mean, left?" asked Ferguson.

"Just what I said. Left last night. Bouncing luggage down the stairs, bump, bump, bump."

"You saw them?" asked Kenny.

"Course I saw 'em! That woman and I guess her boyfriend. Flown the coop. Skedaddled. Vamoosed. Probably done a bunk on the rent. Bums.

Ne'er-do-wells. Gamine and her john. Now get away wit' you. I can't stand here a-jawin.'" She slammed the door shut.

"Hells bells and damnation!" (Kenny); "Shite and bollocks!" (Ferguson); "Shit on rye!" (Kenny) "Feck!" (Ferguson).

"She's done a runner!" exclaimed Ferguson. "I've been out-choreographed once again," he lamented.

"Who do you suppose the boyfriend is?"

"I'd put money on Frank McGinnis," said Ferguson. "But it could be the Randy person, if she's true to form. She likes younger men. Could be Adrian. We should get a warning to Carly and Mona that they might be in for a disappointment. The forger may have gone to ground as well, if Dahlia is back in partners with Adrian. Is Phil in place?"

Kenny consulted his phone. "Not yet, probably. Getting there." But he called anyway. Phil answered. He had just pulled into a lay-by just outside of Rhonert Park.

"Ask him to call the Giacomettis. If they still don't pick up, tell him to call us back. That's our next stop, and we'd better get up there pronto. Oh, and ask him to call Joel or James and find out if they're at the ranch yet."

CAIT AND JESSICA; BRANDON LAIRD; ZOE
GUERNEVILLE, CALIFORNIA: 10:10 A.M.

Zoe had parked around the corner from Jessica's and Cait's studio and remained in the car. Now she saw someone–she was pretty sure it was Laird--park his car out front and approach the studio with a portfolio. Giving him a few minutes to open the portfolio and to unwrap the ersatz Dufy, she exited the car and slowly sauntered to the studio. It was a storefront with large windows. This morning, Jessica, who had been recruited as an additional witness, had not raised the blinds on either the windows or the glass-fronted door. The plan was for her to be seated at her desk at the front of the studio.

Zoe entered the studio. She saw that the painting lay on top of Cait's desk. Cait was holding something. As Zoe entered, Cait glanced at her, then said, "Here it is. Cashier's check for $46,000! That's it! The price of the painting plus broker's fee." As Zoe walked in, Laird looked up, a benign smile on his face. Clearly he suspected nothing. Cait took the painting and held it vertical, then turned it around to show the back. Zoe had one of Jessica's cameras, this a digital one. She activated the zoom. Click, click, click, click. "Hello?" Laird started to approach them. "What is this?" He looked from Cait to Zoe then back to Cait.

"This is documentation of your attempt, Brandon Laird," said Zoe, "to pass off this painting as a genuine Raoul Dufy and to collect a payment for what is probably about twenty or thirty times what it could otherwise be sold for."

"You're crazy! This is a rare piece!"

"It was painted surely within the last year and has an only faintly believable authentication certificate, by one Nicholas Taylor, who has been fiddling such certificates for at least the last eight years," stated Zoe.

"And who are you?" Laird walked menacingly toward Zoe.

"I'm your replacement: Dr. Zoe Dill, visiting assistant professor of art history, Sacajawea and Jean-Baptiste Charbonneau College, with expertise on forgeries and frauds."

CARLY AND MONA; ADRIAN AND ZASSY
10:15 A.M.
SAN FRANCISCO

Carly and Mona followed Ferguson's directions to the house in the Castro district and then his instructions as to how to get into it. They pressed the bells–there were eight of them–in succession, at paced intervals until, sure enough, the fourth one buzzed them in. But behind which door was Zassy?

Stairs led down to the basement. A long hall on the ground floor held four doors. A well-maintained circular staircase led up. As they were puzzling, a man in a charcoal car coat came clattering down the stairs. "Zassy?" Carly said as he approached them. "Upstairs, second door on the left," he replied. He slowed his pace, stopping at the bottom of the stairs, turned toward them.

"Thank you."

"He doesn't like patrons coming to his studio, you know. He sells at several galleries."

Carly nodded. "We know. Thank you!"

The man turned and exited the building. They mounted the stairs and knocked on the second door to the left. "Who is it?" asked a robust voice from inside.

"Zassy?" said Carly.

"Who wants to know?"

"Two ladies who appreciate his fine work and his talent!"

"What do you want?"

"Indulge us. We want to see his studio."

"He's not receiving visitors."

"We won't go away until we can see his studio."

No response.

Carly rapped smartly on the door again. It opened a crack. A youngish man wearing, Carly could see, only boxer shorts stuck his face in the crack. "Go away."

But Carly was too quick for him. She stuck her foot in the door, then her hand in the crack, and shoved. This gesture unbalanced the man a bit and he staggered back. Carly took the side of the door and shoved it open. "Hey!" he said, as she barged in, Mona right behind her. Carly shut the door behind them.

"Thanks! And not to worry. I 've seen plenty of boxer shorts." Another man appeared, in a bathrobe. He stopped. "What do you want?" The first man scuttled off.

"Zassy?"

"Yes ..."

Carly and Mona saw that they were in a large room fitted out as a kitchen, but doubling as a studio, with several easels, paint pots, and canvases in various positions and in various stages of completion and incompletion, in the middle of the room and against walls. A small square table was against one wall. Carly looked left and saw, in another room, more easels, more paint pots, more canvases, and a large unmade bed against the far wall. The first man emerged now also in a bathrobe, from a door in the back of the second room. "Now what is it you want?" He moved aggressively to within a few inches of them.

Carly ignored him and addressed Zassy. "Zassy, you are an incredibly gifted, talented painter. You make your own fine art and you produce Utrillo's, Russell's, Dufy's, Vlaminck's, Modigliani's, Gris, Braque's, Léger's."

"Who are you?" demanded Zassy's companion. *I'll bet anything this is Adrian*, thought Carly.

Carly stuck out her hand. Mona did the same. "Dr. Carly Pinto, art historian. My specialty is the moderns."

"And Dr. Mona Spradley, also art historian, but not a moderns specialist."

Finally, Zassy also shook each of their hands, limply, then dropped them. "We've encountered your work in association with Frank McGinnis and Brandon Laird," continued Carly.

"Oh," said Zassy quietly. "You'd better come in." He led them into the second room and sat on the unmade bed. The second man sat next to him. "This is Adrian," said Zassy. "I suppose you've got the police waiting right around the corner to arrest me, right?"

"Absolutely not!" Carly and Mona stood in the doorway. "Making pictures that look like pictures that someone else made fifty or a hundred years ago is not a crime. It's not illegal. It's a talent that not everybody has. And sometimes it can be challenging, near impossible."

Zassy ran his hand through his already messed hair. "The Dufy was especially challenging."

Adrian cut him off. "Zassy! Don't say anything!"

"And I'll bet he–they–pay you, what? Five, six, eight, maybe ten thousand dollars a painting?"

"We want to go to Europe," replied Zassy. "I want to paint in Paris, where *they* painted. Go to Tunis, to Italy, to all the places that inspired, animated, revealed, motivated. And we've almost got it. We've almost got the means. This seemed like the only way to do it."

Adrian seemed to droop, to cave, to collapse into himself. "Nobody pays him what he's worth," Adrian said, almost in a whisper. "He's finally beginning to gain some recognition, I mean, on his own, for his own art, for what he really does and really is. But it's been slow in coming."

Mona and Carly entered the room. Mona folded her hands across her chest and leaned against a wall. "How does it work? They come to you and say, 'We can move an Utrillo, a Matisse, a Russell, a Dufy, a Léger, a Braque, a Gris, whatever, if you can give us one' and then you go to work and they come around when it's ready? What happens to it then?"

Zassy nodded. "Yes, that's the way it works." Then he shook his head. "But I don't know what happens to them after they take them away." His lower lip was trembling. "I have no idea. They come in, take the paintings, hand me a check or sometimes cash, and take them away."

"You see," said Carly, "unless you're actually selling them as the works of so-and-so, as long as you're selling them simply as paintings that you've done, and that *they know* you've done, there's no crime on your part. There are all kinds of paintings on offer that are 'in the style of' or 'after so-and-so' or 'inspired by.' It's *their* crime. It's *them* that are peddling your paintings as something they're not and getting nice high prices for them."

"What do you want from us," demanded Adrian. "What do you want from him? What do you want from Zas?"

After a moment of silence, Carly said, "An affidavit. A sworn statement. A notarized testimony. Signed by Zassy, attested to by a couple witnesses. Stating when and how and who first contacted him about his doing paintings, and in whose style they wanted them. If possible, how many of each sort he produced. Amounts he was paid are not so important, but it would be useful if he could estimate how much generally or how much for each. The important thing here is that he painted certain ones in certain styles resembling known paintings by known deceased artists commanding high prices and that he was paid nowhere near those high prices, and finally, that it was certain identified individuals who commissioned him to do so."

"And then what?"

Carly paced around the room. She noted a closet with sliding doors. *Wonder if there might be brand new moderns stowed in there.* "Well, we notify the FBI Frauds Division. Maybe, if we can, we identify several probable 'Zassys' that aren't, but are certified as 'in the style of so-and-so'. We then get the owners of those pieces to attest that they paid this-and-that certain sum for each of them. Then we turn over all this information to the FBI and they go ahead with indictments. Or, perhaps, some arrangements could be made just short of FBI notification."

"Kind of like a plea bargain," noted Adrian. He nodded slowly. "I've been there before. But does Zassy have to be involved?"

"Yes, kind of like a plea bargain." Carly nodded. "And I'm not the one orchestrating all this, but I don't think Zassy has to be involved, as long as his notarized statement is available."

"And if Frank and Brandon and Nancy will give back all the money to the people they've bilked," suggested Mona.

"Oh," said Adrian in a small voice. "You seem to know a thing or two."

"Something like that," continued Carly. "But in the meantime, you don't have to give back the money that Brandon and Frank have paid *you*, Zassy. Because you were not a party to the conspiracy to defraud. You just painted the paintings. We'll make sure that's in your statement, too, that you were not told what the ultimate destinations of the paintings would be."

"Cock-foster-fucking-a!" exclaimed Adrian. "They're going to be mad as hatters! We're going to have to get out of here, quick."

"Yes, I'd say that would be advisable," agreed Carly. "But not before Zassy signs this." She rotated the saddlebag hanging over her shoulder, opened it, and retrieved a large manila envelope, handing it to Zassy. "We'll go to the nearest bank, or your favorite bank, and find a notary public and a couple random witnesses and you'll sign in their presence." Zassy blew air out of his mouth and nodded. "You can tell me a few of the paintings and I'll write them into the blank spaces."

22

THEY PULLED INTO THE DRIVEWAY of the San Anselmo house. "What do you want to bet she's changed the lock and the code again," Aimee confided to Paula, in a hardened voice. "Oh! She hasn't!" The code box flashed green and the key turned in the lock. They entered. The house was quiet. They walked down the hall to Nancy's bedroom and cautiously pushed the door open. Nancy was crashed out, in her clothes, on top of the bed. She raised her head as they entered. "Ohhhh," she groaned. "I don't feel good."

"What happened?" asked Aimee.

"I tied one on. At the Yardbird, last night. Ohhhh, do I have a hangover!"

They got Nancy up and into the bathroom where she vomited until she was heaving dry. They changed her clothes and walked her out to the car, stowing her in the back seat.

"Hey, why are you putting me in the car? Where are we going? Where are you taking me?" Nancy asked in a broken, quavering voice.

"To Mavis' house," replied Aimee. "We need you to give us clarification on some things without being interrupted by Frank and his pals."

"Frank!" Nancy held her head in her hands.

"Did you notice? Frank's office door was open and it didn't look like there was much in it," observed Aimee to Paula.

"Where *is* Frank?" asked Paula.

"Frank's gone." Nancy's voice cracked. "That bastard," she spat. "He used me. He was just using me. You know, he hardly ever even fucked me. He just used me."

"Where did he go to?" asked Aimee. Paula started the car.

"Who knows?"

"Why don't we leave it for now," suggested Paula. "Aimee, let's leave. Can you call Phil and give him this–heh, heh–news?" She turned to address Nancy.

"Ohhhh," Nancy groaned when they hit the highway and the car accelerated.

10:25

THE GIACOMETTI RANCH

James and Joel were outside the ranch gate, agitated, milling around, when Kenny and Ferguson pulled up. "We were reluctant to do breaking and entering," said James.

"I think we have to do so. The worst that will happen is the sheriff's department shows up, which might be a good thing," declared Ferguson. He went to the rental car's boot and clicked it open. "Let's hope Alamo supplied me with a crowbar." He snatched it up. Ferguson slammed the boot closed, and walked hurriedly to the gate. "Ah!" he pointed at the lock box. "The light's green."

"That's funny. It wasn't a half-hour ago, I swear, insisted James." Joel added his vigorous agreement.

"'Tis undoubtedly on a timer," suggested Ferguson. "If the occupants of the main house don't do an override, the alarm goes off automatically. Same for it going on."

Ferguson walked swiftly to the house, tried the front door, then charged around to the back door. It was closed but unlocked. "Search the house, also the basement. I suspect they may be locked away and tied up somewhere."

James and Joel did as bidden. Kenny and Ferguson ran to the barn. Swinging the huge door open, Ferguson ran into the barn within the barn. The door was locked and alarmed. Ferguson crow-barred open the door. The alarm went off. He and Kenny rushed inside. The Giacomettis were not tied up. "Oh thank God, thank God!" cried Frances. The alarm continued to clatter and shriek. "They locked us in here. We couldn't do anything!" said Francis. "We don't have the code to the door. We didn't have our phones, and there was nothing we could use in here to pry the door open. This place is totally empty; it's been stripped."

Ferguson handed Francis his phone. "Maybe ye can call the alarm company and tell them everything's okay."

"Sorry. Don't know the number offhand. It's in my phone."

"Let's go into the main house and find your phones." They did so. The phones were out of juice so they plugged them into the chargers. Frances found the alarm company's number and called, but she was told that the alarm was keyed to a pin-code that had to be entered on the alarm panel and without that, even the alarm company couldn't do anything. The person on the other end promised to call the Sonoma County Sheriff's Department and tell them all was okay and they needn't go out.

"Can ye brief us on what happened? What they did t' ye?" Ferguson asked Francis. Frances had disappeared.

"They called us. I guess it was Frank who called us at about 9:30 p.m. Not last night, the night before. Look, I've got to attend to something …" Francis disappeared.

Frances re-appeared. "We haven't had access to the bathroom or food for–what–like, thirty-six hours! There were two water bottles in there, one full of water, one empty. Well, it's not empty now. And it was *cold* in there! Oh, but look, I've got to see to the horses. They have water enough and some food but they should have their stalls cleaned and they'll need more hay soon." Francis reappeared. Frances disappeared again.

"So what did they want with ye?" asked Ferguson.

"They didn't want anything. It was Frank and some woman; we've seen her once or twice before but I don't know who she is."

Ferguson nodded. "Dahlia. Also known as Jane. Whom you would know, if you had been introduced, as Gwen."

"Yeah, anyway, whoever–we let them in, or I did, in the back door. Frank said, 'Where's Frances?' And I said 'Well, she's upstairs.' And he said 'Well can you get her down here?' And I said, 'What for?' and then he got kind o' mean and menacing and said, 'Just get her down here. There's something wrong in the vault.' That's what they called their big room in the barn. So we just followed along, clueless, and we walked in and I asked what was wrong and Frank points to the back of the room and says 'That!' And I said 'What?' and he repeated, strongly, '*That!*' So, dummies, we walked farther into the room, and before we knew it, they'd skedaddled and locked the door and alarmed it!"

"Clearly, they wanted ye out of the way. Nine-thirty. And your outside alarm, at the gate, automatically kicks in at ten at night? And back off at ten in the morning. But o' course ye override it most days and turn it off earlier in the morning."

"Yes. Exactly. Actually it comes on at 10:30. But we'd seen them loading all kinds of stuff from the room into a Budget rent-a-truck all evening. I mean, we didn't really watch them. They would do that periodically–load stuff into their car. Usually it was just one or two portfolios or carrier bags and such. But this time it was lots of portfolios, and lots of luggage, and even the desk and the chairs. I mean, we kind of watched them, but we didn't have our eyes glued on them all the time."

"And when was this?"

"Day before yesterday, right after we'd tended to the horses, and we were having dinner, and then finishing up–so between about seven and nine or nine-thirty."

"Clever," said Ferguson, almost to himself. "Oh, so clever. They were making a run for it. And ye dinna think t' call the one of us?!" he said sharply.

"Well, that was the funny thing. Neither of us could find our phones. We looked all over the house, then out by the pad where we park, then in our vehicles, then all around the place."

"And o' course ye ha'e no land line."

"Nah nah, nah," affirmed Francis. "We got rid of that years ago. Frances' phone is the B&B phone, mine's the personal and ranch phone."

Frances had returned. "By that time it was getting dark, or actually *was* dark," added Frances.

"And looking for the phones took, probably a half-hour," speculated Kenny.

"Yeah. Stupid, stupid, stupid. If we'd missed the phones earlier, we could have driven into town and called you from a café or someplace. You would have known something was up. *We* should have known something was up."

"And o' course while ye were tending to the horses, one o' them could ha' walked in the back door, found the phones, and sequestered them where ye would 'n' hear them if they went off."

"Right," said Francis with a sigh.

"How many of them were there? And who were they?" asked Ferguson.

"Well, it was the Frank fellah, and like I said, this woman, and the other one, that younger fellah."

"Randy," suggested Ferguson.

"You know," offered Kenny, "that day and the day before I sat around in the car just about all day, waiting for that Gwen person to come out of her hidey-hole in San Mateo. Both days I finally concluded she was having a day in, maybe sick or something, and came back home."

"And in reality she had probably already left, perhaps in the middle of the night, picked up by Frank in his car," declared Ferguson. "She could have overnighted in a motel somewhere. Then Frank picks her up again, evening before last. And off they go, paintings, masks, and all, after loading them into the Budget truck." Ferguson shook his head. "Yes, indeed, on that front, we've been out-maneuvered. On the false premise that we had cleverly, oh so cleverly, set up a sting. And because all *our* attention, I mean mine was focused on *that*, I mean on Gwen-Dahlia-Jane, all *their* attention could be focused on making the getaway and making sure you folks, Frances and Francis, couldn't reach us. What a sorry arse of a detective I do be."

Kenny called Phil and gave him the latest news.

GUERNEVILLE: 10:35 AM

Brandon Laird reversed his approach to Zoe, pivoting quickly, advancing on Cait, slapping her hard on the face so that she screamed and dropped the cashier's check. Instantly, Laird swooped down, caught it up, and stuffed it into his trousers' pocket. "Oh, no you don't!" shouted Zoe. Laird charged past her, extending his arm and hand in a fist. Zoe charged after him, tackling him. Her tackle sent both of them to the floor. "Should I call the police? Should I call the police?" screamed Jessica, pressing herself against the wall.

Brandon started to rise to his knees, half turning in an effort to land the punch that he had planned seconds earlier. Zoe drove three knuckles into Laird's left temple. Laird screamed in pain but his punch landed on Zoe's right breast. With both hands she grabbed the offending wrist and gave it a deft twist. Laird screamed again and tried to rise, but fell to his knees again and now tried to get away, crawling. He reached the door, and stood. Zoe raced to the door, dragged him away from it, scraped her right heel down Laird's left shin, jammed into his instep, and then kicked hard at his left ankle. Laird let out a screech. His leg crumpled, he lost his balance, and he crashed to the floor. Zoe pounced on him, grabbed his right arm, twisted, pulled back, then brought her right arm over his head so that her fisted hand was against his Adam's apple with his head now in a modified headlock. She gave her arm a little tug. Laird started to gag. She then pulled her arm, fisted hand still against his throat, toward her. She could see his face begin to darken. He emitted a "graghrg" sound, then another similar one. Zoe tugged again, then released the pressure. She let him go completely, Laird collapsed on his side, gasping and choking, falling against Zoe. They both crashed to the floor. Rolling clear of him. Zoe rose, turned, and leaned against Jessica's desk. Jessica peeled herself off the wall and approached Zoe, who was also panting, although not as badly as Laird.

"Are you okay?" Zoe realized that Cait was also at her side, embracing her and saying, "Oh dear, oh dear, oh dearie! God almighty! Are you okay?"

Zoe caught her breath. "Yeah, yeah! I'm fine! I'll have a boob bruise for a while, but we don't need to call the police."

Brandon Laird was not fine, mumbling between great gulps of air, "You bitch! You bitches! You set me up! You tried to kill me! You bitches! You bitches!"

Zoe dug her phone out of her back pocket, handed it to Cait. "Call Phil. His number's in there. Tell him what happened." Then to Jessica: "Got any rope?" She shook her head. "Duct tape?"

"Maybe. Yeah. Parcel tape, for wrapping." She opened the second right desk drawer and drew out a roll.

"Scissors?" asked Zoe. Jessica handed her those as well. "This won't keep him forever but it will do until we can get him someplace where we can all sit on him if he gets obstreperous." She handed the tape and scissors back to Jessica. "If we stand him on his feet and get his arms behind his back, can you wind a good amount of this around his wrists?"

But Laird, now on his feet, had again reached the door. Zoe, just behind him, banged her fisted hand again on his Adam' apple; he went down in a heap. "He'll be out for a few minutes, but not long enough for brain damage to set in." She rolled him over on his front, got his hands behind him, and held his wrists as Jessica wound the tape round and round and round. Zoe reached into his trousers' pocket and extracted the cashier's check. "This goes back to Ferguson." She folded it into third and placed it in her other back pocket.

Cait took the painting from the chair, placed it back in the portfolio, closed it, took the portfolio, and walked to the door to join Jessica and Zoe.

"You got anything like a hoodie or a big coat?" Zoe asked Jessica.

Laird groaned and tried to sit up. "You'll pay for this! This is kidnapping!" he mumbled groggily.

"Shut your yob!" Zoe said to him quietly, "unless you want me to shut it for you!"

"I think there's something in the car. I'll get it." Jessica returned with a hoodie. "This is Mitch's but he won't mind."

Zoe placed the hoodie over Laird's head and shoulders, hiding the fact that his hands were taped. "Now we're going to walk out the door, to our left, and around the corner to the car. Jessica, can you come along with us?" Jessica nodded energetically. "So Jessica's going to be on one side of you and I'll be on the other side. You're going to be a bit tiddly. You're going to take a misstep or two every now and then."

"Suppose I don't? Suppose I yell for the police, that I'm being kidnapped? That you assaulted me?!"

"First of all, I'll make sure you're a bit unsteady on your feet. Second, if you start yelling, we'll start yelling, something like 'Now, now, daddy, we'll just get you home and you'll be fine.'"

They did so. At one point, Laird opened his mouth and looked as if he were going to yell. Zoe kicked his leg with her foot. He started to crumple. Jessica said, said at a louder pitch than her normal speaking voice, "Now, now, daddy, we'll just get you home and you'll be fine." Despite a few curious looks from passersby, they got him to the car and into the back seat. Jessica hurried back to lock the studio door, then slid into the back seat next to Brandon; Cait was sitting on his other side. Zoe slid into the driving seat. "By the way," said Zoe, "if there's anything in *your* car that you might want, you should give one of us the key and we can fetch it. You're going to be with us for a while; they'll undoubtedly tow your car for parking violation."

Laird sighed and said hoarsely, "Keys in my right-hand trouser pocket. Portfolios in the trunk."

"Ah! Paintings!" Zoe slid back out of the driving seat, opened the door, and came around to the backseat door. She dug her hand into Laird's pocket, fetched out his keys, and asked "Where?"

"White Toyota Century in front of the studio."

Zoe returned with four portfolios, opened the Civic's trunk, and placed them inside, then resumed her place as driver.

23

IN THE TRESTLE GLEN HOUSE, Nancy had been placed upstairs, in bed. Kenny had run out for a mild sleeping potion. "I think I know a drug-store that carries Restorol," he'd said, chuckling. Nancy had not argued when she was offered a cup of chamomile tea with honey and three tablets dissolved in it. Everyone else assembled in the living room. Zoe had removed the tape from Laird's wrists; he now sat on the sofa between James and Joel. Jessica and Cait sat on the small couch. They had brought chairs in from the dining room, now occupied by Zoe, Mona, Carly, Aimee, Kenny, Jessica, and Paula-Mickie. Ferguson occupied the armchair. In several terse statements, Ferguson let everyone know that Frank and Dahlia-Gwen were gone. Carly clung to her saddlebag, which housed Zassy's statement and now also Cait's. Aimee and Paula-Mickie had decided to suppress the details of finding Nancy, saying only that Nancy was upset at Frank's leaving and they didn't want to leave her alone. Zoe had given a truncated report on her tussle with Laird.

"You can't hold me here against my will. When I get out of here I'm going to the police," declared Brandon Laird.

"Oh, and tell them what? This little 110-pound young lady named Zoe beat me up?" suggested Zoe.

"And we can equally go to the police and inform them of your role in unlawful restraint and detaining of the Giacomettis," said Ferguson sternly.

"You can't prove a thing! You can't prove that they didn't go into that room and got locked in because they didn't know the code to get out because they shouldn't have been in there in the first place!" Ferguson knew that, unfortunately, this was true.

But Zoe was not to be deterred. "Let's assume, Dr. Laird, that you want to continue your dual career, your double life, as a credentialed professor of old masters paintings, and also a finder of those paintings for wealthy clients. One feeds the other, right? But if you're exposed as a 'finder' of forged and fraudulent paintings, nobody is going to hire you to teach and nobody is going to believe your Nicholas Taylor authentications, right? And we already have your name on a sworn, signed notarized statement made by Zassy that he has been making paintings on demand for you and Frank McGinnis, in the style of a dozen or more well-known, deceased artists, for three years. We have a sworn, signed notarized statement from Caitlyn Kernberger Murray," she nodded at Cait, "along with photographs of you and the purported Dufy, that you tried to sell her this Zassy-painted Dufy for $46,000. And of course we have a statement which you will sign and which we will have notarized, to the effect that you have knowingly purchased paintings from Zassy over the last three years and resold them as attributed to deceased artists who are not Zassy."

"You're crazy! I'm not going to do that! Why should I do that?!"

"You'll do it because if you don't do it, we'll simply post a website with your name and scans of at least three and maybe four or five sworn, signed notarized statements asserting that you've done just what we have asserted you've done. You can sue us, if you want, but who do you think is going to hire you as a finder, buy from you, hire you as a teacher in the face of that website?"

"And once I sign that statement, I'm a goner! I'm toast! Nothing doing!"

"No. It's our, what you might call, insurance policy. Our warranty. One copy for everyone here. And it's your 'keep out of jail free' card. Because as long as you know we have your statement, and these others, you're going to think twice before you try to pass Zassy's paintings off as something they're not, or try to resurrect your fraud scheme by finding another poor, desperate talented painter to do your forgeries for you. Tomorrow one of us will take you and your paintings back to Guerneville to get your car out of the police compound. Oh, and of course we're giving you back your Zassy Dufy. Just as soon as you sign the statement.

"And we will have another sworn, signed notarized statement from a collector that you bilked matching descriptions of a painting that Zassy did on demand for you, by the end of tomorrow. There is also mounting persuasive evidence that the Léger that Aimee's aunt donated to Sacajawea and Charbonneau College was also painted by Zassy, as was this Braque oil hanging here." Zoe gestured to it. "In fact, neither this purported Braque nor the purported Léger were originally part of the estate sale that all this other stuff"--Zoe gestured again--"came from. Am I right? You 'salted' the estate sale with these two paintings, driving up the price to Aimee's Aunt Mavis, through your stooge, Randy Allen, correct? So we will have at least another, maybe two more statements about un-provenanced paintings that are probably by Zassy."

Laird remained silent, a grim rictus gripping his face.

"And you met Zassy through Dahlia, who met him through Adrian. Am I right?" interjected Ferguson. About three years ago?"

Silence.

"Or you didn't meet Zassy at all," continued Zoe. "You met Frank McGinnis, maybe at an auction or sale. Maybe you met Frank *and* Dahlia at an auction in Paris four years ago? And Frank had already hooked up with Zassy? Anyway, life got easier because you didn't have to go charging all over the place, to estate sales, antiques fairs, and auctions looking for the odd painting that might be okay to get for the college, or maybe some good bargains for the Grassers. I mean, maybe you still did that, but you could do so in the knowledge that meanwhile, the ideal painting from the auction that had not produced one was being prepared. But life also got a bit more complicated. Maybe Dahlia disappeared for a while but then came roaring back, leaning on you and Frank to find a place for her to store her masks. And then, the San Anselmo house dropped into your lap! Aimee moved out! Frank moved in! Frank and Nancy got busy remodeling the house, putting a room in the basement where you and Frank could also store a nice backlog of forgeries! You could keep Zassy immensely busy.

"Then, whoops!! Duncan Pennfield shows up here and innocently, naively, plants doubts about the authenticity of all the stuff Randy got at the estate sale. All you need is for one of those doubts to stick with Pennfield and wind its way to Zoe-the-expert-on-forgeries. The Grassers are already in a snit about the Vermeer, which was not your fault. But all they need is doubts about some of the other paintings you got for them. And those doubts would most likely be provided by Mavis Samuelson or Aimee Garrison, or both. So you had to at least distract them, hopefully disable them, maybe even engineer their demise. You talked Nancy into poisoning Mavis', and by default, Aimee's mint tea with henbane. It worked with Mavis; it almost worked with Aimee."

Aimee gasped. "So you mean he's the one behind this all? Behind the poisonings? He's Nancy's accomplice!"

"Or her mastermind. But then, somebody else pops up who might blow the whistle on the 'estate sale' story, somebody who was actually there. Somebody who could fuel those doubts with information about the estate sale, that the estate sale contained no paintings, only Léger lithographs–no Braque oil, no Léger oil, no Léger lithographs."

"Joel. You ran into him at the college," said Mona. "Or he ran into you. And you panicked and brought that news back to Frank and Nancy. And

Nancy went to work again, doing your dirty work, figuring out where Joel taught and somehow finding out that Joel drank tea all day long and that he kept his stash of tea in a desk drawer in his office. Windfall! Once again, like she'd done with Mavis, she dumped in the henbane. If we examined the back garden of the San Anselmo house, would we find a cluster of henbane plants?"

"What Nancy does or did or did not do is none of my business. You can't pin what she might or might not have done on me!" Laird said forcefully.

"No. You're right," replied Zoe. "We can't pin it on you. We can't even pin it on her. We can't prove anything. But you can bet we're going to ask her about it once she's back up and about. So let's put it this way: we *can* pin all this on you and her, and even if the pins fall out, you've still been pricked."

Silence.

"And when we all showed up at the San Anselmo house," Zoe went on, "Aimee going ballistic about being locked out, and Frank or Nancy told you, you must have flipped! So when we all conveniently disappeared, back into our lives and our day jobs, you heaved a big sigh of relief. You got Randy to sound out the Giacommettis, where he'd occasionally stayed in their B&B, about requisitioning part of their barn to reconstruct your *entrepot* for illicit works. Then, when it began looking like we were going to get on to that, too, and maybe if they knew, the Giacomettis would not be so happy about having their place be a depot for forgeries and stolen ceremonial art, you decided to split up the gang, at least temporarily, and divide the stash among the four or five of you. Maybe you tumbled to the fact that we were indeed doing surveillance on Gwen-Dahlia and on Adrian and Zassy and that the Giacomettis were aware of what was going on. So in the dead of night you all neutralized the Giacomettis, emptied out the vault, and stored the Giacomettis in there, while Dahlia-Gwen and Frank made their getaway, hoping that our attention would be diverted to trying to figure out where Dahlia-Gwen was and what she was up to, and to sussing out Zassy, while you did one last transaction. You, or at least Frank had to do an end-run around Nancy, and that was not in the script, and Nancy has not been happy about that.

"We were only lucky that you never tumbled to the fact that Cait's one of us. That she was a decoy. But what you may have meant to be that one last transaction, giving you a nice going-away present, turns out to be the definite proof of your attempt to defraud and deceive. We don't know what's in these four portfolios." She gestured again to where they had carried the portfolios in and stacked them against the wall. "But I'll wager each one contains a Zassy that strongly resembles paintings done by well-known deceased painters. How many were in the cache all together? Sixteen? Did you divide them evenly? Four for you, four for Nancy, four for Frank, four for Gwen? Or were there twenty? Did Randy get a share? And Gwen--she and Frank have absconded also with the remaining masks, from the auction four years ago. Am I right? How many was she able to sell to one or more of your clients? One to Dora Harris. One to Gareth Foster, who will most likely return it as a donation to the Tribe from which it originated. How many others was Gwen-Dahlia able to sell?"

This time, Laird replied. "There was only one more that I know of, but it's none of your business who that purchaser was. And how do you know that the word of a failed artist that he painted that Dufy is going to carry any weight at all?"

"Ah!" interjected Carly. "But he's not a failed artist at all. He's just coming into his own. He's hot. Zassy paintings 'in the style of' and 'after Utrillo, of Dufy, or Vlaminck, or Léger, or Braque' are going to be as desirable as original Zassys. But only, of course, if he signs them, 'Zassy.'"

"Well," continued Zoe, "you know you're going to get to keep the four paintings in those four portfolios. We're not going to steal them from you. You can do whatever you want with them. But probably, you'd do better to sell them as Zassy paintings, 'in-the-style-of' than trying to pass them off as the real thing. In the meantime, you'll toddle off to you own little bedroom upstairs, with one of us keeping watch to make sure you behave yourself."

"You can't keep me here! You can't keep me prisoner!"

"No, we're not keeping you prisoner. We're providing you with a room of your own, plus, tomorrow, transportation back to Guerneville to get your car.

We'll even bail it out for you from the police station. But before that happens you'll go to your bank and withdraw some cash. You'll put that cash into four cashier's checks. One for Aimee to compensate for totaling her car, one to Paula Cortez Laird as a form of alimony, including enough to cover the costs of the attorney she had to hire to get the complaint against her vacated, one for that couple you bilked, selling them–what was it, Ferguson?"

"A fake Vlaminck. You sold it to them for $18,500, Dr. Laird."

"We will secure a sworn and witnessed statement from the Fosters that you did indeed sell them that painting," affirmed Zoe. "But we will not tell them that it was done by Zassy. We will simply tell them that you mistakenly overcharged them. We will return to them exactly half of that: $9,250. And assuming you probably paid Zassy about half of that or less, another cashier's check for $4,625 will go to Zassy in recognition of his extraordinary talent, which we will deliver to him tomorrow."

"So, how much for you, Aimee?"

"Oh, I'm not greedy. Say, $40,000. I can maybe sell the Subaru for maybe ten and replace the Mercedes that you wrecked."

"What?" yelled Brandon.

"Paula?"

"Well, I know that you're about to get a settlement from the college totalling two years' worth of salary and changing of your severance from a suspension and termination to a voluntary resignation, with the guarantee of a letter of reference. So I think about half of that should go to me, plus $10,000 to cover legal expenses. I've been helped out by ... by some generous friends and I want to pay them back. Your salary two years ago was $96,000. So two years' worth of half of that plus $10,000 is–what? $106,000?"

"That's outrageous! This is blackmail! Extortion! I shell out $150,000 to you pirates? You think I've got that much cash sitting around in a bank account?"

"I think you've got that and more sitting around in a couple offshore accounts," declared Paula-Mickie forcefully. "And it may take a couple days to get it all hauled over here in pieces and made into cashier's checks, but I'm sure your clever bankers can figure out how it can be done. How many bogus artworks have you fobbed off on gallery owners, collectors, maybe even museums over the last three years? At twenty-thirty-forty thousand a pop! I'll bet you've raked in a couple of hundred thousand a year!" Paula's tone of voice was escalating into near-screaming mode. "And what about that Modigliani? And how many more of those did you commission? Modiglianis go for millions! *Millions!* I think you can afford it."

"What guarantee do I have that you're not going to try to ruin me anyway?"

"None," Ferguson answered.

"Then why should I do it?"

"Because if you do not do it, it will guarantee that we do indeed let the Fosters know that you sold them a fake, and we will most assuredly, discretely, but most assuredly, contact the art historian world and let it be known that you have been, and still are peddling forgeries that you have fobbed off on clients as 'finds' from various faked sources. And we can always post the statements that we have taken on a publicly accessible website."

They decided neither Brandon nor Nancy would be left alone overnight. Kenny volunteered to do the Brandon duty and Phil would spell him halfway through the night. Aimee offered to do so with Nancy, with Paula spelling her.

Third Saturday in June
Oakland
7:16 PM

Ferguson had arrived early in the morning, collecting Brandon Laird along with James and Phil. Laird finally did admit to offshore accounts. After they secured the four cashier's checks in a nearby Wells Fargo branch, open Saturday mornings until Noon, they delivered Laird and his four paintings back to Guerneville, to his car, impounded at the police station. Jessica caught a ride back with them. Zoe and Phil followed and secured the smallest of the four checks for Zassy.

The following day, Zoe would load Aimee's Braque into the boot of her car. She and Carly would deliver it to Zassy, who would add his signature to it, and deliver the smallest of the cashier's checks to him. Finally, Ferguson would call the Fosters and find out when it would be convenient to deliver a check to them because of their overpayment for their "Vlaminck", and also kindly request them to affirm, in a prepared written statement, that they had indeed purchased it from Frank McGinnis, and the mask from Gwen-Dahlia. Ferguson would explain that the statement would be necessary for them to claim a tax deduction for donating the mask back to the Tribe from which it had originated. The return would be facilitated by Phil.

By evening, all tasks accomplished and those of the next day arranged, Nancy was brought down and arranged on the sofa. She had slept fitfully, on and off, all day. Paula and Aimee had kept up their vigils alternately, Aimee taking a catnap at one point. Kenny picked up pizza, which waited for them on the dining room table, along with several bottles of wine from Aimee's cellar. The dining room chairs, still arranged in a row in front of the sofa, were now occupied by Cait, Zoe, Carly, Aimee, Kenny, Paula-Mickie, Phil, and James. Joel and Mona sat on the couch. Nancy occupied the sofa. "So here's the jury, right?" said Nancy softly. "And now the defendant is going to get the grilling. Right?"

"We just want some answers," said Aimee quietly. "Or maybe some confirmation of what we already know. Like, the Randy thing. You and Randy weren't really on the outs with each other, were you?"

"No."

"So why the ruse?"

Nancy sighed. "I don't really know. It was Randy's idea. His excuse was to just throw people off the scent, as he put it. He didn't say who 'they' would have been, or what the scent was. But I suppose he thought it was pretty easy for people, someone, to put me and Frank together because we *were* together--we *lived* together. Then I guess it would have been easy for somebody to put Brandon and Randy together because the stuff that Randy found at estate sales eventually made its way to Brandon."

"And every now and then Brandon Laird would claim to have scooped up this or that 'art find' and this or that estate sale and peddle it to a client, right?" added Zoe.

"Yes. That's where Frank and his forgeries came in. And your Nick, too."

"He's *not my Nick*," abjured Zoe, "but yes. So where did they all meet?"

"At estate sales, auctions, I suppose."

"At an auction in Paris, maybe? Four years ago?" suggested Zoe.

Nancy shrugged. "For all I know, Randy met Brandon when he was still back east--four, five years ago. Anyway, I guess Randy and Brandon were getting known for working together at these sales. And Frank was kind of in and out. I mean, I don't know what he did or how he did it before I met him. He presented himself to me as a legitimate art dealer." She shrugged. "And maybe he was. I'm not sure how he met Zassy. Maybe through that Gwen woman? At an auction? I don't know. Anyway, he made it possible for me to quit that awful waitressing job, at the Yardbird."

"No alimony from my namesake?" asked Paula.

"Paul Cortez?" Nancy shook her head. "He's disappeared. I don't know where he is."

"And you met Frank where?" asked Aimee.

Nancy laughed. "Ha-ha! At the Yardbird! Where else? Introduced by Randy, of course. I guess everything else, making that room in the basement, making the house into a depot for forged art, putting the alarm system in, was just him--Frank--taking advantage of an opportunity. Taking advantage of *me*."

"And I was out of the picture. I didn't know and wouldn't have cared, because I was busy with Mavis and when I wasn't busy with her, I was busy with Kenny," affirmed Aimee.

Nancy shrugged.

"So let's get to the dicier stuff," suggested Zoe. "The poisonings. You did both of those, didn't you? Or all three, if you count Aimee. Maybe you knew about Mavis' will and just wanted to hurry her along because you were anxious for Randy to inherit. Maybe he was too much of a loose cannon, and with his own income, he'd be out of your hair. You came to visit Mavis every week, and at some point dumped the henbane into her tea canister. Several days' worth of poisoning did it for her. Then when Randy came to you in a panic about how he'd seen Joel Curwin at Charbonneau and it was obvious he was there a lot and would probably encounter Brandon Laird at some point, *you* panicked and decided Joel had to be strongly discouraged from making so many trips to Charbonneau. So you wandered around Northern Washington University until you figured out where Joel's office was and discovered that he also drank a lot of mint tea. What a coincidence! What an opportunity! So you spiked *his* tea with henbane, too. Little did you know that he was under pressure, like subpoena-grade pressure, to give testimony in an accreditation hearing with regard to a faculty member at Charbonneau working there under a false premise. Maybe with luck, he'd have an 'accident' just like Mavis had had, maybe lose control of his car or some such."

Nancy's lower lip trembled. She blinked back tears. "You think I would do that? What about Frank?!" She turned to Aimee. "Yes, Aimee, you might have gotten suspicious about the two pieces of original art in the estate sale and gotten an expert in to authenticate them or maybe gone directly to the FBI. That would have sunk Randy. And yes, he was a loose cannon. But it was Frank and Brandon who would have been the real losers. How do you know *they* didn't *hire* somebody to do all sneaking around and tea spiking?"

Aimee shrugged. "I guess you're right. We can't prove anything. All we can do is write a script and try to fill in the blanks. Frank's name fits in those blanks as well as yours does, I suppose."

"So you know what?" suggested Carly. "You probably have Zassy paintings stashed away. You know what you might want to do? You might want to try to get over to Zassy before he leaves the country–and he is definitely going to leave the country soon–and have Zassy put his signature on those paintings. Because you can bet Frank and Brandon are going to try to get rid of their forgeries pronto before anyone catches on to what's going on. Besides, it's the honest thing to do."

Aimee rose and strode to one of the two bay windows that looked out upon the street. Then she turned to face the room. "We're not going to try to go to the police," she affirmed. "I'll decide later whether or not to evict you. I have every right to do so, and I should do. But I'll take you back to San Anselmo tomorrow."

⌒⌒

Third Sunday in June
Oakland; San Francisco
Morning

Ferguson had left Brandon Laird in the City, following their bank transactions the day before. It was Zoe, Phil, Carly and James who went to San Francisco, to the Castro district, where they intercepted Zassy and Adrian loading luggage, portfolios, paint boxes, portmanteaus, and boxes into two taxis.

Aimee and Nancy pulled up as well. "This is an awful lot of double parking," mumbled Adrian.

"And are you really off to Paris?" asked Carly.

"You bet!" answered Zassy. "Six o'clock this afternoon, we're in the skies! But I guess we'll detour to the bank to get this changed into cash." He waved the check in the air.

Aimee and Paula ferried Nancy back to San Anselmo through the sea of city traffic. Ferguson had asked Zoe to meet him at the Fosters' place. She, James, and Carly zoomed through traffic in the opposite direction. After explaining that Phil would get the sacred mask back to the Tribe, and introducing James and Carly as "friends", Zoe presented Gareth and Martha with a statement, that they were happy to sign, about how and from whom they had acquired the Vlaminck and the mask, as well as the "overpayment" check. "Don't you just love my Flinck?" Martha Foster had gushed, pointing to the Vlaminck hanging on the wall. "It's like the other pictures–it really brightens things up." *Poor lady*, thought Zoe. *Well, it won't make any difference to her that it's a fake, or to her heirs, since she doesn't have any–just to whoever might come to the estate sale following their demise.*

Outside the Fosters' place, Ferguson gave a little bow and said, "And now I bid ye adieu! Ah think Ah have done meself proud on repaying the debt Ah owe ye. But should ye ever need me again, here's m' direct line." He took out his phone and punched in Zoe's number.

When they all arrived back at Aimee's house, Cait let them in. "Sandwiches and beers on the dining room table, she told them. "Open face on focaccia: cheese, prosciutto, turkey pepperoni, hummus." Aimee and Paula arrived shortly afterwards and declared they needed naps. "That sounds good to me, too," said Zoe. She called Mona, who assured her she and Joel would appear at Trestle Glen for a seven-o-clock repast and rehash of everything that had happened.

"Well!" exclaimed Cait. "Finally I got in on some of the action! I'm so glad I could help!"

EVENING

Paula and Cait volunteered to take on the menu for their last Trestle Glen "sinful Saturday", on Sunday, while everybody else was recovering from their errands. "Why don't you come into the kitchen and entertain us while we cook," suggested Paula.

"Well, we intercepted Zassy and Adrian loading all their stuff into a couple taxis. We introduced ourselves and I told Zassy about Frank's and

Brandon's agreement that they had paid him insufficiently for his work. I gave him Laird's check. "He was jazzed!"

Paula slid half seven summer squashes, the same number of baked potatoes, and two whole broiled chickens out of the oven. Using fork and knife, Cait split the squashes, sprinkled curry powder into each half, mashed it in, and then added a half-dozen pecans into each half, mashing them in. "Those'll sit for a while. Then I'll scoop them all out and chop the skins. Then in they go into a bowl, add some soy milk, into the oven, and that'll be our bisque."

"Then I presented him with Aimee's Braque," added Carly, and he owned up to it being his. "He was happy to sign it." Adrian objected that everything was packed away but then he open a little paint box that wasn't and Zassy signed a bold signature, on the diagonal, at the left side of the picture."

"Then Nancy turns up with four Zassy forgeries!" exclaimed James. "I was astonished! So he signed those too."

Cait split the large russet potatoes carefully, scooped out the flesh, dumped it into a blender with soy milk, salt, and generous amounts of fresh tarragon leaves and some pepper and whirred. She then scooped the mixture carefully back into the potato jackets and laid them on the third rack in the oven to be twice baked.

Paula dumped quinoa into a frying pan on the top of the stove. While the quinoa toasted, she carved the chicken breasts away carefully with a spoon, then carved three slits into each. She inserted a mix of frozen spinach (thawed), raisins, egg, chopped almonds, pine nuts and umami seasoning into each slit, placed them on an aluminum pan, and shoved them back in the oven. "The rest of this mixture goes into the chicken cavities," said Paula. Legs and thighs, dark meat, take longer to cook than breasts so back into the oven go the stuffed skeletal chickens.

"The Fosters were somewhat flummoxed about the 'overpayment check," said Phil, "but they were happy to sign the statement and I assured them they would receive another receipt and a thank-you letter from the Tribal Office of Cultural Preservation within a couple of weeks after I've gotten the mask back to the Tribe."

Paula took the toasted quinoa off the stove and dumped it into a bowl. Cait quickly chopped three cucumbers, scooped the flesh from four avocados halves and chopped them, peeled a and a large mango and chopped it, dumping all of it into the bowl with the quinoa. Paula rinsed out the blender and refilled it with salad with a half-quart of yogurt and added fresh mint and half a "leg" of fresh ginger. Phil had asked that scallops be picked up and at the last minute and now he took on the task of pan-frying them in olive oil with minced garlic, fresh tomatoes and finely diced peppers.

Wines were on the table: two bottles each of a Lerner Project Cabernet Sauvignon, a Clos du Bois sauvignon blanc, and a gewürztraminer.

Now, everything else devoured, the chicken largely a carcass, they were on the quinoa-mango salad, complemented with the gewürztraminer. "We've done better than we'd thought we'd done about our manifold multiplying mysteries!" bragged Zoe. "We can be pretty sure that the decorated skull is Virginia Grimm, whose headless body washed out in a flood in the Santa Cruz Mountains, and who was most probably murdered by Robert Cortez, who, in remorse, decorated her skull in turquois tiles. We know the box that her head was in, and the other boxes, were deposited at Charbonneau by none other than Robert's son, Paula, who is one-and-the-same as the estranged wife of former Charbonneau professor Brandon Laird, known to Carly and Mona as Mickie Laird, now taking her mother's name, DiComo, so now—unofficially because she's still Laird's wife--Paula DiComo." Paula nodded. "We know that she planted the address of Aimee's San Anselmo house, with the odd address 'Suzanne Utrillo', along with the skull, to lead us to the house, because she knew that Frank McGinnis, Aimee's aunt Nancy, and Brandon Laird were all in cahoots in an art forgery fraud scheme. We know now with pretty good assurance that the Léger in Charbonneau's art gallery and certainly the Braque hanging in this house, with authentication certificates by my former boyfriend, Nicholas Zachary

Taylor, are forgeries done by Zassy, who did at least twenty additional forgeries that we've seen or know of. We know that the Zassy Léger and Braque were 'salted' into an estate sale, the price of which was jacked up to give the three players, Randy, Brandon and Frank, a profit of probably twenty thou each, and although she didn't admit it, it's clear that Nancy was talked into doing the two henbane poisonings. By the way, Aimee, what have you decided to do about Nancy?"

"I should throw her out on her ass. But for the time being, I'm going to let her stay. I'll up her rent. I wonder if we might not find Brandon Laird there, getting his wounds licked, with Nancy supplying the licking!"

They all laughed.

Joel shook his head and lamented, "I still find the planning of that whole henbane business incredibly fey." He turned to Aimee. "Did your aunt know that the most logical culprit to get it pinned on was going to be Madison Canter?"

"I don't see how she could have known," replied Aimee. "She knew nothing about what you were doing or even who you really were."

"Yeah," agreed Carly. "She was clueless about Charbonneau except that Brandon Laird had taught there and was now in a bubble of suspicion about his finder-buyer antics because of a painting the forgery of which he actually had nothing to do with!"

"Right, agreed Phil, "it's just like you called it, Joel, only more so. Not only did Joseph Canter get his PhD under a false premise–that he was actually the originator of what was Jane Bennett's work–but also he didn't even forge his dissertation! His wife did it!"

"And it was Madison Canter who had the motivation to get me out of the picture," affirmed Joel. "In her book, I was the baddy who caused all the problems for her and her husband."

"I think we all need a nice break from all this," declared Aimee. "Why don't you stay out here for a few days, spend the Fourth with us, then let's go camping—up north, after the Fourth, when the crowds have gone home. I can take some vacation time. Just us girls—you, Zoe, Mona and Carly and me. Let's go up to the gold country! Colombia, Jamestown, Frenchman's Flat."

"Sounds great! We deserve it. It'll be interesting to see how all this pans out," observed Mona.

EPILOGUE

ZASSY AND ADRIAN SET UP IN PARIS in an atelier in the 13th arrondissement, not far from the Place d'Italie. Dahlia-Gwen and Frank McGinnis along with the rest of the masks went to ground somewhere, whether separately or together was unknown. Having deposited the "bearer" cashier's check into her bank account representing two years of alimony and compensation for legal fees, Paula Mickie Cortez Laird DiComo did not expect to hear from Brandon Laird ever again.

Kenneth Yarborough was accepted to San Francisco State in an accelerated program that would get him a BS, qualifying him to apply for their MBA program. He would take art history courses on the side.

Caitlyn Kernberger Murray rented a car, rendezvoused with Phil for a tour of the Pueblos that included a Saints' Day dance performance at Isleta, made a brief visit to a couple in Corrales–Jen and Thad Pritchard, whom she and her husband Robb had encountered under bizarre and unpleasant circumstances and had afterward found engaging in a quirky way that invited cautious mutual enthusiasm for interaction, if not actual friendship. They were in the midst of renovating a long-abandoned trading post that they were intending to reopen once again as a trading post-antiques-shop-art gallery.

She also visited Coco Vanderjagt in Santa Fe. Her old friend from Croton Corners, Ellie Bortz, had accepted Coco's invitation to move out to Santa Fe permanently and be her roommate; "I need a companion," Coco explained to Cait.

Nancy Allen-Hennessy was surprised to have a phone call from Randy before the month of June was out. He effused enthusiasm for his upcoming internship: eight weeks at a dig in Jordan. Duncan Pennfield was coming down for a farewell visit but might fly over for a rendezvous in Beirut just before Randy's return flight.

Joel Curwin was pleased to be notified that his two articles, one on Jane Bennett's important work from seventy years ago, and the other on the remarkable resemblance of a published monograph by one Joseph Canter to Jane Bennett's thesis and archived notes, along with the narrative of how he had discovered the documents, had been accepted for publication.

It had not taken long for Zoe to find out that unqualified instructors had indeed been the major reason for colleges and technical institutes being de-licensed and, in fact, for the accreditation agency that had accredited them to be de-accredited. She had sent an email to Ferguson quoting from a February 2016 audit report by the State Council of Higher Education for Virginia, finding that, in the case of one college, twenty-two of twenty-six instructors the State Council had reviewed were unqualified to teach their assigned subjects and that therefore the college's programs did not meet standards of quality expected of institutions of higher education. She had let Ferguson do the rest. His report was sufficient to enable Blenheim and Fister to confront Madison Canter with the strong probability that her husband, Joseph Canter, by his own testimony, had not accessed Jane Bennett's archived work or thesis. They cited Ferguson's report that she, indeed, had done so on two occasions, and therefore that it was she, not he, who had written the dissertation and monograph attributed to him, thereby confirming that Joseph Canter had absolutely no qualifications for teaching any course in the field of history, let alone evaluating faculty with higher degrees. They also confronted her with her complicity, along with Joseph Canter and Dora Harris, in placing Herman Shaftley, although having the status of "ABD"–"All But Dissertation"–in the position of doing classroom evaluations of faculty with PhDs and therefore who were, *prima facie*, more qualified than he was to teach in an institution of higher education. Again they cited Ferguson's report on lack of faculty qualifications being a major factor in the rescinding of licensing and accreditation in the case of the "college scandal" of several years previous. The college would have to take measures.

Therefore it was announced that Madison Canter would be joining her husband, Joe, in retirement, and that the history major was being temporarily suspended, although the social sciences major would be retained. It was also announced that the two instructors who had not been recommended for retention in their mid-tenure reviews, Keller and Harley, would be retained for the coming year and some of Herman Shaftley's courses would be re-assigned to them; Shaftley would teach largely introductory, Gen-Ed classes, in order for the social sciences major to be legitimately maintained. A search for a replacement for Joseph Canter, a mid-career candidate for whom hiring with tenure might be a consideration, would be immediately advertised.

What to do with the skull proved a dilemma, the subject of much discussion among Zoe, Mona, Carly and James at their first sinful Saturday after returning to Charbonneau. They finally decided it should be sealed into its hat box along with a narrative, jointly crafted by Zoe and Mona, relating how it was acquired and what their investigations in San Anselmo and Santa Cruz, and the information from Aimee's cousin Stephen, had suggested about who it was and how it came into the "Cortez cabinet of curiosities collection". It would then be deposited in the college Library's Special Collections, with a proviso that the box not be opened until twenty-five years had passed.

"Will Special Collections take an object?" asked Carly incredulously.

"Sure!" replied James. "They have any number of objects. I know at least they have some objects that came in with the Arts and Performances School–Memphis Minnie's washboard, for one."

Zoe, Mona, and Carly agreed that Mona should use the "Joel" spoons at every opportunity, and that their phony status should be communicated to Joel. He laughed uproariously, as did James, when the joke-not-joke was revealed. "In a way, me buying those spoons on the basis of a false premise was what kick-started this whole sleuthing caper, wasn't it?"

"And all the false premises swirling around in our little academic teapot here are going to get you lauded as the Sherlock Holmes of anthropology, aren't they?" quipped Mona.

"I think somebody might already have that sobriquet," he abjured.

"But surely Zoe should be the 'phonies, fakes, and frauds detective'!" insisted Carly. "Excavator and revealer of false premises!"

"Yep," agreed Zoe. "But I guess it's going to be a pretty dull summer," she lamented. "No more mysteries, no more skullduggeries, no more miscreants to expose."

But Zoe would soon discover how wrong that prediction was going to be.

ACKNOWLEDGMENTS

AS USUAL, thanks to my life-long partner, Carolyn, for providing calm insight and enthusiastic encouragement in making important suggestions and comments. Thanks also to my editors, Jennifer and Ellen. The following authors' expertise was drawn upon at various points: Lawrence Jeppson, (*The Fabulous Frauds*, 1970, New York: Weybright and Talley) and Jonathan Lopez (*The Man Who Made Vermeers*, 2008, Orlando: Houghton Mifflin Harcourt). Everything that the narrator and Zoe say about authentication, auctions, forgery, and fraud is drawn from one of the above books. I should note, however, that any errors in that regard are my own.

There was indeed a "Taibo", well known among Paiutes as a visionary and acknowledged as a leader, but he did not travel to London to enlist the sympathies and support of the Anti-Slavery Society for reparations compensating the Native participants in the "Camas War" of 1878 for unlawful seizure of their resources and livelihood. Jane Bennett never existed. Therefore, her personal papers are not to be found in the Beinecke Library. And although the Beinecke did indeed maintain a "log-in" book, it has now undoubtedly been replaced by a computer-assisted sign-in system. "Teas on Telegraph" also does not exist, and any teashop in the shadow of Sather Gate would certainly not carry henbane-tainted mint tea.

www.ingramcontent.com/pod-product-compliance
Lightning Source LLC
Chambersburg PA
CBHW021958260626
47156CB00018B/2129